Susan Sallis is the number one bestselling author of over a dozen novels including *Daughters of the Moon, Water under the Bridge, Touched by Angels, Choices, Come Rain or Shine, The Keys to the Garden, The Apple Barrel, Sea of Dreams, Time of Arrival* and *Five Farthings*. She lives in Clevedon, Somerset.

D0656459

LYDIA FIELDING

Susan Sallis

CORGI BOOKS

LYDIA FIELDING
A CORGI BOOK : 0 552 15017 7

Simultaneously published in Great Britain by Bantam Press,
a division of Transworld Publishers

PRINTING HISTORY
Bantam Press edition published 2003
Corgi edition published 2003

1 3 5 7 9 10 8 6 4 2

Set in 11/12½pt New Baskerville by
Kestrel Data, Exeter, Devon.

Corgi Books are published by Transworld Publishers,
61–63 Uxbridge Road, London W5 5SA,
a division of The Random House Group Ltd,
in Australia by Random House Australia (Pty) Ltd,
20 Alfred Street, Milsons Point, Sydney, NSW 2061, Australia,
in New Zealand by Random House New Zealand Ltd,
18 Poland Road, Glenfield, Auckland 10, New Zealand
and in South Africa by Random House (Pty) Ltd,
Endulini, 5a Jubilee Road, Parktown 2193, South Africa.

Printed and bound in Great Britain by
Cox & Wyman Ltd, Reading, Berkshire.

For my family

One

Lydia Fielding's coming-of-age was celebrated as so many occasions on Exmoor, with a democratic informality unheard of in towns and cities. A party was held in the barn of her father's prosperous farm, Milton Mains, near Listowel village. It was attended by guests from all walks of life, many of whom were not known to Lydia, but came because they could get a lift on a passing wagon and there would be free food and drink and plenty of noise. If they had to walk the night through to return home, they would do it.

Invitations were not sent. News was by word of mouth, even to Sir Henry and Lady Maud at Garrett Place. A reddler in Carybridge might say to a shearer from Tamerton: 'Fielding girl be of age come twenny-third April so I do 'ear. Over Listowel way. Rupert Fielding's girl. Borned forty five if I remembers correck, so that makes it . . . aye, twenny-one. An' there'll be enough cider to drown all your fleas I d'reckon!' And the shearer might call at Garrett Place to make arrangements for his first shearing, and eventually the housekeeper, Mrs Lomax, would rattle her keys as she presented the monthly bills, and say, 'And would it be little Lydia Fielding's coming-of-age, already, ma'am? Seems only yesterday the bailiff caught her wading in the cove and brought her to Sir Henry screaming that the sea belonged to everyone!' And Lady Maud would doubtless smile her horse smile, and say, 'Girl after my own heart, if a little hoydenish. We must put in an appearance. Find her a gift. Something small.'

And over at Mapperly House, built by old George Pascoe with the profit from his sheep trading, the youngest of the three Pascoe boys, Augustus, sent word to his brothers Julius in Bristol and Octavius in Stapleford, to tell them of the party. 'Come alone,' he wrote. 'The local girls are improving. And if I can get an answer from Lydia that night there will be cause for our family to celebrate. Milton Mains will be half hers one day and Rupert runs a tidy herd. We could go into cattle as well as sheep.'

The villagers turned out in force. The dozen families in the tiny hamlet on the edge of the sea knew the Fieldings well. The children had always played with Lydia and her younger brother Alan; the men and women helped on the farm at harvest and lambing and were paid in various gleanings. Even the local Methodies were represented, though such revelries were against their custom; Prudence Peters loved Lydia's mother enough to stand out against her husband and offer her services with the cooking and the serving of the food. She brought her youngest along to help too – or to enjoy some of the celebrating. And, strangely, one of her sons was there with the permission of his father. Wesley Peters, recently back from mercenary fighting in the war made by Mr Lincoln, stood with his back to the wall behind his sister, watching the proceedings through his narrowed blue eyes. Since he had run away to sea five years before to escape his father's religious tyranny, he had seen stranger sights than this; but these were his people and he had returned to them for a reason.

Rupert Fielding held Milton Mains as a copyholder to Sir Henry Garrett, paying a peppercorn rent and certain of the gift of the freehold before his death. He was generous – almost careless – with his good fortune. Nobody asked him a favour in vain; he enjoyed his weekly visits to the cider kiddley in Carybridge; recently he had taken to playing cards with Gus Pascoe; he sent Alan to be articled to a firm of solicitors in Bristol and encouraged him to spend his large allowance freely. Lydia he permitted to do what she liked. Luckily what she liked was everything to do with the farm: she helped her mother with the milking and churning, went out with her father at lambing time, gripped the fat summer sheep between her bare knees when their coats were full and fleeced them without a drop of blood being spilled. She danced around the garlanded pole on May Days, played stoolball with the children among the stubble after haymaking, laughed at the rigid, frigid Methodists who would never join in, yet still made tea for them when they turned away from the cider jar. After painstaking teaching from her mother, she could also manage an arpeggio on the piano, speak a little execrable French, draw and paint watercolours and add a column of figures.

Perhaps it was no wonder that so many came to Milton Mains to wish her well that night of April the twenty-third.

The party was a success. The barn was lined with laden tables and groups of chairs, the middle cleared for the dancers. The huge oak doors were set wide and Lydia stood between her parents, still greeting the guests long after her brother Alan had started the dancing. The food and movement had heated the barn sufficiently to enable most of the ladies to discard their shawls and some of the men to be down to their shirt sleeves, but Lydia and her mother held wraps over their new silk dresses against the dampness of the April evening.

Behind them Amos Pollard, shepherd, sawed industriously at his fiddle and Robbie Roscoe manipulated his squeeze-box with enormous concentration. Alan, home from Bristol for the occasion, sang out in his high clear voice, 'Sets of four for Parson's Farewell, *if* you please!' Everyone laughed and dashed to claim their partners and Alan laughed loudest of all because he had already danced with all the girls from Carybridge and they were beginning to giggle and look at him as if he were one of the Pascoe boys.

Lydia said, 'Shall I fetch you a chair, Mamma? You must be tired standing out here all this time.' She looked over her shoulder, wondering who was still to come. Mrs Pollard and Prudence Peters glanced up at her, nodded smilingly, then went back to the huge saddles of mutton they were carving. Lydia noticed little Marella Peters carrying a tray of pies through the dancers with much shrieking. She must be fifteen now and blossoming fast. Tavvy Pascoe, down from Stapleford, led his sister Joanna into the bottom set and the dance began.

'Mamma, may we join the others now?' Lydia pleaded, forgetting the chair. 'Sir Henry isn't coming. I don't expect the hunt is even back yet. And we're missing all the fun!'

Rupert Fielding settled his stocky body more firmly on his hips and reached out a hand for a tankard of cider which was placed there considerately by his stable lad, Drake.

'Lydie's right, Lucy. Let's get to the party proper-like now. We haven't had food inside us since midday.'

'Rupert! You have been eating and drinking this half-hour since!' Lucy Fielding smiled to soften the severe words. She was a smaller quieter edition of her daughter, content to leave decisions and stern parental discipline to her husband, yet wielding more influence than she guessed. She leaned heavily on her daughter's arm as she spoke. 'You're as bad as each other!

Lydia, you have been chattering to Gus and Robbie and Jinny and everyone else like a magpie! We are missing nothing save the dancing and that will go on past midnight.'

Rupert shook his head. 'You need to sit down my dear, that is certain. 'Twas you we was thinking of.'

Lucy and Lydia both laughed at this but Lydia looked round in earnest for a vacant chair. One of Prudence Peters's boys came forward, pale straight hair and straight Methodist face to match. They all looked the same, dour, even grim. Except young Marella who could not stop her giggles as she passed around the pies.

She looked into the sky-blue Peters eyes, smiling thanks for the chair held between the rigid arms as if to keep a distance between them. No answering smile appeared.

'Er . . . thank you very much.' She widened her face into deliberate brilliance and was glad when he blinked. 'I'm afraid I do not recall your name. Only that Prudence is your mother.'

'Wesley, miss. Wesley Peters.'

He was proud of that name. He had a different assurance from the natural confidence of Amos Pollard and Robbie Roscoe; it was almost aggressive.

She placed the chair for her mother. 'Thank you, Wesley. I hope you are enjoying the party.'

To her surprise his pale face coloured faintly at that and after a pronounced pause he said in a flat voice, 'Thank you, Lydia.'

She flushed too, realizing that he considered

her use of his forename as impertinent. But the Peterses were . . . the Peterses!

She swallowed and persevered. 'Have you eaten? And your sister has finished helping, it would seem. Wouldn't it be brotherly to take her into the dance?'

He said coldly, 'We do not dance. I think you know we are of the Methodist persuasion.'

The air of haughty reproof was infuriating. Lydia smiled. 'I did not realize the original Wesley was against dancing.'

He shrugged. Thin he might be but his shoulders were wide and there was a restrained sinewy strength about him.

'One way or the other, we do not allow it.'

Lydia gave up and turned away, feeling great sympathy for Marella, whose flushed face and tapping toe told their own tale about her natural inclinations. The smug piety of the clutch of local Methodists won no sympathy from the farmers and fishermen of the Moor, and Lydia was of the Moor.

Drake loped through the arched doorway to fetch more cider then glanced back.

'Sir 'enry's 'ere, master,' he called. 'Carriage just drawed up at the house. Will I tell driver to pull round to the barn?'

'Aye.' Rupert held out a hand to his newly seated wife. 'Let us meet them outside, Lucy. Otherwise Lady Maud's voice will stop the music!'

Laughing again because now the party could begin for her, Lydia led the way onto the damp

13

gravel. The haycarts had been ousted for the occasion and stood to one side of the archway. From inside them came scuffling and giggles though some daylight was still left in the sky. The Fieldings tactfully ignored these sounds and hurried forward to the arriving carriage.

This was black and cream enamelled, a magnificent equipage for the Moor. The Garretts were an offshoot of a very old family and their only son, Bertram, was 'something in the Queen's Household'.

Sir Henry scorned help and emerged violently from the swinging carriage door. He was enormous in a many-caped coat and a beaver hat that sat upon his ears pushing them outward in a mass of fiery red veins. He boomed like a foghorn.

'Happy birthday! Happy birthday, Lydie! Happy birthday to you, I say!' And then as he stamped over the gravel and in case no-one had heard, 'A very happy birthday and many of them!' He clasped Lydia's new silk frock to his damp, horse-and-snuff-smelling coat and kissed her cheek with a loud sucking sound.

Sir Henry propped himself on Rupert as Lucy said quietly, 'A good day's hunting, sir?'

'Fair. Fairish. Quite fair, you know. Put up a deer straight off. Lost it over the Heights. Refreshed ourselves at Mapperly for an hour while they found something else for us, then we were going hell for leather through the bracken and Dominic put a foot down a blasted rabbit hole and tossed Lady Maud over his back, as

14

neat as you like. What? No, no damage done, m'dear. Bit of a sore you-know-what. Eh, Lydie? Eh? Sends her apologies. Best wishes. That sort of thing.' He stopped in his tracks remembering something. 'And I'm escorting two ladies instead of one! Hey! Come on Caro! Judith! Where are you, b'God? Not shy – not shy, are you?' He shoved himself off Rupert and stumped back to the carriage. His two granddaughters, twins aged twelve, emerged from the recesses looking over-tall and gauche in identical muslin frills. They stared stolidly with matching brown eyes at the reception committee before them.

Sir Henry bellowed, 'Down at the Place for the holiday. Bored stiff as usual. So I said – what did I say, misses? What did your old grandfather say when he saw you?'

Judith – or perhaps it was Caroline – recited carefully, 'You said it was a damned blessing Lydie Fielding had her party tonight. Give the little vixens something to do!'

Lydia burst out laughing and Lucy protested, 'Sir Henry! How could you! Your own grand-daughters!'

Rupert grinned his wide grin and handed them down. ''Twas a blessing for us too, little ladies. We're glad to welcome you to Milton Mains.'

Lydia shepherded them into the barn and towards the laden tables, while, by the serried ranks of cider jars, Sir Henry said gruffly to Lucy, 'She's a good girl, your Lydia. A very good girl.' He accepted some cider from Drake.

'Like a sparkling cider herself, that girl.' And, pleased with the description, he repeated several times, 'A sparkling cider. That's Lydie Fielding. Her mother's looks and her father's strength. A sparkling cider.'

Lucy let him escort her back to her chair. Her smile was thoughtful as she watched her daughter.

'A sparkling cider goes flat if it is left to stand too long, Sir Henry,' she said in her gentle voice.

He looked at her sharply then followed Lydia with his gaze as she plied his granddaughters with plates of food. He did not make his usual rejoinder that such a beautiful girl would not be allowed to stand for long; he knew what she meant.

'I fancy Gus Pascoe is interested, my dear. Am I wrong?'

Lucy shrugged. 'He has called several times. I think I know his feelings. But Lydie . . .'

Sir Henry said, 'She hasn't got much choice around here, has she?' He blew again, like a grampus. 'What about if she came up to the Place now and then? Looked after the girls for Lady Maud? We might arrange one or two callers.'

Lucy smiled at him and he blinked. 'That would be most kind of you, Sir Henry. Lydia has always been fond of Judith and Caroline and it would give her great pleasure to help with them. And, if you . . .'

Sir Henry wiped his mouth on the cuff of his coat. 'We must see what we can do,' he pronounced. The Fieldings were good people.

16

Excellent tenants. 'Yes,' he said again. 'We must see about it.'

Lydia looked around for someone to fetch mulled cider for the girls and saw that Alan had taken Marella Peters into the set. She smiled, well pleased because the girl looked so happy and Alan was smiling kindly at her. Then she turned to look for Prudence and found Wesley Peters directly behind her, his eyes carefully on his sister.

Lydia said, 'She is young, Wesley, not sixteen yet. Let her enjoy herself.'

She meant it as no personal criticism of his watchfulness, but the eyes were still cold as he glanced at her.

'She is a child, yes. And children must be protected.'

'From what, pray?' She felt a prick of annoyance. 'From my brother, do you mean?'

'Not necessarily.' His eyes went back to Alan and Marella tripping lightly down the long set. 'From danger.'

Lydia was still affronted and would have continued the discussion except that there was a prompting cough from Judith and a deep sigh from Caroline.

'Ah yes.' She smiled apologetically at the girls and then at the unseeing Wesley. 'Miss Caro and Miss Judith are chilled from their ride, Wesley. Would you fetch them some mulled cider from the house if you please?'

He looked at her then and said with astonishment, 'I am no servant, ma'am!'

17

She was pleased to have broken through his preoccupation at last and her smile became gentle as she said, 'But you are a gentleman, Wesley. And these young ladies require a hot drink.' She added quietly to avoid any outright rebellion, 'They are Sir Henry Garrett's granddaughters.'

Prudence, passing with a platter of carved mutton, overheard the exchange and nudged her son with a jocular and ample hip. 'Get on, our Wesley! I'll keep an eye on Marella, never fear!' She looked at the girls. 'And you come on too, little misses. Round by the hot pies and mutton. I reckon you'll be warm enough there while my boy fetches your drink!'

Like her only daughter, Prudence Peters had none of the Methodist dourness and she shepherded her charges behind one of the laden tables and sat them on upturned tubs.

Wesley Peters said stiffly, 'Them being Sir Henry's granddaughters has nothing to do with it.' He glanced again at Marella and Alan. 'I don't know where the kitchen is . . . nothing. 'Tis years since I left Listowel and I never came to Milton Mains at all.'

Lydia took sudden pity on him, though perhaps pity was not quite what she felt. There was an unexpected current of understanding between them so that she could almost feel his tension and awkwardness. She said, 'Come on. I'll show you, then you'll know for another time. You're sure to come up here often if you're going to be home this summer. Everyone comes

18

up here at some time or another to help us out with the sheep or the cows or something.' She went ahead of him through the dancers and the diners and out into the night. It was almost dark and the wide sky was pinpricked with stars. She waited for him and smiled up into his solemn face. 'That's the trouble with a mixed farm. Pa says 'tis better to have your eggs in as many baskets as possible but there are times when you need so much help.'

At last she was rewarded with a glimmer of a smile though he made no comment as they walked across the stable yard and into the kitchen. Lydia went straight to the banked cooking fire, past the table laden with the food which she and her mother had been days in preparing. She pushed two pokers through the bottom firebars and stirred them until a red glow appeared. Then she settled them deeply and fetched a big earthenware jug from the shelf.

'It's as well I came with you,' she said to the silent Wesley as he stood awkwardly on one side of the ingle. 'I thought Drake would be here to help.'

Surprisingly, he said, 'I'd have found what was necessary, miss. I'm used to fending for myself – and others.'

She opened the bung on a cask of cider and filled the jug.

'You can call me Lydia,' she said quietly. 'I meant no condescension when I used your forename. 'Tis usual on the Moor.'

'Aye, I remember.' He seemed to make a

conscious effort to be more relaxed. 'I've come from a war, Lydia. It strings the nerves like fiddle gut. And before I left – ' he took a pot holder and half removed one of the pokers, saw it was still only dull red and pushed it back in. 'Before I left, the Moor folk were against all Methodies.'

'You're a convinced Methodist, Wesley?'

'I'm not religious if that's what you mean, but I believe in people being equal, having the same chance in life. 'Tis what Christianity is about. But the Church, the English Church, makes sure that don't happen. Methodism is something more like.'

'You're interested in politics then?' Sometimes Alan talked of politics and though she was bored by it she had noticed it usually ended in red faces and raised voices.

'I've come from a war to abolish slavery, Lydia. Aye, I'm politically minded.'

It was she who was silent now, only too conscious that she knew nothing of slavery or its abolition and liking the present order of things far too much to want to change it. It seemed to her that was what politics was about: the alteration of the present order.

He said, 'These are ready. Give me the jug, Lydia.'

She watched as he stood the jug in the hearth and plunged the glowing pokers into the cider. There was the usual steam and hissing and for a moment his face was lost in a mist. In the next instant the steam subsided and he was there, his face no longer still and waiting but flushed and slightly smiling. The pale hair was darkened by the damp and curled over his forehead and for a moment he looked like some ancient Northern god hovering over a potion.

As if in tune with her thoughts he looked up, his smile broadening. "Tis an ancient rite, this,' he remarked. 'Strange how old customs can make you feel . . . content.'

She smiled too, noticing the sensitivity in his thin mouth. 'There's nothing wrong with being happy, Wesley,' she said.

'Ah . . .' he was half serious. 'Content is one thing – it does depend on your soul being at rest. Happiness is quite another. Happiness can never give you peace. And it can lead to torment.'

She fetched a clean towel and put it over the top of the jug.

'You sound like your father, Wesley Peters!' she scolded teasingly.

He was silent and she thought she had gone too far. Nathan Peters was the sort of lay preacher known locally as a bible thumper.

She said quickly, 'Let us be content in making these little girls warm with this, shall we?' It was a plea for peace between them and he responded instantly, picking up the jug and opening the kitchen door for her with his foot. It was a small gesture that Gus had picked up from his jumped-up brother in Bristol, but with Wesley Peters it was a natural action. She gave him one of her beautiful smiles. That

21

summed him up. He was natural. A natural gentleman.

As soon as Wesley and Lydia disappeared, Alan led Marella Peters outside to cool off. The first stars shone pale in the April sky and the smell of wet fern was everywhere.

'So. You risked hell-fire, just to dance with me,' he said with some amusement, admiring the creamy column of her neck as she lifted her mane of pale Peters hair to cool her nape.

'You can laugh, Master Alan! I might miss the hell fires but I win't miss a whipping from Father if he do find out!'

'What does he object to? The dance or me?'

'Both,' she said promptly with disarming honesty. 'Dancing is always a sin. And you – leaving the land and going off to Bristol to study the law . . . Father do say law and justice is two opposites.'

Alan lifted a shoulder. 'He's not entirely wrong there,' he grinned. 'Quite a character, your father, Marella. I remember he wouldn't let any of your brothers play with the rest of us.'

'He wants us to be like him. We're inde . . . inde . . . pendent, d'you see.' She told the tale parrot-fashion. 'We don't have to touch forelocks to Sir Henry 'cos even if we lives on his land our living is our own. Father owns his boat and will likely be master of another afore long.'

'I see. So he whips you to make sure you stay independent.'

She turned and smiled up at him. Her face was like a marigold, open and radiant. He was reminded that the summer was at hand. She said, 'Don't worry yourself, Master Alan. No-one will tell him about tonight. Mother told me on the quiet that if I could give Wesley the slip I could go on and enjoy myself.'

Alan looked down at her, his smile only just holding. Her bodice had a drawstring at the neck which she had loosened to cool herself. He could see her fifteen-year-old breasts, well developed, not bound or camisoled, thrusting against the butter muslin.

He said gruffly, 'Well, you're doing that, I reckon.' He took her arm. 'Come now. Let's get back to the dance before my sister brings back your brother!' She stumbled against him on the wet turf and her laughter suddenly stilled at his closeness. He felt a tremor run through her and held her off quickly. But not before he felt a thrill of his own. No girl had shaken at his touch before and he felt masterful.

Lydia made Judith and Caroline sip their drink discreetly and then paired them off neatly with Julius and Tavvy Pascoe for the dance called 'Old Mole'. The Pascoe brothers were only too well aware that their partners were Sir Henry's granddaughters and behaved with exquisite courtesy. Well satisfied, Lydia took Gus's arm and found a place for them halfway down the set. She knew full well that Gus Pascoe had taken his turn behind the haywains with half a dozen girls, but he was her childhood friend and she smiled brilliantly at him because she was happy – or content – with everyone at that moment. The music began and Alan led Marella Peters down the set, she giggling and unsteady on her feet. Gus and Lydia fell in behind them. They both arrived by the open doors to find Wesley waiting for them.

He said curtly to his sister, 'Your bodice needs adjustment. And you had best come and help Mother now.'

Alan protested loudly. 'Good God, man, we're in the midst of a country dance! Just this last one—'

Wesley said, 'My sister is accountable to me, mister, and I am telling her to go to her mother!'

Impulsively Lydia pulled Gus from the dance and thrust herself betwen Wesley and Marella.

'Wesley! I do declare – you want to dance and will not!' she rallied him, relying on those moments of closeness they had shared in the house. She put her hands on his forearms, very conscious of his bones through the thin serge of the jacket he had not taken off. 'Come Wesley. Dance with me!'

Gus spluttered resentfully from behind, 'Hey Lydie! We were dancing this one!' And Alan, seeing his chance, almost scooped Marella back along the tunnel of arms and rustling skirts.

Wesley took a step backwards, as if he would follow them, but then said coldly, 'I think you have drunk too much, Lydia. I told you, I do not dance.'

Gus heard the rebuff and laughed loudly. Lydia was suddenly furious.

'I asked you merely to avoid unpleasantness,' she said, breathing quickly. 'But since that is what you want, please go away! Leave my party now!'

He stared down into her eyes. The whole barn was full of noise, music, chatter, raucous laughter and high, feminine giggling, but between them there was silence.

Wesley said, 'Very well, if that is what you wish.'

'It is what I wish.'

'I will fetch Marella and—'

'You will do no such thing. Marella is employed for the evening.'

'I am to watch over her.'

She said scornfully, 'I will guarantee her safety. I hardly think she will come to any harm with my brother in this crowded barn. Your insinuation is insulting.'

For a moment longer he looked at her then he turned and walked through the doors into the night.

'Young pup!' Gus slid an arm round her waist. 'You told him all right, Lydie. My wonderful Lydie.'

Lydia felt no sense of triumph, but defiance upheld her. Earlier she would have removed Gus's hand and told him that she was not 'his'. Now he was a support and she leaned against him and looked at him with enormous eyes.

'He implied that his schoolgirl sister was not safe with my brother!' she said angrily. 'Did I do right to send him packing, Gus?'

'You did right, my dear. These blasted Methodies think they own the district.'

'But I shouldn't have humiliated him.' She wanted to weep.

He said clumsily, 'He should be honoured to be humiliated by you, Lydie.' Her acquiescence to his arm encouraged him. 'Come out for a breath of air, you are overheated. Look at your brother with that little wench. He's enjoying himself, so why shouldn't you?'

Lydia thought Wesley might be lurking outside and the defiance in her rose above remorse. She let Gus pilot her to the furthest hay wain. He was thickset and heavy as so many men who handle sheep, yet he was also a light dancer and nimble on his feet. He polka'd her to the strains of Old Mole and they landed against a cartwheel, laughing breathlessly.

'Oh Gus . . . why should it be wrong to have *fun*?' Her slipper was off at the heel and she held onto him while she hopped about beneath her blue silk skirt. He mistook the meaning of the clutching hand and pulled her to him to fasten his mouth on hers. She struggled free, unsurprised. During the past year, Gus had made a habit of the sudden engulfing kiss and as she was aware of his reputation she took little notice and no offence. But it definitely interfered with what she was doing at the time, and from being an occasional companion well able to keep up with whatever daring she had in mind, he had become a nuisance.

'Gus, will you stop it!' She pretended to be

affronted. 'I am *not* the dairymaid and I wish you would bear that in mind.'

He snuffled a laugh like an eager dog. 'If you were the dairymaid, Lydie, you would not be standing up by now!' He sobered himself with an effort. 'And all that is in the past anyway, my dear. I'm a reformed character now, as I have tried to make clear this winter.'

She laughed too. 'Oh Gus. You've called twice and both times I was out with Father and you talked to Mamma about wool prices! Is that proof of your reformation? I've heard talk in the village of a certain lady—'

'Lydie!' he warned, not entirely jovially.

She did not heed the warning. 'A lady whose name reminds one of an angel—'

He grabbed at her and she eluded him easily and ran up one of the grounded shafts of the wain from where she could look down on him and be out of reach. She was laughing still, enjoying what she thought was their old rough and tumble. 'Let me see . . .' She put one of her capable fingers to her bottom lip and pretended deep concentration. 'Was it Miss Cloud? No, I don't think so.'

He leapt and almost caught her skirt, but she twitched it out of reach. 'You are not to talk of matters that do not concern you, Lydie! It is unseemly. We were talking of us. You and me!'

'Were we?' She looked perplexed for a moment then clicked a finger and thumb as adeptly as Amos Pollard. 'I know. Harper. Miss Harper – that was the name. I understood she was mad for you Gus, followed you everywhere in fact—'

He charged up the sloping shaft like a bull, seized her round the waist and tipped her over into the remnants of last year's hay. A shuffling at the far end of the wain showed that they were not the only occupants.

Gasping, Lydia hoisted herself into a sitting position.

'Really Gus! My best frock . . . and where is that slipper! Oh, thank you!' She took it from him and tapped the back of his hand with it. It checked the next ardent kiss. She went on quickly, sensing that the situation was getting beyond her. 'Papa will be looking for me to lead the Lancers. I am supposed to be hostess, Gus!'

She made a great fuss about putting on her slipper and trying to stand up. Belatedly, still panting, Gus got to his feet and pulled her upright.

'Lydie. You manage to ruin all my intentions.' He glanced sideways at her as they both leaned on the rail getting their breath. Her dark golden hair was piled on top with ringlets appearing behind each ear. He longed to bring it tumbling down. He longed to do many things.

He took a deep breath. 'Lydie, I want this evening – I want very much to make you a serious proposal. Of marriage. You must know how I feel. You are of age now and will make me a good wife. A partner. A helpmeet. A—'

'Oh Gus.' She noticed he said nothing of love.

'It sounds dull?' He snuffled another laugh.

'Not with me, Lydie. It won't be dull with me!' He slid an arm around her waist again and she felt it would be unkind to remove it, so there it stayed. 'I'm a passionate man, Lydie, and I know you could be a passionate woman. Marry me. I won't let you stagnate at Mapperly with my sister. You shall come with me to Stapleford and Bristol and – and – even London!'

She was touched by this. 'Ah Gus. I am honoured. Truly. I know you could set your cap at Sybil Lambourne—'

'She is a child, Lydie.'

'But she will grow older and would be an excellent match for you, Gus.'

'It's you I want, Lydie. You.' He pulled her against his side ardently and she could smell him. It was not unpleasant, she was used to strong smells. His hand dug into her hip and his fingers reached across her pelvis, massaging persuasively. That was not unpleasant either. She knew suddenly that if this had happened earlier in the evening she might well have accepted Gus's proposal.

She said breathlessly, 'Gus, my dear. I am so fond of you. We are like brother and sister—'

'I do not feel brotherly towards you, Lydie. Can you tell me you feel like a sister to me?'

'Please, Gus. Please stop it. I must be honest with you. I do not want to get married.'

He had her clamped to him and now he twisted abruptly so that they were facing. His hands slid down the silk of her gown and back again.

He whispered, 'You want me, Lydie. Admit it. You want me.'

'Gus . . . I do not know. But I do know that marriage is not for me yet. I am too content as I am.'

He began to kiss her. Not the enveloping kisses she knew but quick, light touches over her face and neck. He said, 'You are twenty-one today, my dear. It is no longer young. Do you want to be an old maid like my sister Joanna?'

'No!' She liked Joanna and added gaspingly, 'I admire your sister. But some day, I would like to be a wife.'

'And some day you will lose your beauty and no-one will want you!' He laughed again to take the sting from his words and moved his mouth to her ear: 'Some day, you will have half Milton Mains, Lydie. We can be the richest landowners on the Moor.'

It was the wrong thing to say. She pushed at him and gained herself a few inches.

'You say nothing of love, Gus.'

He was astonished. 'Have I not told you how I want you? Over and over again? And can't you see with your eyes and feel with your body—'

'Want!' She spoke with simulated scorn because she had felt only too well the terrible power of physical emotion. 'Want! That is not enough, Gus! There must be more than that for marriage!'

'Let me prove otherwise, Lydie!' He snatched at her and held her still with his huge arms and wide mouth so that she was unable to move a muscle. Then suddenly, at once a rescue and an abysmal humiliation, Wesley Peters's voice spoke from the ground below.

'Can I help you, Miss Lydia?'

Lydia jerked away from Gus as his hold loosened for a second. She gasped and put her hands to her ringlets. Finding them intact she stared angrily down at the strangely dignified figure beneath her.

'I thought you had left!'

'I have left the party, Miss Lydia. I am waiting to escort my sister and mother back to our cottage.' He came closer. 'Let me give you a hand down,' he said calmly.

Gus put a proprietary hand on Lydia's shoulder. 'Clear off like Miss Fielding told you – young pup! Go on! Clear off before I thrash you!'

Lydia said quickly, 'He means well, Gus. And it is time we went back in.' She picked up her skirts and stepped nimbly over the rail, intending to jump past Wesley, but his hands went immediately to her waist and she was forced to put hers on his shoulders and let him take her weight. He was stronger than she had imagined. His thin arms had tensile power and he did not even take a breath as he set her on her feet. But he was no match for Gus.

She said coldly, 'I will send Marella out to you, Wesley. Prudence will doubtless stay the night to help my mother.'

Gus scrambled down to her side and she kept herself between them.

Once inside the barn, Gus said furiously, 'How could you let him interrupt us like that? Before you had even given me an answer!'

She looked around the barn. There was no sign of Marella or Alan. She felt suddenly weary; Wesley Peters would doubtless blame her for his sister's waywardness. She said, 'I think I did give you an answer, Gus.'

'It wasn't final,' he maintained stubbornly. But he knew Lydia well enough not to press the matter further. 'I shall ask you again, Lydia. And maybe, next time, you will be only too glad to say yes.'

Fulminating, he led her into the dance. He knew that if it hadn't been for that whey-faced Methody, he would have had her. And he had told his brothers it was a sure thing.

As soon as they were on the grass, Alan stopped and took off his coat, wrapping it around Marella's shoulders.

'I should have asked Lydia if we could borrow a shawl,' he said uneasily. 'She might misconstrue the two of us going over to the house and taking one.'

'I d'reckon she was behind the haycarts,' giggled Marella. 'I don't reckon she'd have wanted to be asked anything. She was with young Mr Pascoe.'

Alan looked in the direction of the carts. They were silhouetted against the lighted barn and he saw Lydia and Gus clasped together into one figure. He stared incredulously.

Marella said with a slight lisp, 'In any case, Master Alan, once I gets in the warm house I'll be all right. I dare say Mrs Pollard has kept the fire in your bedroom. I'm that grateful to your sister for sending our Wes off home like that. There'll be no fire at the cottage and it gets cold these spring nights.'

'We're not going to my room, Marella,' Alan said automatically, still watching those black figures on the haywain. Surely Lydia knew about Gus Pascoe?

Marella said childishly, 'I did want to see your room, Master Alan. I'd like to think to myself where you do sleep. All by yourself like. I sleep with Ma and Pa and Mercy and Luke and Wesley.'

He returned to her. 'All those people, Marella? Surely not?' He was shocked but also amused. She seemed to make everything innocent.

'Not always Mercy. She only bin married to Luke these two year. But before that, there was Benjie too.'

'Is there only one bedroom in the cottage?' he asked. Robbie and Jinny Roscoe had partitions in their loft to give them some privacy and he had assumed all the villagers did likewise.

She laughed and tugged him on. 'Oh no. Six or seven at least! Come on now, Master Alan. It'll be you catching cold without your coat!'

There was no more argument; they went straight to his room. The fire was burning low and he made it up with logs and stood looking into it while she walked around examining his things with enormous interest. He thought: Lydia and Gus Pascoe. Surely not. Yet there they had been.

Marella said, 'You can read all these books, Master Alan?'

'Stop calling me Master Alan. Just Alan will do. Call me Alan.'

He looked up and saw her gazing admiringly at his bookshelves. His coat had slipped from her one shoulder and dragged the butter muslin with it. Her shoulder was perfectly rounded; a work of art. 'Go on, call me Alan,' he repeated roughly.

She looked at him fully, then dropped her eyes. 'Can you read them all, Alan?' she asked softly, her lower lip very full and trembling slightly.

He went to her and took his jacket and flung it on a chair.

'Yes, I can read them all, Marella.' He put his forefinger on her shoulder and moved it to left and right. Her skin was so smooth it was slippery.

She whispered, 'You're very clever. The cleverest man in the world, I reckon.'

He felt like a giant, powerful yet gentle.

'You're such a child,' he said tenderly.

She looked up quickly. 'No. No, I'm not a child, Alan.' With a swift movement she pushed the dress from her other shoulder. 'You see? I am not a child.'

He was dry-mouthed. 'Marella. You are fifteen.'

She stood still, waiting and submissive.

'You ain't much older. Eighteen, is it?'

'Nearly twenty. Oh my God – pull up your dress – ' He jerked the flimsy muslin to her neck and tried to pull on the drawstring. It did not help. Now that he had seen, he knew.

She sobbed like a child. 'You're hurting, Master Alan! You scratched somewhere! My back – please look – I think 'tis bleeding.' She dragged the dress down again and turned one shoulder. 'Can you see owt? It do hurt something awful.'

'I did scratch it – Marella I am so sorry.' He was a helpless midget now, flapping his hands futilely. 'I have some salve somewhere. Wait . . . Let me . . .' he fetched some jars from his closet and found something that Mrs Pollard made up from camomile. 'This – this will do. Take it.'

'Can't see, Master Alan. Can you rub it in for me?'

She twisted herself again, trying to see her shoulder blade. He got behind her and dabbed at arm's length and she relaxed immediately, closing her eyes like a satisfied kitten. Very gently he rubbed in a circular movement. She made a sound of repletion and leaned back against him. He could see her face upside-down against his shirt front, her eyes closed, her lips slightly parted. His hand slid beneath her arm and cupped her breast as if coming home. Very slowly this time, the dress slipped to the ground and she turned in his arms and lifted her mouth, smiling.

He carried her to the bed thinking: if Lydie can do it, so can I. It was a defiant thought that helped him over the first difficult moments. But as he slid into her, he knew that he had deliberately misled himself. First of all, Lydie never would . . . never with Gus Pascoe anyway. And secondly – and this brought a measure of relief – Marella, fifteen or not, was certainly no virgin.

Two

A summons came from Lady Maud the next day.

Lydia was not a bit pleased. The summer stretched ahead of her, packed with work and incident, but free; she felt that by going up to the Place to nursemaid she would lose it.

'If only it were to teach them something! They're too old and too wayward for a nurse. And I'm not good enough to be their governess – my position will be unbearable, Mamma, surely you see that?'

Lucy did not pause in chopping rhubarb for preserves.

'Dearest, you are doing Lady Maud a great favour. That is the way you must look at it. You will be occupying the young ladies during the day—'

'Because their grandparents – even the maids – cannot be bothered with them. Have you forgotten why they were brought to my party, Mamma? To give them something to do!'

Lucy took some of the precious ginger root

Alan had brought her from Bristol and added it to the preserving pan.

'Now Lydie. That is how things are arranged in such households. You cannot expect those two girls to be permitted to run wild as you were.'

'They'd be all the better for it,' Lydia protested but with acceptance in her voice now. She was lively and rebellious to a certain extent, but she had been brought up to appreciate the order of things. If Lady Maud wanted her help, Lydia knew she must give it.

Alan, descending the back stairs in his bed gown although it was nearly midday, came and sat blearily at the kitchen table, head in hands.

'Loud voices . . . not seemly at this hour. What's to do, Lydie? Surely your birthday humour has not wore off already?'

Lydia told him tersely that the Garretts needed a nursemaid for Judith and Caroline. He listened to some more wrangling and gradually relaxed against the chairback and studied his sister. He was still feeling no end of a dog after his conquest last night. As he had hurried Marella to the end of the combe he had made one more assignation with her before his return to Bristol. It had all been wonderful and exciting: the wide night, the smell of summer coming in, the murmur of the sea. Marella had assured him that old Nathan Peters and his two other sons were somewhere out there, casting their nets, and that had made him feel perfectly secure. He had negotiated the climb back to

Milton Mains with a certain amount of caution in case he bumped into Wesley. He had not. It had all been easy . . . and very successful.

Perhaps because of it, he saw Lydia in a different light. She was attractive in the same way as Marella, all sea, fresh air and country flowers; but she had a refinement Marella did not. Marella spoke of independence and had none; Lydia never mentioned it because it was innate. She was a free spirit.

He said tentatively, 'Could you not look on it as a challenge, Lydie? Give the two Garrett girls a taste of our ways. Within reason of course.'

She stopped badgering her mother and looked across the table at him. 'Take them to Jinny Roscoe's for a lesson in net-mending?' she asked, doubtful and therefore sarcastic.

'No. But you could take them to one of the coves. Let them run wild on an empty beach. Teach them to swim, perhaps. You could do it, Lydie.'

She sat down in surrender, and sighed from her pattens up.

'You know I've no choice. So you try to make it sound interesting. I thank you for that, Alan.'

He laughed, feeling again the sense of mastery – superiority – and this time over his sister who usually wielded the authority.

'Maybe a summer in another place won't do you any harm, Lydie. Give you time to think.'

'What about?' she asked suspiciously.

'Your future. You're of age now, my dear.'

'You sound like . . . someone else.' She picked

up a stick of rhubarb, dipped it into the sugar tin and passed it to him. 'I don't want to plan my future. I want it to happen.'

'Here at Milton Mains?' He chewed, screwing his face against the sharpness. 'Nothing will happen here, my dear. Except that the years will go on and you will grow older.' He felt old himself and very wise. 'You might meet someone interesting up at the Place. And if not . . . you will have the chance to see things in perspective. Like I do at Bristol.'

She did not answer but picked up her mother's knife and began the job of chopping. Lucy stirred her preserving pan and smiled quietly. Alan ran his fingers through his fine brown hair and let it fall over his brow. Lydia had told him once he looked like Lord Byron and since he had lived in Bristol he had trained the stray curl assiduously.

He said, 'Did Gus Pascoe ask you to marry him last night?'

Lucy stopped stirring and Lydia looked up from the chopping board with a startled expression, then smiled ruefully.

'Guessing games, Alan.' She gathered some rhubarb leaves and pushed them into the trough of kindling where they would dry for firing in the range. 'Well, yes. He did. And I turned him down. Properly this time.'

Alan went on in the same direct manner. 'Why?'

'His reputation is not good. Jinny Roscoe tells me that there is a Miss Alice Harper up

Carybridge way . . . respectable too. Besides, I don't think of Gus in that way.'

Alan let out a guffaw and she coloured slightly, guessing he had seen something of her tumble in the haywain.

He said sarcastically, 'And how do you think you should think of him then, sister mine?'

Her flush deepened and she was conscious that her mother was still listening by the range.

'There is no understanding between us. No tenderness. No sympathy at all, Alan.'

Lucy's slight smile returned. She tapped her wooden spoon on the side of the pan and came to the table for the rest of the rhubarb.

'Come now, children, there has been enough discussion on this matter. We are agreed that Lydia might well find her work at the Place interesting. It will certainly be a change for her. And, as Alan says, change gives a different perspective on everyday affairs.'

'So that she might realize after it, that life as the wife of one of the Pascoe boys – who have many fingers in Bristol pies as well as up here, sister – is not to be turned off lightly!' said Alan, unable to relinquish another comment on the situation.

Lydia said nothing. Lucy shook her head at her son. 'Lydie knows what she is looking for, Alan. And she has no need to make a marriage of convenience. You are both well provided for.'

Alan dropped his pose and became Lydia's younger brother again as he stood up and put an arm over her shoulders.

'If you decide to be an old maid, Lydie, I'll look after you and make something happen for you!' He was teasing again, but there was a hint of seriousness in his brown eyes as he looked down at her. 'We'll go to America – what do you say to that? As soon as I can put up my own brass plate, we'll go over and make a fortune out of the litigation that's going on over there. It's the day of the black man, so they tell me. If you're willing to defend them they will find money from somewhere and you can be a millionaire in five years. What d'you say, Lydie, eh? What d'you say to that?'

To his surprise his enterprising sister kissed him lightly and gratefully but then shook her head.

'Dear Alan. I could never live anywhere but Exmoor. I think if I dipped my hands into the earth for too long they'd grow roots and pin me here for ever.'

He said, 'You sound so sure. When did you discover this?'

She thought seriously, a faint frown between her eyes.

'Yesterday,' she replied slowly. 'At my party. Last night. When I spoke to Wesley Peters.' She smiled at her brother and then turned to Lucy and with her old frankness said, 'That was when I knew I couldn't marry Gus Pascoe, too.'

Alan laughed and kissed her cheek indulgently. He had enjoyed himself last night but he knew that Exmoor was not for him any more;

not when it rained and blew and snowed for months on end.

Lady Maud met Lydia's suggestion that she should not live in, with relief. It was arranged that Lydie would arrive at the Place by ten o'clock each morning and leave again at five when Judith and Caroline were taken over by their maid. Lady Maud wanted to accommodate the Fieldings; she was as appreciative of them as was Sir Henry, but Lydia Fielding could be wild. And Lady Maud's daughter-in-law would not brook anything but the most genteel manners in her twin daughters. As for Lydia, seven hours seemed just about bearable. She set off on her first day with trepidation but no dread.

It was four miles to the Place and she walked it, leaving Milton Mains soon after eight on a perfect May morning. She crossed the meadow where the small Fielding herd grazed day and night all summer long and had just returned after milking. Then she struck up towards the Heights through one of the dense bands of gorse and bracken that covered vast tracts of the cliffs, using a sheep track just wide enough for one person. Already it was difficult to determine where the sea ended and the sky began. The ocean sent up its distinctive smell: mixed with the new green fern everywhere it was heady stuff. She took enormous breaths and thought that if she'd been picking redcurrants with her mother she could have stopped and stared and thought her own thoughts and talked nonsense without having to mind her accent. But she was determined to get the young Garrett girls out into the countryside anyway, so there was half her desires granted and, as for chattering, it would do her no harm to guard her tongue for once. And then, as her thoughts gave themselves to the sheer enjoyment of her surroundings, her eyes met those of a stag. Everything else went from her consciousness. She froze where she was.

He was about twenty yards away, couched in shoulder-high fern, his antlers seeming part of the bracken as he watched her. Lydia stayed very still, staring back at him, knowing that he was aware he had been discovered, waiting for him to break cover. He did not move. He was wary but not afraid of her.

It seemed an endless time she was motionless, not wanting to frighten him. She had never been so close to a stag before unless he was at bay; this stag was not at bay. Calmly he looked at her, accepting her as part of the Moor with the same rights as himself. Gradually she relaxed and let her facial muscles lift very slightly. The giant head moved half an inch as if in acknowledgement. She smiled fully, beaming at him, secure because of his acceptance. Moving slowly and still holding his gaze, she backed away until she was on the road running along the Heights. She lifted her hand fractionally in a salute, then steadily walked on. After a dozen paces she risked a backward glance. He was still there.

She hurried on, ridiculously cheered by the encounter. If she stayed the rest of her life on the Moor, unmarried, it need not be a stagnant fate. Something happened every day and every hour out here in this wild and beautiful country. All that was required of her was to live.

Garrett Place was guarded by a long avenue of aspens, whispering even in the still May morning. On either side lay the famous park, dotted with rookeried elms and flanked by the imposing E of the Elizabethan manor house. Lydia's nerves tightened again as she paced sedately along the avenue – surely the longest part of this four-mile walk – and almost snapped when the oak door swung open long before she used the knocker, to reveal, not the London butler sent down by Bertram a year ago, not the imposing but familiar figure of Mrs Lomax, but a twittering maid.

'We been watching for you, miss,' she said, her eyes wide and curious. 'Master and Mistress be gone out and I'm that thankful you've come. The little ladies is hard to please.'

Lydia took a deep breath, searching her memory to put a name to this local face. 'Thank you, Bessie. Bessie Tongie, is it? I remember Sibbie your sister who went to Squire Lambourne's.'

'Aye, that's it, Miss Lydie. I was just a littl'un when you did used to call for our Sib to play. I'm thirteen now and Sibbie is twenty and married with four of her own.'

Lydia let her breath go. Sibbie Tongie with four children – and she was a year younger than Lydia herself.

'Well, take me in to the young ladies then, Bessie. I've no shawl – no, nothing for you to take, thank you.' She should have brought books and her old slate in case the girls refused to go out. There would be better books at the Place but hers would have been familiar.

Bessie opened the door into a small sun-filled morning room and immediately Lydia was surrounded by dogs. They yapped and leapt on her and she stood still, touching their noses and letting them get her scent while she surveyed the girls beyond. Both of them were dressed in dimity, with caps, aprons and patent slippers. Nothing could have been more demure. They sat side by side on the windowseat, straight-faced and solemn, only just able to contain their rabbit teeth.

Lydia waited for them to call off the dogs and when they did not she pointed to the hearth and used the voice she kept for her father's old sheepdog. 'Sit!' They obeyed.

Judith – Judith had worse teeth than Caroline, Lydia recalled – said with surprise, 'You're not frightened of them, Miss Fielding.'

'Of course not. Are you?'

'No!' said Caroline immediately.

Judith temporized more honestly. 'A little. They're so messy and they smell horrid.'

'That's not being frightened,' Caroline maintained. Then she added haughtily, 'You're late.'

'Am I?' Lydia looked for the sun through the window. 'I took no account of the time in my walk. I saw a stag.'

46

'You walked? It's miles!' There was another hint of admiration in Judith's voice and Lydia smiled, sensing an unwilling ally.

'Four, to be precise. An hour's walk. But the stag delayed me. He wasn't frightened, you see. Usually they run as soon as they get the scent of a human being. We watched each other for quite a long time. It was . . .' she searched for a word. 'It was quite thrilling.'

Caroline wrinkled her nose superciliously. 'We see them sometimes and Grandpapa becomes excited. What are we going to do now?'

'I thought your grandparents would give me instructions.' Lydia stood inside the doorway still, the lack of welcome like a wall across the room. 'Bessie tells me they are not at home. Will they soon be back?'

Caroline said condescendingly, 'Oh, do you know Bessie?' And Judith said, 'They left early for Stapleford. To get out of our way, probably. Grandfather has to see the Toryman. What is a Toryman, Miss Fielding?'

That was twice Judith had called her Miss Fielding. Caroline had called her nothing so far.

'Something to do with politics, I believe,' she said vaguely, wishing for the first time she had listened when her father talked of such matters. Wesley Peters was interested in politics. She stared at the girls and they stared back. One of the dogs lifted a heavy eyelid at the silence then dropped it again. She must think of something to do; now, at this very moment.

'Have you any older clothing? Stronger shoes?

47

Or pattens?' She made herself move forward and stand among the dogs. 'I would like to take you out into the air.'

They exchanged glances. Judith said doubtfully, 'Mamma says ladies always wear—'

Caroline interrupted with an unequivocal 'No!'

Lydia stared at them and still they stared back. It became a contest. She said firmly, 'Very well. We will walk as you are. And please observe everything very carefully as I shall ask you to write about it this afternoon.'

She pulled the bell with a confidence she did not feel and was not comforted when Bessie arrived so promptly it was evident she had been listening outside the door. Lydia's voice went up a semi-tone as she asked Bessie to inform Sir Henry and Lady Maud that Miss Fielding had taken the girls for a walk to Garrett Cove.

The footpath down the combe to the cove had obviously not been used for a long time; it was completely overgrown with cow parsley and nettles and awash in several places where the streams ran from the watershed of the Heights. Lydia had never used it herself and was soon regretting the impulse which suggested it. Her own shoes were soaked through and she dared not look at the squealing girls in case she faced outright mutiny. Her only hope was in keeping up a patter of conventional observations as if every walk they took was bound to be accompanied by wet feet and scratched arms. 'Kindly observe the bluebells, girls. They are very early this year. And there goes a butterfly – now which of you can tell me the name – '

'I've got to look down all the time,' snapped Caroline irritably. 'And I've just been stung on the back of my hand.'

Judith yowled abysmally. 'Miss Fielding, my shoe has gone again! Wait a minute till I pick it up. We'll never get back home . . . shouldn't have come . . .'

'We're here,' Lydia said, trying not to sound relieved as she parted some fronds of alder and saw the beach ahead of them. 'Come on, Judith, give me that shoe and let me clean it on some seaweed. Off you go, Caroline – run – enjoy yourself!'

The tiny cove was full of gently shelving shingle leading to gritty sand below tide level. The sea was a long way out. Lydia wiped off Judith's shoe and stared around her curiously. Although this cove lay next to Listowel it was strictly private and could only be viewed from the sea. It was pleasantly sheltered and would be ideal for bathing.

Caroline had remained next to her sister, apparently unable either to run or to enjoy herself.

She said now, 'Shall we go back?'

Lydia forced a laugh. 'Of course not, we've only just arrived. I want to explore – this is the first time I've ever been to Garrett Cove. How quiet it is. Do you swim here?'

'Papa used to. We do not. There are no bathing machines.'

'Bathing machines? What are they?'

Caroline exchanged a glance with her sister. 'Little houses which can be wheeled into the water, of course.'

'But why?' Lydia was bewildered.

'Ladies can get into the sea without being watched.' Caroline arched surprised eyebrows. 'There are many of them at Brighton. And Weymouth. Have you been to Weymouth, Miss Fielding?'

Lydia half smiled. Caroline had used her name at last and she was not to be classed with Bessie after all.

'I've never been further than Stapleford. But there are no . . . bathing machines there. Yet people swim.'

'It is not genteel.' Judith hopped as she replaced her shoe. 'Shall we go back *now*?'

Lydia took another breath. She was tired, as she would never have been at Milton Mains picking currants.

'Not yet. We are going to start a shell collection. So while we explore we must pick up all the shells we see. Now. Take off your slippers, roll up your drawers and let us start.' She leaned against a rock and unbuttoned her own shoes. 'We will also look for crabs, limpets, anemones . . . how do you spell anemone, Judith?'

The startled silence continued for three seconds then Judith spelled anemone.

'Well done!' Lydia straightened and, not looking at the girls, led the way to a shallow pool. 'Come along. The water is almost warm and – '

she bent quickly – 'here is a razor shell!' She
stared at the two still figures. 'Caroline? You're
not frightened, are you?' It had been Caroline
who had refused to admit fear of the dogs.

The mob cap jerked up. 'Of course I'm not
frightened!' The slippers were placed neatly
beside Lydia's shoes; stockings were rolled inside
them; the dimity skirt was held high. 'O-o-h, it
tickles! It's lovely! Judith come on! It's not like
Weymouth!'

Once into the water there was no stopping
either of the girls. Beneath their snobbishness
they had inherited the fearlessness of their
grandparents and they waded deep into the sea,
their cheeks afire with the sun, the hems of
dresses and drawers sopping wet. They confessed to Lydia that at Weymouth where they
had to huddle in the bathing machines with
Mamma's irritable maid, they did not enjoy the
sea. But here when they simply held up their
skirts –

'Not quite high enough it would seem,' Lydia
said drily. She smiled at them. 'If we used the
rocks instead of bathing machines, would you
like me to teach you to swim properly? Not
just splash as your mother's maid taught you
but proper strokes. Right out to the headland,
perhaps.'

Caroline did not even glance at her sister. 'Yes
please, Miss Fielding,' she said. It was the first
time either of them had said please.

Lydia called a halt at last.

'We've followed the tide almost past the point,'

she showed them. 'Look, our shoes are a long way back.'

'Just a few minutes more, Miss Fielding,' begged Caroline. 'If we could reach that rock we could get right round the point and into the next cove.'

Lydia shook her head. 'There are only rocks until the combe at Tamerton. Our feet would be cut about if we tried to clamber over them.'

Caroline stayed where she was, shielding her eyes, staring. Judith caught Lydia's hand as they turned back. 'It's been a pleasant walk, Miss Fielding. Better than riding with Tranter. Or visiting the tenants with Grandmamma to give out jam.'

'I hope you will still think so when you have committed it all to your diary, Judith.' Lydia smiled warmly down at the rabbit teeth and swung the small hand companionably. 'Have you any paper for writing and drawing?'

Judith returned the smile. 'Oh yes. Grandmamma gives us heaps and tells us to amuse ourselves. But it's difficult when you don't know what to draw or write.'

'We'll make some into diaries.' Lydia felt ideas coming thick and fast now. 'Then we can show your grandparents exactly what we are doing each day.'

'Mamma keeps a diary,' said Judith. 'All ladies do. We shall be proper ladies, Caro. Caro, we're going to make diaries and . . . Miss Fielding, where is Caroline?'

Lydia turned and stared around the confines

of the cove. There was no sign of the other twin.

She picked up her skirts again with vexation. 'She has gone around the headland, I suppose!' She started back towards the sea. 'I distinctly told her it was no use trying to go round there!'

Judith loped by her side. 'She is a very head-strong girl, Miss Fielding,' she panted. 'I am the amenable one. Caroline the headstrong one.'

Lydia might have smiled at this a few minutes before. Now she wanted only to have Caroline in front of her and dress her down. It was well past midday and they had a half-hour's climb back to the Place before they could refresh themselves. She had no wish to present Lady Maud with her granddaughters before they had changed their clothes and shoes.

She said curtly, 'Wait here, please – I mean that! If you are not on this very spot when I return I shall be extremely angry.'

She just had time to register Judith's surprise and dawning respect before she set her face to the tumble of rocks below the sheer drop of the headland to the west. She gathered her skirt and tied it in a huge knot before her, leaving her hands free, then ran quickly through the shallows and began to clamber among the sharp, limpet-studded boulders where the tide guggled with a distinct threat of menace. When she reached a vantage point she stuck her knee into a crevice and cupped her hands to her mouth.

'Caroline!' her voice bounced off the cliff and slapped back at her. 'Caroline! Where are you?'

Immediately, blessedly, Caroline's voice answered. The girl sounded excited and not a bit frightened.

'I'm here, Miss Fielding. Just below you. And you were wrong – there is a little beach and a cave! I can see it from here – a proper cave!'

Lydia looked down. Around the point in a jumble of rocks she could see Caroline's figure soaked to the skin, waving back at her.

She yelled furiously, 'Come up towards me! At once! Do you hear?'

The girl's attitude showed her shock; only her grandparents used that tone. She shouted back in her high voice, 'There's a cave, I tell you! And a beach! And anyway I can't climb up there – the sea is between us.' As she spoke a surge of water swept almost to her waist. She screamed and scrambled inland and out of sight. Lydia could hear her outraged squealing.

She shouted again, 'Listen Caroline – wait there! The tide must be coming back in and wc shall have to climb farther up. Just wait!'

But she could not go higher; not even her moor-toughened feet could manage the sharp pinnacles and knife edges of the headland. She had been right: the tide was coming in. The place where Caroline had been standing five minutes before was now covered in sliding green water.

Biting her lip, Lydia scrambled into it, letting the water fill her billowing skirt and buoy her up so that her searching feet could get purchase without taking much of her weight. Ahead of her on a tiny beach of shingle, Caroline hopped about triumphantly. Lydia dragged herself – heavy now – out of the sea, and joined her.

'Do you realize we are going to have to swim back?' she panted furiously. 'I told you we could not get around this point—'

'But we did!' Caroline said with her dreadful logic. 'And there is a beach. And a cave. So you were wrong.'

'There are hundreds of caves all along here,' snapped Lydia. 'But they are all covered at high water and are extremely dangerous. Now, remove your dress and roll it up—'

Caroline stared. 'My dress? But why? I told you I cannot swim very well.'

'Then I must swim for the two of us. Hurry, Caroline. The longer we wait, the further we must swim.'

Caroline continued to watch as Lydia stripped off her own soaking dress. 'Isn't there another way?' she asked at last in a small voice. 'If we stayed here Grandfather would send round a boat—'

'A boat.' Lydia finished tying her dress into its sleeves. 'There may be a boat in the cave. I remember your father used to row around to the harbour for fresh fish sometimes. Come on!'

She strode up the shingly beach ignoring her smarting feet. Caroline scrambled along behind her, partially regaining her old hauteur. They pressed between the giant rocks that guarded the cave entrance, over more boulders, and were inside a low damp passage, slimy with weed and smelling rank. Caroline hung about near the entrance while Lydia went on her hands and knees into the darkness, one hand stretched before her, the other trying to take some of the agonizing pressure off her bare knees. There would be a boat only if the back end of the cave was dry at high water. At last she came upon the brittle wrack left by the spent sea. After that the pebbles were ice-cold, but dry. And there was no boat.

Caroline's voice wavered from behind her. 'Miss Fielding? Is there a boat?'

There was no room to turn around. Lydia started to shuffle backwards. 'No. There is no boat, Caroline,' she panted.

There was a long silence while she decided to roll over and travel on her bottom. Then Caroline said in a very small voice indeed, 'Miss Fielding, I am sorry.'

Lydia smiled to herself in the darkness. It was almost worth her skinned legs and ruined dress to hear Caroline say that. She reached the cave entrance and led the girl into the blessed warmth of the sunshine while they removed her dress and tied it into the bundle of Lydia's.

'Takes courage to admit you're wrong, Caroline,' she said briefly. 'And after all, you did agree to take swimming lessons from me, though I hardly thought they would begin so soon.' She smiled reassuringly. 'We'll trail this bundle behind us, it will float if we tie it to some driftwood.' Caroline found half a dozen pieces eagerly. Lydia made clothes and wood into a small raft while she issued instructions. 'Don't struggle if the water laps into your mouth. Stretch out as far as you can on the sea. Don't hug me – just touch my shoulders with your fingers so that your head is clear.'

Caroline's confidence came back with a bounce in the safety of the shallow water. 'It's not difficult,' she pronounced autocratically. 'I expect I shall improve as we go along.'

'I hope so,' Lydia replied drily.

She swam with short, rapid strokes, Caroline trailing behind her as instructed. As they moved slowly and jerkily out beyond the protection of the headland they became conscious of a strong current; luckily the tide was now coming in and they were pushed towards Garrett Cove rather than out to sea. It proved a safe, even an easy journey, though they were nearly half an hour in the water. Lydia found time and energy to note with amusement that at last Caroline was obeying her to the letter; she did not speak once and the pressure of her small hands on Lydia's shoulders was constant. Perhaps something good would come from this disaster of a day after all.

Judith leapt through the shallows to meet them.

'Caroline, you are a wicked girl!' she greeted her sister smugly. 'When Miss Fielding tells Grandfather what has happened, he will punish you severely. He may even whip you!'

Caroline and Lydia collapsed onto the sand and concentrated on recovering. Judith took the clothes and struggled with the tied sleeves.

'Just look at these dresses. They're ruined with sea water! And you should see your hair!'

Lydia gasped, 'Spread them on a rock, Judith. Bessie will wash them for us when we get back to the Place.'

'She'll tell Mrs Lomax too. And Mrs Lomax will tell Grandmamma.'

'No she won't. Not if I ask her to keep silent.' Lydia scooped her hair over one shoulder and twisted some of the water from it. 'You forget, I know Bessie. She is my friend.'

'Oh. Oh yes.' Judith glanced at her sister. 'Aren't you going to tell Grandmamma and Grandpapa yourself, Miss Fielding?'

Lydia, fully recovered, also looked at Caroline. 'There will be no need to worry them, will there?' She pursed her lips judiciously. 'That is, of course, if you both promise me you will obey me instantly in future – and without question.'

Judith said swiftly, 'I wasn't naughty. I didn't go round the headland—'

Lydia said, 'Yet you are still very wet, Judith.'

Caroline took a last sobbing breath and let it go.

'It is very difficult to make promises like that,' she began haughtily. Judith rounded on her instantly.

'Miss Fielding just saved your life! You ungrateful child!'

Lydia stood up hastily and began to struggle into her soaking dress. 'Well?' she prompted.

'I promise,' Caroline said a little sulkily.

Judith slipped her hand into Lydia's. 'And I

do,' she smiled like any little girl of twelve years old and her prominent teeth looked suddenly charming. 'Poor Miss Fielding, you do look funny all wet. Won't it be fun creeping back into the house – won't it be a lovely secret?'

Caroline pulled at her frock irritably. 'Grand-papa certainly would not whip me. But it is only fair to promise, I suppose.'

Lydia said diplomatically, 'We will have fresh milk and bread and honey when we return. Then there will just be time to make our diaries.'

Judith's smile vanished. 'We don't like milk. Mrs Lomax will have cold meat ready—'

Caroline said triumphantly, 'You promised to obey Miss Fielding without question! *I* will drink milk and eat bread and honey – even if it makes me sick!'

Wrangling amiably, they began to climb the combe. The journey was twice as difficult as it had been coming down, yet there were no grumbles. Lydia was well satisfied.

She was not alone in this. When Lady Maud sent for her granddaughters on her return, she was delighted, and surprised, by their enthusiasm for their new companion. She smiled her gracious, horsy smile at Lydia and introduced her to Mr Warren – the Toryman – as 'our new governess'. Lydia made her curtsy, fully realizing the honour bestowed on her. Mr Warren, listening to Caroline and Judith expounding on the beginning of their shell collection, commented knowledgeably, 'Ah . . . modern methods of education, Miss Fielding. Very interesting. Very interesting indeed. I have acquaintances in Bristol who run a Ragged school on similar lines. Beginning with the environs of the child, I believe?'

Lydia swallowed and made do with a smile while Lady Maud neighed a laugh. 'Lydia prefers to be out of doors herself, that's the truth of the matter, Mr Warren. She has no modern educational nonsense in her head, I do assure you.'

Lydia found it best to keep her smile in place until it became sphinx-like. Mr Warren did her arguing for her and the discussion moved away and into the window embrasure, while Sir Henry listened amiably to the girls. Lydia murmured excuses to no-one in particular and retreated. As she began the walk back to Milton Mains her satisfaction became nearly smug. What had seemed like a fiasco had been turned to her advantage and the girls in their separate, contrary ways, were on her side. What was more, quite inadvertently, she had used approved methods. Already her mind teemed with ideas. She would see Lady Maud about suitable clothing for swimming; she would teach the girls to play hide-and-catch among the rocks to warm them after the sea; they could begin a pressed flower collection and mount their shells in a bed of clay. They would learn . . . well, at least they would learn how to enjoy themselves.

As she reached the place where, this morning – only this morning – she had seen the stag, she stopped and looked around, half hoping he would be there again. Of course he was not. It was somewhere between five and six o'clock, and the midsummer heat had lulled everything into complete stillness. Not a frond of fern moved, the brilliant yellow gorse was petrified, even the land itself seemed somnolent. The deer, ponies, rabbits, the myriad small animals of the Moor, must all be sleeping. Lydia smiled again as she stared around her, relishing anew the sense of belonging. Then she too froze: twenty yards behind her, the way she had just come, a single fern-head sprang up as if it had just been released from a crushing pressure.

She kept her eyes glued to that fern. Nothing more happened. Could it possibly be her stag? Had it ever happened that a stag – any animal – would lie in wait for a particular human being? It was a wonderful thought . . . but a foolish one. Lydia moved on, taking the almost invisible sheep track between shoulder-high bracken that would lead to the pasture around Milton Mains. She trod carefully with a deliberate rhythm designed to soothe any wild animal in the vicinity. A quarter of a mile from home the sheep track opened into the farm pastures and the smoke from the cooking hearth could be seen apparently rising from the ground itself. Milton Mains, like all big farms, was sited within a fold of land to protect it from the weather and was invisible until you were almost on it.

Confidently Lydia walked across the pasture to the gate by the rhododendron hedge and looked back. The ground was clear and empty behind her; no stag. But as she opened the gate she caught a glimpse of russet movement in the woods to her left which came down almost to the kitchen garden. It was ridiculous; a trick of the dipping sun. No stag could work out that he could keep her in sight by branching upward from the bracken and taking to the trees.

All the same, after she had greeted her parents and told Mrs Pollard that they did not serve food as good as hers at the Place and read a letter which had arrived from Alan that day, she asked her father whether there was news of a lone stag in the district.

He shook his head. 'They'll be inland now,' he said. 'Plenty of food up on the Heights for them. The one you saw would be on his way to join the herd.'

Lydia nodded. 'Yes, I suppose so. But he gave me such comfort – I confess I was nervous this morning.'

'And tired and bedraggled tonight,' Rupert observed disapprovingly. 'Looks as if you've been picking currants instead of teaching two young ladies. You'll have to mend your appearance, Lydie.'

Suddenly Lydia was too tired to recount the afternoon's adventure. Besides, perhaps it was a secret for herself and the girls only. Her mood of satisfaction was disappearing as her weariness increased.

Lucy leaned forward worriedly. 'Yes, you do look tired indeed, my child. To bed with you.' She recalled her conversation with Sir Henry last month and could not resist adding, 'And they introduced you to Mr Warren, did they? He was a pleasant young man? Married?'

'Mr Warren? Oh, the Toryman. Yes, he came back for dinner and was introduced. I cannot recall . . . he was about fifty, I imagine.' No real interest could be heard in Lydia's voice. He had approved her methods with Caroline and Judith but probably it had been just polite talk. So much talk . . .

She took her mother's advice and went to bed. And she took Alan's letter with her to re-read. He sounded different. His letter reminded her in some odd way of Caroline Garrett. High-handed and consciously superior. Not that it mattered. Nothing mattered except sleep. She closed her eyes and almost at once began to dream. Of the stag and its protection.

Three

It was a good summer. By mid-June, Rupert
Fielding had made two fields of hay, reared most
of his lambs, had his cows in the high summer
pasture and was finishing up last year's cider
with anyone who cared to join him. Gus Pascoe
had made him a better offer than usual for his
wool and he had sent half a dozen cartloads
to the warehouse in Stapleford, where Octavius
Pascoe – Tavvy to everyone on the Moor – would
have it sorted for shipment to the Yorkshire
mills via the Bristol office and Julius. Rupert was
convinced the good price it fetched was something to do with Lydia's influence on the
youngest Pascoe boy. He began to link their
names affectionately and when he went carousing in Carybridge and met up with Gus, he
greeted him as one of the family and ended
up the evening weeping on his shoulder. Gus
did nothing to change this state of affairs. He
grinned and patted Rupert's back and said of
course he'd look after Lydia and be good to
her. He called at weekends when she was home

and courted her assiduously, not in the least discouraged by her coolness.

'Get this school-marming out of her system and she'll come running,' he confided to an apologetic Rupert. 'I could tell at her birthday party. She's a late starter is your Lydie, but once she's in season there'll be no holding her!'

Rupert knew it was only Gus's way of talking and after a slight hesitation he laughed as raucously as any Pascoe, and when Betty Sperring, who lived at the Carybridge kiddley, passed by with a tray of cider pots, he pulled her onto his lap and squeezed her breasts until she screamed. Everyone enjoyed that and slapped him on the back and – if he'd realized it – he felt just as his son had felt last April the twenty-third. No end of a dog. Just like one of the Pascoe boys.

Lydia was soon very thankful for her work at the Place. It enabled her to push thought of Gus and his unwelcome attentions right away; and it was fascinating for its own sake. As her rapport with the girls increased, they became more amenable, not only to her but to their grandparents. This meant that once or twice each week they spent the day with Lady Maud and Sir Henry, so Lydia was free to follow her own pursuits. She helped her mother as much as she could and saw that this was still not enough; Lucy grew tired too quickly these days. When Prudence Peters visited Mrs Pollard next, Lydia asked her whether Marella could be spared to live in for the rest of the summer and help out where need be.

'I know how Nathan feels about it,' Lydia said hastily, anticipating refusal. 'But I do assure you that my mother would care for her as a daughter while she was under our roof. And I am home in any case each evening so—'

'I d'reckon her pa 'ud be glad to see her settled and bringin' in some wages of her own,' Prudence said surprisingly. 'He'm wanting to get off on the preaching circuit now Wesley be back 'ome. An' certainly our Wes got better things to do than follow his sister around all day. Yes. I d'reckon Nathan might be glad to lend 'er to 'ee, Miss Lydie.'

Lydia was silent. She had thought of asking for Marella's help as a link between the families, and had wanted Wesley's name to come up. Now it had, she could think of nothing to say.

Mrs Pollard nodded sagely. 'Certainly your ma needs somebody by her more often, Miss Lydie. I does the rough and what else I can, but she won't let me near the cooking stove and with all the fruit to be preserved this year, she don't hardly move away from it!'

Prudence put a greasy hand on Lydia's arm. 'Don't worry about it no more, my girl. Marella shall be at the kitchen door first thing tomorrow morning. An' if you can give her a bed and keep her with you, it will be a blessing all round.'

So Marella Peters came to work at Milton Mains and proved cheerful and biddable. Yet, in spite of her tumble of golden hair being confined in a cap and the drawstring being pulled tight to her neck and an oversmock covering her to her knees, she still managed to look a minx. As they cleared supper one night Lydia tried to draw her into the family conversation.

'Do you think it is possible to be followed every day by a stag, Marella? The same stag?' It pleased her to indulge her fancy that the stag was still keeping her company though she knew it was impossible.

Marella looked at her knowingly with her sky-blue eyes. She replied in a saucy voice that surprised Lydia. 'Aye. Aye, I think that very likely, Miss Lydie.' Her smile widened. 'Specially if he's a two-legged animal!'

Only Rupert laughed at this sally. Lydia wondered what Wesley would make of it. And Lucy looked anxious.

So the summer went on. The Garrett girls finished their shell collection and their carefully annotated book of pressed wild flowers. They learned to swim like fish, to play tick-tack-toe and stool-ball on the privacy of the beach and to 'draw perspective', frowning at Lydia's description of the disappearing point as 'nothingness'. For their part, their grandparents tried to fulfil their side of the bargain. Twice more they produced Anthony Warren for inspection. Then he became betrothed to a young lady in Bristol with pronounced radical views and his career as a Toryman, let alone Lydia's suitor, was in jeopardy. After that they arranged for a stalwart, middle-aged dairy farmer from the Somerset Levels to inspect their herd and asked Lydia to tell him something of the Fielding heifers. She did so obligingly but showed no more interest. Without hope they introduced her to Squire Lambourne's eldest son; the Lambournes were far above the Fieldings, but more unequal matches were known. Lydia described him to Caroline as a milksop and Caroline passed on this opinion to her grandmother.

Lady Maud said to Sir Henry, 'I give up, my dear. The girl is courted already by the youngest Pascoe, and that would be a most suitable match.'

Sir Henry looked doubtful. 'Fielding would like it, that's for sure. But Lucy Fielding . . . I ain't sure about her feelings. As for the girl herself, she professes to despise the Pascoes because of their hold on the wool buying.'

'Nevertheless I understand from Mrs Lomax that the Fieldings got a good price for their wool this season.' Lady Maud sniffed. 'I think we'd best leave young Lydie Fielding to work out her own life. Seems she isn't doing so too badly.'

After this exchange, it was logical that Sir Henry should send a messenger to Mapperly House requesting Mr Pascoe to carry out a head count on the Garrett flocks at Tamerton. This entailed two days' work, during which time Gus was invited to lunch on the terrace. It gave Gus a certain status as an accepted friend of the 'governess', as Lydia was officially known. She felt herself being edged into an embarrassing situation, underlined by Judith's aside on the second afternoon: 'I hope you don't marry Mr Pascoe, Miss Fielding. I'd prefer you to stay an old maid.' Which made Lydia want to laugh and cry at the same time.

His task finished that second day, Gus walked home with her along the Heights road. He led his horse, the animal's nose reassuringly between their shoulders, and asked after Alan and, more closely, after Lucy. Lydia relaxed slightly and tried to remember how companionable he had been in the days when Alan was home.

'I miss Alan a lot,' she confessed. 'He will have been with Mr Swallow a whole year come Christmas. And Mother . . . she tires so easily. I do not think she is well.' She had not voiced the thought before and it terrified her with its own certainty. She went on quickly, 'How is Joanna? Julius? Tavvy?'

Gus shrugged. 'Joanna has taken the running of Mapperly out of Mother's hands, it is her reason for life now. When your – er – charges have returned to London, she will call and you can talk. She can tell you about Mapperly. And anything else you wish to know of our affairs.'

Lydia was about to reply sharply that she had no wish to know anything of the Pascoe affairs when her eye was taken by a movement in the fern. They had reached the junction of the road and the sheep track and she halted quickly and kept her eyes on the place.

Gus said, 'Well? Aren't you going to ask me to supper, Lydie? I promised your father I would accompany him to Carybridge tonight and – what is it, Lydie?'

'Nothing at all. I must hurry, Gus. Mamma

needs help with supper.' She turned as she spoke and almost ran a dozen steps into the midst of the fern. Over to the left there was a rustle.

Gus said quietly, 'All right, my dear, I am behind you. We will keep walking at a steady pace. Talking normally. When we have rounded the bend I will drop behind and you will go on with the horse.'

She said, 'No, Gus. Please. It's a stag – he's followed me before – '

'Don't be a fool, Lydie. More like a gypsy. Now. Where were we? Ah, Julius. Anne has just had another laying-in. Julius keeps busy. They have been married four years and this is the fifth child.' He sniggered and Lydia quickened her pace desperately. 'As for Tavvy – he connives, as usual.'

'Connives?'

'With politicians. With influential women.' His voice dropped an octave. 'Here, take these – ' he thrust the reins into Lydia's hand. 'I'll drop behind some fern and wait. Continue talking as if I were with you.'

She had no choice but to go on ahead but she did not like it, though she could not say why. He had no gun so he could not hurt the stag, yet still she did not like it. It was an invasion of something very secret and very precious.

However, there was nothing for it but to plod on. Occasionally she glanced around but there was nothing to see. Gus was as used to the Moor as was the stag and he did not need to move.

Small groups of gnats danced here and there in skeins and clusters; there was a heaviness to the day that had pressed them earthwards. She hoped it would do the same for all the other animals. She hoped they would lie couched and still and watch her approach her own pasture land. Or perhaps cut across to the woods as before and disappear on the endless barren stretches of the Heights.

Then, suddenly, there was a cry behind her.

She stopped and pushed against the horse. She heard it again. A triumphant bellow that was definitely Gus, then a choking, strangling sound, animal and desperate.

She dropped the reins and ran, panting back up the steep slope, stumbling, half falling, grabbing at the fern roots to pull herself up and along. She rounded a bend and there they were.

Gus was upright, leaning back slightly, holding against his shirt front – clamped to him with one massive arm – a shape that at first to Lydia's startled eyes did indeed appear to be a stag. Then she saw that the red torso was a russet smock and the aureoled head almost buried in Gus's shoulder was a man's. She stared, horrified. It was Wesley Peters. That fair hair and those blue eyes were unmistakable. He was her stag. He had watched protectively . . . been aware of her . . . just as she had been aware of him ever since their first meeting.

'Got him! Got him, Lydie! This is your stag – some stag indeed!'

Gus panted the words triumphantly, ending

with a grunt of pain as Wesley jabbed fiercely with his elbow. Although the smocked figure looked slight against Gus's barrel chest, it was obvious it had only been captured and held there by sheer surprise. Wesley had a lean hardness tempered into steel by endless hours at sea.

Gus tightened his arm viciously and crooked his knee against his opponent's spine, bending him like a sapling. Lydia choked a cry of protest.

'What'll I do with him?' Gus was exuberantly joyful, the victor and the rescuer.

'Let him go!' Lydia put her hands to her face. Her cheeks were burning hot. 'For God's sake – let him go!'

Amazement made Gus slacken his hold slightly. 'Let him *go*?' His face was purple above the straw-pale hair. 'He was following you, dammit! He might have grabbed you, Lydie—'

'Be quiet, Gus! He had no such intention!' She could have wept. He was still her stag and he was trapped.

'How do you know his intention? Don't be a fool, Lydie. He must be whipped – made an example – '

Wesley, who had bent so pliantly to his captor, took advantage of the respite to heave himself forward. Gus stumbled and it was enough. The wooden pattens thrust into his shins, two russet-clad arms came up and grabbed his head and with a jerk of the back, Wesley sent Gus's heavy figure hurtling forward to land with a sickening thump in the bracken. He lay there winded and after the first horrified glance, Lydia's gaze went back to Wesley.

She said rapidly in a low voice, 'Are you all right?'

'Yes.' Wesley stared back at her, panting only slightly. 'Is it true you're going to marry him?'

'No. It is not true.' She swallowed and spared a glance for Gus who was groaning and beginning to retch. 'Have you done this often?' She was going to ask 'Have you followed me?', but changed it to 'Have you been with me on the way home before?'

'When the tide allows.'

His voice was deeper than she remembered, husky with slurred sibilants. Lydia recalled that he was a fisherman and would be in his boat for twelve hours out of the twenty-four.

'Why?' she asked.

'I want to be near you.'

She gasped at his directness and found she could no longer hold his steady blue gaze. She was conscious of herself and then of him, two bodies displacing air, in relationship to each other. She had to breathe carefully. This was all too soon, too quick, she did not know what to say or do. There were no rules any more.

In the bracken Gus finished retching and got to his knees beginning to curse.

Wesley said quietly, 'Lydia. Be wary of this man. He cannot control his passions.'

It was a reminder to her and she advanced towards Gus. 'Go quickly,' she hissed over her shoulder. 'I will make sure he says nothing – go now!'

'And leave you with him?'

'I shall be all right – I have known him since we were children – please go, Wesley!'

Whether it was her look or tone of voice she did not know, but after another uncertain look at the bull-like figure in the bracken, Wesley did indeed turn and disappear into the opposite wall of fern.

Lydia knelt by Gus and supported him. Her heart beat with heavy, hard strokes; she hardly felt the weight of his winded body; she could think of nothing but Wesley Peters. The link with the stag was curiously strong. There were many stories on Exmoor of men changing into stags and she almost wished they were true.

Gus slobbered onto her shoulder and gasped, 'I'll kill him! Just let me get at him! Let me—'

She spoke calmly into his ear. 'He has gone, Gus. And it was you who attacked him – and came off worse.' She got to her feet, crouching above him. 'Now, come. Stand up and let me get you to your horse.'

'You're for him! My God, Lydie, you're for that damned vagrant – after he followed you and would have raped you, given half a chance!'

Her face flamed but she said, 'Ridiculous! Really, Gus – in broad daylight on my own ground? And he is not a vagrant. He is a fisher-man—'

'A mealy-mouthed Methodist! Yes, I recog-nized him, don't think I didn't! That blasted

74

Peters whelp, the one you sent packing from your party. Have you forgotten that, my girl? He wanted to pay you out for that! Stag, indeed . . .'

Somehow she got him to his horse while he spoke, and shoved at him until he put a foot into the stirrup and levered himself into the saddle. She was panting herself.

'Listen, Gus. You did not cut a pretty figure back there. I will say nothing about it if you will keep silent also.' Somehow it was vital to keep Wesley's partisanship a secret. She did not know why.

He fidgeted in the saddle, regaining some composure.

'I should have thought you'd want your father to horsewhip him.' Gus stared down at her, his eyes jealous. 'All very romantic you think, don't you, Lydie? I can read you like one of your Gothicks.'

Somehow she met his eyes. 'The whole incident would worry Mamma very much. I would prefer it not to be spoken of.'

'Ah. So you ask my confidence as a favour now?' He leaned down. 'Favours must be paid for, Lydie. Come here.' He encircled her with his arm and pulled her up till the tips of her toes brushed the dusty path, then he kissed her wetly.

Her own physical awareness stimulated by Wesley made Lydia terribly conscious of Gus's iron-hard arm forcing her breasts upwards, pressing her against his thick leg so that the horse fidgeted and she was tossed helplessly about, her sunbonnet knocked askew, her mouth open beneath his, invaded. When he released her, the horse's shoulder knocked her onto the soft fern and for a moment she lay there feeling so exactly like a plucked and discarded flower she could almost feel the pain of severance. Above her Gus laughed.

'Now you have a small idea of how I felt, my dear.' He slid off the saddle and pulled her up. 'Angry? Hit me if you like.'

Strangely, she wasn't angry. If that was the price of secrecy, she had paid it. She said, 'I don't want to hit you, Gus. Let it be pax now.' She dusted down her skirt and settled her bonnet. 'Come. They will wonder what has happened to me.' She led the way ahead of him across the pasture and through the side gate. There was no flash of russet in the opposite belt of trees though she stared till her eyes ached.

It was taken for granted that Gus would stay to supper and he and Rupert went to the fields to see to the cows while she helped her mother and Marella. She hardly noticed the conversation during the meal nor the way Marella giggled when Gus pinched her waist. Her whole mind was occupied with Wesley Peters and . . . and what would happen next. When Gus took Rupert off to Carybridge she was forced to notice Lucy's sudden tiredness amounting to a near collapse. She called Marella out of the scullery to help her undress her mother and put her to bed. In spite of Lucy's assurances, she was worried.

'Is she often like this, Marella?' she asked. 'When I am at the Place?'

Marella shrugged. 'She do get tired. Ah. Oftentimes. But 'tis Master. Goin' off like. That's what upset 'er tonight.'

'But . . . but he often goes in to Carybridge. He was with Mr Pascoe.'

Marella giggled, unconcerned. 'That's the trouble, Miss Lydie.' She saw Lydia's incomprehension and shook her head. 'Don'ee worry about it. No 'arm. No 'arm at all. You'm looking tired yourself, miss. Get you to bed while I clears up down b'low.'

Lydia was thankful to do so. There was still some light in the sky and it was Saturday tomorrow so she could spend time looking after her mother. Two whole days before she took the Heights road again. She tipped her head and brushed her hair from underneath. It sprang up with a life of its own, crackling around her head like fire. She felt on fire, wanting something she could not quite identify, something great and wonderful. She lit a candle and carried it to the window to pull the curtains. There she paused. It was a beautiful night, darkness settling on the earth but the sky still pearly with one or two stars showing above the Heights. The woods were a solid block of black against the greys and she stared at them until her eyes ached, recalling the first time she had seen her stag. He must have cut right across Milton Mains's boundary and down to the village a good four miles away. Unless he had come through the rhododendron hedge and skirted the kitchen garden to pick up the path again at the main gate.

Her eyes flickered over the garden, following his possible route; then stopped. Somewhere between the stick beans and winter cabbage, there was a movement that was at once familiar, exciting and soothing. She stared again. She was surely seeing what she wanted to see; he would not still be here.

Yet he was. She blew out the candle and withdrew slightly behind the curtain. For a long moment nothing happened, then a figure crept out of the shadow of the rhododendron and loped towards the gate. The moon rode up from the Heights and silvered his straw-coloured hair. The gate swung silently and he was gone.

Lydia sat on the edge of her bed. She smiled into the darkness. He was her own. Her knight. Her stag. She drew the sheet to her chin and her last waking thought was that she was pleased that it was summer and she was wearing her cambric nightgown. And that she had brushed her long, autumn-coloured hair till it must have been shining with a light all its own.

The next day Lucy seemed perfectly normal. Pollard was out milking because Rupert was still abed and Lucy was determined that he was to be undisturbed.

'Let me take him some food, Mamma,' Lydia suggested helplessly. 'No need for you to run up and down the stairs more than once a day.'

'He'll be down soon,' Lucy replied calmly.

'Now, child, were you planning to pay a visit to Jinny Roscoe this morning? Because if so you can bring back pilchard oil and take some preserves.'

'I had changed my plans, Mamma. I want you to rest while I see to things here.'

But Lucy would have none of it. She had already packed a basket and almost hurried Lydia out of the kitchen door. Marella, lugging linen to the wash-house, paused and watched the small scene with what appeared to be amusement.

'Your mam dun't want you to see your pa like 'e is,' she said as if offering comfort. ''E'll be all right by midday. Usually is.'

Lydia was horrified. 'Does this happen often, Marella?' she asked unguardedly.

Marella shrugged. 'Not often. No. Once, twice a month. 'Im and Mis'er Pascoe do meet up for cards and one thing do lead to another. You know.'

Lydia wished she had not asked. She must speak to Gus. And she must do so in such a way that it was not another favour she asked. As she started across the yard Marella said, 'I needs to talk to you, Miss Lydie. Serious like.'

Lydia looked over her shoulder, surprised then confused. Could it be something to do with Wesley? She wanted to see Jinny Roscoe with a view to questioning her about the Peters family in general and Wesley in particular, but she couldn't bear to discuss him with Marella.

She said, 'I have an errand for my mother. In the village.'

For a moment Marella looked stubborn, then she shrugged again.

'When you comes back then, eh? Looks like I'll be spending the day in the wash-house so if you comes straight there . . .' It was almost a command. Lydia watched the smocked figure sway through the door and turned away, frowning. She had a suspicion Marella was not pulling her weight at Milton Mains and her familiarity was beginning to border on the impertinent. Even Wesley's young sister could not be allowed licence.

It was a relief to spend two hours in the company of straightforward Jinny. The two girls had always got on well; they were both capable and supremely well adapted to their wild environment. When Mrs Roscoe had died in childbirth leaving Jinny to look after the family at only twelve years old, Jinny had done that without fuss. It had kept her out of service and given her some status very early in life. Lucy had helped out where she could and Lydia had taught Jinny and Robbie to read and included them in picnics and fishing expeditions so that there had been plenty of joy in their lives besides hard work.

After the girls had exchanged gifts – fish oil for preserves – they stepped out of their pattens and lifting their skirts waded out through the tide pools to the nearest upturned boat where they settled themselves like gulls for a talk. Robbie and Pa Roscoe were mending nets in the cottage and further up the beach the local children scrambled among the shingle for fish-head bait or shells, according to their preference. The girls knew from past experience where to look for privacy.

Lydia was bursting with news, but, as usual when she had a precious secret, she hugged it to herself for as long as possible and asked for Jinny's news first.

'What has happened over Tom Johnson?' she enquired. 'What with the wretched Garretts I have not seen you all summer and would not have been surprised to hear you were married!' The Johnsons were labourers on the Lambourne land and the youngest son had taken to walking down to Listowel on Sundays all last winter to court Jinny.

She did not colour as usual. 'Pa told him to find someone else. Their cottage is full and overflowing and Pa says I should be just a drudge up there.' She looked regretful; she was a drudge for her father and brothers and Tom Johnson might have offered compensations they could not. 'Pa went to see old Nathan Peters. Wesley – the youngest – has been home since last spring and Pa thought—'

Lydia said, appalled, 'They're Methodies! And everyone knows what a narrow-minded old man Nathan is!'

Jinny was practical to the core. 'I wouldn't be marrying Nathan. An' Wesley's able to provide a separate cottage. Maybe more than a cottage. He's got wonderful plans has Wesley Peters – something to do with politics – I don't rightly understand—'

'Has he talked to you of these plans?' Lydia felt as if their upturned boat were on the high seas.

'No!' Jinny laughed. 'It's got no further than talking between Pa and Nathan. It's what I hear, though. All the small sheep farmers are grumbling about the hold the Pascoes got on the wool buying – well you know your own pa can't abear it, can he? Anyway, Wesley Peters talks about a co-operative. He'd run the wool up to the Yorkshire ports direct, see, and then divide whatever he got between—'

'He can't do that! The Pascoes will squeeze him out – ruin him! Don't you recall Mr Drewitt? He piled his fleeces on four wagons and tried to drive them into Bristol and they ended up at the bottom of Tamerton Cliff?'

'That's why it has to be a co-operative. And done by sea.'

Lydia swallowed and stared at the jetty, wondering whether one of the assembled net-menders could be Wesley. He was pitting himself against the ambitious Pascoes, which meant danger. Especially as Gus already had him marked after yesterday. Rupert, her own father, played cards with Gus two or three times each month . . . so where was she in all this tangle? And what did it matter if a match was being arranged between Wesley and Jinny? Her best friend.

Jinny said, 'And what of you? How are your charges?'

Lydia was thankful to be able to speak of Caroline and Judith, a far cry from stags who suddenly changed into knights errant. She expounded at some length until quizzical Jinny openly laughed.

'I never thought to see you turn into a schoolmarm, Lydie!' she teased. 'I confess I hardly understand some of the ideas you've been trying, though I can see it is all interesting. But I also hear that in spite of such business, you have time to entertain Mr Pascoe to supper?' She laughed again at Lydia's expression. 'Robbie met Amos Pollard last night and he passed on the news – no secrets in Listowel, Lydie.'

Lydia bit her lip, knowing that to be true and wondering whether anyone else had seen her 'stag'. She dismissed Gus's courtship decisively but admitted that the situation was becoming difficult.

'Everyone – certainly Father – even Sir Henry and Lady Maud – seem to think it is settled,' she complained. 'I've no wish to offend Gus mortally by sending him packing, yet because I accept him as a friend—'

Jinny said definitely, 'There is no such thing as friendship between men and women on the Moor, Lydie. You should know that.'

'I will show that there is! I can be friends with Gus Pascoe without wanting to wed him!'

'But can Mr Pascoe be friends with you?' Jinny slid off the boat and wrung some wet from the hem of her skirt. 'I think if it were not for his reputation, you might look kindly on him, Lydie. It would be a good thing for Milton Mains. And an interesting life.'

'It depends what you mean by interesting.'
Lydia shook her head. 'Not for me, Jinny.' She
too lowered herself into the incoming tide.
'They'll be going out this afternoon and staying
all night, I suppose?' She referred to the small
fishing fleet.

Jinny nodded. 'It's been a good year. We've
salted enough barrels to last till January and the
gleanings from Sir Henry's corn were sufficient
for two sacks of flour.'

'The Lambourne orchards should be ready for
clearing in a few weeks.' Lydia grinned at her
friend. 'We'll go as usual, Jinny? I shall finish up
at the Place in another month. October . . .
apple time . . . ducking in the tub.' She lifted her
face to the summer sky, relishing the delights of
autumn in spite of her confusion over Wesley
Peters. After all, it sounded as though Wesley
with his politics spelled change, and hadn't she
decided she wanted nothing to change?

She ate pilchards with Jinny at midday and
walked back up the combe, arriving at Milton
Mains at four o'clock. It was mid-August, yet a
mist was beginning to collect along the tumbling
waters of the Stowe river as it swept down the
combe towards the village. She stood at the gate
and looked down on it, smiling slightly because
it heralded all the things she and Jinny could
share. It had been a better summer than she had
imagined at the Place, but the winter would be
even better. Her stag had been flushed into the
open now; Wesley must declare himself. She bit
her lip as she remembered that Jinny's father

84

was negotiating with old Nathan Peters to make a match for his daughter. Would it make any difference to the long friendship between the two girls?

Still frowning, she took the fish oil into the kitchen for her mother, pleased yet anxious too to find her sleeping in the wooden armchair next to the range. Quietly she put the kettle on the trivet to boil for tea and crept out into the yard again, remembering Marella. She found the wash-house door propped open and Marella inside. Having progressed to the ironing, the girl was red-faced and perspiring in the heat from the furnace. The rack holding the irons against the fire-bars was full and on the whitened scrub boards lay Rupert's best suit. Marella spread a wet cloth over it and fetched an iron. She recoiled slightly from the hiss of steam then looked up and saw Lydia.

'I bin at it all day,' she excused her ineptness defiantly. 'The lines up the croft are near touching the grass with the weight of it all! And now your pa comes storming in wanting 'is suit for a funeral.'

'Let me – ' Lydia sidled behind Marella and took the iron and cloth from her. 'You look faint. Go and stand by the door while you tell me whatever it is you have on your mind.' The girl went immediately outside, gulping air like a fish; she was not made for Lucy's kind of house-keeping, that was for sure. Prudence Peters's slap-happy methods were as much as Marella could manage. Lydia did not care for her obvious resentment. 'Whose funeral is it, do you know?' she asked, hoping to avoid any overt complainings.

'One o' they reddlers,' Marella replied without interest. 'Your pa says 'e were only drinkin' wi' 'im last week. Now – phut – he's gone.' She looked back lugubriously as Lydia slammed down the iron, lifted it onto the trivet, turned the cloth, slammed again. ''E won't be the only one at this rate, neither.'

Lydia tried to laugh. 'We're not working you that hard, Marella,' she protested. 'Surely you had to help at home?'

'Oh aye. But I were strong enough then. 'Tis different now.'

Lydia looked up in surprise but Marella's eyes had shifted beyond the garden wall to the woods. Lydia changed the iron and finished her father's suit, folded the cloths, hung the suit on the horse and riddled the furnace. 'Well?' she prompted.

''Tis more difficult than I thought . . . I'll put the horse in the sun, Miss Lydie.'

The girl came in and lifted the wooden frame through the doorway then sat on the yard wall pushing her hair beneath her cap and glancing again at the wood. 'I did think I saw Wesley up there a minute ago. My brother.'

Lydia, following and leaning against the rough stone, felt her heart leap and then settle into a hard beat.

'The tide is coming in. He'll be getting ready to go out with the other boats, surely?'

'Unless 'e lets Benjie take over. Father ast 'im

to watch me an' so 'e does. All the time. Almost as if 'e knows.'

Lydia took a deep breath. 'Knows? Knows what, Marella?'

Marella seemed to gather herself together. She said flatly, 'I'm in trouble, miss. In the family way.'

Lydia stared at her, horrified. She remembered Wesley's concern and how foolish she had thought it. And he was still watching his sister . . . He had told Lydia he wanted to be near her . . . yet his father had gone on a preaching mission and had instructed him to watch Marella . . . not Lydia . . .

She forced herself to deal with one thing at a time. She and Alan had listened at the door when Lucy dealt with this kind of thing in the past. How did she go about it?

'Are you . . . is it . . . far gone, Marella?' she enquired at last.

'Four months,' Marella spoke sulkily now. 'And don't ast me why I an't got rid of it before now. I went to Tamerton and saw old Mrs Nancombe and she—'

'I wasn't going to suggest that,' Lydia interrupted quickly. 'What you are suggesting is far too dangerous – don't you recall Nancy Quick? She died of putrefaction after she'd gone to Stapleford to try to lose her baby. Don't consider that, Marella.'

'Mrs Nancombe only gev me seaweed pills.' Marella's full mouth drooped sullenly. 'An' I only tooked one an' I were sick.'

Lydia sawed at her underlip. 'Um . . . er . . . the father. Will he marry you, Marella?'

'I don't know.' Marella looked up and at last her blue eyes filled with tears. 'I'd marry 'im tomorrow. Any girl would.' A childish hiccup jerked her milky throat. 'But 'im . . . I don't know. Mind, our family – we're not servants. Not gen'lly. Father don't like me being 'ere. He 'drather I mended the nets and salted the fish down. But course I knew I 'ad to get away for a bit till things could be sorted out. 'E'd 'ave discovered 'ow I was – early on when I were bein' sick.'

'Yes. Yes, of course.' Lydia felt herself on firmer ground. 'Your father is a proud man and rightly so. But your . . . the father of *your* child – he will be proud too. Proud to marry you. Mrs Pollard says you are learning to be a good little housewife.' Mrs Pollard had said no such thing. 'He'll be glad to look after you too. Why, this is something to be pleased about! Don't cry, Marella.'

The blue eyes were drowning. 'Whether 'e be proud or not, Miss Lydie, 'tis 'is duty to marry me! 'E put the child inside me and—'

'Quite.' Lydia wanted to end the interview now. The kettle would be boiling . . . her mother would know what to do. 'Could you not confide in your brother? Ask him to speak to the young man if you think there may be . . . difficulties? I hardly think I am the one—'

'But you are, Miss Lydie!' Marella got down, and, as the smock caught on the rough wall,

88

Lydia could indeed see a thickening in the young figure. 'You are the only one. That's why I ast you. Can't you see what I'm a-trying to tell you? I'm four months gone. Four months ago it was your birthday party in the barn. And Master Alan took me to the house to get a shawl.' She giggled. 'But he kept me warm other ways.'

There was a long silence. Lydia stared at her, appalled. At last she said thickly, 'Are you trying to tell me that Alan is the – the – '

'The father. Aye. He is.' Marella bridled. 'I 'aven't been with no other man, Miss Lydie. Master Alan swep' me off my feet that night. I loves 'im dearly and that's the truth of it.'

Lydia whispered, 'I can't believe it.' Yet she knew it was true. It accounted for Alan's naive arrogance.

'Believe it or not, I dun't care.' Marella's flush was angry. 'I thought to save your ma some pain, but if you wun't plead with 'im for me, I'll 'ave to see 'er.'

Lydia put out a hand. 'No – no, don't do that, Marella. I'll tell Mother – or Alan can. You might be wrong, Marella.'

'I'm not wrong.'

'Dear God. What can we do?'

Marella said, 'You must write to your brother. Tell 'im to come 'ome and marry me.'

'Of course. You can't write.' Lydia held the wall, staring up into the woods. Naturally old Nathan and Wesley knew Marella better than she did; knew that she had to be watched.

She said, 'You are sure no-one else knows about this?'

'No-one knows, Miss Lydie. Just you an' me.'

'Then . . .' She lifted her head high. 'Then, tell no-one. Alan shall come home and marry you as soon as possible. No-one need know that you are . . . as you are.'

She left Marella where she was and walked slowly across the yard and into the kitchen. She had been a fool twice over, a stupid, romantic fool. Wesley was no wild stag protecting his lady. He was a suspicious brother who knew his wayward sister only too well. And Alan . . . oh dear God, Alan, her own baby brother, had got himself into this. She glanced back at the woods and was thankful to see no flash of russet.

Silently, she made tea and drank a cup with her mother. Then she went upstairs to write to Alan. There was nothing else to do. Alan was nineteen and old enough to deal with his own problems.

Four

The chapel at Carybridge was on the outskirts of
the village, set on the road that crossed the
Heights and dropped down into the lush,
protected valley that held Mapperly House and
the comfortable thatched cottages around the
ancient Saxon church. The land had been given
by the then Squire Lambourne nearly a hundred
years ago when John Wesley had preached in
the village on his way to the wilds of Cornwall;
his converts had used the stones from the
Moor to pile up a meeting house famous for its
draughts and hard seating. The present Squire
had never been inside the chapel and employed
no Methodists in his house or on his land. They
tended to come from the lonely cottages on the
high Moor where perhaps the only consolation
for the hard life on this earth was the hope of a
better place in Heaven.

On this day at the beginning of September
they crowded into the tiny interior and quickly
filled up the bride's side, over-spilling behind
Lydie, Rupert and Lucy and impregnating the

draughts with an acrid smell of sheep and fish. Lucy, her face chalky white, dabbed at her nose with a handkerchief and Rupert looked as though he might be sick. In spite of suddenly inclement weather, Lydia had put on her blue silk dress with the flowers, the one she had worn for her party. She had dressed her hair in ringlets and wore her bonnet well back to show them off. There was an air of defiance about her as she gazed around the congregation.

In the front pew, Alan sat with his elbows on his knees and his head drooped between them. He had made no secret of his unwillingness to marry despite his sister's pleas not to worry their mother. Lucy, who could have condoned a love match between her son and the kitchen maid, had visibly wilted over the last three weeks. It had been arranged that Alan and Marella should share old Granny Peters's cottage until after the baby's birth. By that time Alan hoped to have found suitable rooms in Bristol. Mr Swallow had graciously conceded that if the article fees continued to be paid regularly he would be generous with time for 'our young man to make his arrangements'. Rupert had nodded curtly at this letter and passed it to Alan.

'You can still become a lawyer at any rate. It will be harder but you can do it.'

Alan had made no promises. He said airily he might take a 'long honeymoon' until the Hilary term. He could not imagine Marella in Bristol. He could not imagine a baby. When he had received Lydia's letter, he had returned home immediately and accused Marella of duping everyone. But she had wept prodigiously and cast herself on his shirt front and he had found himself kissing her . . . and more. Lydia, who might well have got the truth out of her, had proved strangely intractable. Nothing would do but that the banns be called without delay. Prudence, hastily summoned to the farm, had seemed his only ally. 'Are you sure, Master Alan?' she had asked, not even looking at her daughter. But Marella had got between them, tucking her smock under her sudden bulge and giggling, 'Course he be sure, Ma. You can see for yourself!' And Prudence had turned away, flushing unaccountably, seemingly embarrassed for him. Even old Nathan, preacher and patriarch, had appeared grudgingly pleased at the thought of having Alan for a son-in-law. He had harangued him, told him to 'treasure this vessel of immortal life' and himself gone to see the Carybridge minister.

Alan, as usual, had let the tide of events take him. His disgruntlement showed only when he referred to his forthcoming marriage as 'Lydia's wish'. It was a slight comfort to lay all the responsibility at her feet.

Lydia had thus been forced into a position of determined optimism in order to reassure her parents and herself. She wanted Alan's marriage to be a success for her sake as well as his. Once she had got over the initial shock of realizing that Alan had actually made love to Marella under her brother's nose, she could see no reason why it should not be a good match. She deliberately did not think about Wesley Peters now, so it could not occur to her that her anxiety to legalize Marella's position might be something to do with him. She said encouragingly, 'This will be an excellent thing for you, Alan. Marella is quick and able and loves you dearly. She will promote your career – of that I am quite certain.'

Rupert was inclined to agree with her, though whether it was to calm Lucy's worries Lydia could not be quite so certain. Lucy was very quiet. She had had more to do with Marella than any of them and was afraid that her sixteen-year-old shallowness might never deepen.

They had arrived early at the chapel on Lydia's insistence. She regretted it now, ashamed of Alan's whipped-dog look. When Mr Dunwiddie from Tamerton hurried in, adjusting his plain white surplice, she dug Alan's back. 'Sit up!' she begged in a whisper. 'Look proud!'

Alan glanced around, startled then resentful, but straightened his back nevertheless. Mr Dunwiddie smiled absently at the four of them, swept the rest of the congregation with a harassed gaze and stuck two half-burnt candles in the sconces. His hands were still dirty from weeding his garden. After the long summer and damp autumn the Lord was providing well and Mr Dunwiddie was obviously wondering how quickly he could get back to his winter greens. It was the end of the summer and the daylight faded fast.

Marella came down the aisle on Nathan's arm at last. Like Lydia, she was unsuitably dressed, in a muslin frock which revealed her pregnancy for all to see. Nathan wore a thick stuff jacket and a pair of dark trousers and looked grim. Marella on the other hand was smiling widely; as Alan stood up she took his arm and her whispered giggle filled the silent chapel.

'Dearly beloved, we are gathered here together in the sigh-a-God to join this man . . .' Dunwiddie rattled along at a great pace, yet at every comma there was a loud chorus of 'amens' from the bride's side which inevitably delayed him.

Lydia turned her head slightly and tried to see past her parents to the assembled Peterses. Wesley was unfamiliar in a decent suit with his hair plastered to his ears. He stared ahead and did not join in the next response. The other brothers wore ancient frock coats. Prudence and her daughter-in-law, Mercy, were enveloped in cloaks. If this was what they wanted for Marella they did not look cheerful about it.

'With this ring . . .' Alan's voice was almost inaudible. He had asked no-one to stand by him and Lucy had passed him her grandmother's ring moments before. He made no attempt to slide it over Marella's knuckle and she released him long enough to do so with a loud sigh. Lydia flushed and glanced sideways again. Mercy had her head down and was making a fuss about crying. Wesley stared. Prudence was watching Nathan with an expression of acute anxiety.

They prayed standing up and Dunwiddie was about to turn to the corner where the Parish

Register lay open on a table, when Nathan said sonorously, 'We will sing – All those who are Righteous in the Lord – take the melody from me.' He immediately sang a note and was followed raggedly by everyone except the Fieldings – and Prudence. Lydia, still watching, noticed that Prudence kept her mouth tightly closed.

The signing was a brief affair, crosses one side and Alan and Rupert's signatures the other. Marella sidled over to Lydia and put her arm around her.

'We're sisters now, Miss Lydie. I never had a sister and no more 'ave you, so 'tis something special today, isn't it?'

'Something special,' echoed Lydia. 'And you mustn't call me Miss Lydie any more. Just Lydie.'

Marella giggled. ''Twill soon be Aunt Lydie, wun't it?'

Alan said roughly, 'Go and get in the dogcart, Marella, it's waiting at the gate.' He turned to his parents. 'Mother – Father – thank you for . . . everything. I will return the cart tomorrow.' He ignored the assembled Peterses and strode ahead of his new wife to fling open the chapel doors. Marella ran after him, giggling again as if it were a game they were playing. Lydia went too; Marella's hand on her arm was impossible to loose.

'Wait for me, Master Alan!' Marella's giggle had a hint of desperation in it. 'You can't honeymoon on your own!'

He went on through the treeless, lonely grave-yard to the gate where the dogcart waited with Blackie in the shafts. He climbed into the driver's seat, leaving Marella to sit with her back to his. With Lydia's help she clambered up and sat there blowing kisses while Lucy threw a hand-ful of rice and Alan tried to get Blackie moving. At last the cart lumbered slowly along the Heights road, Marella still facing the small crowd and thoroughly enjoying being the centre of attention.

The early afternoon was closing in around them. Far below, a few white horses rode the grey sea. Rupert said heavily, 'Let us get on. You're cold, Lucy. And you must be frozen in that ridiculous dress, Lydia. Thank God the Methodies want no jollifications.'

He helped them into the wagonette and they followed Alan. Sitting sideways, Lydia watched the Peterses crowd out of the gate. Ahead of them was Wesley. He set off at a brisk walk and until they reached the branching of the ways at the old hanging stone, he kept them in sight. Lydia tried to keep her eyes away from that doggedly following figure but they were drawn back time and again. She wondered what he made of this marriage, whether he had blamed Lydia, whether he had realized she had done her utmost to right a wrong. She had seen nothing of him since that day – only four weeks ago – when she and Gus had surprised him. It was an anticlimax; she had expected something to happen afterwards.

She found she was staring at him again. He was waiting by the hanging stone as Rupert negotiated the narrow Stowe bridge. She had seen him twice – today was the third time – yet already his lean, whipcord figure was achingly familiar to her. She wanted to talk to him, about America or his ambition to form a wool co-operative; about anything. Especially she wanted to ask him whether he had in fact been following her as she walked to and fro from the Place that summer, or whether he had been watching his wayward little sister.

Suddenly, as Rupert slapped the reins and 'gidduped', Wesley lifted his hand in a salute. He did so just as Lydia remembered that Pa Roscoe was trying for a match between him and Jinny . . . She turned away, sharply.

The Peters family filed solemnly through Gran's tiny hovel to wish the newly-weds well. It was a strangely formal procession; Alan and Marella sat at the deal table with their backs to a scorching fire, facing the open door. Shoved into a corner behind them, Granny Peters crouched on a stool, pushing the kettle on and off the trivet as a reminder that she wanted her tea. Nathan sat on one side of the table intoning passages from the Bible, head tipped back, eyes half closed, his free hand clamped over Marella's as it lay on the pitted wood. Edging sideways around them came the family and others of the Methodist persuasion who could spare an hour. They rounded the table crab-wise, silent, eyes reverently downcast, laid their palms for a moment on the two heads and passed Nathan with stomachs held in, to file out of the door once more.

Alan did not know whether he wanted to laugh or weep; the whole scene had a dreamlike quality that was not entirely unpleasant. He felt so superior to everyone here but their presence did not irk him as he had imagined it would. They were his minions; even Nathan. He looked sideways and caught Marella's bright blue gaze on him and knew that she wanted him and could hardly wait for this charade to be finished. He smiled slightly at her, reminded of that evening in April, knowing what was to come. He could have married well if he'd waited . . . perhaps. But no well-born wife could give him what Marella could give him, that was certain. If only he hadn't been stampeded into the wedding by Lydie . . . by Marella herself . . . by this damned pregnancy . . . He'd sworn at Marella, accusing her of losing her maidenhead to someone else, probably the child's father, but she had wept and wept and at last whispered to him how she had done it herself. The confidence had inflamed his passion to such a degree that he had forgotten the interesting experiences he had been courting in Bristol during the past few months and had thought of little else besides Marella – though to all outward appearances he was accepting the inevitable situation with sullen acquiescence only.

He lifted his eyes and met Wesley Peters's stare. There was a triumph in having filched

Marella from his dog-like care. There was rivalry too. Alan frowned. Was Wesley a little too fond of his sister, perhaps? Or was the rivalry because Wesley felt Alan's sense of superiority? When Nathan paused, Wesley was the only one besides Alan himself who did not murmur 'Amen'. No-one appeared to question his silence; it had to do with natural dignity and not inarticulacy. Alan watched him narrowly as he left the small, dirt-floored room. He was no minion.

Nathan led a last loud amen and closed the bible. Prudence waited for him by the door but he seemed loath to go.

'Be good to 'er, my son, and 'er'll be good to you,' he said solemnly, not taking his hand from his daughter's nor standing up.

Alan, remembering, grinned. 'I've no doubt of that, Nathan,' he said in Gus Pascoe's jovial tone. 'No doubt at all!' He slid an arm around Marella's waist and drew her to him. She yielded like a sapling and he laughed and put his other hand on the thin muslin between her breast and the baby. The effect on Nathan was startling. He gripped the hand he was holding and pulled Marella towards him so sharply the table moved and dug into the stamped dirt. Its edge cut into her side so that she gasped.

'What the devil are you doing?' Alan said angrily. But Nathan was standing at last, tugging Marella to him frantically.

'A vessel – ' he panted. 'A sacred vessel for immortal life, to be treated as such! Respeckful like – '

Alan leaned over and wrenched Marella away and Prudence hurried forward and tugged Nathan backwards. It was almost a scuffle but over as soon as begun.

'Stupid ole man!' Prudence fumed at him. 'Stupid and jealous!'

Nathan hung onto the door, determined not to be swept out like flotsam on the tide. Marella put out a hand to him pleadingly.

'It has to be, Father,' she said. 'The baby . . . it has to be!'

All at once he slumped and let himself be pulled out. Prudence reappeared and pulled the door after her.

'Take no notice,' she advised. ''Tis right and proper and that's an end to it.'

Alan was angry as well as bewildered. 'What did she mean? By God, we're married now, we don't have to wait for permission to bed! And as for your crazy father – '

Marella soothed him. 'That's what she meant, Master Alan . . . just what she meant. Take no notice of Pa. 'Tis the religious tantrums gets into 'im sometimes. That's what she did mean.'

She wound her arms around his neck and began to kiss him. Gran said testily, 'Will 'ee be wanting tay? We've waited long enough, I reckon.'

They took no notice of her and she stood up and pushed the hissing kettle onto the table beneath their noses.

'Upstairs then, if that's what you want,' she advised. 'Dun't want to scald yourself. Upstairs with you!'

On the other side of the fireplace was a ladder leading to the loft above. In spite of her girth, Marella showed a clean pair of heels as she took the rungs two at a time. Alan stared at Granny Peters helplessly, knowing that she would hear every sound they made.

'Tis my cottage,' the old woman said defiantly.

He swore gently under his breath. Why hadn't he taken Marella to Milton Mains, or Bristol? He fished in his pocket and held out half a guinea. 'You could drink tea with the others?' he suggested. She took the money and bolted so quickly he guessed she had angled for it all along. Well, if it was money they wanted, he supposed he could find it. Enough to impress the Peterses anyway. He put his foot on the ladder feeling powerful again. Being married to Marella might have its advantage; the Peters clan could work for him and no-one would ever blame him if he took some of his pleasures elsewhere. Not even Lydia. Not even Wesley with his cold, critical eyes.

The girls presented Lydia with a tiny Italian cameo of a classic Roman head. Judith pinned it to the dove grey dress which she had taken to wearing since the cooler autumnal days. Lady Maud, in velvet and a bonnet, beamed approvingly.

'Most suitable – they picked it out themselves, Lydia. Most suitable, is it not?' It came of course from Lady Maud's own collection.

Lydia smiled. 'I have always admired them.'

'Really?' Judith was anxious. 'I thought it was a little ordinary.'

'Nonsense, child. Lydia is not the kind to wear anything gaudy.' Lady Maud swept through the hall to where the landau waited on the gravel. 'Are we ready? Boxes . . . portmanteaux . . .'

'My pressed flowers,' wailed Caroline.

'They're with mine.' Judith clung to Lydia's hand. 'You will come to see us in London, Miss Fielding?'

Lydia hung back behind Mrs Lomax. 'There will be no need. You will come to the Moor next summer.' It seemed a long way off; almost another life. She shivered as if with premonition.

Caroline said, 'I don't want to go. I do not want to return to Mamma. Nothing will ever be the same again. Next year we shall be older and you will be married.'

Judith put in, 'Not to Mr Pascoe. You said you would not marry Mr Pascoe, Miss Fielding.'

'That I will not,' Lydia reassured her with a smile. But she went no further. Surely this time next year she would be married . . . to someone. She controlled another shiver. She too wished the Garrett twins were not leaving; she had enjoyed being with them all summer, but during the last five weeks they had been an escape from her own confusion.

Caroline stuck out her bottom lip until it almost covered the rabbit teeth. 'Then you will be an old maid, which will be worse! I really do not want to go back to London. There will be a new governess and fittings for new clothes and it will all be perfectly horrid!'

'But,' Lydia put in rallying her, 'it will also be very exciting and you will have lots to tell me when you write. You will write?'

'Of course!'

Mrs Lomax herded them through the door and into the landau. Lydia stood back with Bessie Tongie while Sir Henry grunted his way inside and gave the order to be off. The clatter of hooves and iron wheels was deafening across the cobbles, then the horses turned into the gravel between the aspens and the coach gradually receded into the distance. Bessie fished for her handkerchief and shed a few easy tears and Mrs Lomax said briskly, 'Off with you, girl. You've got work to do, haven't you?' She turned kindly to Lydia. 'Will you dine with me in my room, my dear? You're in no great hurry to get home, I suppose?'

Lydia declined gratefully, explaining that her mother was not entirely well and there was no help at home now.

Mrs Lomax smiled. 'I heard that your brother took little Marella Peters for a wife. Well, it has happened before and it will happen again. Try not to grieve, my dear, and tell your mother the same.'

Lydia tried to explain. 'We are not . . . truly, Mrs Lomax. But everything is somehow different.' She fingered the small cameo. 'Particularly that Mamma is without help. So I will make my way home and thank you for all your help.'

Mrs Lomax inclined her head graciously and Lydia set off, trying not to stride or break into a run. It was over. So much had happened since her twenty-first birthday: Alan, Marella, Gus, Wesley. And all the time the stimulus of Judith and Caroline, forcing her to think ahead so that sometimes her head ached. Now Alan and Marella had gone; surely Gus had gone – he had not called since that day. And Wesley – had he gone too?

As soon as she entered the bracken and took the sheep track she knew he had not. The fern was crisp and yellowing yet there was not a crackle, not a movement in it. All the same she knew he was near at hand and stood quite still, heart thumping, trying to discover how she knew and why she was so certain. There was no answer. She just knew.

She said clearly but in a low voice, 'Wesley. I know you are there. Please come out.'

There was a sound behind her and she turned and saw him part the fern and step onto the track. His russet smock was covered in bits of dried grass and stalk, his trousers tied with cord just below the knee, yet something in his bearing transcended his country clothes. He took off his wide-brimmed hat and his hair was gold against the grey of the sky.

He said, 'I'm sorry, Lydie. Did I frighten you?'

She wished she could match his calm natural-ness, his complete assumption of his right to be where he was and to act the way he acted. She remembered the pettish way she had turned

from his salutation after the wedding and dis-
liked herself.

'No. You did not frighten me. I knew it was
you.'

To be so honest made her feel vulnerable and
her face reddened with embarrassment. But he
smiled.

'Thank you. Will you let me walk with you,
then? Just as far as the pasture?'

'Yes. By all means.' She had to walk ahead of
him because of the narrowness of the track and
she took off her bonnet knowing that the red-
gold of her hair looked good against the grey
alpaca dress. 'What are you doing hereabouts,
Wesley?'

'I came a-looking for you, Lydia. Alan told me
it was your last day at the Place and I thought to
have a few words with you.'

'Indeed.' She wound the string of her bonnet
around her forefinger tightly. 'Well, you have
found me. Of course, you knew where to look.
We have met on this track before.'

'Aye. That we have. You've not been troubled
by Pascoe since.'

It was only when she answered no that she
realized it had not been a question and she turned
sharply to look at him. 'He came to supper that
night. Since then . . . no. Did you make it your
business to see him again?'

'Mebbe. But he is only scotched. Mind him
when I am away, Lydia.'

She was partly flattered, partly outraged.
'We – his family and mine – we've been friends

for years! What right have you to warn him off?'

He looked at her directly; his eyes were darker than Marella's and very steady.

'None as yet. Save that we are connected by marriage.'

She said breathlessly, 'That was not so. At the time.'

'Your parents permit you great freedom, Lydia. And your brother was away. I was in any case watching over Marella—'

'Two birds with one stone!' she tried to laugh.

'If you like. There might have been danger for you that day.'

'Absurd! I was quite safe with Gus. It was you . . .' She found she could not look away from his straight gaze. She swallowed. 'You said you were going away?'

'Aye. To Yorkshire. I want to see the wool masters myself, supply them direct from our farms. By sea.'

'Jinny mentioned it. A co-operative.' She noticed the width of his shoulders beneath the knee-length smock.

'Jinny? I see . . .' he smiled slightly. 'I understand Tom Johnson is calling on her again.'

Somehow Lydia turned and began to walk down the path again, shamed because he had followed her thoughts so accurately. She hardly knew whether he was still behind her until they entered the pasture and he drew alongside.

He said matter-of-factly, as if in connection with Jinny, 'I shall be in no position to keep a wife until this business is settled. Say two years or more.'

She strode across to the gate and would have opened it and passed through except his hand was on the latch. She said, 'Is that what you wanted to talk about? Your absence?' She hardly knew why she was annoyed.

He said, 'Yes. And to ask you to speak to your brother.'

She was surprised. 'Alan?'

'You have influence with him. Marella told me.'

She flushed. 'It was only right. Then. But now – he is none of my business.'

Wesley shrugged. 'He will not listen to me. And I am going away – my father and brothers will not be so reasonable with him. He talks of staying on the Moor until the baby is born. January. He should go back to Bristol, Lydia.'

'But surely Marella will want to stay with her mother for the birth? And a husband's place is by his wife.'

'Lydia. You must know how he is conducting himself. Not three weeks wed and he is carousing with—'

She interrupted haughtily, 'I am afraid I do not know what you mean. Alan has called to see my mother twice . . . three times. And we do not listen to gossip.'

He said levelly, 'It pleases Alan to treat us as servants. Well, that is his bringing-up I dare say. Not his fault. But Marella is his lawful wife, Lydia, and he should keep his other wenches out of her sight and hearing.'

She gasped. 'You blackguard him behind his back!'

'No. I have spoken to him. He offered to hit me. Perhaps you could fare better.' He pushed open the gate for Lydia but held her arm to detain her a moment longer. She shrank at his touch, much too aware of him. 'Listen, Lydia. While I am there I can protect Alan. But afterwards . . . don't you see, if Marella is wronged in any way, my father will kill him!'

He stared at her for a significant instant to make certain of her comprehension then he let her go and turned back. She watched him run lightly over the pasture towards the steep banks of the Stowe. Like a running deer.

Two years. He could not support a wife for two years.

She turned into the stable yard and saw Gus Pascoe's horse; the increasing sense of anti-climax lifted slightly. According to Wesley Peters, Gus spelled danger. At least danger meant excitement.

Gus looked far from dangerous sitting in one of her mother's armchairs in the sitting room overlooking the combe. He was dressed in a suit which looked too tight for him across the shoulders and thighs. His neck was bright red above his stiff collar and he had pomaded his dark hair to a sleek cap. As she came into the room he levered himself laboriously from the chair and took her hand.

'So formal, Gus?' She sounded pleased to see

him and he was encouraged to press her hand intimately.

'Came on a formal errand, Lydie. I quite forgot you were taking your leave of the Garrett brats!'

Rupert laughed and slapped his knee. Gus grinned. 'Connected with them in a way – this invitation I mean,' he said.

'Invitation?' Lydia fingered her cameo rather than rub her hand after Gus's grip. The door opened and Lucy came in with tea things. The two women laid the side table and busied themselves dispensing refreshment. Lucy smiled encouragement at her daughter so that Lydia would know any suggestion from Gus had her approbation. Gus explained heartily and indulgently, obviously expecting Lydia's gratitude: 'The invitation comes from Sir Anthony Warren. He's the Member for Stapleford, y'know. Knighted. Tavvie knows him well of course, he's returned on the vote of the wool-staplers and likes to show his appreciation when he can. He holds a reception on Michaelmas Day, straight after the hirings. Asked Tavvie if me and Julius would care to attend with our ladies. Tavvie said Julius and Anne would be delighted – just caught Anne in between confinements, which is a miracle – ' Rupert's laugh rang out anew and his knee must have ached with so much slapping ' – and that I'd enjoy it too but I would be on my own. At which point . . .' Gus accepted tea and looked significantly through its steam at Lydie, 'Aye . . . Whereupon, Sir Anthony suggests that

Miss Fielding might like to accompany me!? What do you say to that, eh Lydie? You made a good impression I'd say, wouldn't you? Remembered your name and that you were what he called a "new educationalist" whatever that means!'

'He said that?' Lydia was immensely flattered. She had been on the point of turning down the invitation, which would mean a night in Stapleford just when she wished to be home with Lucy. This last compliment made her pause.

'He did indeed. It seems he's engaged to a Bristol girl. Fanny Parmenter. The Parmenters have a reputation for philanthropy – Merchant Venturers – wealthy. This one runs a Ragged school by the docks, so Warren is suddenly very interested in such things. He wants you to meet this Parmenter girl.'

Nothing could have been better for Lydia's self-esteem. To be wanted, not as Gus's partner or Alan's sister or even a prospective wife in two years' time . . . but as herself. For what Rupert called her crack-brained ideas on governessing.

Lucy smiled at her again and said, 'There is that silk foulard Alan brought from Bristol. Just time to make it into an evening gown if you would like, my dear.'

Lydia said, 'Would we come back that same night, Gus?'

'Lord no, Lydie. Tavvie will give us a bed.' He saw her expression and added hastily, 'Joanna is coming, of course. And Julia and Anne. But there will be room enough if you will share a bed with Joanna.'

Lydia looked at her mother and permitted herself to smile. 'Yes. Naturally. I thank you, Gus. And Tavvie. It will be very . . .'

'Exciting,' Lucy supplied. She patted Lydia's arm. 'Lady Maud and Sir Henry have gone to London, I know, but most of the County will be there. The Lambournes and the Crowleys – '

'The Pascoes!' said Gus.

'And one Fielding!' Lydia capped him.

'And half the politicians from Devon and Somerset by the sound of things,' Rupert said. 'I did hear as Toryman Warren wanted to change his coat now he's took up with this Parmenter lady. He won't get far on the Moor if he has to do without Garrett patronage.'

'He'll tire of Fanny Parmenter quick enough,' Gus said reassuringly. 'She's mettlesome, but political women are always boring.'

It was Lydia's opinion too, but she would not agree with Gus openly on it. She retired to the side table again for a biscuit, then she and her mother enjoyed a conversation about the silk foulard while Gus and Rupert went from politics to wool prices until Gus decided to take his leave. He did so just as formally, though when Lydia walked to the stable yard with him there was ample opportunity for his usual familiarity. He must have sensed her surprise as young Drake helped him to mount, because he laughed and leaned over his horse's neck to seize Lydia's hand and shake it vigorously.

'I can be as proper as any man who goes courting, Lydie! I did it wrong before – admit that. But we'd been childhood friends and I overlooked the fact you had grown. Different now. You'll see.'

She watched him clatter out of the gate and along the lane to the Heights road. She wondered what, or who, had been responsible for such a change in attitude. And she wanted to giggle. Was it possible, just possible, that she was being 'courted' by two men? And was it wrong to enjoy the attentions of both?

Very much later that night, Wesley Peters lifted his head from the straw-filled bolster he shared with his brother and listened hard. Then he rose and slipped from the cottage like a shadow, intercepting his brother-in-law at the entrance to the muddy track known as Peters Lane.

'What you doin'? Still spying on me?' Alan's speech was slurred and his efforts to throw off Wesley's restraining arm were clumsy and in-effectual.

'Be quiet!' Wesley spoke authoritatively. 'You damned fool – why do you do this under my father's nose? D'you think he'll ignore it much longer?'

Alan's muttered defiance was lost in his own gasps and groans as Wesley frog-marched him past the Peterses' cottage and on to Gran's. They almost fell into the midden before finding the front door and shoving through it.

'Blasted upstart!' Alan crouched over the deal

table, heaving, looking malevolently at Gran's hunched figure by the fire. 'What d'you expect – no privacy – no comfort – '

'Get up to Marella!' snapped Wesley. 'And tomorrow you go up and talk to your sister and listen to her. You should go back to Bristol and do some of the work you're used to!'

Alan grabbed the ladder for support and rounded on his tormentor. 'Keep away from my sister!' He felt on safe ground there. 'She's a virgin – not like your sister – just keep away, d'you hear?' He saw the look in Wesley's eye and began to climb the ladder. 'You want her for yourself – that's it, isn't it?' he hissed from the trapdoor. 'Well, you can't – you can't have her!' He did not make it clear to whom he was referring and Wesley stared at the closed trap furiously.

Behind him, Gran said, 'Keep out of it, our Wesley. Husband and wife . . . keep out of it. Nothing to do with you.'

'Pa will kill him, you know it,' Wesley said tiredly.

'I know it. But there'll be a warning first. Nathan gives a powerful warning. Just keep out of it,' the old woman advised again.

Wesley clenched his hands. 'Too much bad blood between our two families would not be a good thing, Gran,' he said.

She stared up at him. 'So . . . the Fielding boy was right.' She cackled and fetched the teapot. 'Never mind, our Wesley. I'll talk to our young man. You go off and rest your bones. I'll see to it.'

Upstairs, Alan finished his heaving into a basin and said exhaustedly, 'For Christ's sake, 'Rella. What's sauce for the goose should certainly be sauce for the gander. Whatever you tell me, I know you've had your fun, so let me have mine, will you!'

Marella watched him warily as he staggered to the bed.

'I dun't know what you mean, Alan. All I know is I loves you an' I dun't care if you 'as other girls, so long as you always comes back to me.'

He sat on the edge of the bed and looked at her. 'D'you mean that? If you mean it, we could manage very well . . . very well indeed.'

For answer she held out her arms and he went into them gratefully. And after he had slept and been comforted again and slept again, she whispered, 'You can't do without me, Alan. Can you? Can you?'

He did not answer, but he smiled with his eyes closed and she kissed him and laughed against his mouth, the gay, pseudo-innocent laugh that had attracted him first. He slept yet again, convinced that his way was the best . . . there was no such thing as wrong. And no such thing as right. The only thing was fun.

Five

It was after midday on the twenty-ninth of September when Gus negotiated the narrow lane from the Heights road and drove the landau into the yard at Milton Mains. The hood was down. Joanna stayed where she was and enquired for Lucy's health with far more condescension than did Lady Maud. Rupert and Drake pushed Lydia's straw basket containing the new silk foulard, her nightclothes, curling tongs and extra wraps next to Joanna's, and Lydia followed. The weather was fine but grey and chilly and she was glad Lucy had insisted on a muff; the grey alpaca, topped with cape and bonnet, was barely warm enough.

Gus, somewhat subdued before his sister, drove expertly as usual and looked almost a gentleman in a beaver and caped greatcoat. Lydia, excited, smiled brilliantly at him and did not withdraw her head when he pecked at her cheek. The past week had been entirely taken up with preparations for the reception. She and Lucy had cut, stitched, fitted and stitched again;

looked out the freshest lavender bags; curled Lydia's hair into immensely long ringlets, even buffed her nails with wads of raw sheep wool. There had been no word from Alan and no news of Wesley's possible departure. When Lydia thought of either, she felt her emotions in a turmoil. It was convenient to put this down to the prospect of the outing to Stapleford. So that by the time she settled herself next to Joanna and looked at Gus's broad back, she hardly knew how to sit still. Luckily, Joanna found this perfectly natural and rattled away, dispensing hardly heard information in an effort to put Lydia at her ease in company to which she was not used.

'Julius and Anne have met the Parmenters several times, my dear, and found them perfectly approachable. I understand Miss Parmenter is perhaps a little out of the run.' Joanna glanced deprecatingly at Gus's rear view. 'Women's rights. Just a passing craze, I dare say –'

Gus laughed jovially. 'Not too certain of that, Janna. I hear she's converting our very own Toryman!'

'I should think it more likely that she has decided to please her family.' Joanna turned confidentially to Lydia. 'Julius will have it that she has made a bargain with Sir Anthony. If they marry he will do his utmost to secure votes for women! Have you ever heard of anything so ludicrous?'

Lydia had to admit she had not. 'Surely she would not be so frank about it? Mr Warren used to visit the Place before he was knighted and I should not have thought he would agree to a marriage such as this one sounds to be.'

'Unless his head was completely turned, my dear!' Joanna gave Lydia a roguish look as if she would know all about such things, then, significantly, began to discuss the running of Mapperly. 'Such an enormous old place, my dear, fifteen bedchambers would you believe it! And when the doors are open between dining and drawing rooms, we have space enough for a ball.' Her look deepened to coyness. 'Of course with two women to run things we might indeed give balls. How exciting that would be, Lydie, to be an important hostess on equal terms with the Lambournes even!'

In the midst of her schoolgirlish happiness, Lydia felt a small cold drop of discomfort at the assumptions that must have been made among the Pascoes. She could almost hear Julius's superior voice in between snuff-taking, saying, 'You could do better, Gus. But you could do worse. With her share of Milton . . .' And Tavvie guffawing heartily as he nodded. 'Practical wench too, Gus. Turn her hand to anything.' She frowned slightly, annoyed with herself. It wasn't possible to be assumed into a marriage, after all. Determined not to let such thoughts spoil the joy of the day, she looked about her and pointed out to Joanna the signs of the changing season. And Joanna, eventually balked of her audience for gossip, nodded and exclaimed over the early hazelnuts scattered in the road and the gorse blossom lying in drifts in the wheel ruts.

In spite of this determination to enjoy herself, Lydia was impressed into silence by Tavvie's house. She had imagined a bachelor villa such as Alan described in Bristol; instead, the red-brick house with its view of the harbour stood four square behind a thick hedge. Shaven lawns reached to its long windows. A gentleman's house and all for one gentleman. If Tavvie Pascoe could be described as a gentleman.

He was as she remembered: a smaller, quieter but coarser image of Gus. He was likely to snigger his ribaldries behind his hand. Lydia thought she would prefer Gus's bold appreciation to Tavvie's all-seeing stare as he shook her hand.

'Welcome . . . *most* welcome, Lydia dear. As beautiful as ever, I see. Champagne. To be drunk slow.' He ran his tongue around the outside of his mouth and smiled secretly at her as Gus slapped his thigh and gave a roar of laughter. 'And sister mine, respectable in black as befits the chatelaine of a big house.' He kissed Joanna and waited while a servant took their things, then led them into a small warm sitting room behind the arching stairway. 'Tea for the ladies, madeira for the men, I think. Lydia, you know Anne and Julius, of course.'

Anne Pascoe had been from Devon, and of the same social standing as Lydia; she never forgot how lucky she was to be taken up by Julius and babbled incessantly about the social life she enjoyed at Clifton Village in Bristol. She was thin and yellow-looking after too many pregnancies but was proud of these also.

'The next one will be called Lucius – to keep to the Roman names, you know,' she confided to Lydia as Joanna dispensed tea.

Lydia raised her brows. 'Oh. Are you . . . again?' she asked delicately.

Anne laughed a high-pitched trill. 'Who knows, my dear. I dare say – it is, after all, two months since my last confinement.'

Lydia, used to farming ways, was anxious. 'But surely while you feed the new baby it is not advisable—'

'We have a wet-nurse. Julius brooks no excuse!' Anne giggled again and then looked solemn. 'The Pascoe line must be continued, Lydie. That is our duty. You must accept that.'

Lydia looked at suave, snobbish Julius, standing with his back to the fire discoursing on the latest Court news, and felt sick.

After the tea, it was time to retire to their rooms and prepare for the evening. Joanna accepted the help of a maid specially imported for this purpose, but Lydia heated her tongs on the gas jet and crimped her ringlets more firmly into place by herself, then slipped her new dress over her head and was ready. She laid herself carefully on the big double bed which she would share with Joanna and watched the other's preparations while composing herself as Lucy had instructed. The silk dress was green and her black satin slippers with the ribbons crossing on her ankle just showed beneath its full hem. Lucy had not permitted the bodice to be too low, but it was low enough to show off Lydia's amber necklace to perfection. And her gloves were made from real Honiton lace. Lucy had said, 'You need not be conceited about these things, Lydia dear, but you *may* rely on them – you may permit them to give you confidence. Even, if necessary, a touch of aplomb.' Lydia smiled as she recalled her small, neat mother; as companion to a connection of the Lambournes, she must have attended many functions before she accompanied her mistress to Carybridge and met Rupert Fielding.

'Why are you smiling, Lydia?' Joanna asked, twinkling knowingly again.

Lydia replied honestly, 'I was thinking of my mother.' She swung her legs to the floor and sat up straight. 'My mother is a lady, Joanna. A real lady. I do not think I have always appreciated that.' Joanna nodded, confused by the abruptness of the reply and Lydia went on, 'I shall devote myself to her this winter. I shall take over the house and her other work and *force* her to rest!'

'I suppose, well, yes, I suppose you can do that.' Joanna agreed doubtfully. 'But I hope you will spare a day each month to come to Mapperly and let me show you how we do things.'

Lydia adjusted her wrap and moved to the door. 'There will be no need, Joanna.' She looked directly at the other woman. 'I think you misapprehend me. I have no intention of marrying your brother.' She left the room and went slowly down the stairs. And felt full of . . . aplomb.

The Assembly Rooms milled with people and, while the Pascoe party waited to be presented to their Member of Parliament, Anne was pleased to point out some notables. The Lambournes had sent their elder son to squire his young sister, Sibyl. Lydia noticed with interest her overskirt in rich satin caught up at the rear on a sort of cage. 'The bustle, my dear,' breathed Anne. 'The very latest thing from the Court.'

The Member for North Devon was looking very solemn and tugging his mutton-chop whiskers as if to remove them altogether. 'As well he might,' sniggered Julius. 'If Lord Derby throws in the hat, he'll be stuck with the Jew, Disraeli.'

'And there is Miss Parmenter!' Anne said excitedly. 'You are lucky to be with us as we know her quite well and can introduce you.'

But as it happened Anne's patronage was not necessary. Sir Anthony clasped Lydia's hand warmly, paid her the usual compliments and said, 'I particularly want you to meet my future wife, Miss Fielding. I have spoken of you and your work with Sir Henry's granddaughters and she is most interested.' He promptly led Lydia away from the others and took her to a group of chairs overlooking the ballroom. A small, dainty woman immediately stood up and smiled at them. She was plainly dressed in pearl grey silk with a fichu surrounding an unusually long neck and proudly held head. Her face was unremarkable and her thick, abundant brown hair arranged in two coils without curls, but there was something in her bearing that set her apart.

'Fanny my dear, this is Miss Fielding of whom I have spoken to you. And this is my affianced wife, Miss Fielding. Miss Fanny Parmenter.'

The two women clasped hands and smiled. Miss Parmenter said, 'Yes indeed, Anthony has told me about you most warmly. Will you sit with me for a while and let us talk?'

'I should be most happy to do so.' Even so, Lydia looked around for the Pascoes. Sir Anthony laughed.

'I will look after your party for you, Miss Fielding, never fear. And when you have had your talk, perhaps you and Mr Augustus Pascoe will come in to supper with us?'

Overwhelmed, Lydia allowed herself to be seated comfortably next to Miss Parmenter and half screened by that lady's fan.

'I expect Mrs Julius Pascoe has spoken of my radical views, my little school down on the docks, my lodge for fallen women in Hotwells!' Miss Parmenter gave a laugh that was nearly a giggle. 'Be assured, Miss Fielding, if I hadn't the most respectable family in the world, I would be a social outcast!'

Lydia blushed but laughed too, unable to completely refute Anne's gossip. 'I know nothing of

the fallen women. But the others – the school –
must command admiration, surely?'

Miss Parmenter looked quizzical. 'What of the
radical views?'

Lydia shook her head. 'I know nothing of
politics. My life is content. I do not want it
changed, so I cannot offer an opinion on
radicalism.'

'Yet you tried to change the lives of your
charges this summer, did you not? You conducted many of your lessons out of doors. You
taught them to swim. These are very radical
educational methods!'

'You are teasing me, Miss Parmenter. The
Garrett girls have everything that money can
buy.'

'Yet still you changed their lives. You improved their lives, I would say. Improved the
quality. Simply because they are wealthy and
belong to what we deem to be the upper strata of
society, you do not look on your methods as
radical. Yet radical they are, do you not agree?'

Lydia stared at the small, humorous face
before her and considered carefully. At last she
nodded reluctantly. 'Yes, I see what you mean.'

Miss Parmenter tapped the back of her hand
with her closed fan. 'My radicalism is easy. The
children I teach are in such obvious need of
improvement that everything I do is radical.'
She smiled. 'Yours was more difficult. Your
pupils apparently needed nothing changed. Yet
you saw that in some ways they had . . . nothing.'
She opened the fan again and held it between

themselves and a group of people approaching. 'Please tell me about it. Your first day – did you intend to do something unusual with them? Or did it happen gradually? Anthony tells me the change in them was enormous. From spoiled brats they became contented little girls.'

Haltingly at first, then in a rush, Lydia spoke of her summer at the Place. It was exhilarating to talk to someone who was interested and completely understanding and who put flattering constructions on what Lydia had done without thought. All too soon Sir Anthony joined them with Gus and suggested they lead the way into the supper room. There was new respect in Gus's dark eyes as he offered his arm and said in a low voice, 'You have pipped Anne until she is green with envy! And Joanna has told me not to value you so lightly!'

Lydia could think of nothing to say to that and as she was very hungry by this time, she devoted the next hour to enjoying the enormous variety of food laid out for them and trying to remember it for her mother's later delectation. From the shrimps rolled in fine paper to the anchovies on tiny triangles of toast at either end of the board, there was hardly a space. Tureens of stewed ducks with olives, plates of forced turkey with mint sauce, enormous platters oozing boiled mutton and caper sauce, and so many open tarts, plum puddings, preserved ginger, nuts, oranges and raisins that Lydia lost count. She ate heartily and could not help remarking that Miss Parmenter did exactly the opposite.

'Please do not let me spoil your appetite, Miss Fielding.' Miss Parmenter gave her a small smile. 'It gives me great pleasure to see you enjoy this food. Even though I cannot.'

Lydia, stricken, said, 'Is it because your small charges are probably near starvation, Miss Parmenter?'

'Guilt?' Fanny Parmenter let her smile widen. 'I hope not, my dear. Abstinence because of guilt makes for speedy self-righteousness. There is a lot of self-righteousness among the phil-anthropists of Bristol and I would not like to think I am going the same way!' She leaned close. 'My reluctance is purely physical, my dear. For this evening my enjoyment must be vicarious.'

Lydia smiled sympathetically. She thought Miss Parmenter must be referring to an upset stomach and did not pursue the matter further.

Afterwards she danced a polka with Gus: the Lancers with Julius; a country-dance set with Sir Anthony himself. She could not help but know that she was a success; the Lambourne son and heir, who had ignored her at the Place, thought fit to introduce his sister and it was obvious that many of the matrons were asking about her behind their fans. It was an exhilarat-ing experience, but by far the most interesting aspect of the evening had been her meeting with Miss Parmenter and their friendship. Lydia hoped it was not one-sided and wondered whether she dare ask Miss Parmenter whether she might correspond with her during the winter. She had joined her again and they were strolling outside the Rooms along a terrace which overlooked the harbour, when something happened which precipitated their relationship into a deeper understanding.

From around the corner, out of their sight, came sounds of altercation which Lydia would doubtless have tactfully ignored, but which seemed to rivet Miss Parmenter's attention immediately. A male voice, obviously belonging to one of the many flunkeys, said severely, 'You cannot come in 'ere, missis! 'Tis a reception being held by the political gentlemen of the district and is by invitation only.'

The female voice which interrupted him was cultured, though distressed and desperate. 'I do not wish to attend the reception! I have explained – I wish to see Mr Augustus Pascoe and I understand he is inside. If you would only give him a message . . .'

'That I 'ave done, missis. I can't do more.'

'But what did he *say*? He must have said something!'

At the mention of Gus's name, Lydia glanced in alarm at her companion and saw that she was alert and listening unashamedly.

The flunkey said doggedly, 'He didn't say nothing. Shrugged. Bid me go. That was all.'

There was a repressed sob. 'But he will come? He must come and speak to me, surely?'

'Twenty minutes since I gave him your message, missis. He's still dancing. Why don't you go away and call on him tomorrow morning?'

'I cannot. I have been to Mapperly House and been sent here from Mr Octavius Pascoe's house. I must return home this evening – I must.'

There was a silence; clearly the flunkey, not entirely without sympathy, did not know what to say next. Miss Parmenter put her mouth to Lydia's ear.

'My dear, we are eavesdroppers and therefore faced with a decision. Do we offer our help to this lady? You are with Mr Pascoe, so it is for you to say.'

Lydia needed only a second to make up her mind. It was her evening, everything she did was tinged with success; she could help this poor creature without difficulty. She nodded and the two women walked on around the terrace to the steps and pillared portico of the Rooms. The terrace had been lit from the tall windows of the ballroom, but this area was in semi-darkness; two gas jets either side of the double doors cast inadequate pools of light which emphasized the slight mist creeping up from the river mouth. In one of these pools stood a respectable-looking woman in a warm woollen cloak and bonnet, drooping slightly with tiredness and discouragement.

Miss Parmenter nodded to the flunkey, holding him back while Lydia approached the woman.

'Excuse me . . .' Lydia realized Miss Parmenter was leaving the meeting to her. She did not wish to appear uncertain yet hardly knew what to say. 'I . . . overheard you asking for Mr Augustus

Pascoe. I am with the Pascoe party. Perhaps I may assist you?'

The woman looked up, rejuvenated with hope. She was much younger than Lydia had imagined; perhaps younger than Lydia herself. The woman said timidly, 'I wished to talk to Mr Pascoe. On a personal matter. But I am afraid he is not available.' She looked at Lydia's face and saw something there to give her courage. 'Are you Miss Fielding?'

Surprised, Lydia nodded.

The woman said, 'He told me that you were to be married. I – I – '

Miss Parmenter approached, the flunkey behind her with a chair.

'You are not well, my dear. Please sit here.' She took the woman's arm and manoeuvred her into the chair.

'Forgive me.' The bonnet brim dipped down. 'I must not say anything. I must not stay here. I should not have come. But when he said he was to be married, I thought it was my duty to warn someone.'

Miss Parmenter said kindly, 'What is your name? Perhaps we can persuade Mr Pascoe to join you.'

'My name is Alice Harper. My father is vicar of Downes Steps, a very small living on the Heights.' There was another sound like a sob. 'He will not see me. I have sent in my name. He knows . . . what I want.'

Lydia felt her body go rigid with shock. Alice Harper. It was the name with which she had goaded Gus last April. A girl, a respectable girl . . .

Miss Parmenter went on in the same gentle tone, 'He will certainly come out if he knows you are in converse with Miss Fielding, I fancy.'

The girl looked up at that and the light reflected fear from her brown eyes. 'You must not tell him! He will realize that I planned it – he will kill me!'

Miss Parmenter picked up one of the small hands. 'Then we will not tell him.' She looked over the bonnet at Lydia and said quietly, 'You are expecting his child, Miss Harper?'

Lydia took a quick breath and swallowed. There was a groan from the girl. 'Is it that obvious?'

Miss Parmenter gave her half-smile. 'Not to anyone else. But I have met other girls in your situation.'

'My father will disown me!' Miss Harper was openly weeping now. 'What else can he do? A parson's daughter – not yet twenty-one – '

Miss Parmenter said, 'Do you wish Miss Fielding to fetch Mr Pascoe out here? She can do so quite easily.'

The bonnet was shaken vigorously. 'I thought . . . I thought . . . to force him to marry me. But I cannot. I cannot. I hate him so much now. Oh God, I do not know what to do!'

Lydia felt all the power gone from her. Her knees shook weakly, yet she had to do something, say something.

She stooped and looked at the young face

covered in tears. 'Miss Harper, I am not betrothed to Mr Pascoe. I have never had any intention of marrying him. I have told him so several times and only this evening informed his sister of the true position.'

Miss Harper reached inside the muff on her lap and produced a sodden handkerchief. 'It makes no difference. Not to me. But I am glad for your sake.'

Lydia looked across at Miss Parmenter again. 'What's to be done?' she asked, anger beginning to tighten her muscles. 'This cannot be allowed to happen – it cannot!'

'Ah . . . the number of times I have said those words, Lydia. But it does happen. Often.' She knelt on the cold stone steps. 'Listen, Miss Harper, by the greatest good fortune you have spoken to us tonight. Miss Fielding is grateful to you and I . . . I am in the lucky position of being able to help you. If you will let me lodge you tonight, you may return with me to Bristol tomorrow morning where I can offer you help until after your baby is born.'

'With you?' The girl looked up. 'I am able to cook and sew—'

'Not actually with me. I am patroness of a home in Bristol which I rented and staffed especially for people in your predicament.'

'A home for fallen women?'

Miss Parmenter looked at her steadily without flinching. 'Yes.'

'Oh dear God . . .'

'It is a sanctuary. Somewhere you can live and

work for your keep. Think of it like that. Not as a punishment.' She went on talking soothingly for a few moments more then took a businesslike breath and changed her tone. 'Now. That is settled. I have had enough of this reception and will plead a headache and take you immediately to a lodging. You need not see Mr Pascoe, nor indeed anyone if you do not wish it. Perhaps you can compose a letter to be delivered to your father – we will work all that out after you have eaten something and are warm and comfortable.' She mounted the steps to the waiting servant. 'Fetch me a hansom or a carriage of some sort as soon as may be, please. And attend this lady while I fetch my things.' She drew Lydia with her into the warmth of the Rooms again. 'My dear Lydia, it is best you leave this matter entirely to me now, otherwise you will be accused of interfering. Feel no responsibility and try not to be distressed. I am thankful you never had any intention of a marriage with the Pascoe man so that you are not heart-broken.'

Lydia said dazedly, 'I am shocked and appalled. I have heard of this girl before now but I never imagined . . . it was a sort of joke.'

'Oh yes. Men – gentlemen – make a joke of it. But, as you see, it is not amusing.'

Part of Lydia's shock was directed at herself; she remembered her instant reaction when Marella had been in a similar plight. But that reaction had been for the wrong reasons. She saw that now with sudden clarity; she was ashamed.

Eagerly she said, 'I want to help, Miss Parmenter. Is there something . . . may I come with you and settle Miss Harper?'

'Please call me Fanny. We are meant to be friends.' The full smile was turned on Lydia. 'As for helping, I think not. Between us we might overwhelm the girl. Besides, Anthony is used to my foibles and the Pascoes might well take exception to your sudden disappearance.' She clasped Lydia's hands. 'Say goodbye now, Lydia, return to the dancing and try to go on enjoying yourself – you radiate happiness like a fire radiates warmth. Say nothing of this in case the resulting acrimony extends to you.' She pulled Lydia towards her and touched her lips to her cheek. 'I will write to you and tell you how Miss Harper goes on.'

'Thank you. Thank you . . . Fanny.'

Lydia did as she was bid; Miss Parmenter's authority was implicit. But she was unable to obey the command to enjoy herself. For the first time Gus's physical presence filled her with loathing. She remembered his engulfing kisses, the way he had manhandled her on the Heights path . . . She shuddered. Only once did she permit him to lead her into the dance again and that was for a square in which she knew she would rarely meet him. Fortunately Sir Anthony, who might have been apprised of the facts by Miss Parmenter, presented her to several partners and she was able to dissipate some of her uneasy spirit in sheer physical effort. So much so that, as they waited for their carriages,

Anne remarked acidly that personally she did not care for the feminine cheek to be over-flushed. 'It becomes coarse. That's my opinion only of course, but—'

'Aye. It's certainly not mine,' Gus said bluffly. 'I like an apple with rosy cheeks. That's when it's ripe for plucking!'

He guffawed raucously and Tavvie joined him, Julius hiding a more decorous smile behind his glove. Lydia did indeed flush then, and furiously.

'How grateful I am that I am not an apple,' she said lightly to Joanna. 'I can think of no fate worse than being plucked and eaten by your brother!' The insult was not veiled. Gus fell moodily silent and remained so during the short drive to Tavvie's house.

Lydia was unable to sleep much that night. For one thing the double bed with Joanna in close intimacy was strange and unfamiliar, for another the sounds from the harbour were noisy compared with the sibilance of the sea at Listowel; but mainly her sleeplessness was due to her churning thoughts. Alice Harper and Fanny Parmenter moved constantly into her mind. The phrases 'radical politics', 'fallen women' and 'Ragged schools' recurred again and again like tolling bells in her ears. She was forced to review her life in a different light; she wished to stay at Milton Mains . . . talk to Wesley Peters . . . perhaps wait for him. But had she any right to such placid contentment? Beside her, Joanna groaned and flung out an arm heavy in folds of flannel. Lydia turned her back and closed her eyes determinedly. The very next instant she was opening them again to grey but broad daylight! She could hardly believe her senses had betrayed her so completely. The room, with its heavy curtains pulled back, was unfamiliar again, and the little maid brought in last night to help Joanna was gone, replaced by a gaunt figure in black, lugging a jug of hot water to the wash-stand.

Lydia struggled up in the feather bed. 'Where is Miss Pascoe? What time is it pray?'

The woman held her mouth disapprovingly. 'Miss Joanna has been gone with Mr Julius and Mistress Anne this past hour. 'Tis almost ten o'clock, miss. Master Augustus sent me to waken you and to ask you to be ready in an hour.'

Lydia said stupidly, 'I can't have slept until nearly dawn . . . of course, we are to return home today.' Her clogged brain registered a fact. 'Did you say Miss Joanna had gone with Mr Julius?'

'Mistress Anne asked her to return to Bristol with them to see the new baby.' The woman finished laying out washing things and turned. 'Is there anything you want, miss?'

'No. No thank you. It is just Gus – Mr Augustus – and myself will be returning to Listowel then?'

'So I suppose.' The woman went to the door. 'Breakfast is still held over in the dining room if you wish it.' It was obvious to Lydia that she was being an unmitigated nuisance and that Gus had enjoyed sending his peremptory message; also

135

that he would doubtless be delighted to drive her home on his own. And probably pester her.

She tightened her mouth as she began work with her wash-cloth. Fanny Parmenter had advised her to keep her knowledge of Alice Harper to herself, but if Gus did begin to pester her yet again, she determined to accost him with it and to flay him with scorn for his insensitivity and cruelty.

Neat in her grey alpaca again, she went down-stairs to find Tavvie still breaking his fast, his plate heaped with kidneys like shining brown pebbles from the beach. He gave her his sly, knowing smile, grease glinting at the edges of his mouth.

'Ah, Lydia. You've slept late, my dear, which is a great compliment to my feather bed and the air of Stapleford. You must come often, Lydie. In the future. You and Gus may share the bed perhaps, hey, what?'

Lydia ignored this and went to the sideboard to help herself to eggs, almost ashamed that her appetite was undiminished by last night and her short sleep. 'I understand the others have already left? Joanna too. I wonder that Joanna did not wake me to apprise me of her plans and to say goodbye.'

Tavvie's smile widened. 'We thought it more unselfish to let you sleep on, my dear. I tried to persuade Gus to stay until at least mid-afternoon. But he would have it that he must get you home in the full light of day. He takes his responsibilities very seriously.'

Lydia could not quite stifle an exclamation of disgust at that last remark but turned it into a cough. She should be grateful at any rate that Gus was harbouring no thought save for her welfare. She ate her eggs in unsmiling silence, leaving Tavvie in no doubt of her mood. When Gus appeared impatiently in the doorway, Tavvie said warningly, 'I'm afraid her good sleep has done nothing for Lydia's temper, Gus. Treat her carefully, dear boy. Very carefully.' He laughed at this as if he had said something amusing and followed his last two guests to the door where he lounged and watched them load their baggage, apparently unaware that their silence was grim. As Gus climbed into the landau and took the reins, he disappeared suddenly into the house, re-emerging seconds later to throw a handful of rice at them and stand holding his sides as they moved slowly up the drive then quickened into a lively trot on the road.

Lydia would have hated it even more had it not been for Miss Harper. Last night's events had made the possibility of marriage with Gus so much out of the question that these constant assumptions by the family meant nothing any more. She brushed the hard grains from her bonnet brim and muff and was almost surprised when Gus turned around with an unwilling grin.

'I think Tavvie's trying to tell us something, Lydie. Quarrels don't mean much between lovers, eh? Perhaps it confirms that they are indeed lovers?'

It was a question and Lydia answered it briefly. 'Don't be absurd, Gus.'

He retired into an angry silence again and concentrated on his driving. They rattled cautiously over the enormous stones of the harbour and through the narrow tunnel of Fore Street past the scene of last night's reception. The horse slowed to a plod as the real pull began to the top of the combe and Gus broke his silence to make encouraging noises. The air was growing colder by the minute; Lydia pulled a rug over her lap and shrank into the upholstery, wishing she could ask for the hood to be raised. Once on the Heights, an unseasonal greyness pressed around them and when the sea came into view above the receding roofs, the horizon was indeterminate with fog. They rattled along at a good rate, but it was a three-hour drive and the time stretched endlessly ahead.

At last Gus cleared his throat. 'There'll be snow for the early lambing,' he said experimentally. 'Hard work for you but good news for me. Plenty of snow in winter means a good fleece in summer.' There was not much to be said to this and Lydia said nothing. Gus did not wait too long. 'Damned cold. Yes. Damned cold. Are you warm enough, Lydie?'

Lydia took her hands from her muff to pull her bonnet firmly over her bunched ringlets and tuck the rug around her waist again.

'Perfectly, thank you,' she said formally.

It was too much for Gus. 'Good God, Lydie! What's the matter with you? Spoiling for a row –

is that it? Well then, let's have it and be done, for God's sake! You've been like a crab-apple ever since you queened it over everyone at the reception last night – did it go to your head, madam?'

Lydia's temper flared to meet his. 'Your attitude doubtless made me seem a crab-apple, Gus! I seem to remember a remark you made about apples which might well have made me sour! As for queening it – '

'I'm sorry, Lydie,' Gus interpolated hastily. 'I withdraw that. You were an enormous success last night and I do not grudge it you. Far from it, it did my heart good to see Anne's snobbishness put in its place. As for the other . . . the apple . . . I thought you could joke with me as we've always done.'

She felt suddenly weary. Lack of sleep and the shock of her meeting with Miss Harper, with all its very personal implications, took away her temper as abruptly as it had come. She said, 'Oh Gus, it is true, we were friends once, weren't we? I am grieved, yes grieved, that you could behave so. That any friend of mine could behave so.'

He said, 'You are grieved because I take a few liberties in my speech with you?'

'Gus! Do you not know what should lie on your conscience? Can you really bandy stupid words like this and not know?' Her grief was quite sincere, she could have wept. For Miss Harper and for Gus himself.

He said with laboured patience, 'Just tell me.

Just tell me, Lydie – what is it that should lie on my conscience? I am curious.'

She looked at him. 'Miss Alice Harper.' He stared back at her. 'Yes,' she said quietly. 'Alice Harper came looking for you last night, Gus. And found me instead. Now do you see why I want nothing more to do with you?'

He said sharply, 'Alice? Alice was in Stapleford? When – why was I not told? Where is she now?'

'You were told, Gus. The lackey at the Assembly Rooms found you and gave you Miss Harper's message—'

'Dammit, Lydie, I got no message!' His voice rose. He checked the horse viciously and turned to face her. 'Do you think I would have risked . . . discovery . . . by ignoring her?'

That sounded feasible. She said hesitantly, 'What would you have done had you known she was outside the Rooms?'

He smacked his riding whip on the leather seat. 'Sent her packing of course! She has plagued me since last Christmas, Lydie – you have no idea. Following me wherever I go, fawning on me like a bitch on heat – '

'Be silent, Gus! How dare you speak of her so? She is a respectable girl, younger than me. The daughter of a parson—'

'And the heart of a whore! Do not speak of things you do not understand, Lydie. I have tried to be kind to the girl – let her down lightly, but she will have none of it—'

'She is pregnant, Gus!' The words leapt from

Lydia in a simple effort to stop his smug flow of excuse. 'She is with child and alone and frightened. And it is your doing!'

Again he was shocked, but only for an instant. 'She does not know that it is my doing. Naturally she will try to foist the child on to me because I have money and position.'

Lydia was outraged. 'You cannot bluster your way clear of this, Gus. It was obvious to Miss Parmenter and me that Miss Harper was a good woman led astray by you!'

Gus went white. 'Do you mean to tell me that Miss Parmenter is in your confidence? How dare you tell tales, Lydie—'

'I have told no tales, Gus. We saw Miss Harper together. I certainly could not have dealt with the matter and might well have come to you and accosted you then and there! It was your good fortune that Miss Parmenter was with me.' Lydia took a deep breath. 'But enough of these recriminations – are you telling me that you will now look after Miss Harper? Offer for her hand?'

'Most certainly not! The girl is a nobody. A stupid nincompoop—'

'Who loved you enough to believe your promises – oh yes, I can imagine the promises you made to her, Gus.' Lydia was filled with bitterness. 'Then you are again lucky, because Miss Parmenter has taken poor Miss Harper and will look after her until your child is born. I hope that will help you to sleep at nights!' She jerked herself sideways and stared out at the grey fog-filled sea. 'Now let us get on. I find your company insupportable.'

There was a tense silence for perhaps two minutes. It was the longest two minutes Lydia had known. She had no more stomach for haranguing Gus; he seemed past logical reasoning, let alone humane feeling. She managed to spare a grateful thought for Alan, who at least was not so self-centred as to think of no-one and nothing save his own inclinations. She bit the inside of her mouth, breathing fast but shallowly. She could not wait to get home. She would call on Marella; take the girl under her wing; teach her . . .

Gus said grimly, 'So be it. You will regret this, Lydie. But it is your own choice.' He turned and laid on the whip and the carriage moved forward with a bone-shattering jerk. Faster and faster he drove as if in an effort to frighten her. Occasionally the iron-rimmed wheels came out of the mud ruts and threw the landau about helplessly. Lydia removed her hands from her muff and gripped the sides and said nothing.

Then abruptly, they slowed for a gradient. Gus shouted at the horse, but it was to no avail. The creature was blown, its side heaving and glistening with sweat. Muttering a curse, Gus jumped down and led the equipage off the road to a patch of the wiry cliff grass. Lydia leaned back and relaxed slowly, determined not to betray any nerves and even more determined not to speak another word until she said good-bye at Milton Mains.

Gus said with horrible sarcasm, 'Will Milady step down and stretch her legs while I rest the horse? It would doubtless be a relief to remove herself from any unwelcome presence for ten minutes or so.'

Lydia opened the door and jumped down unaided before the end of this speech. She crossed the road to where an outcrop of rock rose like a coastal fort and scrambled around it until she could look out to the misty sea. Somewhere out there, the Peterses' fishing boat might be drifting for fish with Wesley aboard. Freed at last of his dog-like guardianship of his sister. How strange it all was. Alan and Marella. Perhaps she and Wesley. Perhaps.

Gus's voice spoke at her side.

'Still the hoyden, Lydie? Clambering among the rocks, fording rivers. You'll never change. Last night may have given you ideas above your station, but you'll never really change. You belong to the Moor, Lydie, and so do I. You belong to me.'

She did not turn her head nor reply to him and wondered later if it had been a mistake, for her silence seemed to madden him.

He said tightly without any of his usual bluster, 'You're still asleep, Lydie. These high ideals of yours – just because you forced poor Alan to marry the Peters girl you think I should also wed Alice Harper, is that it? Men have always got girls into trouble and always will. They do not marry them afterwards. It's a fact of life.'

Still she did not speak and suddenly he swung round in front of her and grabbed her shoulders. She struggled furiously but it was hopeless; she had always recognized Gus's great strength.

'It's ironic, is it not my dear, that Alice follows me around begging for a marriage ring, while you turn me down? Yet, therein lies the solution, does it not? Can you see it as clearly as I can see it, Lydie? Can you – can you?' At each reiterated question, he shook her hard. Her bonnet fell back and her ringlets jumped against her face. She screamed at him to let her go.

'So. You cannot see, or you don't want to see. Then let me spell it out for you. Just like the spellings on your schoolgirl's battledore. Plain and simple. If I fill *you* with child then you will follow me around just like dear little Alice, begging – pleading – wanting me – '

She felt hysteria erupt in her head. Her nostrils were full of the smell of him; she could only just focus on his eyes and register that they were mad; the eyes of a mad dog. She turned her head abruptly and he buried his face into her hair, literally slavering.

She said on a near scream, 'If you do not let me go – this instant, do you hear me – I will never speak – never see—'

His wet mouth ran the length of her neck and back to her earlobe. Her voice ended in a shudder of disgust.

'Oh Lydie – ' he was actually laughing. 'If I let you go now, my darling girl, you will never speak to me again. That is logical. There is only one way now that I can arrange for you to speak to me . . . to beg me for marriage as Alice begs me—'

As if she were a cork on water, he lifted her bodily and slammed her back against the rock face. The breath left her body and his weight crushed her agonizingly; she opened her mouth wide, fighting for air and his mouth was on hers instantly, his laughter vibrating in her own throat. Her senses were going; when he lifted his head her body hung limply sideways from the waist. The damp air rushed into her lungs; she waited desperately for enough of it. Gus's feverish mouth and tongue were on her throat and descending; she realized he had exposed one breast and felt sudden pain as his teeth found her nipple. Her whole concentration was bent on summoning a scream.

When it came it seemed to split the quiet grey day in two. It lent her strength, a sudden frenetic strength that jerked her knees upward and her arms out. Gus took a staggering step back and in that instant's respite she leapt sideways, screaming still, and crashed down from the rocks and into the bracken by the edge of one of the many small hidden streams draining the Heights. She knew she felt pain but gave it no time to register before she was clawing in the mud for handhold. Then she felt her cape ripped from her and cast aside and Gus was straddling her, his hateful laugh in her ear as he pinioned her with his weight and pressed her face into the damp fern roots. There was a long sobbing, gasping silence. Gus shifted himself slightly so that he knelt on the back of her legs, pinioning her arms behind her at shoulder height and shoving hard now and then so that the agony would remind her to keep still. She had no choice; it was nearly impossible to breathe, her eyes were full of gritty bits of growth, she could taste earth in her mouth and wondered whether her teeth were broken. Terror was uppermost; her anger and outrage gone. This was no longer Gus Pascoe astride her; this was an insane stranger. She recalled once standing aside for the hunt to pass her in full cry. A rider, teeth bared, eyes alight with an unholy fire, had leaned forward suddenly with his whip and slashed at her as he went by; senselessly, needlessly.

Above her came Gus's voice again, whispering, laughing, incredibly enjoying this.

'What did I tell you, Lydie. Like an apple ripe for picking. Just like an apple . . .' He lowered himself onto her and she screamed again but her clawing fingers did not push at him: now they clung to his shirt sleeves as if she were drowning. Every breath was a scream but she was no longer fighting him. Then, before she could accept the full horror of that, the very earth seemed to thud as if with its own violent heart-beat and Gus was torn from her by a giant hand and thrown away. Lydia herself was rolled onto her side, her hands still reaching for him, the sudden emptiness making her want to wail with animal loneliness. Instinctively she pulled back her arms and protected her head from the unknown attacker, and as she did so, she heard Gus's body crash among the dying undergrowth as he emitted a great shout of shock and outrage. She did not see what leapt across her body and threw itself on its victim; but she knew, immediately she knew, it was her stag.

Through her encircling arms she could hear the dreadful sounds of struggle; grunts and the repeated thudding earth sounds, as if the Moor itself were fighting. It went on and on and she drew up her bare knees, curling herself into a protective ball, pressing herself double, smelling her own blood which was everywhere, holding herself against vomiting. Her shoes and stockings were falling from her, her drawers were gone; she was sore and aching and the terrible emptiness was in the core of her body, shaming her, humiliating her beyond bearing.

At last there was a silence. She lifted herself and looked. It was he; just as she had known it was; she could not bear it. Wesley stood over Gus, not even panting after that one mighty kick that had sent him flying.

Lydia took it in with one glance then turned away with a moan. Immediately Wesley was by her side.

'You're all right, Lydia?' The Somerset burr was strongly pronounced but was the only sign of anxiety. He did not touch nor look at her and through the numbing relief of her rescue came shame. She remembered the whispered giggles of the villagers over a girl, supposedly raped three or four years ago. Even fair-minded Jinny had grimaced and said, 'It couldn't 'appen – you couldn't be forced agin your will, she must've given in.'

Lydia looked sideways, trying to see Wesley without turning her head, hoping his hand would be extended towards her, or at least the knuckles white and clenched. All she could see was her own outstretched leg, the grey travelling dress rucked above her knee, remnants of a stocking clinging to her calf. She drew the leg inside her skirt, sat up and clutched both knees with all her strength, pressing her forehead inside her arms, escaping inwards.

'Lydia,' Wesley's voice held a touch of impatience. 'Lydia, just tell me. Are you all right? Nod or shake your head if you can't speak.'

Convulsively Lydia jerked her chin up then down. She could smell herself. Or Gus. The sounds of his continued retching made her want to vomit too. Pain was everywhere in her body but was surmounted by the nausea. She fought not to heave.

Wesley left her and returned to Gus. He caught hold of him by the collar and trouser band and hauled him to his knees, then to his feet. The trousers provided leverage for the ensuing ungainly progress through the bracken and back to the landau. Gus made occasional efforts to resist, frustrated by such ungentle treatment from his captor. It was no longer clear whether he was retching or sobbing; when he called Lydia's name at intervals the choking was accompanied by tears but, as his flailing attempts at retaliation earned him repeated kicks, the tears need not have been for Lydia at all.

Wesley thrust him onto the driving seat with all the force left in his body and Gus slithered and fell to the far side, crouching while Wesley unhobbled the horse, led him to the middle of the road and flung the reins back.

'Take these!' he ordered curtly. 'Drive to Mapperly House and stay there until Miss Fielding decides what to do with you. Do you understand?'

There was no reply and Wesley stood on the wheel, took a handful of Gus's hair and jerked him upright. Gus howled like a stuck pig. 'I said – do you understand? Good. Now listen well, Mr Pascoe. It may be that Miss Fielding will want nothing said of today's happenings. In which case, you will remain silent. If a hint of it gets around the parish I shall hear and come for you. Do you understand *that*?'

Gus nodded his head against the remorseless hands. 'Yes – yes, blast you! For God's sake let me go – I'll have you for this, Peters – for Christ's sake – '

'If she does not wish to keep silent, remember I shall be a witness for the prosecution. Remember that, Mr Pascoe!'

He released Gus and sprang back to the road. Gus fumbled for the reins as the horse sidestepped in the shafts. 'Damn you!' he sobbed. 'Damn you to hell, you interfering, narrow-minded Methodist hypocrite! She was enjoying it, I tell you! Christ, d'you think I don't know how to handle a woman by now? They all enjoy it – '

He got no further. Wesley hit the horse's rump with his open hand and the creature leapt away as if at a pistol shot. Gus's shirt flew open against his waistcoat buttons and he wrapped the reins around his hands frantically, bracing his legs with the automatic expertise of the natural driver. Wesley watched the landau sway perilously away and then click itself into the wagon ruts of the road and disappear around the shoulder of the hills steadily. He turned and ran through the bracken again, halting abruptly as he came on Lydia in the same foetal position as before. Her arms tightened as he approached more slowly and he said, 'Don't worry, Lydia, 'tis me. He . . . he's gone. Taken the coach. Gone back to Mapperly. You need not see him again. Not ever. Not unless you want to.'

She spoke in a voice stifled by the folds of cloth. 'I do not want to . . . I do not want to.'

'That is good.'

He sounded glad; relieved. She said, 'Did you doubt it?' Yet even as she spoke she knew he could not help but doubt it when he had seen her . . . not resisting . . . shame rose again like bile in her throat. She dropped her head further and squeezed her eyes shut.

He said slowly, 'If you wanted to see the black-guard in gaol, Lydia, you would have to see him again. But it would not be only your word against his. I am a witness and I will testify – '

'No!' She held her knees to her head, her head to her knees. 'No! Never that!' Her forehead turned as she repudiated the very thought of the magistrates at Stapleford. 'No! I can't bear – can't bear – ' her voice rose to hysteria.

Wesley said quickly, 'No. 'Twouldn't do. Your father 'ud kill him – you're right. It would mean trouble all ways.'

She grabbed at the excuse. 'Yes. Yes, Father . . . and Mother. Oh Mother – it would kill her.' She was still, thinking of her mother, wanting her with all her soul and knowing she was the one person who must not know of this.

Wesley said unexpectedly, 'I'll fetch your brother. Wait here. I'll be very quick.'

'Alan?' She lifted her forehead slightly but could not turn to look at him. 'It will be dark before Alan can get here.'

He moved so that he stood before her. She could see the ragged hem of his smock; his trousers tied below the knees.

'He's down in the combe, Lydia. I'll fetch him.'

She frowned, trying desperately to concentrate her thoughts. 'If he's just below why didn't he hear me? Why hasn't he come with you?'

'He was . . . occupied. Besides, I was higher up. Above him.' He waited for no more questions but turned and strode into the bracken, then paused and picked something up. Lydia stretched her aching neck at last and saw him shoulder an ancient blunderbuss before disappearing into the undergrowth. She was incurious. A blunderbuss would disintegrate a rabbit, and in any case the villagers snared rabbits. A blunderbuss might destroy a man's arm or leg . . . She frowned again. It was too difficult, everything was too difficult. But if Alan was arriving directly, she must do something. Move. Fetch her drawers, muddied and torn, pull up what remained of her stockings and button her shoes, look for her bonnet to hide the wet lank hair. She explored her hair and realized all vestige of the party ringlets had gone. Of her muff there was no trace and the buttons of her dress were missing but by the time she had fastened the sodden cape and rinsed the blood from her face and hands at one of the many streams, the pain was more localized and she hoped faintly that her recent plight was not immediately obvious.

Alan arrived in a great flurry, hatless, his hair in disarray. The sound of his horse pounding along the Heights road terrified Lydia anew until his familiar, 'Halloo! Lydie! Where are you – halloo there!' galvanized her into running to meet him, glad that he was not to find her at the scene of her terrible struggle. He dismounted and ran beside his horse, coat flying open, face wide with anxiety. 'Lydie, my dear, Wesley says there has been an accident. What the deuce – ' he was silenced as she cast herself on him, in tears at last. For a few moments he had his hands full with prancing horse and weeping sister. Even when she had recovered sufficiently to speak, she said only, 'Oh Alan, my dear, you are wearing your wedding shirt and I have quite spoiled the ruffles!' Then she looked up at him and seeing his predicament, smiled through her tears. 'Alan, do not look so, I am all right. And it is so good to see you.'

He relaxed slightly, relieved, then flung the reins over a rock and led her away from the horse.

'I have never had such a welcome before, sister, so perhaps you are not entirely all right!' He tried to return her rallying smile and then the full extent of her state registered. 'Dear God, Lydie – what kind of accident? Were you on Blackie? Did she bolt?'

It was useless to lie too much. She told him about the reception at Stapleford and Gus's actions afterwards, but only up to a point.

'Wesley arrived before – before – anything . . .' she reiterated again and again in the face of his horror and black anger. 'I do assure you, Alan, I could have dealt with Gus. But Wesley intervened.'

'Aye, that I can believe!' came the bitter interjection.

'He sent Gus away and then came to fetch you. Because, obviously, Alan, you do see, don't you, no-one must know about this. Papa would go to Mapperly with the horse-whip and Mamma—'

'Yes, I see. Of course, my dear. And we can rely on Gus's silence if he is sufficiently ashamed. And ashamed he must be! Your dress is torn and you are soaked.'

'I fell, my dear. My clothes caught in a rock as I rolled down the cliff. I lost my bonnet and ended up in that stream. Alan, take me home. And help me to put Mamma off the scent.'

He nodded and lifted her onto his horse, straddling bareback behind her. She had often ridden with him thus, her skirt kilted by the horse's mane, yet now she had a new and terrible self-consciousness and tried to pull it over her knees. Alan hardly noticed, setting the horse at a brisk gallop between the wheel ruts and muttering occasional imprecations. 'Damn Gus!' Then, 'Damn Wesley! Not much to choose between them.' She might have argued fiercely with this, if complete exhaustion had not been dragging her into a bottomless pit. And the shame, which had been so obvious to Wesley, began to turn into resentment against him. It hadn't been her fault . . . had it? None of it. Yet everything was spoilt.

Following her dreary line of thought, she said suddenly, 'Alan, what were you doing with Wesley in the combe?'

Alan steadied the trot into a walk as he turned the horse into the track for Milton Mains.

'I was not with Wesley, my dear. I did not know Wesley was within six miles of me. He was spying as usual.'

'Spying? Spying on you? But you are married now.'

'Aye. Just as you wished.' Lydia flinched at the tone of bitterness but did not have the spirit to protest. 'Married. Tied up. Tricked. Aye, I was

tricked. And so were you, Lydie. She had someone before me. I guarantee that baby will be
dropped long before January. I'll take a bet on it
if you like!' He tried to lighten his words with a
laugh but it sounded hollow. Lydia said nothing
but cowered before him, unable to take in all the
implications of what he said, yet knowing there
were many, many implications and a lot of
them centred around Wesley. Alan said, 'Don't
be shocked, my dear. It's happened before and
it will happen again. And in spite of it all . . .' he
swore and finished fiercely, 'Dammit, I do love
her. She sets me on fire. More than any of the
others—'

'The others?'

'I've sampled a few. Yes. Why not? I'm no
Gus Pascoe, Lydie, they're willing enough. They
think I'm no end of a dog! And what's sauce for
the goose is certainly sauce for the gander.'

She said hoarsely, 'You mean Marella is un-
faithful?'

'She's still seeing her lover. I'd stake my soul
on it. I can tell – sometimes when I'm back from
a day's rough shoot . . . I can tell.'

They crossed the pasture in silence and
clattered into the stable yard. Drake appeared
and held the bridle while Alan slipped down and
lifted Lydia to the ground.

'So that was why Wesley was watching you,' she
said quietly. 'You were with another girl.' He
shrugged, looking significantly at Drake as he
led the horse to the trough. She shook her head;
Drake was simple. 'Oh Alan, please be careful. I

155

cannot hope to fathom the rights and wrongs of this. Perhaps time will prove you mistaken about Marella. I hope so, as you do truly love her. But be faithful to her for the sake of that love and that doubt, my dear. And because – because – Wesley was carrying a gun today. And he is as devoted to his sister as you are to me!'

She turned and went into the house and knew immediately from the very smell and silence that it was empty. Never had she been so grateful for her parents' absence. When Alan joined her five minutes later with the news that Rupert and Lucy had taken the wagonette down to Taunton early that morning, she felt only relief and no anxiety or even curiosity as to their errand. Alan was sweet and good to her as he had been when they were children. He pumped water and blew up the fire to heat it then went into the pantry while she washed and bathed her many cuts and bruises and emerged half an hour later with game pie and pickles on a tray and their own russets to push into the embers and eat with a spoon when the inside flesh was a sweet froth.

By the time Lucy and Rupert returned, she was in bed and asleep and Alan told the tale they had concocted of the spilt landau and the remorseful Gus. And, probably because they themselves were worried, no questions were asked and Lydia was cosseted for a chill. Her terror and shame subsided to dull hatred of Gus, while her resentment against Wesley strengthened as she convinced herself he had been censorious and that he was involved in some plot to trick Alan. On both counts there was humiliation for her. She drank her mother's nettle tea and stayed in bed without argument but the humiliation did not diminish. It grew progressively with each hour.

Six

Even after a day in bed Lydia found herself quite unable to enter into the affairs of the house. She remembered with some sadness her determined little speech to Joanna about helping her mother; she had been a different person then. She looked back over the past two days and saw herself as she had been: vital, complete in herself with half-repressed romantic hopes and a belief in the goodness of life. Above all, innocent. Now, because she was tarnished, so was all else. She saw her feelings for Wesley as childish and entirely unreciprocated. She saw all men as predators and all women as victims. Even Alan and her father were infected. Life was too worthless to strive for, and as for getting any satisfaction from looking after the house, that had been another romantic fiction.

So she moped about, getting in Lucy's way and causing Mrs Pollard to tell her she needed an emetic. When Rupert came in from the evening milking, he followed her into the big, empty dining room, little used but giving a downstairs view of the combe and any possible visitors from Listowel, and asked her what was the matter.

Rupert hated illness in his family and ignored it when possible; so Lydia, even in her dreary state, was surprised by the enquiry.

'I . . . there was this accident, Pa. I thought Alan had told you.'

'Aye. But that has gone and over with. And there are no bones broken, it seems. I fancy poor Gus must have fared worse else he'd have been over to ask for you.'

She swallowed. 'I think he was all right. He could drive.'

'Aye . . . well. Has your mother told you why we went down to Taunton, then? What did you think?'

She looked up at him, noticing for the first time that his eyes were narrowed with strain. He met her gaze, saw that she knew nothing and walked jerkily to the window. It was almost dark but he shielded his eyes with one filthy hand as he stared down the combe.

'She's been coughing blood, Lydie. Keeps to her own room . . . oh, I know you all think that's because I'm the worse for cider. No-one stops to think why I go to the kiddley with Gus.' He sounded angry. Rupert always became angry when he was puzzled or hurt. 'A man's got to have something . . . something.'

'She was ill?' Lydia said urgently. 'Really ill?'

'In the night. While you were at Stapleford. I got the trap ready first thing, wrapped her up, we were at Dr Mount's by a quarter-past ten.'

159

'Dr Mount?' Lydia tried to swallow again and could not. If her father was worried enough to take Lucy into Taunton to see the doctor when they had Dr Tarling in Carybridge . . . and if her mother actually consented to go . . .

'I wanted to get Tarling but she kept on about this fellow in Taunton. He dealt with the Lambournes years ago it seems and has some newfangled notion he can cure consumptive lungs. It was a bee in her bonnet of course. He cannot do anything for her.' Rupert hunched his shoulders angrily. 'Rest. That's all he could say. Rest and fresh air. He was as pleased as Punch when I said we lived seven hundred feet up. Let her sleep outside, he said. Outside! I ask you! With winter coming on!' He rounded on Lydia. 'I did think you would have asked her how she got on. Tried to give her a bit of a hand.'

'I didn't . . . I'm sorry.' Lydia looked down at her hands on the enormous dining table; they were clenched and white-knuckled. 'Oh Pa . . . Pa, what shall we do?'

At this cry from the heart, Rupert crumpled suddenly. He got to one of the high-back chairs and sat in it, putting his head on the table. Horrified, Lydia saw the tears gather in small globules on the polished wood. She had never seen either of her parents weep, and at first the sight frightened every other thought from her head and she stood and stared through the murky gloom while Rupert's breath gathered itself into a sob. Then some sort of despairing strength came to her. Her mother was mortally ill and her father could not manage. Alan was a married man. That left her. All at once her own misery seemed mere foolishness and she could dismiss it and think entirely of her parents. She took a step towards Rupert, half expecting him to leap up and deny his tears. She put her hand on his shoulder.

'Papa, listen. If Mother believes in this doctor – Dr Mount – then let us do so too. She needs rest and fresh air. We can arrange that. It is winter, certainly, but we have sunny days in winter. And it is a quiet time of year. We can make sure she does absolutely nothing – there will be time enough for me to read to her and we will play backgammon again and . . .' She rambled on, talking while he recovered himself, providing them both with reassurance.

Eventually he sat up and clasped her around the waist, pressing his wet face to her bodice.

'Lydie, Lydie . . . you are so like her. So very like her when she was young. If you can . . . do this . . . take over . . . it will be – might be – bearable.'

She leaned down and put her lips to the rough, dark hair. 'I will do my best, Papa. Dear Papa.'

It was a promise and she felt honoured, almost exalted, by it. It was not until later, when she tried to talk seriously to Lucy, that she wondered whether it was a promise she might not be able to keep. Lucy turned her stern commands away with her usual small smile, but as they said good night, she touched Lydia's hand gently and said,

'Your father is a volatile spirit, Lydie. A creature of impulse. Like Alan – yes, very like Alan. I would like to think that, in the future, you would not tie yourself to his every whim. I would like to think you would leave Milton Mains, perhaps the Moor itself, and make a life for yourself.' Before Lydia could protest or question this, she started up the stairs, hand cupped around her candle. 'Tomorrow you must tell me more of Miss Parmenter. She sounds a woman I would admire.' She turned and smiled fully at her daughter. 'I would admire any woman who so obviously admired Miss Lydia Fielding!'

Over the next few weeks, there were many such talks. Lydia even told Lucy of Alice Harper in an endeavour to show the full extent of Miss Parmenter's goodness. When a letter came from that lady reassuring Lydia of Miss Harper's welfare and fairly calm resignation, it was possible to show it to Lucy and discuss the matter further. Lydia was surprised at some of her mother's opinions. 'Yes, you would certainly like Miss Parmenter,' she exclaimed. 'And she would pronounce you a radical!' They laughed together. They laughed a great deal and what might have been a melancholy time was quite otherwise. A routine was established which suited them both. Lucy was 'allowed' to come down-stairs each morning and make her own day's supply of camomile tea. Then she retired to the upstairs parlour which was warm and draught-proof, and rested on the sofa until teatime when she came to the window to watch the blood-red sun disappear into the sea. In the evenings Lydia would read to her or they would all three play a board game. So far as Lydia knew, there were no more bleedings and no more evenings at the kiddley for Rupert. In fact, Lydia was tempted to believe she need not set eyes on Gus again and part of her humiliation was alleviated. She tried never to think of Wesley Peters.

During the last week of that precious October, they had a rare caller. Jinny Roscoe brought pilchard oil and a cape for Lucy knitted from the oiled wool used in the fishermen's jerseys. Delighted, Lydia took her upstairs and left her with Lucy for a while, made a proper tea and laid it on a tray with a cloth in honour of their guest.

Jinny, neat as ever, smelling cleanly of fish, brought them up to date on the village news, keeping her own until last.

'I've really come to tell you – ' she helped herself to some of last summer's ginger preserve – 'and to invite you, o'course. I'm a'getting married at long last. 'Tis to be this Saturday down at Listowel, if we can get the vicar out of bed long enough to say the words!' She laughed nervously and bit into her bap, her brown eyes on Lydia asking for approval.

Lydia gasped a short breath. 'You said before . . . your father was seeing old Nathan.'

Jinny laughed again, coughed a little and swallowed. 'That came to nothing, Lydie. I thought you must know. Tom Johnson came calling again and this time I persuaded Pa to look a bit more kindly on him – '

Lucy broke in with congratulations and Lydia jumped up and hugged her old friend. Her pleasure ballooned with enormous relief which she dared not acknowledge, but before Jinny left she found herself asking: 'And who else will be at Listowel church on Saturday? Alan, I hope. We have not seen him for over three weeks. And perhaps some of Marella's family?'

Jinny fastened her shawl over her head. 'Robbie has asked Alan, of course. But I'm not sure . . .' She avoided Lucy's eager gaze. 'He might find it a dull occasion.'

'Ridiculous child!' said Lucy. 'If I am not strong enough to come, Alan and Lydia will represent all the Fieldings. We have always looked on you and Robbie as a second family, Jinny, you know that. When you are living at Lambourne House you must come and visit us often.'

Jinny smiled her pleasure and Lydia persisted, 'And will Marella accompany Alan?'

'The Peterses' will not enter our church, so I am not sure.'

'Marella is a Fielding now!' Lydia was sharply annoyed by this evidence of Alan's status as Marella's husband. Perhaps she could understand a little of Alan's stupid retaliatory behaviour.

Jinny shrugged. 'I hear Nathan expects her to attend the family prayers still. And if she does not, he goes to Gran's cottage and reads them there!'

Lucy said nothing, tightening her lips anxiously, but Lydia was less guarded. 'Nathan is ignorant! Bigoted and stupid! But the others – I thought Wesley had more intelligence than to permit himself to be treated as a member of a – tribe!'

Jinny shot her a look full of curiosity as she tucked the ends of her shawl into her skirt band. 'Wesley Peters has but one interest in life, Lydie, and that is forming this co-operative for wool trading. It suits him to be one of a tribe.'

'I did not realize his plans were so far advanced.' Lydia went to the tray and tidied the teacups as if her life depended on it. 'So, he has not yet left for Yorkshire?'

'It is to be next week, so I understand. I have not heard much about it. Your brother spoke to mine. Neither of them think it will work.'

Lydia put the tray on her hip and went to the door with Jinny. She tried to laugh lightly. 'I suppose if he is involved in his co-operative, he cannot be spying on Alan at any rate!' she said.

Jinny went ahead down the stairs without further comment and Lydia closed the door gently on her mother, smiling reassuringly at the questions on the well-loved face and angry with herself for provoking them. She kissed Jinny goodbye, feeling a terrible sense of loss in spite of herself, then she spent the next two hours preparing supper and food for the next day, leaving her father to go upstairs alone and deal with Lucy's questions. As she listened to the voices droning from above, it struck her that he was doing so fully. Perhaps he knew more of the situation in the Peters camp than she did herself. She gave a sigh of exasperation as she lugged the stewpot onto the fire. Even in her thoughts, she called the two cottages in their own lane 'the Peters camp', as if they were at war. She shook her head as she dippered some broth into a basin for her mother; she would think about what she would wear to Jinny's wedding. The grey alpaca would have been excellent and Lucy had mended it beautifully, but she would never wear it again. It would have to be the snuff-coloured linen from last winter which was very suitable but not attractive. However, if Nathan forbade Marella to attend the wedding he would certainly not permit any other member of his family to go. Lydia spilled some hot broth on her hand and exclaimed sharply.

In contrast to the bare chapel at Carybridge, Listowel church was decorated and colourful with its stained glass and brass lectern. Lydia arrived early with arms full of late roses and chrysanthemums and found the other women of the village laying garlands of old man's beard along the window ledges and chancel steps. It was good to work with them again. Her popularity as a hoydenish schoolgirl had waned during the last year. They probably thought she had tried to rise above her station in life by governessing the Garrett girls; her brother was a solicitor in Bristol; her father took his pleasures with the Pascoes in Carybridge. Alan had married a local girl but was still not one of them. But now that Lydia had arrived early for the wedding of her best friend, rolled up the sleeves of her plain dress and dressed the church with the rest of them, they warmed to her instantly again.

She thought she was to be the sole representative of her family but when the candles were lit and the rest of the congregation standing with the groom, there was a rustle at her pew door and Marella, huge with child, pushed through sideways, smiling her bright, confident smile and followed by a sheepish Alan. Lydia felt a surge of pleasure which surprised her. She had not seen them together since their wedding day and all her good intentions to visit Marella and 'educate' her had come to nothing. She renewed them quickly to herself as she reached for Marella's small, icily cold hand and squeezed it. Yes, her first duty was to Lucy, but she could still find time to walk down the combe twice a week and visit her strange little sister-in-law. She met Alan's eyes above the blond, Peters head, and was warmed again by one of his old sweet smiles.

Everyone agreed it was a 'lovely wedding'. Jinny wore a dark blue serge dress which would do nicely for Sundays in the years to come. Her bonnet was covered with a piece of blue lace and her red hands were half hidden beneath mittens of the same, leaving her fingers free for Tom's heavy gold ring. He was younger than she was; the same height, wide shoulders and stocky farm labourer's body, unlike the thinner wiry fishermen she was used to. His pride seemed to shine through his red face, lighting it like a beacon in the grey old church. Identical smiles appeared on the faces of the watching matrons, even on Robbie's long mouth; Lydia could feel herself smiling too and was not surprised when Marella began to sob quietly.

There was not room in the Roscoes' tiny cottage for more than four people at a time and there were ten times that number of well-wishers. Robbie lit a fire on the shingle above the tide line and rows of mackerel strung on fishing lines sizzled and spat their oil and were eaten between doorsteps of fresh bread and washed down with mulled cider. Robbie produced his squeeze-box and where the shingle changed to dry, packed sand they tried to dance, shuffling around in the flame-shot gloom, laughing and calling to Tom and Jinny as they stood, silent and shy, holding hands and staring into the fire. Before it was fully dark, Lydia took her leave of Alan and Marella, promising to visit them during the next week. She started back up the combe, stopping frequently to scan the darkening bracken, angry with herself for doing so. She felt softer, easier than she had done since that awful time at Michaelmas; if Wesley had appeared they might have talked again calmly. But he did not appear.

She went into the house by the kitchen door and was surprised to find Mrs Pollard still in the kitchen.

'I'll see to my mother's supper, Mrs Pollard.'

She smiled as she untied her bonnet. 'It was good of you to miss the wedding so that I could go.' She prepared to satisfy Mrs Pollard's curiosity, but that lady immediately left the fire and donned her own bonnet.

'I'm that glad to see you, Miss Lydie. Your pa hasn't been in since you left and I cannot face your dear ma again with no news – besides which my Amos has had to do the evening milk and I must get back and see to 'im.'

'My father – didn't he come in at midday, Mrs Pollard?'

'Never seen 'ide nor 'air of 'im, Miss Lydie.' The bustling Mrs Pollard, smelling of onions as usual, paused at the door. 'We both know where 'e is, dun't we? But 'ow can I say that to the missis? An 'er sick like this too. I think a great deal of Mr Rupert m'dear, you knows that, but I think just now . . . at a time like this . . .'

'Yes. Thank you, Mrs Pollard.' Lydia felt her cheeks warm. She was deeply angry with Rupert but could not discuss it with the shepherd's wife. 'As you say, there's no need to worry.'

'Oh aye. We know that. Mr Pascoe will bring 'im 'ome. An' put 'im to bed if need be I don't doubt. But 'ow can you say that to your ma?' The shawl was girdled tightly and Mrs Pollard opened the door. 'There's arrowroot there. And fish pie. An' she should 'ave some of that pilchard oil – build 'er up a bit.'

'Yes. Very well, Mrs Pollard.' Lydia held the door and watched the matronly figure bustle across the yard. All her thoughts crowded around that casual remark: 'Mr Pascoe will bring 'im 'ome.' Was it just possible that Gus would be with her father when he came home? It had happened in the past, but surely things were different now?

She went straight upstairs to her mother and was relieved to find her sitting by the window for the last of the light on her book. She looked the picture of tranquillity.

'And how did it go, Lydie?' Lucy's gentle face was warm with interest. 'I want to hear everything. Sit by me where I can see your face. No need to light up yet.'

Lydia made up the fire and complied willingly. Of course Gus would not have the temerity to come to Milton Mains again, for whatever reason. Lucy appeared to be completely diverted by Lydia's account of the wedding and was genuinely pleased to hear of Alan's obvious contentment – exaggerated a little by Lydia. It was she who told Lydia not to worry.

'If your father is talking wool or politics – and they are both the same at present – he might not be home till midnight.' She smiled up at her tall daughter as Lydia rose to go downstairs. 'Leave a storm light by the kitchen door and bring supper up here, my love. There's nothing to worry about.'

Reassured, Lydia went down to the kitchen and straight outside to check on the yard before the last light went. Amos had not sluiced the byres; the pails of milk were in the dairy as usual but on two of them half a dozen mottled leaves floated. She took them out, put on the covers and went to the stable for fresh straw for the cows. Rupert was proud of his herd and had never employed a cowman: Amos was a shepherd. Lydia laid the straw as best she could and ran back to the house before her mother could miss her. As she hung the lantern on the hook outside the door, she heard the unmistakable sound of her father's voice raised in song.

'She were a fair pretty maid were she – '

The words were shouted from the track leading to the Heights road and were immediately followed by Gus's raucous laugh. Lydia froze where she was, half in and half outside the door, then realizing she was silhouetted by the storm lantern she whipped into the kitchen and shut the door. From being warm with her hurried efforts in the byre, she became clammily cold. She ran her tongue over her lips and tasted salt.

'He were broad and 'ansome were he – '

Rupert's voice was nearer home now. They would come through the gate and around to the front of house to the stable yard. Then they would have to see to Blackie . . . they would be ten minutes at the very least. Galvanized into action, Lydia shovelled fish pie, arrowroot and cider onto a tray, kilted her skirt over one arm and hurried upstairs to her mother. She was trembling as she closed the door and leaned on it defensively.

Lucy looked up from her bible, surprised.

'Is something the matter, Lydie? My goodness, you're as white as a ghost!'

Lydia forced herself to move forward and put the tray on the side table. 'Nothing is amiss, Mamma. I think I hear Papa coming home, but there is food below if he is hungry.'

Lucy said quickly, 'Yes, my dear, let him help himself. He is better alone on these occasions.'

Lydia brought her mother's supper to her without further comment. She might have been shocked by Lucy's acceptance of the situation had she not been far more shocked at the thought of Gus's nearness. They ate in silence and in darkness, both unwilling to show a light beneath the parlour door and attract attention. At last they heard what they had been listening for: the kitchen door opening with a crash and the subdued but nonetheless riotous entrance of Rupert. Then Gus.

Lucy said immediately, 'You did not say Gus was with your father. That is all right, Lydie, he will be all right with Gus. Light the lamp, my dear. No, I will not take arrowroot tonight . . . It is some little while since Gus called. Not since your father took me to Taunton, I believe.'

It was significant that she did not say 'not since he spilled you from the carriage'. Lydia adjusted the lamp flame and closed the curtains against the mist rolling up from the sea.

Lucy said hesitantly, 'Did Gus speak to you in Stapleford, Lydie? I may as well tell you that when you were out the evening he called with the invitation he asked your father whether he might court you properly.'

Lydia helped her mother into a chair nearer the fire and adjusted her shawl. 'Yes, he spoke. He has spoken before. I turned him down as usual.' She spoke steadily but as she lifted Lucy's feet onto a stool, they both felt the trembling in her hands. She straightened and forced a smile. 'That is why I would like to leave you now, Mamma. I would rather not see Gus – he has been avoiding me, I think, so it would be an embarrassment to him also. Can you manage?'

'Yes . . . yes, certainly, Lydie.' Lucy caught the fluttering hand and put it against her cheek. 'My dear girl, I pray you will find happiness. Remember, remember that will always be my dearest wish, Lydie. Never mind the opinion of others. Choose happiness.'

There was something in this kind command that was prescient but Lydia could barely spare the time to kiss her mother's forehead before making for the door. She slid through it and closed it quietly, standing still and listening to the sound from below as her father obviously lugged a cask of cider from the pantry. She was halfway along the landing before she saw the shadowy outline of Gus waiting almost nonchalantly outside her bedroom door. She stopped, then began to back towards the parlour again. Gus moved towards her. She felt behind her for the doorknob and whispered in a strangled voice, 'Keep away – keep away from me, d'you hear? My father might be drunk but between us I think we could overpower you – '

He came into the pool of light thrown up from the kitchen, still smiling and at ease.

'Oh, come now, Lydie. Enough histrionics. Is it likely I would try to take you here and now?' He passed her and descended two steps, then paused and looked up at her. His eyes travelled from her face to her feet and back again and his smile widened. 'How the bitch trembles when the master comes near! I wanted a word and that is all. Just a word. To tell you that I shall kill Wesley Peters. When I am ready I shall kill him.' He ignored her sound of protest, descended two more steps and turned with an afterthought. 'Also, when I am ready, Lydie, I shall come for you. You are already mine – you know that, do you not?' His eyes met hers. 'Yes. You know it. So you will wait for me. Do you hear me, Lydia Fielding? You will wait until I am ready to come to you.'

He went on down the stairs and she heard her father greet him, then both men apparently turned their attention to the cider cask. Lydia stayed where she was, listening yet not hearing. Her ordeal was over; she had met Gus and had been insulted yet again and she could now go safely to her room and read until bedtime. She told herself that, yet when she found the strength to move along the landing and open her door, it was to make immediately for the china basin and hang over it, retching desperately. And then at last she lay down, still trembling and very cold. Was it true? Is that what happened to everyone? Did she in fact belong to Gus? Suddenly burningly hot, she turned her head into her pillow, sobbing hysterically.

It was still dark when she woke. Immediately she recollected her distress and was amazed that she had fallen asleep fully clothed. From the texture of the silhouetted window frame, she saw she had almost slept the night through.

She no longer felt devastated; as before, after the actual event, her nature found a childish relief in transferring blame. Somehow it was Wesley's fault for not having rescued her sooner. She knew very well this was unjust; yet it was also true that Wesley Peters lay at the very root of her uncertainty and disorientation.

Then came again the sound that had wakened her, the particular sound of a clod of wet earth hitting her window pane.

She was off the bed in an instant, heart thumping again, hardly knowing whether to be terrified or just excited. There was no moon or stars but dawn was not far off and the upturned white blur of a face belonged to neither Gus nor Wesley. She opened the casement and leaned out.

'Alan!'

He put up a restraining hand. 'Hush, Lydie, for God's sake, hush!' Alan's voice was a thread, barely distinguishable from the sough of the breeze. 'Let me in – kitchen door – quick!'

She stared for a moment longer then withdrew her head and went silently to the landing, where she paused to listen in case Gus was still in the kitchen. The thick darkness convinced her that below-stairs was empty and she went down quietly, feeling her way from the newel post along the dresser to the door. When she slid the bolts and eased it open Alan whipped inside and helped her to relock. Then he put his mouth to her ear.

'Back to your room, Lydie. They will be here at any moment – your room is my only chance!'

Bewildered, Lydie followed him back up the stairs and along the landing. She went straight for her candle but he stopped her with a quick word and felt his way clumsily to the open window where he leaned out, listening hard, then shut the casement quietly.

Lydia said, 'Alan, what has happened? Who is coming? Close the curtains and let me light up—'

'No! It will be seen, Lydie. They mustn't know I've been here . . . oh my God, Lydie – please hide me! I cannot go back – not after – not after – ' He left the window and fumbled his way to the bed where he collapsed in a heap, making a horrified moaning sound that frightened Lydia anew. She went to him and gripped his shoulders.

'Alan, you must tell me what has happened. Otherwise I cannot help you, my dear. Is it some silly quarrel with Marella? This afternoon I thought you looked happy, reconciled. She is such a child, Alan, can you not make any allowances for her?'

He groaned again. 'Allowances? Oh Lydie, you do not know how many allowances I have made – you do not know. I had even reconciled myself to the fact that the baby was not mine. It was still Marella's, after all, and I loved her . . . God you do not know, Lydie!' He lifted his head and she saw tears on his face. 'Yes, it was a quarrel, of course. We quarrel often and then we make it up. Sometimes I despise myself for making it up, but I cannot help it. She rails at me for running after the Tamerton wench, then I rail at her for cuckolding me, and the next instant – oh God, Lydie, you cannot imagine, you cannot understand – '

She dabbed at his face with a corner of the sheet. 'Perhaps I can. Yes, I think I can.'

'It is a battle – a duel! All the time. Which one can injure the other the most. And then tonight . . . tonight she won. She dealt the – the final blow.' He took a deep breath and sat up and his voice was suddenly calm. 'I cannot go back to her, Lydie. I cannot. Nathan, Benjie, Luke, Wesley, they are all after me. I can't get along the Heights road in either direction. They know every track and sheep trail. And I cannot go back with them. They will have to shoot my legs off with that old blunderbuss and carry me before I will go with them!'

Lydia tightened her grip on his shoulder. 'Wesley? After you too? How dare he – my brother – how *dare* he!' At last she had a reason for all that unreasonable resentment. She put her face close to her brother's. 'You shall hide here, Alan. No-one will make you do what you don't want to do any more. I promise you.'

He stared at her in the darkness, full of hope for a wonderful moment, then slumped again. 'Oh Lydie, if only. If only. It's no good, my dear. Nathan will have half a dozen other Methodies with him by now. They will search the house – Pa will have no option.'

She said, 'He is drunk. I had forgot – he will be in no state to resist Nathan.'

'You see? I had best take my chance on the Heights road. I must just give them the slip and get down to Taunton. If I could get back to Bristol they would not dare try anything.'

'If Wesley is scouting in that direction, he'll find you, Alan.'

'I know. I know it.'

Her anger bubbled into action and she stood up like a released spring. 'What can they do to you? If they find you here and you tell them you have left Marella . . . what can they do?'

'Escort me back. To talk things over. Besides, Lydie, I struck her.'

She felt her eyes open wide. 'You hit Marella?'

'Yes. She is all right. Breathing still. Old Gran Peters ran like a banshee, wailing she was dead. But I know—'

'But Alan, why? It is not in your nature to hit a woman. Why?'

There was a pause then he sighed deeply. 'She told me who the father was. Taunted me that it

178

had been a trick. That he still saw her. Whenever he wished.'

She waited. Then breathed, 'Well? Who is it? Who *is* it, Alan?'

'Wesley Peters. Her own brother, Lydie.' He sobbed again. 'I should have gone to him and killed him. But I did not wish to set eyes on him. Let him have her. Let her have him – they are a good pair. I just want to be gone. Gone from their hypocritical denials and bible thumping. Gone!'

There was another pause. Lydia wondered whether it could be her own heartbeat thudding inside her head. It increased to a crescendo of sound that rocked the house itself, and a bellowing roar accompanied it.

'Fielding! Rupert Fielding! Come out here, man! Come out here and give us back our property!'

Alan's eyes flashed again as he looked up.

'They've come, Lydie,' he said, quietly. 'That's Nathan. I'll go down and let him in – no need to upset Mother. Perhaps I can placate him.'

Lydia put her hand on his shoulder and held him where he was.

'No.' She felt suddenly calm and sure, though as yet she had no idea what to do. 'No. You are not going back to that. Wait. Perhaps Father will wake and go down. Wait.'

Seven

The few seconds stretched into a minute . . . and another minute . . . and still Nathan hammered on the kitchen door and still Lydia restrained Alan as if she knew some kind of respite was at hand. And then from the attic storey where Alan had always slept, a door burst open and footsteps descended and passed them and went on down the back stairs. A fresh outburst of knocking elicited a roaring reply from the kitchen, 'Wait, can't you? I'm coming – for God's sake, wait!'

Lydia's hand clutched Alan's shirt. 'It's Gus! He brought Father home earlier and he must have . . .' She leaned down so that their faces were close. 'Alan. Gus will see to things here – better than any of us. Quickly – we must get down the front stairs before Gus comes to rouse me, as he surely will do.'

Alan started to protest but Lydia was already flinging her cloak over her shoulders, pulling the blankets from the bed, shovelling candles into a bag.

'Hold these,' she hissed. 'I'll go ahead of you. Trust me, Alan. I know somewhere you can hide – just trust me!'

She lifted the latch with care, eased open the door and slid through it and along the landing to the stairhead. Below her, Gus had found a candle and was shielding its guttering flame with one hand while tugging at the bolts on the door with the other. The light, shining up from the flagged floor, cast upward-slanting shadows on Gus's irritable face that made its usual bucolic cheerfulness look diabolical. Lydia shivered and glided on to the top of the front stairs. Behind her, Alan stumbled on a drooping blanket but the sound was thankfully lost in the sharp report of the bolt sliding back below them. Lydia turned and snatched some of the bundle from him then ran lightly down to the hall and began work on the front door. Muffled but unmistakable came Nathan's sonorous voice demanding Alan, interrupted by Gus's furious indignation at a disturbance at such a time. 'Thought at least it was a matter of life and death!' he bellowed as Lydia began on the top bolt. 'A man has got a right to leave his wife if he wants . . .' The door swung open and the fog fingered its way into the hall. Lydia removed the rarely used key, pushed Alan outside and joined him. ''Tis a matter of life an' death!' boomed Nathan. 'My daughter be taken abed before her time – ' Lydia closed the door gently, locked it and pushed the key beneath as she and Alan had done so often on midnight escapades when they were children.

Alan blurted, 'She's gone into labour – did you hear that, Lydie? Marella. It must have been the blow I gave her. Oh God.'

Lydia took his arm and urged him along to the gate. 'You said the child would be born before January,' she hissed. 'You said it yourself! This is no premature birth, Alan!' She felt cold and clear-headed. Alan could not go back to that situation. Incest was by no means unknown on the Moor, but Wesley and Marella . . . it was unthinkable.

He got himself through the gate then leaned on it despairingly.

'It's no good going up to the Heights, Lydie. I explained. And am I to be taken back ignominiously? Would it not be better to return myself? Lydie, I should have taken her to Bristol immediately. It's my fault – I thought I could lord it over the Peters, have a good time like the Pascoes do. But I'm not like them. I should have taken her back to Bristol – brazened it out – I was ashamed. Oh God!'

Lydia seized the rest of the blankets and rolled them into a manageable bundle. 'We're not going up to the Heights, Alan. We're going down the combe. They've followed you up, so they won't be searching it any more. We're going to get a boat, or swim. I know somewhere you can lie up until this awful business dies down.'

'I cannot desert her, Lydie. Not now.'

'You are not deserting her! You are giving yourself time to think, to plan, and then to decide. They are not going to hunt you like some animal and drag you back there, Alan – not the Peterses. And if you go back freely now, you are condoning . . .' she swallowed. 'You are condoning the situation.' Behind them, a light came on in her own room. 'Alan, quickly. Gus has gone to fetch me and they will realize now what has happened. We cannot *allow* ourselves to be caught! Please, Alan – '

He released the gatepost at last and plunged after her.

It was a mile-long descent to the beach at Listowel by a footpath that ran above the small torrent of the river. The sound of the water covered their progress and visibility was so bad that they would have had to cannon into someone before being seen. Even so, Lydia, knowing Wesley's tracking experience, felt her nerves stretch like wires each time she touched one of the alders which fringed the path, and her ears hummed with trying to listen above the river sound for a snapping twig or padding feet.

It could have taken them only fifteen minutes to reach the wide, sandy track that spilled over onto the shingle of the beach, but it seemed like hours. They stood getting their breath, re-distributing the blankets, peering through the mist for any boats drawn up on the pebbles.

'We're going to make a fine old clatter hunting around for a boat,' Lydia said in a low voice. 'Tide's right out now. Can you remember whether there was anything near at hand earlier?'

Alan said, 'If we could find the fire Robbie

made . . . there was a flatner nearby. Upturned. 'Rella and I sat on it to eat our mackerel. Just a few hours ago.'

Lydia ignored the pain in his voice and moved to the left. 'The fire was near the Roscoe cottage. Are those embers glowing over there?'

They made their way through the sand towards a faint glow in the murk; it was indeed the remains of the fire, ashy and white around its two driftwood logs, dully red in the centre. They took to the pebbles, wincing at the rapid fire of sound as they ploughed down the beach. The flatner was there, light and easy to turn, its single oar lying beneath it. They threw their bundles inside, then picked it up between them and began to run at a stagger towards the invisible sea. At one stage Lydia thought she heard a cry behind them and almost gave up. Then her foot slipped into the low-tide mud and with a gasp of thankfulness she released her end of the boat and it slid gracefully – as it was meant to – over the mud like a sleigh. She jumped into it, Alan gave a final shove and joined her and the first of the tiny wavelets bore them up and floated them out. The silence was blessed. There was no sound of pursuit. After a precious moment of listening, Lydia fitted the oar into the niche on the stern and, standing like a gondolier, she took the tiny boat through the darkness to the headland looming near them. Once round that, in Garrett Cove, she felt safe.

She rested, crouching to speak to Alan where

he knelt in the bows. 'We shall be all right now. We can take this boat right up to the rocks – it draws less than six inches. We'll creep over to the other side of this cove, then just follow it around.'

'That brings us into the open sea and this thing won't stand up to it, Lydie. You know the Atlantic rollers come right in to Stapleford—'

'Dear, we are going no further than around Garrett Cove. On the other side there is a cave. It's hidden by a rock – Caroline Garrett found it the first time I went to the Place last summer. It's Garrett land, so no-one will think . . . you will be quite safe there, Alan, just for a day or two. Peace. That's what you'll have, my dear. Don't you think it's the very least you deserve?'

There was a sound like a sob. 'Lydie . . . you are so good. I've tried to blame this whole fiasco on you, my dear. But always you have acted only in my interest.'

'Please, Alan. I am not proud of persuading you into this marriage. Not a bit proud. We always said the Methodies were mad. We weren't so wrong, my dear, were we?' She patted his shoulder, unable to hug him. Then she took up the oar again and rocked with it while the flatner bobbed along the surface of the water towards the looming cliff over which she had clambered so crossly that day last summer. Her thoughts were confused and jumbled, kept at bay by the physical effort of rowing, but she knew that the perfidy of Wesley surmounted in sheer horror Gus's dastardly attempt to rape her at Michaelmas. She knew that the driving need to outwit him now, at all costs, was the force that was guiding her to the rocky shore of the 'secret' cove. She even let herself believe that Caroline's discovery had been destined for this very contingency.

With all her considerable expertise, she steered her little craft alongside the cliff letting the jagged rock-face guide her around to the next headland. It was dangerous; Alan hung over one side up to his shoulder in the sea, gauging the depth beneath the frail wooden hull. And then he would grunt and swing the boat outwards as he caught a projecting pinnacle beneath the surface. When they reached the point, the open sea caught them and swept them away from their landfall. Frantically, Lydia turned the prow and rowed hard again until Alan's gasping cry warned her they were almost aground. Then it was a question of going with the quiet swell until the pebbles knocked on Alan's outstretched fingers and he could leap over and pull the boat gently up the shingle. He secured it safely against Lydia's return while she gathered their things and began the struggle up the beach. It was very much easier than it had been before when she had been bare-footed, but even so she was panting by the time her hand reached the sharpness of the rock guarding the cave entrance. She leaned on it, hanging her head and waiting for Alan to join her.

'Sis – ' his groping hand found her cloak and

hung onto it. 'These pebbles are wet. The tide must sweep right in and halfway up the cliff.'

'It does.' She straightened her back and took a deep, steady breath. 'That's why no-one will suspicion you are here. But the top of the cave is dry and we shall be able to tell from the candle flame whether there is an air hole.' She let go the rock and clasped his arm. 'We're safe, Alan. Take heart, my dear. We're quite safe. Come on.'

Once again she scrambled ahead of him, finding the cave entrance without too much difficulty and entering its clammy blackness without obvious hesitation. She talked as cheerfully as she could to encourage Alan, whose muttered curses told clearly when he fell foul of projections and small pools. Then, at last, she felt the dry seaweed of the tide line and crouched on the sand beyond, searching in the bundle she carried for matches and candle. Once lit, the flame burned steadily, its smoke ascending straight to the darkness above them and illuminating a tiny area of tumbled rocks among the sand. Lydia waited no longer than it took to glance around her, then she began to gather the dry weed into a heap. 'We'll light a fire, Alan. Dry you off,' she panted. 'You need warmth outside as well as in.' She pushed the bundle towards him and a bottle emerged from the tumble of blankets. 'Take some of Father's brandy, it will steady you. And take off your boots.'

The seaweed ignited easily and crackled

fiercely and by the extra light Lydia found enough driftwood to keep it going for an hour or two. She packed it around with large pebbles which would retain their warmth afterwards.

'No food. I did not dare delay us by going to the pantry. But there's a mackerel line here. You can fish tomorrow when it's light. Get more wood. Drag it in here to dry. I'll come again as soon as I can, Alan, but if the Peterses prove hard to convince it might be two days. Even three.'

Alan swigged the brandy and watched her morosely. 'What will you tell them? They'll know you're lying whatever you say.'

'I shall tell them the truth up to a point. That we took a flatner intending to row round to Stapleford and met up with a trawler. From . . . Rosslare. Yes, Rosslare. You're on your way to Ireland, my lad!'

She forced a laugh but he did not respond. Shock had taken him into himself and he stared blankly at the leaping flames as if they had hypnotized him.

She kissed him hurriedly. 'Alan. Listen, my dear. Can you manage here, alone, for as long as two days? You have the brandy and there will be fresh water running from the cliff you can collect. And the fishing. Will you be all right, Alan? Mother will be so terribly worried, what with Nathan stamping around and Gus shouting.'

He roused himself sufficiently to nod. 'Of course, Lydie. Mamma – I had forgot Mamma.

Give her my love. I will wait for you, dear girl, then we can go to Mamma together and put her mind at rest.'

She made him stay where he was, his boots drying on the warm pebbles, his trousers steaming on his legs. When she looked over her shoulder as she crept back down the cave, his face looked luminous in the firelight and terribly vulnerable. In spite of everything, he still loved Marella. She felt a constriction in her chest. Love made Alan vulnerable . . . it made everyone vulnerable.

Dawn was turning the fog pearly white as she rowed back across Garrett Cove. She was unbearably tired now; the walk back up the combe was impossible, yet it had to be done for her mother's sake as well as Alan's. She rounded Listowel point slowly, holding her elbows to her side and using her body to move the heavy oar back and forth, back and forth. This time yesterday she had been getting up, going into the garden to pick the few remaining flowers for Jinny's wedding. Had it been only twenty-four hours ago?

A wave rose beneath the boat and carried her smoothly forward for two or three yards and she could have sobbed with relief. Then she realized she was still gliding effortlessly towards the beach. She glanced over her shoulder and gave a cry of sheer terror. The flatner was being towed in. A man up to his armpits in the sea was walking slowly towards the shore, the mooring rope over his shoulder.

Lydia dropped the oar with a clatter and collapsed where she was, clutching her knees. Even before the white mist outlined his hair, she knew the man was Wesley Peters. Her awareness of his identity was frightening in itself; his silence, his inexorable progress, was a separate terror. Beyond that cry she could not speak. Until then, she had realized only too well that the awful hunt was a nightmare for Alan, but for her it had been a battle to be won. Now she entered Alan's nightmare and until the flatner grounded and he turned and lifted her bodily onto the dry shingle, she was immobile with shock.

His hands on her waist altered that.

'Let me go!' She struggled free and moved back three quick steps from him. He looked at her steadily for a moment then turned and saw to the boat. She said, 'There was no need – I was rowing. I could have done it.'

He began to walk up the beach then stopped to wring out the hem of his smock. 'It was obvious you were going to go into the sea at any minute. Tired out, aren't you?'

She wanted to weep and wail. She loved him. Like Alan loved Marella in spite of everything, she still loved him.

She said as levelly as she could, 'He's gone, Wesley. Alan has gone. I rowed him out to an Irish trawler. They took him aboard and will land him in Rosslare.'

He paused in his wringing and stared at her for another moment as if he could read the truth in her face. Then he shook out his sodden smock.

'That is that, then. There's no more to be said or done in that direction and Marella must manage alone.'

She felt herself begin to tremble with relief; instinctively she knew that in spite of Nathan's trumpetings, Wesley was the true force in the Peters household. If he said she was to be believed then she would be believed. She swallowed and gripped her frozen hands in front of her.

'Marella?' she said stupidly.

'She is in labour and it is proving difficult. She chooses to believe that the child will not come unless its father be present. She will have to do without him.'

An obvious retort sprang to her lips and might have been uttered had she not been so near to collapse. Instead she hung her head and simply stood there.

His voice was gentle. 'Come. Come now, Lydie. I will help you up the combe. There will be a bed waiting for you and food.' He held out a hand. 'My father will make no more trouble, I promise. You did what you had to do. He will see that.'

She almost took his hand, then his forgiving words struck her with renewed irony and she stifled a sob and turned on her heel.

'I do not need your kindness, Wesley Peters! I do not need you. Get back to your sister, where, it seems, you belong!'

She stumbled over the shingle and past the now dead fire, pain and anger lending her strength. Once clear of the beach the fog was no more and the daylight was almost too bright to bear. She shielded her eyes and stared up the tunnel of the combe, near despair. When Wesley took her arm and led her to the river's edge, she protested no more. There was not a soul about; the track leading to the two hovels owned by the Peters was deserted: not even a gull wheeled overhead looking for pickings. Through this empty, quiet landscape, Lydia and Wesley trudged, archetypal travelers looking for rest. Everything was so unreal that Lydia was drained of emotions and leaned more and more heavily on Wesley until by the time they reached the gate at Milton Mains, her feet were dragging and he was almost carrying her. Her body was aware of his; there was comfort there but also a terrible, forbidden attraction. She let her fingers clutch his wet smock and her nose smell the salt sea smell of him; felt his hip on hers and his whipcord arms around her waist holding her up, and though her tired mind refused to think about it, her body knew only too well that she would never love anyone else with such tenderness and such knowledge.

As the gate slammed back unheeded, people came running at them. Two men she had never seen before but recognized as Methodists from their shorn hair, followed by Nathan and Benjie Peters. Wesley freed one of his hands and held it up.

'She is his sister. She got him away. That be only natural, brothers. What we woulda done in the same circumstances.'

Nathan stopped before her and bunched his hands by his side. He seemed to knot and swell with emotion and she expected at least that he would spit at her. But he controlled himself and gradually relaxed. The others, save for Wesley who still supported her, gathered around him and she understood only too well how he could gather and hold a congregation. But when Nathan spoke his voice was bewildered.

'She keeps a-callin' for 'im. 'Er mother be with 'er. My mother too. But all she do want is your brother.' Suddenly there was hatred in the quiet voice. 'The day she set eyes on Alan Fielding was a bad day for 'er! A bad day for all the Peters. Our two families should never be joined – not by marriage, not by friendship, not by nuthin'!' He turned his eyes, blue and crazy, on Wesley. 'You shoulda killed 'im! That day you saw 'im and followed 'im down to Tamerton Combe – you shoulda killed 'im then! But you wanted 'er! Didn't you? You lusted after the Fielding girl just like 'er brother lusted after 'Rella. So you spared 'im.'

Lydia tried to stand up and away from Wesley but he held her tightly to him.

'Enough of that, Father. It's over – can't you understand that? It was a match that should never have been made but it has given the child a name. Now it's over. Let it be done with!'

Father and son stared at each other, Wesley's

strong will keeping the old man silent. Then there came a cry and the group of men parted and looked back to see Lucy stumbling from the house.

The sight at last gave Lydia back her reasoning powers. She freed herself from Wesley somehow and took a step forward.

'Mamma . . .' She wanted to cast herself on those frail shoulders and weep and be cared for, but could not. 'Mamma – you should not be out here. It is damp! Please, Mamma.' They met by the glossy rhododendrons and clasped each other. Lucy was shaking in every limb and Lydia was forced to support her back into the house. At the open front door she glanced over her shoulder and her eyes met Wesley's. He had followed close behind, ready to help if need be, but now he smiled very slightly at her and turned to herd his companions back along the path and through the gate. Lydia closed the door. They were gone. He was gone.

She said, 'Mamma. I am so sorry. It has been a terrible time for you but there was no way I could warn you.'

'Dear child. So long as you are safe. Come into the kitchen. You must tell us everything.'

They went through the cold dining room and into the welcome warmth of the kitchen. At the fire Mrs Pollard was frying ham and everything was as neat and orderly as it usually was at this time when Lucy had her short spell in her own kitchen.

'Your father and Gus Pascoe are doing the

milk, dear child. Mrs Pollard, bring Miss Lydie some hot tea and then tell Mister Fielding that she is back, safe and sound.'

Lucy sat knee to knee with Lydia, touching her skirt or her arm now and then as if for reassurance, while Lydia let the blessed steam of the tea thaw out her stiff face and fingers. She had not reckoned on having to face Gus again, though she should have guessed that he would be bound to stay at Milton until there was some news of Alan or herself. It seemed days since they had crept along the landing and she had been grateful then for Gus's aggressive presence. She looked at the tall old clock under the stairs: it had all taken less than three hours.

When the two men finally erupted into the kitchen, Gus had the decency to stand back by the fire while Lydia told her prepared story. It did not take long; Rupert and Lucy of course accepted it without question. What took the time was trying to explain the dire situation between Alan and Marella.

'Is Alan convinced the child is not his?' Lucy asked in a withdrawn voice. 'How can he be certain? She is so young.'

'It seems she has taunted him with it, Mamma. I do not understand fully. But Alan was terribly provoked.'

'But striking her! In her condition!'

'The Peterses joined together to trap him into marriage, Mamma.'

Rupert said, 'Aye. I can see that, right enough. The way they came after him – if Gus hadn't been here I'd have taken my gun to them, Lydie, I do assure you of that! He wouldn't let them over the doorstep – came to rouse you and realized then what had happened. But he wouldn't give an inch! Apprised me of what was happening and I went to your mother – naturally they'd awoken her with their roaring! Gus kept them at bay. But they were all around the house waiting for Alan to come out – didn't believe a word we told them!'

Lucy said painfully, 'Marella has been taken to bed with the baby and is calling for Alan, my dear. It is natural – '

'Damned upstarts! He is well rid of the lot of them.'

Lydia said wearily, 'He may return to Bristol as soon as he can and then he would send for her. If they are away from the Moor they might well manage to make a separate life for themselves and be happy.' She remembered Alan's confession of love and tears rose to her eyes.

Gus said tactfully, 'I had better leave you to rest – all of you. There will be no more trouble by the sound of things.' He came to Lucy and took her hand. 'I am thankful I was here, Mrs Fielding, and able to help. In a small way.' Lucy tried to speak but he smiled and turned to Lydia. He took her hand and held it very hard. 'I will call on you in two or three days, Lydie.' He did not ask permission; it was a declaration of intent.

She could not be frightened or even repelled. She was too tired.

*　　*　　*

In spite of that, she did not sleep the clock round and the few hours' rest she did manage were disturbed by frightful dreams of Alan being killed by Wesley; of Wesley being killed by Gus, sometimes urged on by herself. She woke to find Lucy sitting by her bed, leaning forward and frowning worriedly.

'Lydia, my dear, I was about to wake you. You were crying out pathetically in your sleep.'

Lydia turned her head wearily into the pillow and reached for her mother's hand. 'Mamma . . . I am sorry. I had a nightmare. I will get up now.'

'No, Lydia. Please. It is only two in the afternoon. You have been asleep no more than four hours. I am afraid you have a slight fever – doubtless going out in that fog and getting wet.'

Lydia forced herself to sit up and smile reassuringly. 'Darling Mamma. You know I am as strong as Blackie and never get fevers or chills! Now, let us go to the parlour and sit together by the window. I will fetch the tea things and we can take up our routine as if last night never happened.'

Lucy allowed herself to be persuaded and when they were settled in their usual chairs and the fire burning brightly, she encouraged Lydia to talk of her experience and release some of her tension.

'I had to help him to get away, Mamma – I feel partially responsible for Alan's marriage. I was so determined he must do the right thing by the Peters family.'

'You were right, Lydie. Alan would have eventually seen that by himself, I feel certain.'

'Yes but when he told me that they had all conspired to trick him so that the baby would have a respectable father, I felt we must outwit them at all costs.' Lydia twisted her hands restlessly and stared at the window where yesterday's mist seemed like an evil dream and the sun shone brightly on the alders lining the combe. 'It seems rather silly now. You see, Alan still loves Marella and I think after the baby has been born he will decide to take her back with him to Bristol. He could just as well have stayed hidden in my room as Gus told old Nathan he had, then by now he could have returned calmly . . .'

Lucy said quietly, 'I don't think Alan should see Nathan for some time, Lydie. I am afraid the old man is a little mad and might seek to do him an injury.'

Lydia looked sharply at her mother, who never exaggerated. She remembered the blunderbuss and old Nathan's words earlier this morning.

She said weakly, 'Nathan does a lot of talking, Mamma.'

'I saw his face yesterday. Once or twice. Through the parlour window. He stared through, hardly seeing me, looking for Alan. He had eyes only for Alan.' Lucy drew her shawl closer. 'I think you did the right thing, Lydie. You took Alan out of the path of a mad bull.'

Lydia got up to tend the fire. She had been about to say that Wesley could control his father.

Then she remembered that Wesley's behaviour was described as insane by many people. Just for an instant she let her mind picture Wesley with Marella . . . the two pale heads in close confusion. She put a hand to her throat.

Lucy said anxiously, 'Lydie, I think you should take to bed for a day or two. You are not well, my child.'

Lydia stood up and went to her mother. She put her lips to the brown hair in front of her cap. 'Mamma, I am quite well. And I need to be very well indeed. You see, Alan is not bound for Rosslare at all. I have shown him a cave on the other side of Garrett Cove, where I am certain he will be safe. As soon as Marella has given birth to this child, I shall go again and fetch Alan here.'

She felt Lucy's gasp. Then the calm, well-schooled voice said, 'Then I agree, you are in the pink of health, Lydie. And perhaps you should not mention this to your father. He has sold some sheep to Gus – quite a big flock I understand – and when they meet next time there will be money to be spent. Your father might become indiscreet.'

Lydia stared down at the netted frill of the cap, wanting to ask questions but knowing that her mother's loyalty would not permit her to answer them. She clasped the thin shoulder to show her agreement and went to the window, frowning. Why would her father be selling any of his sheep at the beginning of winter? And to Gus, who bought wool, not livestock?

Then all questions were forgotten as she stared down at the rhododendrons and saw someone walking through them. The next instant Wesley's old felt hat emerged from the foliage and he strode to the front door and lifted the knocker.

Lydia turned. 'It's Wesley Peters.' Her mouth was suddenly dry. 'Shall I go, Mamma?'

'Do, child. Mrs Pollard isn't there. He may well have come to tell us the baby is born.' Lucy checked Lydia's departure. 'Bring him upstairs, Lydie. He is the only one who has behaved well throughout this business. I believe him to be genuinely loving to his sister.'

Lydia felt a sharp pang at those words from her mother – who never exaggerated. She should have seen it for herself right from the very beginning. Why else would he have shadowed his sister so protectively? She dreaded seeing him again.

Nevertheless her heart leapt as she dragged at the heavy oak door and there he was, standing with his hat held before him and the same smock which had dried on him and showed salt stains up to the neck. His white-straw hair, blue eyes, the taut skin over the angular bones of his face . . . they were all so dear to her. She loved him and she wanted to scream and run from him.

He said quietly, 'Thank you for coming to the door. I thought you would be abed and I wanted to see you.'

She could not reply. She hung onto the door

like a stupid schoolgirl and stared at him with all her eyes.

He said, 'Lydie . . . Lydie, my love. My beauty—' He stopped as an involuntary cry came from her lips. 'All right . . . all right, Lydie. I will not speak. Not now. Just tell me where your brother is. Where is Alan, Lydie? Tell me, please tell me.'

Another cry, like a moan, came from her. She gasped, 'Alan? You are still searching for Alan? I told you – oh God, I told you – '

'We both knew that was not true, Lydie. I wanted Alan gone – right away – so I said no more. But we both knew – ' He took a step inside as she tried to slam the door, then, when she abandoned that and turned to flee he gripped her by the arm, twisted her to face him and held her close. 'You have to tell me, Lydie. Marella cannot go on like this. She wants Alan.'

His hands hurt; his face was two inches away; that beloved face belonged to a man who could only love his sister, yet could still speak words like . . . Lydie, my love . . .

She drew a breath and somehow gasped, 'If you did not believe me then, Wesley, how can I make you believe me now? Alan has gone. You will not see him again. I can say no more.'

Again he stared into her eyes as if he could find the truth there. Gradually his grip relaxed; he bent his head and very gently put his lips to hers.

As if he had touched her with a naked flame, she leapt away from him and backed to the huge table, standing there, scrubbing at her mouth with the back of her hand.

His blue eyes gazed at her. 'I thought – I thought – '

She tore her hand away and choked at him, 'Understand this – I hate you, Wesley Peters! You disgust me! I thought at first you were a stag – an animal with an animal's natural feelings! And I was right, oh God, I was right! You are nothing more than an animal! You have an animal's urge to – to—'

He interrupted her fiercely. 'Lydie, I know, I understand how you feel. After what happened I can only suppose that any man is hateful to you. But I will wait, my love. You will forget Gus Pascoe and see that—'

She almost spat at him. 'How dare you mention . . . that! How dare you even speak of it! I *have* forgot! I have forgot entirely – there are other things in my mind now.' She sucked in a huge breath, turned and walked unsteadily to the front stairs. 'Please go,' she said hoarsely. 'Your father was right when he said there should be no connection between our families. There is something . . . wrong . . . evil . . . about it.'

She began to climb the stairs but stopped when he spoke from directly beneath her.

'Lydie. That is all nonsense – but we will speak of it later when you are rested. Now, may I speak to your mother instead?'

'She is unwell. She cannot be burdened much more.'

'I think she will be glad to see me.'

Lydia did not argue further but continued up the stairs with him behind her and went directly along the landing to the parlour. Her mother looked up, expecting him, smiling a welcome.

'Wesley. Is there good news of Marella?' she asked, indicating a chair near the fire.

Wesley dipped his head in a kind of salute; fleetingly Lydia remembered his proud independence and knew she should be touched by his evident respect for her mother.

'No news as yet, Mrs Fielding. But I've come to ask whether Miss Lydia be allowed to attend my sister. Marella has always had a leaning towards her – right proud to be her sister, she is.' He glanced at Lydia's set face. 'You see, she calls all the time for your son. We – I – thought Miss Lydia might set her mind at rest on that score.'

Lucy sighed deeply. 'Lydia is tired Wesley, very tired. But I do not see how either of us can refuse your request. Poor little Marella. I would come myself if I thought I could help her.'

Lydia started forward, words of protest and refusal on her lips. Then she stopped. It was true; Marella had always seemed fond of Lydia in her shallow way. And Alan loved her. And it was Lydia's doing that Alan could not be with her at this moment. The chain of events again semed to end with her; the responsibility was heavy but inescapable.

She said dully, 'I will fetch my cloak.'

She went to her room and put on her shoes. She stood up and said aloud into the empty, familiar space, 'I cannot bear this. I cannot *bear* it!' But there was nothing else to do.

They walked down the combe in the same caul of silence that had enshrouded them before but this time there was no physical contact between them and after the first time Wesley's helping hand had been rejected he did not offer it again. Yet it was as if the space between them was charged, and Lydia felt a physical ache in all her bones which she knew would be assuaged by closing that space.

By the time they had picked their way past Nathan's midden and reached the open door of Granny Peters's cottage, the afternoon light was fading and it was difficult to discern who was in the tiny downstairs room. Against the light of the fire, Lydia could see Mercy settling a pan of water on the trivet, and around the table were several male figures she guessed to be Nathan, Luke and Benjie. As they looked up at her arrival, sounds came from above and they all froze. The ladder at the back of the room led through a hole in the ceiling to the attic above and from there came an encouraging voice followed immediately by a quick panting then a terrifying, animal scream. Luke and Benjie still sat stolidly at this; Nathan bowed his head to the table and covered his ears. Wesley shut the door sharply on the greyness and stood defiantly at Lydia's side.

Mercy said sharply, 'What's *she* doing 'ere?'

Wesley's voice was flat, the Somerset burr

hard. 'We can't get her brother. Seemed to me she were next best.'

Nathan lifted his head and seemed to gather his anger around him. 'What good will that do? 'Tidn't 'er our maid do want. 'Tis that cursed brother – oh merciful Lord – 'ark to 'er!'

Marella's cries rang out anew, starting with fierce grunts and ending in high-pitched screams.

Lydia said, 'Let me go to her. She turned to me once before.'

'She cannot birth without 'er 'usband!' Nathan roared, leaning halfway over the table. 'She cannot birth—'

Wesley caught his arm. 'Father, be still. Let the girl go up. No 'arm can come of it.'

Mercy's sudden sobs added to the general noise and confusion. Through it all, Luke and Benjie sat. There was a scuffle from above and Prudence's head appeared in the loft opening.

'Hot water, quick, Mercy – ' She hung her head down, extending an arm for the pan. 'Nan is going to try a cup of nettle tea.' She caught sight of Lydia and paused. 'You be come, eh, miss? Well, come up then. Tell 'er some lies about Master Alan. Quieten 'er if you can.'

Lydia pressed past the table and climbed after Prudence and into the cramped loft. There was no window; the only light came from two wavering candles. The wooden bed was pushed to the middle of the floor where the pitch of the roof allowed the women to stand almost upright. Marella lay, propped high with pillows, a thin blanket covering her legs, her shift torn and pulled down to show bruises on her arms and shoulders. Her neck plainly bore the marks of Alan's fingers. Lydia averted her eyes. She had borne similar marks after her struggle with Gus.

'Lydie?' The voice was a thread of its normal self. 'Lydie, is that you?'

Lydia came close and saw that the wizened figure kneeling by the bed was Nan Nancombe, well known throughout the district for her birthings, layings-out, love potions and abortions. Lydia leaned over her and took Marella's tiny hand. It was cold with sweat.

'Yes. It's Lydie.' She felt her voice catch in her throat as she stared at this girl who was Alan's wife and her sister-in-law. The face was like a waxen doll's, the blond hair lying in plastered strips close to the scalp.

'Lydie . . . Lydie . . .' the hand gripped hard. 'Tell Alan – tell him – ' The wide eyes lost their hard-won concentration and distended with terror. 'It's coming back . . . Ma . . . Nan . . .' She tore her hand from Lydia's and reached for more familiar comfort. The two women crowded over the bed, pulling the girl almost upright.

'Push hard!' Nan's voice rasped out an onion breath. 'Come on, girl – now – *now*!'

Prudence gasped, 'Try, Ella. Try for Ma – '

Lydia drew back, her head pressed hard against the straw of the thatch, her own face contorted in sympathy. The grunting screams started again and, as if in sympathy, the smoky lights dipped and swayed ghoulish shadows over the loft. There was a final agonized shriek, then another panting silence. Marella collapsed on the straw pillows, Prudence huddling one side of her, Nan the other. Then they both turned to the pan of steaming water on the floor; the acrid smell of blanched nettles filled the roof space.

Lydia crouched again and took the limp hand from the blanket.

'Marella, listen to me.' She put her mouth close to the tiny ear and whispered urgently, 'Alan is waiting for you. He wants you to get this over quickly so that he can send for you and the baby.' She swallowed. 'He loves you, Marella. Can you understand that?'

The long blond lashes flickered.

'We done wicked things, Lydie.' The whisper was haunted. 'Both of us done wicked things. But I do love 'im good and true.'

Lydia bowed her head to hide tears. Behind her, Prudence murmured to Nan, 'We've got to do something. She can't stand much more of this. Twelve hours of grunting and groaning and no further forrad. Let one of the boys go for the doctor.'

Old Nan said calmly, 'She's nigh on ready now. If she can sup this and try again, we shall 'ave a crowning. An' a boy, I'll be bound.'

Lydia supported the sticky blond head as Nan held a cracked cup to the parched lips. The steaming green brew ran down Marella's chin and into a cut and tears trembled on the long lashes.

They waited together, the four women.

Occasionally Marella would rouse herself and begin again the preliminary gasping screams of fear and pain. And then at last Nan motioned Lydia away and whipped off the blanket, standing ready by the bare bent legs. Marella reared up, bracing herself, pulling with an unbelievable strength on her mother's hands. A scream burst from her with renewed force.

Nan said hoarsely, 'The next time. The next time I'll be able to reach the 'ead.' Lydia glanced down and saw, sickened, that the arm, brown and stick-like, was buried inside Marella. The candlelight wavered, throwing a merciful shadow; Marella groaned and lifted herself and began again.

Afterwards, Lydia never knew whether it was ten minutes or an hour before Nan's triumphant hiss. She knew she would always see the old woman braced against Marella's bare feet, both hands working between the pale thighs. The leathery face seemed all sucked into the inverted lips and the greasy black head covering had slipped low over the forehead.

Then at last the sibilant whisper of triumph – 'I got 'en. Firm and square, I got 'en. Push 'ard now, my beauty.'

As if obeying the command, Marella came up, her pretty doll's face lolling on its neck. Her hands whitened on her mother's, her legs pushed on Nan's skeletal shoulders. She screamed, a mere echo of her previous shrieks so that it was possible to hear Prudence shout for God's help. Feverishly, Lydia grabbed a candle and held it for Nan. Her stomach fluttered against the automatic retching at what she saw. Elbow deep in blood, Nan held grimly onto a head emerging from the smallness of Marella. It was the biggest head Lydia had ever seen on a baby. Gently, very gently, ignoring the kicking feet, Nan turned the head and eased out a shoulder. The baby slithered onto the bed.

'Sheeting. Calico. Anything.'

Nan bundled the child into the blanket and put it on the floor. A dark river was flowing from Marella. Lydia turned frantically and felt something put into her hand. Above the sheet she met Wesley's eyes for an instant as he reached through the trapdoor. They held no expression at all.

She turned and thrust the cloth at Nan and crouched again by Marella. Prudence put her daughter's head back on the pillows, her cheek pressed to the waxen one, her lips murmuring endearments. Marella sighed a long sigh.

'Better now,' she whispered. 'No pain.'

Lydia picked up the hand and put the fingers to her lips, tasting her own tears.

'Tell Alan . . .' Marella's eyes were wide again, looking at something beyond Lydia's head. '. . . loved him. Always loved him.'

Nan whispered, 'Nowt else we can do, Wesley. Leave it. Leave it be.'

Then Marella gave a sob and whispered, 'Nathan!' and closed her eyes. They waited for a long moment though they all knew she was dead. Then Prudence took her daughter's hand from Lydia's and placed it on her breast and stood up.

'I had three girls and this was the last,' she said steadily. 'But I would not wish her back into this world.'

Lydia looked at her, horrified. Prudence's lips were set in a straight line and her eyes were expressionless, like Wesley's.

Lydia whispered, 'I'm sorry, Prudence. I'm sorry.'

Prudence ignored her and turned to Nan Nancombe. 'What of the child? 'Twere a boy, I seed. Is 'e dead?'

Nan reached down her gory arms and picked up the bundle.

'Aye. 'E never took breath and I never 'elped 'im. 'E's a muckle-ead. Better dead than alive. An' 'e took 'is mother too.'

They all stared down at the gross infant. Lydia remembered a small boy in Carybridge once; water on the brain they called it; and he hadn't been able to speak or feed himself.

Wesley said roughly, 'Wrap him again and put him by Marella. We'll have to send for old Tarling now.' He gestured at Lydia. 'Go on down, Lydie, wait outside. Go on. Now!'

Somehow Lydia climbed down the stairs. The men sat around the table just as before and only Nathan turned his head to ask a silent question. Lydia avoided his eyes and as she put her head down to press past them to the door it flew open and, incredibly, Alan stood there. He was wet to the skin, his face livid and seeming terribly

210

sunken since she had last seen him. He stood still, holding the lintel above his head, swaying, his eyes on Lydia beseechingly.

'I couldn't stay there . . . I swam over with the tide and went straight up to Milton. Mamma told me. How is she, Lydie? Tell me how she is.'

Lydia held the ladder behind her for support.

'Oh my dear . . . oh, Alan . . . she is gone. I am so sorry—'

Alan said, 'Gone? Gone where?'

Lydia saw the white blur of Nathan's face just out of her vision. 'She died, Alan. The child was so big . . . she died.'

There was a roar from the table and pandemonium broke out. Nathan leapt to his feet and his two sons jumped too like dogs obeying their master. The table was flung aside with a splintering crash. It was only as Nathan leapt that Lydia saw the flash of steel in Nathan's hand: then he and Alan were clasped together as if in friendship and Nathan's roar had deepened to a growl. Together the two men slid very slowly down the door jamb to the earth floor, Nathan on Alan's breast. Alan's mouth opened to echo the old man's animal sounds, but only a sigh emerged; a long, long sigh that went on and on and ended in a gurgle of blood. His eyes, wide with surprise, widened further and stared sightlessly at the plank ceiling. And Nathan knelt there, still pressing the knife into Alan's chest as if he would drive the haft right through to the ground, the growls like sobs, the attitude horrifically incongruous, like a lover above his loved one.

Mercy started to scream.

Lydia felt hands on her shoulders and knew that Wesley had slid down the ladder behind her and put her to one side as he moved swiftly to the doorway and lifted his father with the same ease he brought to everything. He crouched over Alan, one hand staunching the blood around the knife, the other supporting his own ear as he listened for a heartbeat. Prudence spoke from above, demanding to know what had happened but her only reply was the gibbering of her husband in a corner of the room. Still Mercy screamed.

Wesley looked up and straight at her.

'Lydie . . . he's dead.'

He said something else but she did not hear him. She too was sliding down the wall into blessed oblivion.

Eight

The next day began the terrible winter of
'66 and '67 that was to decimate the Exmoor
flocks and scour the thin soil of half its holding
bracken and gorse. The sea mist lifted but the
cloud came down low over the Heights and an
icy rain blew straight from Ireland, smashing the
moored boats in the tiny harbours up the coast
and wreaking havoc in the orchards and gardens
that clung to the south-facing slopes of the
combes. Tales were told of uprooted cabbages
bowling along the lanes like footballs; of a hail-
storm of turnips; of a horse lost in the quagmire
of the Moor. Misfortunes did not come singly;
foxes, starved of their normal prey, came
down to the farms for chickens and reports were
heard of mangled sheep. The Garretts, back
from London, were incensed by the increase in
poaching and when Sir Henry sat on the Bench
at Stapleford such crimes were liable to be
punished with harsh prison sentences. Nathan
Peters was to be tried for murder and was in
Taunton Gaol gibbering and mewling and

cursing the Fieldings. While Lydia Fielding lay in her room at Milton Mains not much better; her eyes open after twelve hours of unconsciousness but staring at the ceiling without expression.

The funeral of Alan and Marella Fielding took place the following Thursday. The open coffins had been placed on the dining table at Milton Mains the previous day and all who wished to pay their respects could do so. Many came from sheer curiosity to stare down at the ill-fated couple, beautiful even in death; already a legend was growing of their love in the face of the enmity between the two families. Though Mercy, Prudence and Lucy sat together in the kitchen, it made no difference. Old Nathan Peters had cursed the match; he had not allowed the Fielding boy to take his bride to Bristol; he had virtually kept them both prisoners in Granny Peters's cottage; when his daughter had died he had killed Alan Fielding where he stood. If Lucy or Prudence heard any of this they made no attempt to put it right; the truth was stranger than the fiction and less credible. Even less creditable. As Prudence said steadily, 'They played a silly game – both of 'em. And they died because of it.' Lucy nodded and let the fiction grow in kindness to the two silly children who had indeed played with fire. There was a deep sadness in her; but her anxiety was for Lydia and Rupert. And perhaps Nature was healing Lydia. Rupert tried to heal himself with his old medicine, and failed as usual.

On the Thursday, Lucy, Mrs Pollard and Amos worked hard to get him ready by midday. He stood by Lucy's side in the dining room gazing down solemnly while Mr Salmon from Carybridge screwed down the coffin lids. Lucy stepped forward and touched Alan's forehead with her fingers and then, as an afterthought, made the sign of the Cross on the baby's head, which was laid across Marella's feet. Unwanted, unchristened, he was already forgotten, his only hope of Heaven his careless little mother and Lucy's blessing. Rupert made a sound of disgust at her gesture and turned away quickly.

'Cause of all the trouble!' he said thickly. 'And nothing to do with us. Nothing to do with poor Alan!'

Lucy pressed his arm warningly, glancing at Mr Salmon and the bearers. But if they heard they gave no sign. The legend already had roots, and nobody wanted to know about the baby now.

At Prudence's unexpectedly earnest request, the funeral took place at Carybridge Chapel where the couple had been married only months before. But it was a weekday now and people were at work; Mercy, Prudence and the two Peters boys huddled on one side of the aisle; Rupert and Lucy the other. There was no sign of Wesley, and Lydia had no idea what was happening. When they stood around the double grave, the wind dropped momentarily, and though the rain still descended, it was possible to hear Mr Dunwiddie's words, 'Dust to dust', and the splash of the mud on the coffin lid where the brass plate read ALAN RUPERT FIELDING 1847–1866.

No tears were shed until they reached the gate, then Prudence touched Lucy's arm and held her back briefly.

'Missis . . . when they 'ang my Nathan, will they let me cut 'im down after and bury 'im like these two bin buried?'

And when Lucy had to confess she did not know, then, at last, the two women wept.

Wesley Peters was already well known in the small tin chapel by the City Docks in Bristol. He was not an avid attender like some of the Bristol Methodists, but he had come to their meetings once or twice to spread his ideas about shipping wool direct to the Yorkshire mills and cutting out the dealers. They respected him because his plans were carefully cut and dried and his contacts in Yorkshire were firm. Also he was not hypocritical; he did not pretend to religious fervour. He had been brought up a Methodist and approached them because – truthfully – he knew where to find them and when, but more than that, because their beliefs were genuinely classless. The powerful Merchant Venturers would not deal with a fisherman from Exmoor who had lost touch with his own country after three years fighting in America in the mistaken belief that he might help to free all slaves. Methodism was his only key to a great many doors; and he was quite honest about that – he intended to use that key.

One man who attended worship at the Mariners' Methodist Chapel as irregularly as did Wesley was a lawyer; a man called Bennington. Wesley sought him out the following Sunday and put Nathan's case to him. He shook his head doubtfully.

'Almost a crime of passion. Perhaps better than that. An English jury would never be sympathetic to the complete *crime passionel*, but the love of a father for his wronged daughter . . . yes, we might do something. And he is quite mad now, you say?'

Wesley's face was expressionless. 'He is obviously mad now. I believe he has been mad for some time.'

'That is best left undisclosed, Mr Peters. In any case some of our lay preachers are apt to be carried away with their own oratory. It is our weakness.'

Wesley said, 'If you hope to present this as a religious killing, you will lose instant sympathy with the jury. The Methodists are not popular on Exmoor.'

'But if we had a Methodist jury, Mr Peters.'

'Is that possible?'

'Everything is possible in the law, sir. Now. Will you leave this with me for a while. I take it there will not be enough money for silk?' Wesley looked his incomprehension. 'Queen's Counsel, Mr Peters. Besides, they too tend to be unsympathetic to our religion. But I know of a junior barrister whose great-grandfather was a preacher with Wesley himself. Could you afford that?'

Wesley shrugged. 'A great many small sheep farmers are trusting me at the moment, Mr Bennington. By the New Year I should have payment from the mill captains and there will be commission for me. Will you trust me until then?'

Bennington smiled. He had taken the trouble to investigate the wool-trading enterprise and thought that this raw-boned young man with his commonsense ideas would be wealthy one day.

He said, 'I will, sir. And may I say that your filial regard does you great credit. I do not imagine your father has been helpful or even encouraging towards you since your return from Mr Lincoln's war?'

Wesley shrugged again. 'Eventually persistent injustice corrodes the spirit, Mr Bennington. Perhaps that is what happened to my father. But my wish to see him have a fair chance is a selfish wish. There has been a lot of wrongdoing over this matter and I have tried and failed to put it right. Perhaps if I can do this I shall have an easier mind. I do not know.'

Bennington looked up sharply. They were walking along Hotwells and almost immediately he stepped in mud and stifled a curse.

'Nothing, 'tis nothing, Mr Peters. The road-sweeper has not been at work here.' He glanced at a gaunt building opposite the riverbank. 'Not surprising. That is a home for fallen women. There is a crude joke going around the city about them falling outside their own home. However, I admire a conscience, sir. But will it extend to a hand-picked jury? It is your father's only chance.'

Wesley's smile was cold. 'We live in an unfair society, Mr Bennington. Sometimes unfair means are called for.'

Bennington laughed. 'A man after my own heart in all respects.' He halted and held out his hand. 'I must leave you here, sir, and take a hansom to Clifton Village where I live. But may I offer you some advice? Entirely gratis. It is this. You are going to come up against strong fire when your venture gets under way and is seen to be successful – and I believe it will be. Political fire. If you hope to survive, you must fight with the same fire. You would get a great deal of support if you took up residence in the City and stood for the Council. As a Radical.' He saw Wesley's impassive expression change. 'Yes sir,' he went on. 'I am quite serious. We have a strong element in the City who would welcome new blood from the – er – rank and file, if I may say so. For instance, Miss Parmenter, who administers this home behind us, has been fighting for the feminine vote for the last ten years – philanthropy is her weapon. The Parmenter family are powerful and though they disapprove of her opinions they still support her work. You could do worse than offer your help in some form or other. To her, personally.'

He shook Wesley's hand vigorously and crossed the road to Jacob's Wells where two hansoms waited. Wesley stood and watched him climb into one, the wooden traps slapping into place over his knees, the driver opening the roof trap to hear the address. He remembered standing sightlessly like this, eighteen months before. It had been in Boston, Massachusetts, and he had just got himself a berth in a ship bound for Liverpool, when the newsboys had erupted onto the wharf waving the sheets which proclaimed the death of President Lincoln. Wesley had stared at the headlines without seeing them and thought of the man who had been born in a log cabin and had freed thousands of slaves. Now, for the first time, he wondered about himself. Could he . . . was it possible that an unschooled boy from Exmoor could help to free some of the slaves in his own country?

Very slowly he retraced his steps, staring at the home for fallen women as he went past.

On the tenth of December, the first snow fell. There was nothing soft and blanketing about it, it fell in hard, icy spits like handfuls of frozen grit and lay in gullies and wagon ruts as skids for the unwary. Lucy and Mrs Pollard entered Lydia's room as usual at half-past eight with hot water and fresh linen and talked brightly in an effort to rouse her to participate. She sat on the edge of the bed and washed with the soaped rag like an obedient child and their words passed over her head as if she were at the bottom of a well.

'My Amos birthed the first lamb in the night, Miss Lydie.' Mrs Pollard made up the bedroom fire and swept the hearth. 'Said it was froze solid as it came out. Shows you 'ow cold it is, dunnit? 'E just laid the poor little beggar on the ground and – whop – it was froze!'

Lucy put a fresh nightdress over her daughter's head. 'I dare say it was stillborn anyway, Mrs Pollard.' She smiled at Lydia reassuringly. 'Papa brought me in the two others at first light and I'm suckling them with a bottle. Strange how a sudden snowstorm brings the first lambs.'

Lydia said nothing and Mrs Pollard removed the bowl of water, placed it on the stand and washed her own hands. 'It will be a good summer for wool too. They allus grows twice the fleece in a bad winter.'

Lydia frowned slightly. She had heard those words before.

Lucy said eagerly, 'Perhaps you can help Papa with the shearing. Like you used to. D'you remember?'

Lydia nodded slowly and stood up while they put wraps around her and led her to the fire. They began on her bed. Lucy coughed a little at the blanket fluff and stifled it hastily with a handkerchief.

Suddenly Lydia said, 'Is Nathan Peters hanged yet?'

Both women jumped and turned together, then exchanged glances. Lucy went to the fire and knelt by the huddled figure.

'Dearest . . . the trial began three days ago. It should have been over by now but the – the – defence is very sympathetic. Sir Henry was in

Taunton yesterday and told your father that the jury cannot agree.'

Lydia said woodenly, 'He killed Alan.'

Lucy moistened her lips. 'Yes, Lydia. But . . . he thought Alan responsible for the death of his daughter.' She took Lydia's cold hands between hers. 'What good will more killing do, my dearest girl?'

'This is Wesley's doing. It should be Wesley on trial beside his father. He is to blame for everything.'

It was Lucy's turn to frown. 'Lydie . . . not many were blameless that day. But surely Wesley of all of them did his best—' She stopped speaking. Lydia had leaned back in the chair and closed her eyes. She would not hear what was said now. Lucy stood up slowly and painfully and went back to the bed. She and Mrs Pollard completed their task in silence then Lucy took a chair opposite her daughter and picked up her bible. Mrs Pollard took the empty log box and crept from the room. Lydia had barely spoken to them before this but the bitterness of her words now gave them little to hope for.

However, almost against her will, she did begin to recover after that day and by the time Christmas week arrived, she was able to see Lady Maud for ten minutes when that lady made her annual visit.

Lady Maud swept into the bedroom above the combe like a gale of wind, smelling of snow and horses, indeed clad in a riding habit although she had arrived in the crested coach full of presents for her tenants.

'Lydia . . . no, don't get up, my girl. Your mother says absolute rest is what you must have and I suppose she knows best.' Lady Maud sounded doubtful about it. 'I bring greetings from Caroline and Judith and a small sampler they stitched between them.'

She displayed a framed sampler: the alphabet and half a text, 'Blessed are the Meek.' It was dull, unadventurous stuff far below the standard they were capable of. Lydia felt a faint stir of annoyance quite separate from her soul-consuming bitterness against Wesley.

Lady Maud swept on. 'I am sorry to say their mother was not entirely pleased with some of the habits they had acquired at the Place during the summer.' A tiny smile appeared in the faded eyes. 'They were presented to the Princess of Wales one evening and when asked what she would like to do when she was grown up, Caro replied she planned to open a school to teach young ladies to swim!'

An answering smile appeared on Lydia's face and Lady Maud was encouraged to lean forward and ask directly, 'Lydia. When do you intend to go downstairs and take over the household reins again?'

Lydia lowered her eyes and made an inarticulate sound.

Lady Maud said, 'I understand you had a terrible shock, child. Do not think I am unsympathetic. But you are young and resilient and will get over the fearful death of your brother – you were always the strong one, even as a child.' She sat up straight as if dealing with a mettlesome horse. 'Now, Lydia, listen to me. You have two duties. To your parents and to this farm. And you are failing in both. Your mother is very ill, that is obvious. Your father sees no reason to keep the home together without her so he is doing his best to send it to the dogs. Yes, you may look at me, miss. It is perfectly true.'

Lydia, whose eyes had flown open at such frankness, lowered them again. Lady Maud pressed her lips together.

'Also it *is* my business whatever you may think! You are Garrett tenants still – do not forget it!'

There was a short and angry silence, then Lydia said in a faltering voice, 'Are you saying that my mother is going to die?'

Lady Maud softened instantly. 'Of course she will die. One day. What I am saying is that you could delay that day.' She stood up briskly. 'I shall expect to hear that you cooked the Christmas dinner, Lydia, and cooked it well.' She went to the door and the fire cowered as she opened it with a jerk. 'And should you be tempted to feel as your father evidently does, let me tell you that Lucy Fielding has put her heart into this farm. It is her legacy to all of you. If you throw it away you will do her a great disservice.' She went out on the landing, then reappeared to say kindly, 'You should marry the Pascoe boy, Lydia. You could eventually run this place then. It would make up for your brother's death. Your duty is plain before you. Do not pretend you cannot see it by closing your eyes.' The door slammed shut and the fire flared.

Lydia did her best. The very next day she descended the stairs and began the slow process of trying to make Lucy rest. It was hopeless. Lydia lacked her old driving force and there was a change in Lucy too; she seemed to relax only when Rupert was out of the house. As soon as dinner or supper time was near, she was trying to usher Lydia upstairs while she presided over the kitchen. Lydia did indeed cook the Christmas dinner but only because Rupert was in the cowshed battling with a difficult calving. She and her mother ate it alone. Mrs Pollard had gone to Listowel to her sister's and Amos was to join her as soon as his work was finished in the cowshed.

Neither of them talked much, but that too was not unusual. Conversation, especially at Christmas time, was dangerous; either of them might inadvertently mention last Christmas and the carol singing at Listowel Church. Alan had been with them then. Lydia contented herself with saying, 'Papa will enjoy the beef. Let me cut another slice and put it in the side oven.' And Lucy nodded. 'It is a pleasant change from mutton, certainly. Now, dear girl, I would like you to go up to the parlour and put out wine and nuts. I will join you directly.'

Lydia assumed her father would also join them. She heard him come in, the murmur of her mother's voice and his abrupt rejoinder, the clatter of his plate. Then the kitchen door closing again. She was curious enough to cross the landing into her mother's room overlooking the stable yard. After a few minutes Rupert led Blackie out of the stable already saddled. Amos followed him and went to the pump to wash. He did not look at his master. Rupert mounted Blackie and walked him around to the front of the house; the familiar bang of the gate made Amos look up from the pump handle. His face was long and disapproving, his mouth tight. He dried his hands on a sack and, walking with care over the frozen snow, he too made for the gate and the footpath down to Listowel. Lydia hurried back to the parlour just ahead of Lucy.

'Well, isn't this nice?' Lucy lifted a log with the fire irons and sparks shot up the chimney. 'Nothing to do, my dear, except amuse ourselves! Papa has gone calling on the Pascoes and Amos is to come back to do the evening milk. Now . . . would you like a hand of piquet? Or shall I fetch the backgammon board?'

It was indeed restful. But it was also incredible that the two of them were alone on Christmas afternoon. For the first time, Lydia realized their isolation. There had been no wassailers this year; no Jinny and Robbie Roscoe calling for them to go gleaning for nuts. Lady Maud had come as usual, but with warnings and forebodings. And now Rupert had gone to find his own company. And the snow bound them where they were as much prisoners as was old Nathan Peters in Taunton Gaol.

Lydia woke with a start. It was still dark. She lay on her back on her horsehair mattress listening to the creakings of the house and knowing they were not what had wakened her. Her father had returned at midnight and had gone straight up to Alan's old room; could it be him stumbling downstairs to the privy? Then the lowing of a cow in distress broke through the ordinary night sounds and she sat up in bed listening intently. It came again, a long moan ending in a cracked cough. Was something wrong with the cow who had calved yesterday morning?

The noise became continuous and she swung her feet out of bed, feeling for her old pattens. Perhaps this was her chance to help her father directly; to show him he was not alone. She pulled a shawl over her nightgown and lit her candle hurriedly. There was no sound on the landing; quickly she slipped down the back stairs and through the kitchen, shivering as the icy air ruffled goose pimples onto her arms. A sly wind blew straw in wisps about the yard and the horses stamped in the stable as she hurried over to the barn. The lowing was urgent now, frightful, hacking sounds that the other cows took up in sympathy and fear. The new calf bellowed back its insecurity. Lydia held the storm lantern high and wedged the small door in the enormous double entry. Everything was covered in a skin of ice; already her hands were numb and clumsy.

Amos and Rupert had made a pen in the corner of the barn, lined it with straw and left water and hay. The mother and baby should have been comfortable there until the morning. As it was, they were both fidgeting around and already the cow's legs were beginning to buckle under her.

Lydia opened the pen and led out the calf, afraid it would be injured if its mother collapsed on it. She found a rope and tethered the calf to the wall of the barn, murmuring endearments and stroking it soothingly. Then she hurried back to the mother who still circled around, her legs trembling and bending precariously. It was a pathetic sight. Lydia forgot the cold, forgot everything in her need to help the animal. She pushed her against the side of the pen trying to hold her there long enough to draw off some milk from the udder. But she did not have the strength against the cow's urgent need to keep moving. Trying to keep clear of the feet, she lifted the tail and bit her lip at the sight of the thin stream of blood pouring down the rear legs. She knew what was wrong now. The cow needed to be cleansed. Rupert should have done it before now.

Lydia had twice watched a cleansing of the afterbirth in a cow and knew how it was done. It did not occur to her to go for her father or Amos. Certainly she had never seen a woman cleanse a cow but then, she had never seen any other woman shear a sheep. Determinedly, she hooked her shawl on a nail and seized a sack, tying it around her waist somehow. She rolled up the sleeves of her nightgown to her armpits and shoved her hair behind her ears. Then she went back into the pen, got to the rear of the cow and began to move with it.

Probably had she been less tired she would never have attempted a job which, in her experience, had taken two people, both strong men. But her mind was not functioning at its best and she suddenly wanted to find her old place at the farm: a her father's substitute for a son. She worked for half an hour, circling with the anxious cow, soaked to the waist in blood, her pattens long lost in the mess of dung among the straw. Twice she thought she had it, then the slimy mass under her frantic hand slithered away and the cow's tail thrashed her head and she had to stagger to the wall and dry her sweat and draw deep breaths of cold air from the open wicket before returning. She tried to remember the last cleansing she had seen before her mother called her away. It had been quick and easy. A long arm sliding into the cow, the mass of liver substance emerging to slop onto the floor to the accompaniment of ribald noises from Alan and herself. Nothing could have been simpler. Drake had held the tail, Amos the head . . . of course . . . the cow had been *still*.

She fetched another rope and tied it around the horns and onto the side of the pen. Yet another rope pinioned the tail to the slats of the pen. The cow called shudderingly and the calf replied. Lydia said, 'It's all right, it's going to be all right.' She rinsed her hands and arms in the water barrel then went back to work. Five minutes later, the afterbirth slithered out and there was blessed silence in the barn. For the first time since Alan's death, Lydia felt she had achieved something. She looked at the mess on the floor, then at the ridiculously tethered cow, then at the calf. Tears of exhaustion sprang to her eyes and she staggered to an upturned bucket and crouched there, crying freely and with an overwhelming sense of release.

She was still sitting there when she heard her father cross the yard. She went quickly to the wicket.

'It's me, Pa. Lydie. Everything is all right. You can go back to bed.'

He stopped in his tracks and stared as if she were a ghost. She too was shocked by what she saw. In the fitful light from the lantern he stood swaying, his thatch of brown hair standing on end, not even a pair of trousers pulled over his nightshirt. His mouth was slack and wet; the stink of him reached her nostrils even through the other pungent smells of the barn.

He looked past her and took in the scene slowly. 'You done this?' His voice was slurred and had reverted to pure Exmoor. She nodded briefly and he stepped through the wicket and looked again. 'Christamighty, Lydie. Christamighty.'

She tried to smile. 'I'm sorry everything's a mess. I had to cleanse the cow. She was going to drop.'

He went on staring. She could hear his breathing. Then quite suddenly he stumbled towards the upturned bucket and collapsed onto it. And then began to weep.

Lydia reacted very similarly to the way she had reacted when he had wept at Michaelmas as he told her about Lucy's consumption. At first, fright and horror made her tense; then the weight of responsibility seemed to move her way and again she rose to meet it. She put a blood-caked hand on his shoulder.

But this time her touch apparently yielded no comfort. He looked up and the bitterness she glimpsed so often when she met his eyes across her mother's protective head was there plain to see.

'Christamighty, Lydie,' he repeated thickly. 'My daughter . . . look at you – look at you!'

She became conscious of the bloodstained sack, her nightdress pulled over one shoulder. She flushed and drew at the string quickly.

'You taught me to shear a sheep, Father. You said I was more of a farmer than . . .' Her voice faltered and stopped.

'Than Alan?' His voice sharpened. 'Yes, that was true. Alan went a-whoring among the Methodies. And you – ' he stopped himself.

She swallowed fearfully. 'What do you mean?'

He said fiercely, 'Gossip – I would have put it down to gossip! They didn't know me over at Tamerton at first so they spoke freely and I soon shut them up, believe me!' He hiccuped a sob. 'But then Wesley Peters brought you home that dawn, my girl. I could see the way he looked at you. And during those weeks you lay there mad, you called his name. Over and over. And Gus. I thought it would kill your mother – kill her!'

Lydia said through stiff lips, 'I thought I was in love with Wesley Peters. But he was responsible for Alan's death and—'

'I told Gus about it! I had to talk to someone and his name was in your mouth as often as the Peters whelp!' He ignored her moan and twisted himself on the bucket so that he could not watch her cowering before him. 'He told me . . . he told me that he and you – *and* he's still willing to marry you, Lydie. In spite of the gossip about Wesley Peters! He's a good man – he told me tonight – just tonight – that now you are recovered he would call again!'

'How could you – how could you, Pa? Gus Pascoe . . . oh dear God I cannot bear this.'

Rupert was angry again. 'You will 'ave to bear it – just as I've borne it. Head down, hear nowt.' He looked over his shoulder and his voice softened slightly. ' 'Twill be better when you'm married, girl. Then you can face 'em out. Just get a ring on your finger now you'm recovered. You must be recovered to do this – ' he swept the filthy pen with a wavering hand. 'So it will be all right now. You can fix with Gus, fix with Gus.'

'It's not true about Wesley. I don't know how the gossip started but it's not true.'

'He followed you everywhere, like a dog after a bitch. The bailiff at the Place saw 'im waiting for you in the bracken often.'

'It's not true! Can't you believe me, it's not true!'

' 'Tisn't me to be convinced. It's Gus. 'E knows full well you went willing with 'im and 'e 'asn't got to do much reasoning to come to the conclusion that if you go with one man you'll go with another.'

She was sobbing hysterically now, crouched as she had crouched before, clutching her knees. 'He's a liar! He wouldn't marry me – wouldn't have thought of marrying me – if he didn't want Milton Mains!'

Rupert said, 'I've got no son now. If you have the place you can't run it alone. He's got money to put into it. He's a good sort. It was always a good match. I reckon now, it's the only one you will make.'

'I can't – I can't – ' It was as if she heard Gus's voice again telling her that one day she would beg him for marriage. All the many roads she had taken since her twenty-first birthday had led back to this. Marriage with Gus.

Rupert got heavily to his feet. 'If you're nursing hopes of the Peters boy, let me tell you we shan't see him in these parts any more. Julius Pascoe writes that he has taken the freehold of a tumbledown cottage this side of Mr Brunel's suspension bridge in Bristol. He's not a popular person, it would seem, undermining all the proper traders, getting his murdering father out of the hangman's noose. The Pascoes have got inside knowledge . . . knowledge . . . they'll see to Master Peters right enough.' He stumbled to the wicket. 'You'd best untie that cow, Lydie, and put things straight in here.'

Lydia raised her tear-clogged face and stared after him disbelievingly. If she had needed proof of Lady Maud's accusation that Rupert was letting the farm go to the dogs, she had it now. The herd was Rupert's pride and joy – or had been. It set him apart from a dozen other sheep farmers. Yet he wasn't interested in helping her to put things right in here.

Drearily she stood up and went to untie the cow. Only after she had washed in the barrel and was shivering with cold, did the full implication of her father's words strike her. They were going to kill Wesley. The Pascoes were going to carry out Gus's threat. She should be glad of course. Wesley was directly responsible for Alan's death. Wesley and Marella . . . she shuddered as the familiar pictures formed behind her eyes. Then she slithered and stumbled back to the house. Dawn was not far off and the snow showed grey in the combe. She began to riddle out the ashes from the cooking fire. She was not tired enough to go back to bed. It was the feast of St Stephen and she would make griddle cakes for breakfast and do the morning milk. At last she had need of her natural strength; today Gus was going to call on her and Gus tired very quickly of unattractive women.

He came after dinner and found them all together in the parlour as they had been in the past. Already Rupert looked less bitter; he had come downstairs to find his work done and a good breakfast ready for him and Lydia looking better than she had looked for two long months.

It was her way of telling him that she was sorry and she intended to obey him in future; it had always been her way. As impulsive as his dead son, he was quite willing to accept her acquiescence without deeper thought. After breakfast he had gone with Amos to carry hay for the snowed-up sheep and brought back another lamb and tales of another sheep mangled by foxes. But the news exhilarated him now; the prospect of Pascoe money was a good one.

Gus had not seen Lydia since the night old Nathan had besieged the farm and it was evident he was surprised at her changed appearance. She had indeed taken care with it, using the curling tongs and rubbing at her cheeks until they burned with colour. She made a greater effort to appear vivacious and was soon rewarded by Gus's undivided attention.

'The book was a birthday present from dear Mamma – ' she was describing one of Mr Dickens's publications. 'It concerns the vagaries of a young man's life from boyhood. He is obsessed with his love for his childhood sweetheart – '

'How well I understand that,' Gus interpolated.

'But finally realizes that he has been entirely wrong—'

'Rubbish! Poppycock!' Gus immediately lost interest and raised his glass of madeira. 'Let us drink a toast to young love that survives all the troubles that life can throw in its face.'

Lydia studied him as he tipped up his glass.

He had been drinking that morning and, she guessed, much of Christmas Day. She wondered objectively whether she could bear to live with such a man then knew that it did not matter. Inclination for anything was gone. What remained was duty. Lady Maud had outlined that very concisely last week; her father last night. She refilled Gus's glass and let her eyes come up with the bottle to meet his avid gaze.

'By God, Lydie,' he said in a low voice. 'I'd swear you were still in a fever if your pa had not assured me otherwise. Your cheeks are as bright as that fire and your eyes . . .'

She could not bring herself to tell him that she might well be in a fever with him calling on her, but she turned up her mouth in the semblance of a smile and did not shrink away when he put a hand to her brow mocking old Dr Tarling.

''Tis leeches I prescribe for you, young miss – ' He took her wrist portentously while Rupert guffawed applause. 'And as they be all died on me, I must do the best I can without.' He put his mouth to her jumping pulse and began to suck vigorously. Lydia discovered that though she might have no definite inclinations she had some very strong disinclinations. There was something predatory in all Gus's actions and now his teeth sank hard into her frail skin and it was as if indeed he could suck out her very life blood.

Lucy rescued her with her usual gentle tact.

'You may be right, Gus. I quite agree Lydie is looking flushed. Sit here by the window, child, and drink your tea while the men talk sheep. And Gus, will you take some of Mrs Pollard's Christmas cake?'

She rearranged the room to give Lydia some breathing space. It was Lydia herself who insisted on going down with Gus when the time came for him to leave. Lucy was surprised; Rupert the same, but pleased. Neither of them raised objections. Lydia paused at the door and glanced at her mother, hoping for something. Lucy had her underlip between her teeth and returned her look anxiously. Lydia closed the door and wondered what her mother had made of the ramblings of delirium; if she had guessed at Lydia's feelings for Wesley Peters and could not approve them. But apparently Lydia had also called for Gus. It was no wonder that Lucy was bewildered.

Gus led his horse to the mounting block by the kitchen door.

'Well now, Lydie, so you are recovered.' He settled the capes of his greatcoat and tugged at his gauntlets. His grin was open and candidly relieved. 'Recovered from . . . everything?'

The intense cold struck through her shawl to her very marrow. She smiled at him, trying not to shiver.

'By God, Lydie, I thought you looked burnt out when I saw you first. But now . . . I confess I find this older woman even more fascinating than the young one.' He took her hand in his hard leather glove and drew her towards him. She steeled herself. He kissed her. 'By God . . .

by God, Lydie.' His mouth slid to her throat. 'You're shaking, you're on fire!'

She drew back. 'Not too quickly, Gus. Please. Not this time.'

'But I may see you? Often?'

'If you wish.'

'I wish. How I wish.' He drew back and laughed thickly. 'I knew how it would be. Didn't I tell you that day, Lydia? You want to marry me now, don't you?'

She kept the smile in place. She could taste his saliva.

'Maybe.'

'So it is to be a game, is it? Very well, I will play for a time. But when I tire . . .'

'The game can end when you wish it, Gus. But meanwhile – ' she stepped over the threshold and stood close to him. 'Meanwhile Gus, I have a whim.'

'What is that, my lovely?'

'I cannot play the game – any game – if there is more bloodshed.'

'I will not hurt you this time, darling. I promise it will be only pleasure.'

'Peters's blood, Gus. I cannot be happy with you if it means another Peters must die.'

'A . . . a . . . ah. Wesley. I told you I would kill him.'

She took his face between her hands and her shawl slipped to the ground. Very gently she touched his lips with hers.

'Too many people have suffered already, Gus. All that must end before we can begin.' She felt his breath quicken and become hot and she stood away. He grabbed at her but his fingers were clumsy in their gloves and she eluded him easily, laughing as she bent to pick up her shawl.

'Bitch,' he hissed, but laughing too. 'You always were. That's why I want you, of course. Kiss me and then I'll promise.'

She gave herself into his embrace and let him do what he would. Then he stepped onto the block, laughing breathlessly.

'No harm shall come to the Peters whelp. I promise. But you must keep your side of the bargain, Lydie – and I will see to it that you do!'

He was gone, the snow splintering icily beneath his horse's hooves. Lydia went into the kitchen and wept again.

'What am I going to do?' she whispered to herself. 'Oh dear God, what am I going to do?'

There was no answer.

Nine

Strangely, as the terrible winter isolated each and every dwelling on the Moor, Gus's ardent courtship was a comfort. He would emerge from the snow every three or four days, stamp his feet in the kitchen and stand steaming by the fire while he regaled Lucy with the news from Mapperly and made Rupert laugh at his latest innuendo. The price to be paid for his company – a hurried kiss in the stable, sly references to their 'bargain' – became nearly acceptable. He was like an excited dog, leaping around her and licking at her face. Or so she told herself. Where it was leading and whether she would marry him eventually rarely crossed her mind. She tried not to think; every avenue of thought led to misery and horror. The snow fitted in with her mood; she buried herself at Milton Mains with her mother, trying by sheer hard work to forget everything else.

Nevertheless when there was a blessed lull in the blizzards for two days in mid-January, she was delighted to see Jinny Johnson – née Roscoe

– trudging the track from the Heights road, and ran to the front of the house to greet her at the gate.

'Jinny . . . Jinny . . . this is wonderful indeed!' The girls embraced fervently. They had shared so much of their lives until Lydia's twenty-first birthday and their rare meetings since served to emphasize how much they missed each other. 'Come on inside! Oh my dear, have you walked all the way from Lambourne? And in this snow – such heavy going. Come inside and sit by the fire.'

They went into the kitchen and Lydia took Jinny's cloak and shook it over the half-door, smiling her delight. It was wonderful to feel again such unshadowed happiness.

'Your mother?' Jinny put a hand to her side, still panting, and took the chair by the fire gratefully.

'In the parlour. We will go up in five minutes, I promise. But I must talk to you first. Oh Jinny . . .'

'I know.' Jinny reached up and caught her friend's hand. 'Poor Lydie. I wanted to come but Tom said best keep away. They said you were in a trance for weeks on end.'

'I don't know. I cannot remember. I still cannot believe Alan is no longer on this earth.'

'Nor me.' Jinny put the work-roughened hand to her cheek and gazed into the fire. 'I was so jealous, Lydie. I never thought he would marry a girl from the Moor, otherwise I would have set my cap for him.'

Lydia drew away and looked down into the dark eyes. 'You? You felt for him, Jinny?'

'Always. But I was a fisherman's daughter and older than he was.' Tears came to Jinny's eyes. 'I would have cared for him better than Marella Peters, Lydie.'

There was silence while Lydia accepted all the implications behind this confession. Then she echoed her friend's words. 'Poor Jinny . . .' She swallowed. 'But you do love Tom Johnson? You both looked so happy, my dear – you made me happy that day. Alan too . . . yes, he was happy for you, I'm sure of it.'

Jinny smiled. 'I am glad. And of course I love Tom. I would love anyone so good and true who loved me so earnestly.' Her smile turned wry in the face of Lydia's surprise. 'I was always the practical one, Lydie. What else was there for me besides marriage? I would rather look after Tom than Robbie and Father.'

'I – I suppose so.' Lydia sat down slowly.

Jinny said reassuringly, 'His love kindled mine. I admired him, I knew he could give me a home and protection and – and children. And his love for me is unwavering. It survived the talks my father had with Nathan Peters.' Her smile turned to a laugh. 'That was important to me – his steadfastness.'

'Yes. Yes, I can see that.' Lydia looked into the fire and her thin cheeks flushed. 'Jinny, tell me true now. Did you . . . when the match was not made between you and Wesley Peters, did you blame me?'

Jinny's surprise was completely honest. 'You? How should I blame you, Lydie?'

'You never heard any gossip which linked our names? Wesley Peters and mine?'

'The only one your name is linked with be Augustus Pascoe, Lydie. You should know that. I told you before when we talked on the beach.'

'Yes, you did. And you have heard more on that score since?'

It was Jinny's turn to flush. 'Aye. Well . . . it is put about that you are another Pascoe conquest. I know better than that of course and have put folks right about it.'

'Oh, it is true, Jinny. Gus pressed his . . . attentions on me back last Michaelmas. I thought I could not bear to see him or speak to him ever again. Yet he comes a-courting each week and I do not turn him away.'

Jinny was silent now, digesting this. At last she said quietly, 'Sometimes the sheer force of a man's love makes him do things that he regrets later.'

'Gus does not regret what he did to me. He thinks it binds me to him. Perhaps it does.'

'Not unless you wish it, Lydie.' Jinny tried to take Lydia's hand again but Lydia withdrew it.

'I do not know what I wish any longer. And Gus Pascoe has been steadfast in his feeling – whatever that may be – for me. Everyone says it would be an excellent match.'

Jinny chewed her lip. 'I think . . . yes I am sure . . . you would know if you did *not* wish it,

Lydie. Perhaps that is enough to make a match possible. I cannot say.'

Lydia stood up and swung the kettle over the flame, fetched the teapot and laid a tray. Then she cupped Jinny's face and kissed her.

'You have told me of your feelings, dear friend, and I must make up my own mind. Thank you, Jinny . . . thank you. Now let us go upstairs and drink tea with Mamma and you must tell us everything about the Lambournes and Tom and all your new relations.'

They trooped upstairs. Lucy was delighted to see Jinny and the clatter of teacups and feminine laughter took them all back to the days when Jinny and Robbie had joined Lydia and Alan once a week for lessons.

Jinny assured them that she did not have to return to Lambourne that day. 'I am to spend the night with Father. Tom said I had best take the news in person before a passing reddler told it for me and offended the whole of Listowel for ever more!' She smiled widely at them. 'Have you not guessed? I am expecting Tom's baby!' She put an automatically protective hand to her abdomen. 'Not until July month, but I have wanted to bring the news this past four weeks and Tom would not let me venture out until the snow stopped blowing!'

'I should think not!' Lucy exclaimed. 'Now, put your legs on that footstool at once, my girl and do not wait on me as if I were an invalid!'

Lydia hugged her friend anew. 'Oh Jinny . . . Jin, my dear! You will be such a wonderful mother. What a lucky baby! Two such dear parents and the Moor to grow up in. What more could any child wish?'

Jinny subsided with much laughter, and the talk turned to babies and their clothes and their food until it was time for Jinny to go. Then it was Lucy who asked tentatively, 'Jinny, dear child, we have had no connection with Prudence Peters since . . . you know. If you have time and the weather keeps clear would you take our good wishes to her?'

'Aye, that I will.' Jinny put her face to Lucy's and her eyes shone with tears. 'The story is that there is great hatred between your families. I knew that you could not hate . . . whatever cause you had.'

Lucy said reasonably, 'I have great pity for Prudence. She has lost a daughter and a husband besides a son-in-law.'

Jinny said hesitantly, 'The story also goes that Nathan will not now be hanged. The jury at last said he was not guilty of murder and the judge has imprisoned him for the rest of his life. He does not understand what has happened to him.'

'I heard that also.' Lucy spoke calmly still. 'Sometimes madness must be a blessing rather than a curse, Jinny.'

'I do not doubt it, Mrs Fielding.' She glanced at Lydia. 'Have you also heard that Wesley now lives in Bristol and has formed a co-operative for selling wool in Yorkshire? He will go to the North in May with the first of the summer's wool.'

Lydia was conscious of her mother's eyes looking at her. She said, 'It will be interesting to see
how the others are surviving with Benjie and
Luke as their sole support. Neither of them
seemed capable of doing anything without a
command.'

'Interesting?' Lucy's voice held faint reproof
but it was covered by Jinny's laugh.

'If I remember, Prudence Peters is well able to
give commands, Lydie! And Wesley had already
stepped into his father's shoes. He uses the
boat to call at every harbour between Bristol
and Stapleford, organizing his co-operative and
taking samples of fleece. He is well able to look
to the rest of the family; do not worry on that
score.'

'I was not worried,' Lydia said more sharply
than she had intended. 'Indeed, if they were not
so rotten and corrupt I might find it amusing
that the Methodists, who seem to have taken a
pride in their poverty and independence, are
willing to use our business methods to their own
ends.'

Lucy frowned and Jinny said awkwardly,
'Naturally you feel . . . I agree that often they are
hypocritical. But—'

'You do not like the word corrupt?' Lydia
glanced at her mother reassuringly and smiled
at Jinny. 'We cannot all be like Mamma, dear
friend. I admit I feel hatred. But do not let us
talk of it now. I will walk halfway down the
combe with you and admire the icicles on
the alders.' She too kissed her mother. 'It has

been a happy afternoon, Mamma.' It was half a question.

Lucy smiled. 'I did not think we could be so happy again. It is very necessary to let love into our lives, Lydia dearest.'

'I know. I know, Mamma.'

Two days after this delightful interlude with Jinny, Mrs Pollard went to the pump and slipped down with a pail of water. The general dampness, the caterwauling, the immediate incontinence and then increased wailing hid the fact that she had seriously hurt her ankle. Only when Lydia, Amos and Drake between them had got her by the fire and Lydia had changed her skirts and petticoats for a warmed sheet, did anyone notice the size of her foot.

'Look at un, missis,' Drake said, awed. ''Tis like the man with elephant legs at the circus!'

Mrs Pollard aimed a swipe at his head and caught sight of the foot herself. Fresh lamentations broke out. Amos cut away the bursting stocking and Lydia fetched snow from the yard and packed it around the ankle while Mrs Pollard's shouts turned to tears of pain and fright.

'We must send for Dr Tarling,' Lydia said. 'Drake—'

'No, missis.' Amos sat down by the foot and looked at it gloomily. ''E couldn't tell you no more than I can. Been looking at sheeps's legs all me life and they ain't so different from yumans. Can't tell whether owt be broke – neither could the doctor, mind you – not till the swelling do go down. But she got to keep it up, that I do know.'

'Ow can I keep it up?' howled Mrs Pollard. 'With you and Drake to look after, both as selfish as the sheep you do look like—'

'We must get her down to her sister, Amos,' Lydia said. 'And we must do it quickly before the snow comes again. Take the gate off and I'll wrap some bricks from the fire to keep her warm. My father and Mr Pascoe will be back soon and they can help.'

'An' 'ow will them two lummocks manage in that cottage by themselves?' demanded Mrs Pollard.

'We shall manage, wife,' Amos grunted. 'Looked after us selves afore you came along and us'll do it again.'

'I'll keep an eye on them, Mrs Pollard,' Lydia said quickly before the next swipe developed. 'Now, I'll fetch some shawls and blankets and you must have a hot drink.'

So it was arranged. Rupert and Gus arrived back in time to take a corner each of the make-shift litter and Lucy and Lydia watched anxiously from the parlour window as they eased their burden through the gateway and began to slip and stumble down the combe to the accompaniment of shrieks from their passenger. When Lydia went back down to put the stewpot over the fire against their return, two things occurred to her. The first was that she and Lucy would be entirely alone for most of the daylight hours now. The second, that both Amos and Drake had called her 'missis', a term kept previously for Lucy.

The next day the blizzard began again. Nothing could be done while it blew; Rupert chafed about indoors, mending a few bridles, soaping the saddles on the kitchen table and getting in Lydia's way. The men had spent the few open days carrying wattle fencing to the sheep and making pens which they hoped would give some shelter against this fresh outburst of weather, but as it continued unabated through the night, hope dwindled that any of the flocks would survive. Before it was light Rupert was shaking Lydia by the shoulder.

'It has eased slightly, Lydie. Amos is here and we are starting off for the slopes below Carybridge. You must see to the morning milk and if Gus should call ask him to follow us as soon as he can.'

Lydia, struggling with a thick sleep that had been disturbed by the howling wind, raised herself on one elbow.

'It is still blowing, Papa – you cannot go out in this. Wait until I cook some ham—'

'Don't be a fool, Lydie. Come on, get up.'

'Even if Gus calls in this, he certainly won't follow you,' she grumbled, feeling for her felt slippers beneath the bed, while her father took the candle to the window and peered through.

'He damned well should do – half the cursed sheep are his now!' snapped Rupert, striding to the door. 'And he's quick enough to help me spend the money for 'em!' He rounded on Lydia as she drew in her breath sharply. 'And we both know why I do that, don't we, girl? To keep him up to scratch – that's why!'

'Oh, Papa—' Lydia began, distressed past her usual determination not to think at all about the future. 'Papa, I had no idea you were still selling to the Pascoes! You must not!'

'If I am to keep your mother in comfort, it is the only way.' Rupert opened the door with a jerk and the candle blew out in the draught. 'Now get up,' he whispered. 'See to the cows. We still have them!'

The door closed in the pitchy blackness and he was gone. Lydia drew on a shawl, caught up her clothes in a bundle and followed him slowly.

However, Gus did not come and by midday she knew he would not. It was as well; the snow had certainly lessened, but the wind howled unremittingly and any tracks Amos, Drake and Rupert might have made were covered by the shifting surface; even the stable yard and the route to the pump were constantly swept and a fresh carpet of fine snow laid. Lydia went about her chores slowly and methodically, finding her usual satisfaction in them. At two o'clock she went upstairs to be with her mother and found Lucy sitting anxiously by the window.

'There is more snow on the way,' she said, pointing to the north-west from where the weather had been coming. 'You had best put as many lanterns out as you can before it gets dark, Lydie dear. I will come down and help you.'

'You will do no such thing, Mamma!' Lydia brought another chair and sat down where she could watch the low, yellow sky. 'Father will be home before dark. And if not, then will be the time for the lanterns. It is not like you to fret, dearest.' She laid a hand on her mother's. 'And you are cold! Come nearer the fire – ' She half rose to help her mother across the room and got no further. Without warning, Lucy gave her usual faint cough into her handkerchief and instantly, horrifically, the white linen turned bright red.

'Mother! Oh my God – ' Lydia pulled at her own handkerchief and dabbed frantically where the rushing blood ran down the tiny, pointed chin. 'Lie back – lie back, Mamma. Oh dear God, let it stop, let it stop!' She pushed her mother back against her chair, then tipped her head further still. Immediately the white face suffused desperately and Lucy began to choke on her own blood. Lydia pulled her forward again, panic making her clumsy. The tiny frail body fell about without volition; Lucy's eyes closed, her cap slipped sideways and she lost consciousness.

It probably saved her life. With her head resting on her shoulder and her mouth open, the blood flow gradually reduced to a trickle and then stopped while Lydia grabbed at cushions to support her. The breathing was shallow but regular. Lydia somehow controlled her own frightened sobs to listen hard: yes, the damaged lungs were taking air again. Trembling, she crouched by the chair, massaging the limp hands, watching and waiting for she knew not what.

After a very few minutes, the eyelids fluttered and Lucy gave a deeper breath, automatically caught a cough before it could be born and looked at her daughter. She smiled, the small, heart-breakingly familiar smile that had been the comfort of Lydia's childhood.

'Don't look like that, Lydie. It happens sometimes and means nothing. No more than a scratch from a nail.'

'Mamma, I did not know. You should have told me. You must have Dr Tarling – and soon.'

'Why, Lydie? To be cupped and lose more blood still? It is just this damp air, dearest. Once the snow gives over and we have some spring sunshine, I shall be myself again.' She moved a cushion and sat up straight. 'Help me onto the sofa, child, and read to me for a while. Then you must see to those lanterns.'

Lydia did not wait for her mother to raise herself further. Impulsively with a command of all her old strength, she slid her arms beneath knees and shoulders and lifted Lucy over to the sofa opposite the fire. She silenced the protests with a quick word, appalled at Lucy's lightness, and covered her own breathlessness by fetching shawls and coddling her mother against any possible draught. But she had only just turned away for the copy of *Great Expectations* which they were reading, when the same small sound came from behind her and, turning, she saw Lucy holding one of the coverings to her mouth again. This time the attack was not followed by a faint but she was quite unable to speak and there was no question of reading to her or pretending that anything was normal any longer. Lydia sat on the floor by her mother, holding her hand, praying for her father's return; even Gus's usual call. No-one came. It began to grow dark.

'Mamma . . . can you hear me, darling? I will go down now and light the lanterns and bring some hot tea.' The hand she held was cold in spite of Lydia's rubbing. 'And some hot bricks too. And when Father comes in, Drake shall be sent for Dr Tarling.' Lucy made no sign she had heard but the brown eyes stayed open and the breathing was regular.

Lydia took the stairs two at a time, frantic in her haste. She plied the bellows on the dying range, fetched the storm lanterns from the entry, lit a row of them with a taper and hung them at the front door and back, in the tree beyond the wash-house and at the gate to the combe. The yellow sky was almost upon them. She tried some loud halloos into the grey and white wasteland at the other side of the river but received no answering shout. Her own panting breath interfered with her hearing and occasionally she held it, listening for something – her father, a horse, her mother . . .

She took hot bricks out of the oven, wrapped them in flannel and put them in the capacious pocket of her apron; then she made the tea. Going back upstairs, slowly now, she told herself everything would be all right. Apparently her mother had weathered such attacks before; soon the men would return and Drake would go to Carybridge with the wagonette and bring back . . . she opened the parlour door and was immediately assailed by the smell which had seemed normal before but after the icy air outside now struck her as fetid. Her mother lay as she had done, on her left side, her right hand touching the rug on the floor. Lydia began to speak in a high, unnaturally cheerful voice.

'Here we are, Mamma. Lanterns lit. Papa on his way home—' She stopped as she turned from the side table. Lucy's eyes were closed and her face a waxen yellow; from the corner of the open mouth a thin stream of blood trickled inexorably.

Lydia heard her own cries as she went to her, terrified that the precious life had gone while she was below. But Lucy still breathed. Lydia hardly knew what to do. She adjusted the dear head so that the blood could come away freely; and freely it did come. She packed the hot bricks where she could, fetched smelling salts, dabbed – always dabbed; finally she sat back on her heels weeping hopelessly. Was she condemned to sit and watch her mother's life blood trickle away?

And then, at last, just before darkness was full, Lucy opened her eyes. Lydia sobbed with relief and bent close.

'Mamma, listen. I must get Dr Tarling – I

must. Do you hear – do you understand? This is no ordinary blood flux.'

Lucy's face twitched as she tasted her own blood. She forced her mouth into a shape and Lydia put her ear to it.

'Go. Go now. I will be all right while you are gone. I promise.'

Lydia waited for no further encouragement. She seized her cloak from the hook on the landing, ran back down and scratched a message for Rupert on her old school slate. She still hoped to meet him within a few minutes of home; she hated to leave her mother, indeed was torn in half by the necessity to go and the desire to stay. The murky yellow light illumined the snow fields to silver and made the Stowe river a black trickle in their midst. Lydia was reminded of the ever-flowing trickle of blood leaving her mother and broke into a run as she went through the gate. Almost immediately she fell headlong and slid down the side of the combe to the river's edge, fetching up against a rock with a painful jolt. But the fall shook some of her hysteria out of her. She sat up, rubbing her hip, recognizing the real danger of the cruel weather; planning what she had better do.

In the end she crossed the Stowe by some stepping stones and struck up through the snow-packed bracken on the other side to meet the Heights road a mile further on. It was heavy, exhausting going and she was thankful for the hard work of the past three weeks which had given her back her strength; she needed every ounce of it. She counted her steps, closing her mind to the thought of the four miles ahead of her if she did not meet Rupert. At every fiftieth stride, she stopped and called, cupping her mouth and turning in each direction. Nothing disturbed the smothering silence. She struggled on again, counting stubbornly, sometimes forgetting the number she had reached as her boot went through the crisp bracken and she was up to her waist, floundering in snow. By the time she reached the road she was sweating profusely beneath her clothes and forced to stop for a few minutes' precious rest.

The road was discernible only as a shallow shelf in the leaping land mass; even the usual wagon ruts were filled and obliterated. But small indentations, almost faded, showed that someone had passed this way, and within an hour too because it took the wind just that long to sweep in fresh snow. Holding her side and breathing deeply, Lydia followed them trying to see from the print which way they led; had their originator been walking away from Milton or towards it? After a few yards they took her to the other side of the road and into the wild land that went on up to the very top of the Moor and was inhabited by animals only. She felt hopeful, knowing that some of the Milton flocks ran this way. Silently now, grimly determined, she ploughed on; below her she could see the faintly flickering lights of Carybridge; ahead the white wilderness disappeared into night.

When she was directly above Carybridge

village, she heard sounds. It was completely dark now and if she put her foot into a rabbit's or fox's hole, she was lost. She stopped and listened, remembering terrifying stories of the ghosties of the Moor and no longer caring. The sound came again: a gasping laugh ending in a small scream. Then . . . a guffaw.

She had been about to call but the twin sounds stopped her and she stood stock still in the early dark, a new fear gripping her. Nothing happened and she took a step forward, then another. Looming above her was the wall of a hut. A shepherd's hut; the kind that dotted the Moor. She could smell smoke now. To the left a faint glow came through the opening of an unglazed window and lightened the snow slightly. She edged towards it but before she got there a voice said loudly and clearly, 'Will you lie still, Betty Sperring? I won't ask you again!' and the laughter followed. A country voice replied, 'Ow can I keep still, Rupert Fielding, when you're a-doin' what you're a-doin'?'

Lydia half fell against the rough stone of the wall and pushed her hand to her mouth to stifle her cry of pain. She had known when she had heard the guffaw . . . known and not believed. She felt the sweat cold on her body and sudden pain which she had not noticed before struck up through the soles of her feet. Other sounds followed. She looked up wildly, recognizing them against her will, then pushed herself off the wall with new convulsive strength and plunged downhill towards the lights of the village.

They found her outside the kiddley and two labourers who knew her half dragged, half carried her along to Dr Tarling's house on the edge of the village. He dosed her with brandy and shouted to his boy to harness up his trap and within half an hour they were on the road back to Milton Mains, blown there by the blizzard which had started again in earnest.

Lucy had not been able to keep her promise. When they went into the parlour Lydia knew immediately that her mother was dead because the loved presence was nowhere there. She stood stiffly by the banked-up fire, while Dr Tarling made his examination and pronounced the obvious, then she collapsed where she was, just as she had done nearly three months earlier in Granny Peters's hovel. There was no hope of Dr Tarling returning to Carybridge that night. He had a patient on his hands anyway; he carried Lucy into her bedroom and laid her out with none of Prudence's expertise. Then he put Lydia on the vacant sofa and made up the fire and sat with her until the next morning when Rupert was brought home drunk by Amos Pollard and young Drake.

Lucy Fielding was laid on the dining-room table in her open coffin just as her son had been. The snow kept away the curious, but her friends came in spite of the weather; the whole of Listowel village, many from Tamerton and Carybridge, the Lambournes with Jinny up beside them in their coach, Rupert's friends, the Pascoes with

Joanna veiled and in black. Prudence Peters stayed for half an hour on her knees by the table leg, her face set in a mould of bitter resignation. Then she sought out Lydia in the kitchen.

'You are older now, my girl. You thought life easy. Now you know better.'

Lydia said woodenly, 'How are you, Prudence?'

'They tell me I am well. They tell me I can afford to move further up the combe out of the sea mist. That I can buy butcher's meat and factory clothes. But if I did any of those things my man would not know me when he came home.'

Lydia looked at the hooded eyes but could read nothing. She turned back to the table where she was preparing the funeral meats. Perhaps senility was catching. Perhaps consumption was catching too; she hoped it was and that she would die very soon.

Just the villagers were at the church to see Lucy laid to rest. The combe was too difficult in the snow for outsiders and Lydia was thankful for it. As it was, she and the Pollards had great difficulty in supporting Rupert. His grief had made him physically heavy; he could not pull himself upright to don his jacket so Amos dressed him like a baby.

'I cannot bear it . . . cannot bear it . . .' he repeated over and over again. 'The light of my life has gone out. Where is Gus? He should be here to help me . . . help me.' Everyone had to help Rupert; he was suddenly incapable and no-one would permit him to dose himself with a drop of brandy.

That night Lydia heard him sobbing in the room he had shared with Lucy a year ago. Her mother had hated no-one and Lydia tried to recapture some of her old careless affection for her father for Lucy's sake; but she could not. Last year Betty Sperring had been the May Queen at Carybridge and had been crowned with flowering thorn and driven along the Heights road in a high wagon while people had showered her with blossom. The spirit of a virginal new summer. And now, because of Rupert Fielding, she was a virgin no longer. Lydia went no further than that. If she let herself wonder for a moment whether her mother's life could have been saved had her father come straight home that night, she knew a stab of such hatred that must surely lead to Nathan's madness.

For a week Rupert nursed his grief to fever pitch. He ate little and drank a lot. Amos and Drake were doing the best they could for the sheep; Lydia milked twice a day and did the best *she* could, making butter and cheese. Rupert never enquired about the animals or the people around him. It did not occur to Lydia that guilt was gnawing into his very soul and some of her own grief was absorbed by her bitter anger.

At the end of that week things came to a head. Amos had dug them out that morning with the news that the flock above Carybridge had been frozen solid yesterday; not a single ewe left. Rupert, humped over the cooking fire, his tea laced with brandy, looked up with something like alertness at last.

'Can't be,' he said flatly. 'Saw to 'em myself only yesty. Got them all behind the shippen and fenced them in with wattle.'

Lydia was wrapping shawls around herself ready to go to the barn for the first delayed milking. 'That was ten days ago, Father. You haven't been out since then.'

'Haven't been out?' He looked at her, the whites of his eyes flecked with red. 'Haven't been *out*? What do you call that walk down to Listowel then? What do you call that, Miss Hardface?'

She stopped by Amos, horrified at his tone.

'Apart from that. You know very well you haven't been to the Carybridge shippen since the night Mother . . . died.'

His glance focused sharply on her. 'How do you know that? Come on, out with it! How do you know that?'

Lydia crossed the ends of a shawl over her chest and tied them behind her back. Amos rescued her. 'You an't bin to any of the sheep since then, master. Miss Lydie be right.'

Rupert said stubbornly, 'I fenced 'em in by the shippen there—'

'That were ten days ago,' Amos said firmly. 'You be mazed with grief, master. That flock be froze to death now. We could see some return on 'em if we could get hold of the new co-operative – they're paying for meat and winter fleeces on carcasses frozen hard—'

There was a roar of fury from Rupert, and

Lydia slipped out under cover of it. She battled her way to the barn where the cows were shifting uncomfortably with the weight of their milk. For the first time since Lucy's death the awful emptiness of Lydia's grief was invaded by a faint curiosity. So Wesley had organized the 'co-operative' far enough to be making offers for frozen stock. She wedged the stool in between the welcome warmth of the cows and pushed her head into an accommodating flank as she began to milk. What did it matter? What did any of it matter? The world contained no more Lucy, no more Alan. It was lonely and cold . . . Even her father had become alien.

She went back into the kitchen to find him trying to get his feet into stiff boots. She thought her unwary remark was to be tactfully forgotten, but Rupert had been fermenting it in his mind with the gall of bitter guilt and as soon as she shut the door behind her on another flurry of snow, he began.

'Spying on me now. Is that it?' He tugged furiously then stood up and stamped his heel down. 'How did you know I was in the Cary-bridge shippen that . . . that night?'

Lydia put a pail of milk beneath the table and sat down by it wearily. 'You told me, Father. Before you left, you told me.' She looked up at him and managed to smile. 'It doesn't matter surely? Not now?'

He started on the other boot, pulling then stamping, his face red above his shirt.

'A man has got to have some comfort,' he

panted. 'A woman too, it would seem – *you* should know that.'

'Father, please – '

'No blame. No blame, my girl. I forgave you for that when you promised you would marry the man concerned.'

'Father! I made no such promise! You know I did not!'

He rammed his heel into the boot and tugged at his trousers angrily. 'You have led Gus to believe so, Lydie, so do not deny it. I have seen with my own eyes how you have led him on.'

She stood up, tearing at her knotted shawl. 'Gus grabs . . . mauls . . . oh, he has not been unwelcome this winter perhaps, as much for Mamma's sake as anything, but the one time I really wanted to see Gus, when Mamma lay here coughing up her life's blood, then he did not come! No-one came! Oh God, if only someone had come then!'

'Are you harping on that again, girl?' Rupert heaved himself into his coat. 'Am I to live always with your face telling me I killed your mother?'

'I did not mean—'

'I am going to Mapperly now, Lydie. There is a chance Gus can dispose of the frozen flock. Then I shall go to Carybridge where I am welcomed with smiles instead of whey faces.'

'Smiles from Betty Sperring?'

Lydia heard her own voice, choked and full of hate, and knew she had gone too far. Her question fell between them solidly. After the first startled moment when her father stared at her wide-eyed, his gaze dropped to the flagged floor as if he expected to see her words lying there. Then he went to the wall and took down his crop and came for her. She cowered where she was, her arms over her head. The blows – just four of them – were random and undirected; immediately Rupert realized what he was doing, he stopped. Her shoulders burned . . . her upper arms . . . her back . . . The kitchen was filled with the sound of his panting breath and her terrified sobs.

He said thickly, 'I will come home tomorrow, my girl. And we will have this out. I shall expect something different from you by then. Think about it.'

He opened the door and went through without closing it. The snow blew in and by the time she heard the clink of Blackie's bridle as she was led around the front of the house, there was a small drift against the milk pail beneath the table.

Gus found her huddled by the dead fire as the last light struggled through the snowstorm in the middle of the afternoon. She had closed the door and taken off her shawls so that she could rub feebly at her sore shoulders; otherwise she had done nothing since her father left. Tears streaked her face and her hair was awry. She looked up without surprise or interest as Gus entered; there had been a faint momentary hope that it might have been Mrs Pollard limping up from her sister's; or even Jinny. When she saw it was Gus she returned to raking at the fire bars.

Gus put his cap on the table and swung out of his cape.

'Rupert told me you were on your own. Not right – not right for a girl to be alone and unprotected.' Lydia raised her eyes, expecting him to come to her and kiss her and wondering whether she had the strength to tell him to leave. But he picked up a sack from the pile in the corner and put it over his head. 'The cows need milking, Lydie. I'll do that. You kindle the fire and boil some water – broth, if you have any. Wash your face and hands and see to your hair. I will bring fresh logs in when I come.' He went to the door again without pausing. 'Put out some food and we will eat together.'

The door latched shut after him and Lydie stared at it, surprised at last out of her lethargy. Fumblingly, because there seemed nothing else to do, she began to obey his instructions. Birch bark in the kindling box burned steadily as it always did, wet or dry; she piled on sticks and old candle ends then some logs. As soon as the kettle steamed she poured water into the wash bowl, stripped to her petticoat and worked slowly and painfully with the soaped wash cloth. She fetched a clean lawn blouse from the press and fastened it high on her throat with the Garrett cameo, wrapped a fresh shawl over her shoulders, bundled her hair into a tidy knot above her ears. She warmed some of the milk, added yeast and corn and set it aside for fermenty, cut ham and bread and fetched gherkins pickled by her mother last summer . . . only last summer. Some of the terrible loneliness that had gnawed at her all day abated. Nothing would ever be the same between Rupert and herself again; it could not be. She had no mother, no brother . . . and now, no father. She had thought there was nobody else. But, of course, there was Gus. She put cushions in a chair for him and knew the age-old pleasure of a woman looking after a man.

He came in, the picture of robust health, alive, a source of energy and warmth. She watched him as if she had never seen him before. He had swilled head and hands beneath the pump and he snuffled into a cloth just like the dog she had always likened him to, but a dog who was loyal, affectionate, had his mistress's welfare at heart. His black hair stood on end in tousled curls and his black eyes sparkled at her approvingly as he threw the cloth into a corner and turned towards the table.

'That's better, Lydie. I hardly knew you when I arrived, sitting there in a trance like old Mrs Nancombe!' He drew up a chair as she placed the fermenty in front of him and added, in an unusually gentle voice, 'You will be happy again, Lydie. Just wait and see. And you need not feel guilty when you do because your mother would want it. Your mother would want happiness for you, Lydie, more than anything.'

She sat down suddenly, lowering her eyes so that he could not see the tears. He spooned fermenty into her dish and shoved it towards her and when he was deep into his she lifted the spoon to her mouth several times knowing that she needed nourishment.

He took ham onto his plate and cut it, speared a piece on his fork and put it into his mouth. The edge was off his hunger and he chewed slowly, glancing at her occasionally as if gauging her mood. When she pushed her dish of fermenty away, he poked his loaded fork at her.

'Come on, Lydie. Eat.'

She shook her head. 'No more, Gus.'

He put the fork against her lips and she opened her mouth, unwilling to throw such kindness back. 'Honestly, Gus . . .' She looked at him at last. 'That is all. Really.'

'A pickle to go with it – ' The sharpness of the vinegar burned her tongue. 'Bread to follow . . .' Her mouth was stuffed full. He sat back, laughing. 'Your cheeks are swollen and plump at last! And by God, 'tis the only way to stop your flow of refusals! Why did I not think of it before?' He got up and went to the dresser, found the cupboard key in the pewter tankard and got out Rupert's brandy bottle. He grinned at her round eyes as he uncorked it and poured some into a cup. 'I know where your father keeps most things now, Lydie, and he would be the first to tell me to help myself.' He waited until she swallowed and stood behind her holding the glass to her lips. Her head was pressed against his waistcoat, her ear against his encircling arm.

'No, Gus.'

'Yes, Lydie,' he said. 'You have obeyed me so far and feel better for it, do you not?' She managed to nod without jogging the cup. 'Then obey me now. Drink.' The glass tipped against her bottom lip and the fiery liquid ran down her throat and had to be swallowed. He refilled the cup and put it by her, then resumed his seat. 'Now, more food.' He loaded his fork.

'Gus, I do not want . . .' Tears of weakness filled her eyes again.

He pretended schoolmasterish sternness. 'Miss Fielding must learn to be biddable. Firstly – laugh!' She was disarmed into a small smile and immediately the fork was between her lips. 'Now eat!' She took the food into her mouth and chewed. It was true: she felt better. The brandy warmed her stomach and sent threads of sensation down her arms and legs. When Gus next held the glass towards her she did not protest. He refilled it again, drank himself, gave her the rest; poured more. She leaned back against the chair, relaxed for the first time in ten days, her eyes half closed. She wanted to sleep.

Gus said very seriously, 'The game we have been playing, Lydie. It must end.'

She misunderstood him and nodded almost gratefully. 'Yes, Gus. Yes. It has gone far enough. I thank you for calling so regular and . . . for now . . .' she swept her hand around the table waveringly; her tongue had difficulty forming her words. 'I might have died without you, Gus.'

'That would not do, Lydie. I want you alive.'

He took her hand, drew her to her feet and held her against him. Her shawl fell back and through the thin lawn of her blouse she felt the heat of his body. It was luxurious and she did not withdraw from it. He kissed her; not his usual engulfing kiss but a light probing with his lips. 'Yes Lydie, the game must end tonight. Now. Do you understand?'

She wanted to push him off. With her mind and with her heart. But he was warm and strong and without him there was nothing and no-one. She closed her eyes and tried to shake her head; her physical being did not want to lose him.

He said, 'You are grateful to me, Lydie, are you not? I have let the Peters family be. Though Julius and Tavvie have wanted them ruined before they come to be competitors, I have insisted that they be left alone. And you are grateful that I am here now, are you not? When no-one else comes near you. Yes, you are grateful, Lydie. You are grateful.' The insidious voice was in her ear now. She could not bear it if he went away; she could not stand without his support. Without his warmth she would die of the cold.

She breathed, 'I am grateful, Gus. Thank you.'

'And this time, you want me,' he whispered. 'You will not cry rape this time?'

She said nothing but her eyes closed.

He kissed the eyelids. 'Then we will go to bed, Lydie.'

He swung her into his arms and climbed the stairs easily, turning her body around the newel post expertly. On the landing it was quite dark but she could still see his eyes when she opened hers. He felt his way along the wall to her room. She wondered why she had fought against this inevitable moment. Gus had always got his way in the end and since her birthday party he had marked her for himself. In the moonlit bedroom she even helped him to undress her and when at last she cried out it was a protest against her own treacherous body which responded to his against everything she held dear.

Ten

Lydia opened her eyes to full daylight coming through the uncurtained window. She was sleeping on the extreme edge of the mattress and turned herself fearfully on one elbow to look over her shoulder. Gus lay there, arms upflung, the bedclothes only just above his waist showing his chest a tangle of black hair. She closed her eyes tightly, wishing desperately it was all a dream, but the soreness inside her and around her breasts told her it was only too real.

She reached for her shift and held it to her while she slid out of the bed and went to the window. It was long past milking time and the cows lowed urgently from the barn. She pulled on petticoats, skirt and an old smock of her father's and went hurriedly downstairs. She threw kindling and logs hopefully onto the ash of the fire and scooped last night's supper dishes into a bowl; the whole atmosphere of the kitchen was musty and unbearable. She remembered the events of last night and wished passionately that she were dead with her mother.

An hour later, Gus found her milking. He lounged against the wicket opening of the barn door, watching her and saying nothing.

At last she could stand his scrutiny no longer. She looked briefly at him and away. 'Cover yourself!' she said with contempt.

He flushed, straightened and buttoned his trousers.

'Love makes you sharp, Lydie.' He came in and closed the door, shivering. 'Or is it the cold? You were soft and docile enough a few hours ago.'

She shifted the pail from the restless hind feet and moved on.

'Was that love, Gus?' She sat down and began again. 'I think it was a need for human comfort, for a harbour in—'

His loud laugh broke through her meditative words. 'Is that what it was, Lydie? A harbour? Comfort? You needed a great deal of comfort, my dear, did you not?'

She flinched and worked harder, watching the milk froth into the pail as if her life depended on it.

'It pleases you to make a joke of it, Gus.' Her stifled voice merely provoked louder laughter. 'After all, you have got your way and will marry me just as you have always said.'

The laughter cut off like pump water. There was a long pause while she milked steadily. Then Gus said, 'Lydie, what I see before me is a slut. Her feet are covered in dung and she smells sour. Would I want to marry a slut?'

She flashed him a burning look. 'What I am, you made me, Gus! And if you enjoy insulting me, remember that I know over half of your desire for marriage is to gain Milton Mains.'

'Ah, so you guessed. No matter.' He kicked at a bucket casually and it fell over, sending a river of milk into the straw. 'No matter at all, Lydie. Because you see, the farm is almost entirely mortgaged to me, anyway. Since last summer I have worked at it very carefully—'

Lydia had jumped up when the milk was spilt. Now she took hold of a rope coiled on the barn wall and hung onto it.

'We lease it only! From the Garretts. Sir Henry will never permit—'

'Sir Henry will be delighted to see me in charge, Lydie. He knows who kept this place together – he knows who kept your father working properly. And your mother is gone now and it is likely that Betty Sperring will take her place. Sir Henry knows that I can manage it. I can pull it together and make it into the farm it once was.'

Lydia held hard on the rope and breathed deeply. It sounded . . . true. She said hoarsely, 'Betty Sperring?'

'Oh yes, you don't know about her, do you? Don't worry, Lydie, I will see you are kept on here. After all, Rupert won't want to get up early mornings to do the milking and you are such an able milkmaid!' He stepped through the wicket and looked back. 'I'm going now, Lydie. You will be here when I come back. If I come back.' It was not a question and she did not reply. After

273

a while she went to the wicket and peered through. Gus had left the kitchen door open and he reappeared capped and cloaked after about ten minutes. He went to the stable and led out his horse, the saddle over his arm. He saddled her expertly, testing the tightness of the girth with a gentle finger. Then he led her around the house.

The farmhouse was quiet and solitary again under the yellow, snow-filled sky. No smoke came from the chimney. Gus had not brought in logs last night after all and there was the water to fetch too. Lydia turned back to finish the milk. She was sick to her soul with what had happened over the last twelve hours at Milton Mains; sick with herself. She went to the pump, washed thoroughly and looked around again at the desolation of snow surrounding her and cutting her off from all human contact. Well . . . loneliness meant freedom.

At the beginning of March Rupert told her, with a certain clownish dignity, that after a suitable period of mourning, he would marry Betty Sperring. The announcement put their relationship on a different footing. Now he was respectable again and practically betrothed, he became pompous and informed her that Miss Sperring would visit them on May Day and would expect a proper welcome.

'You can tidy this kitchen for a start. And mend your clothes. I can't think what has happened to you during the last few weeks.'

She said bitterly, 'Gus tells me that Milton Mains belongs to him. I saw no point in working for his gain.'

Rupert shrugged. 'I have borrowed money certainly. Anyway, Gus tells me things too. I think you had best cast no stones, daughter.' He held up a hand before Lydia could protest. 'I know that you and Gus have quarrelled, Lydie, and I will tell you that he has every intention of giving you a ring before summer is out, but he thinks you need taming. Perhaps he is right. You were always mettlesome . . . always . . .' He looked past her into the nostalgic distance then shook his shoulders. 'I tell you this to put your mind at rest. You will not want to stay here when Betty becomes my wife, I know that. So be assured, your future is quite settled and certain.'

The renewed if careless energy that Gus had given her nearly erupted in temper at her father's sheer complacence. Instead, she took pleasure in scrubbing the flags of the kitchen floor around his feet and making life as uncomfortable as possible for him during the short time he was at home. Later that night, when the full import of his news had been absorbed she sat late in her room by her guttering candle, thinking. At last she got out her writing materials, cleared a space on her dressing table and wrote to Fanny Parmenter in Bristol.

My dear Fanny – for such I call you in my thoughts just as you directed – I thank you for your kind letter on the occasion of my mother's death. Although this was expected, it was indeed a mortal blow, as you say. I dare not dwell on her absence, dear friend, so will pass to the next reason for this letter. My father proposes to remarry this summer and as I would like to leave the farm for he and his new wife to enjoy undisturbed, I am considering other means of employment. You are aware of my limited experience as a governess and you were flattering on that score when we met! Would it be possible to secure a congenial post in Bristol or its surroundings of this nature? I feel certain that I can obtain references from Lady Maud Garrett, but know that your personal recommendation would be invaluable. I should welcome your advice.

Affectionately yours, Lydia Fielding.

The next morning she entrusted the letter to her father to post in Carybridge. He, forgetful of last night's announcement, said truculently, 'What makes you think I'm going to Carybridge?'

She smiled. 'I imagine you would want to visit your future wife regularly, Father.' She heard her own voice, sweet to the point of acidity. However, Rupert did not notice anything amiss and, mollified, kissed her head on his way to the stable. She watched him depart with gratitude, then said guiltily into the blessed silence, 'Oh Mamma. You were right. Somehow, I must let love in.' She crossed to the fire and rattled the bars with the poker. 'And if I cannot do that, then I must go.' She looked up the stairs towards the parlour door. 'I have to leave Milton Mains, Mamma!' she said, her voice suddenly loud and surprised. And then she sat down and wept and in the midst of her tears nausea swept down on her and made her retch.

A week later, the thaw began, Mrs Pollard returned to the farm cottage and Lydia received a reply from Miss Parmenter. The three events happened in that order.

She woke as usual before light and dressed for the morning milk before she realized she was not shivering. As soon as she opened the top half of the kitchen door, she heard it: an orchestra of drips playing slowly but surely. By the time it was fully light the pace had quickened and at midday a weak shaft of sunlight broke through the low sky and Lydia stood outside the front door sniffing with a kind of awe. Could she really smell spring? And if so, what did it matter to her? Yet, in spite of her constant ache of despair, she knew it did matter; whatever happened in human disasters would not stop the world turning and, willy nilly, the humans went with it.

Mrs Pollard limped in – ostentatiously – during the afternoon, and sat down heavily at the kitchen table to watch Lydia making the supper and to recount the village news. They were living on salted pilchards down there, the flour had all gone and the carefully hoarded fruit. The tiny efforts at vegetable growing had come to nothing because of the weather and the fishing boats had hardly put out at all since before Christmas. Robbie Roscoe had walked over to Lambourne to see his sister and she was doing nicely except for the cramps, which, as Lydia probably knew, meant the baby would be a boy. Nan Nancombe was dead. They'd found her body at the top of Tamerton where she went to collect roots for one of her draughts. As for Prudence Peters, she was as mad as old Nathan; she had moved in with Gran and was supposed to be looking after her but more likely it was because she couldn't stand Luke, Benjie and Mercy. Two old witches together, they were; the local children wouldn't go down the Peters track and crossed themselves when they met Prudence down on the shingle at her beachcombing. On the other hand she had rid Bessie Truebody of her warts, saved Mark Wittling's pig and done a bit of got-riddin.

'Got riddin?' Lydia took a leg of mutton from the big oven for basting.

'Nellie Truscombe. You 'eard about 'er?' Mrs Pollard wiped her nose on her shawl with anticipation. 'Got 'erself into trouble with one of the men on the Garrett place. 'Er father took 'er off to Sir 'Enry and 'e said there'd been quite enough of these 'asty marriages what repents themselves at leisure an' she 'ad no proof . . . so Prudence Peters got rid of 'en.'

'Oh.' Lydia basted the mutton. 'Poor Nellie.'

'Poor Nellie? She din't want to leave the village and go to the Place. An' she didn't want no fatherless baby. Lucky Nellie, more like.'

'Yes. Certainly. Lucky Nellie.' Suddenly the sight of the fat slipping over the mutton was obscene. She took a deep breath. 'Will you and Amos have supper here, Mrs Pollard?'

'Nay, Miss Lydie. I must get my own range going.' Mrs Pollard made a fuss about getting to her feet. 'An' you won't 'ave your kitchen to yourself for much longer I do 'ear, so I'd best go.' If she expected any gossip from Lydia she was disappointed. She looked at her closely. 'You'm pale and peaky and no wonder. If I'd bin 'ere, mebbe your dear ma would still be alive today.'

Lydia crouched by the oven and Mrs Pollard got herself to the door, nodding lugubriously. 'Everything's changin'. Everything. And not for the better, I'll be bound.'

Lydia waited until the uneven footsteps had crossed the yard then she hurried outside to gulp in huge lungfuls of the gentle air. It was no good; she went round the corner to the midden and vomited bile. Sweat was cold on her forehead. She crept slowly back to the house and sat down.

Rupert came in with spirits to match the weather. And he had a reply from Fanny Parmenter.

'The snow's off the southern slopes,' he said jubilantly. 'The Tamerton flock are grazing as if nothing has happened! Amos and me will move them up to the Carybridge grounds tomorrow – or half of them at any rate. Even the lambs are full of wool. It's going to be a good year for

279

fleeces. A lucky year, eh, Lydie? Gus rode down today. He's got the price of that frozen stock and it's not too bad. I can afford to get you wed in style, daughter, even if I have to make do myself!'

Lydia could think of nothing to say to that; she smiled faintly and opened Fanny's letter while her father carved the mutton.

'Well? What does your rich friend have to say for herself?' Rupert pulled at a length of crackling and stuffed it into his mouth. 'Has she married the Toryman yet and mended her ways?'

Lydia skimmed the close-written script for items to pass on to her father. 'I think it more likely he will change his views,' she said absently. 'Fanny stipulates they must live in Bristol. There is a vote to be taken in the City Council as to whether female householders may be represented. I do not quite understand.'

'I should hope not, indeed. If she were not so well-born she would be stoned! Wearing trousers next – that's what it'll be, you mark my words!'

'She wants me to pay her a visit, Father. Before summer is out. Would that be possible?'

'I cannot spare you until after the shearing. Then there's reddling. And haymaking. Gus and I thought our marriages would best be left till Michaelmas. Perhaps for a week before then?'

Lydia flushed and folded her letter carefully. 'Perhaps,' she said noncommittally. She remembered Lucy and her half-smiles and cautious replies.

Once in her room that night, she re-read her letter with care; especially the middle page.

'. . . I understand the difficulty of your position only too well, Lydia, as I expect you know my father remarried when I was fourteen . . .' Lydia had not known this and was surprised at further evidence of their similarity.

The Hotwells school is now run by three managers: myself, Sir Anthony Warren and a trading gentleman who is more practical than either of us! I have been running the school with helpers, as you know. Now we hope to install a teacher on a salary. There is a small cottage next to the school hall which we have purchased for this teacher. At the moment, Lydia, we can find a minimal salary which – perhaps fortunately – means we cannot hope to obtain anyone with College qualifications. It seems we have found someone with qualifications of a different kind: practical experience, love and enthusiasm. Her name is, of course, Miss Lydia Fielding! However my dear, though this all sounds well-omened, I would not care for you to launch yourself into it without knowing more. Would you care to stay with me during July and attend the school with me? You would then have a good basis for making up your mind.

Lydia read and re-read this half a dozen times. Then she got ready for bed and lay very still on her back, both hands clasped lightly over her abdomen. Sir Henry was right: there had been enough hasty marriages, especially in this family. But the alternative was grim indeed.

May Day came and so did Betty Sperring. She was an open, naive girl, a year younger than Lydia and already showing the child she was expecting. As soon as Rupert left them alone together she confided candidly, 'Mr Fielding talks of marriage in Michaelmas, but it will be a toss-up whether the wedding or baby do come first!' She giggled without embarrassment, but Lydia, working that out, had to conclude that the conception had taken place before Lucy's death.

Taking her tone from Betty, she asked curiously, 'Do you really want to marry my father? You know the farm is mortgaged to the Pascoes and life here will be no easier than what you are used to?'

'Zackly.' The girl blushed prettily – she was very pretty. 'I'm used to work. And mortgaged or no, this is a step up for me. 'Sides, I want a father for this – ' She patted her stomach.

Lydia could not keep it up and turned away to lay the table for the special meal she had prepared in accordance with Rupert's instructions. She, of all people, should understand her father. Yet she could not. And she was sickened by the way Betty constantly deferred to him. 'If you say so, Mr Fielding' and 'Whatever you say, sir,' was her parrot cry whenever Rupert paused for breath. It stiffened Lydia's resolve as nothing else had. She was almost certain now that she was pregnant herself and had vacillated only because she had thought it her duty to provide a father for the child. Now that alternative was dismissed without difficulty. The choice lay between having the child and living on her father's charity with Betty's permission; or going to Prudence Peters for a 'got riddin'.

The shearing and reddling were well under way when she walked down the combe two weeks later. One of the reddlers was sleeping in the barn and his powdery red ochre clogged her nose and made her sneeze in the May sunshine. She did so with deliberate violence, having heard from Mrs Pollard of a local miscarriage caused by a sneeze. But she knew that after her sin there would be no easy way out for her; she would have to drink Prudence's noxious brew and suffer pains of hell as punishment. She did not care; she wanted freedom again and the opportunity to work as a teacher. A paid teacher.

After the terrible winter, summer was late in coming fully. Even the glittering sea was still iron-cold and none of the sheep farmers had dared drive their sheared sheep through the shallows to clean them for fear of lung death.

Lydia paused by the Peters track and made her repeated bargain with her Maker. 'Dear God. If you will release me from this bondage, I will never sin again. I will be chaste for ever and work only towards your glory.' She looked up at the silvery blue sky and knew it was the kind of thing Betty Sperring might say and having received amnesty would become pregnant again within the month. Yet, wasn't Betty's way more honest than Lydia's? Lydia hung her head, remembering again that night with Gus. She groaned aloud this time, 'Oh God . . . dear God . . .'

Neither Prudence nor Gran Peters answered her knock. She waited by the midden, which was already steaming in the morning sun, then called into the latch. 'Prudence! It is Lydia Fielding. Will you speak to me?'

Eventually there was a creaking sound as of someone shifting in a chair and Prudence's voice came harshly through the wood.

'I have nothing to say to you. My secret shall die with me. Go home, Lydia Fielding!'

Lydia leaned against the door. The decision to come here had been hard to make; the time to do it had been even harder to make. Lydia felt nausea overwhelm her when she thought it was all for nothing. She groaned and began to slip towards the turf. Then the sound of bolts being drawn sounded by her ear; she hung onto the lintel as the door opened a bare six inches and Prudence looked out. Lydia fought for consciousness through the stench.

Prudence's button eyes took in the condition of her visitor and she let the door swing wide and put her skeleton shoulder beneath Lydia's arm. They staggered to the table. Lydia sat on it and began to retch. A pail appeared below her bent head. She clung to its rim and afterwards hung there, sweating while Prudence watched her from the chair.

'Who be the father then?' she asked at last when Lydia straightened with difficulty.

Lydia shuddered convulsively. Everything was the same as it had been that terrible night last autumn: there was the ladder and Granny Peters's chair by the fire and the bare packed-earth floor and the table.

She whispered, 'Gus Pascoe.'

'Did he force you?'

'No.'

Prudence drew in a shuddering breath. 'Little fool. Wun't he marry you?'

'I don't know.'

'You 'aven't tole 'en?'

'No.'

'You dun't want to marry 'en?'

Lydia shook her head.

Prudence put a dipper into the water pail, drank deep and passed it to Lydia.

'And why not? Still hanker for our Wesley, do you? D'you think 'e'll want Pascoe leavings?'

Lydia flinched and cowered, then sipped at the dipper and forced her back to straighten.

'I shall never marry. I shall live without men.'

'Ha!' It was a sound of derision but when Lydia made to stand up Prudence shook her head. 'Wait. I have something. Something you have come for. But it is dangerous if the child be far gone.'

Lydia swallowed; the water tasted bad. 'Three months. Perhaps a little over.'

'Perhaps? What is this – do you go with this man often?' For the first time Prudence sounded outraged and Lydia flinched again.

'Once. I swear. Three and a half months, then. That is all.'

'It is enough. You should have come sooner.' She thrust her chin out. 'Tell him. Tell Gus Pascoe. Marry 'im. 'Tis best.'

'I cannot. I hate him. Prudence, I beg you, for the sake of my mother whom you loved—'

'Silence, girl! Do you think she would permit this? You are more of a fool than I guessed!' But she stood up and went to a chest behind the door. There in the shadows she crouched before the upraised lid and fumbled beneath folded clothes. She produced a stone jar.

'I gave this to Marella to kill her child. In her food. You know what happened to her. Do you still want it?'

Lydia nodded.

Prudence dipped the dipper again and shook the contents of the jar into it. Lydia seized the wet pewter before she could think any more and drank deeply, forcing the liquid down her throat until she had drained the last dregs of gritty powder.

Prudence said drily, 'You wanted that sure enough.' She threw the empty jar into the cold hearth where it shattered sickeningly. 'There. 'Tis gone. I'll never make more.'

Lydia pressed her hand to her dripping mouth as if to keep the solution in. Prudence sat down in the chair again. She was smiling very slightly.

'Repaid the debt. An' in such a way . . .'

'Debt?'

'My family took from yourn.' She looked up sharply as if regretting her words. 'Get off with you, Lydia Fielding. Get you to bed when you reach 'ome. If nothing 'appens by morning, marry the Pascoe boy and make the best of things.'

Trying desperately not to heave the mixture back, Lydia went to the door, remembering just before she went out to reach back and put something on the table.

'Mamma's fob,' she gasped. 'She would want you to have something from her. Goodbye, Prudence.'

There was no reply, but when she reached the end of the track and looked back, Prudence was standing in the door staring after her and holding the corner of her apron to her leathery face.

Lydia never knew how she got home without vomiting again. She did as she had been bid and went to bed, to Mrs Pollard's concern and her father's frank irritation.

'Extra mouths to be fed and Mrs Pollard still lame!' he grumbled. 'If it's the ochre, I'd like to know why it's never affected you before!'

But he used her sickness as an excuse and the next morning he went to fetch Betty Sperring to 'help out'. Lydia stayed in bed that day as well, but nothing happened. At night when she heard Betty and Rupert go into Lucy's room together, she wondered whether there were further depths to which any of them could sink. She got up betimes, convinced Prudence was wrong and she should be active, but though she worked unceasingly all day, still nothing happened. She was trapped. There was to be no teaching post for her in Bristol.

And then Gus called. He had the grace to look a little awkward as he greeted her in front of Betty Sperring.

'And how are you, Lydie? It must be nearly three months since I saw you last. Four? Surely not . . . well, if you say so. We have been busy and I sent messages with your father.'

'Yes, I had them.' Lydia watched him consideringly and he actually coloured under her cool gaze.

Betty giggled. 'Two weddings together. That's what Mister Fielding do say.'

Gus dried the palms of his hands on his trousers. 'Aye. He did mention it to me.' He turned from Lydia and smiled at Betty Sperring. 'I have to offer felicitations, I believe. Mrs Fielding left a gap that sorely needs to be filled.'

Before Lydia could say anything, Betty spoke, distressed. 'Well, 'tis not me that will fill it, Mr Pascoe, sir. Not me that would try to do such a thing!'

Lydia felt a rush of warmth towards her. She had not taken Betty seriously; the position was so ridiculous, a stepmother younger than her stepdaughter. Suddenly she saw Betty as the only possible successor to Lucy because she was not a usurper. Gus was continuing with his empty gallantries but Lydia hardly heard them now.

Hard on the heels of her new feeling for Betty followed a sensation of almost physical relief. Perhaps Rupert's disloyalty was not completely unforgivable?

She walked to the gate with Gus and did not reply to his laboured pleasantries until they burst into irritation.

'If you are trying to punish me, Lydie, you must find some other way!' he snapped. 'I suppose your father told you I planned to marry you eventually, did he? And you thought you had the whip hand again? Not so, my girl. Eventually is the key word. I will marry when I please.'

She said quietly, 'Gus, I am sorry. I was preoccupied. For so long I have been in despair because my heart was full of bitterness. I remember Mamma said once that I must let love in . . .' She gave him one of Lucy's small smiles. 'Gus. I will not marry you. But I will not hate you any more. In the future . . . whatever happens . . . please remember that.'

He stared at her, baffled and angry. 'I do not intend to make any more pleas, Lydie. You know you belong to me whether you will or not. Hate . . . love. They mean nothing when two people are bound as we are.'

She could feel the panic and fear rising in her again and interrupted quickly, 'Do not speak so, Gus! I cannot bear it.'

He laughed shortly. 'Because you cannot face the truth? Face it, Lydie, face it!' They had come to the gate and he swung her through it and into the lane then held her on tiptoe against his body. She gasped with the shock of it, and the memories it brought forth. He had done this before and she had strained against him, desperate to lose her loneliness in him, desperate for him to awaken her to happiness again after so much misery. Would she . . . was it possible that she would do so again? Shame and guilt made her weak and he laughed triumphantly. She pushed at him with a kind of anguish.

He allowed her to go, staggering back against the gate as if she had been too strong for him, laughing again at her renewed anger and distress.

'Oh Lydie . . . Lydie . . . when *will* you admit once and for all that you are mine?' He controlled himself, straightened and pulled his hat on firmly. 'No more arguments, my dear. Your father needs you till Michaelmas, he tells me. We will be married then.'

She said nothing, holding to a leaning alder with one hand, the other pressed into her side as if she had a stitch. She watched him up the combe, then dropped her head and looked at the trampled grass around her feet. Only two minutes ago she had imagined in her foolishness that she could live with Betty and her father, look after her baby and Betty's – let love in. She had thought she had reached the bottom of the abyss and there was no further to fall. Now she saw that was not so. She must indeed belong to Gus Pascoe, there was no way out of that, her own body would betray her every time she tried to stand firm. He might marry her, he might not. But every time he wanted her, he had only to find her. She felt completely powerless against him. She was his chattel; far more in his power than Alice Harper had been.

After a long time she turned and began to walk slowly down the combe towards Listowel. Her sleeve caught on an overhanging branch and tore, unheeded. Unseen brambles snagged her hair and she jerked herself free. When she arrived at the beach, she stepped out of her pattens and continued barefoot over the pebbles, feeling no pain. Not a soul was about but she did not notice that either. She moved in a trance, down past the tide line to the sand, lifting her feet automatically over mooring ropes and beached floats until she came to the lapping sea. She went on until her skirts billowed around her waist and the swell rode up to her neck icily. It shook her out of her dream state, but stiffened her resolution too. She began to swim because there was no other way of going on. Slowly she reached forward at each stroke as if pleading with the sea to take her and slowly she moved inexorably forward, the water often entering her mouth but easily dealt with as so often before. Her skirts, trailing behind her, gradually lost their buoyancy and began to tug her down with their sodden weight. She stopped moving her arms and lay on the water, eyes closed, thinking of Lucy. She felt herself being engulfed, being borne down and she went gladly, opening her eyes and tipping her head back for her last glimpse of the sky. Waveringly, mistily, it was there. A solid sparkling blue promising a wonderful summer. She stared at it wonderingly. It was just as beautiful as it had been last year . . . and the year before . . . She must breathe now; did she open her mouth and take in a chestful of water and die instantly? She opened her mouth. The next instant she had shot to the surface of the sea, coughing, spluttering, wanting only that blue sky that would be there each year whatever happened to puny Lydia Fielding.

The weight of her clothes was no longer friendly. She choked and retched and fought the drag of the water and knew for certain that her life was precious and she wanted it. And she was going to have to fight for it. She gasped in air and struck out desperately for the shore. The cold was terrible now that she no longer welcomed it: it numbed her kicking legs and thrashing arms until it tempted her to give herself to it completely just as she had tried to do minutes before. She might well have succumbed with a kind of resignation then, only her hand struck something solid. It was a cork float, anchored there to mark a lobster pot far below. She hung onto it gratefully; it provided just enough buoyancy to give her a few seconds' rest. Her mind took over again: she gauged the distance to the deserted beach, gathered her strength to a nucleus and swam slowly and calmly as she had done on the outward journey. It took twice as long; she schooled herself not to think of what she was doing but of what she would do. When she dragged herself out of the water at last and lay on the sand, she knew one thing for certain. Her life would be lonely, painful and hard from now on – maybe for always – but it was still worth having simply because every year at some time or another, the sky would be blue and the earth would have turned fully again.

Slower still, but without impatience or even anxiety, she climbed back up the combe. By the time she reached the gate her hair was almost dry and she was able to comb it through with her fingers. The sun was still well above the horizon and her father would be with the men in the sheep grounds. Betty would barely notice her dishevelled state. She was glad however to hear voices – Betty's and Mrs Pollard's – in the pantry discussing the capon which was cooked and waiting there to be dressed. Neither of them heard her go upstairs and when she came back down only half an hour later, their surprise was for quite another reason.

Mrs Pollard spoke first. 'Eh! And what for be 'ee dressed in your grey? An' your bag too.'

Betty followed apprehensively. 'Oh dearie me. Is it because of me? You're never leaving because of me?'

It was almost enough to make Lydia abandon her plan – though plan it was not, simply an instinct at that stage.

She said, 'Oh Betty . . . it is because of you that I *can* leave. Do you mind? Father has said he will need me here this summer, but if *you* are to be here – '

'But where are you *going*?' Betty was round-eyed and worried.

'Father knows. I have had an invitation from a friend in Bristol. A Miss Parmenter, who is highly respectable. He knows all about it and is by no means against it, but he will delay and delay . . .' She forced a smile. 'You know how it is with gentlemen.'

Betty put her hand on her stomach again. 'Aye. I do that.'

Mrs Pollard nodded vigorously. 'You should 'ave a rest, Miss Lydie. I was only saying to Amos last night as 'ow you look fair done in. What with losing both brother and—'

'So you and Betty can manage Father between you, Mrs Pollard?' Lydia said quickly.

They both laughed comfortably, even smugly, then plied her again with questions. She had no answers. She did not know when the postal cart left Carybridge or whether it would take her to Taunton. She had no idea whatever about trains from Taunton. But yes, she had money enough: five sovereigns paid to her mother by Lady Maud for her services at the Place last summer. They both looked at her respectfully; she could get to Bristol and back a dozen times with five sovereigns. She kissed Betty – with more regret than she would have believed possible but with gratitude too – and hugged Mrs Pollard, then she walked back to the gate and up the track to the Heights road. She told herself she was not leaving her home, she was going to meet a new life. Two . . . three hours ago she had thought that choice was closed to her. Suddenly, as she had climbed back to it, sodden yet with life still burning determinedly inside her, she had known it was the only thing to do. There could be no more compromise; no more fobbing off the future. She had to launch out on her own and leave the harbour which had proved so treacherous. The home for fallen women was a safer harbour by far.

It seemed as though Fate was smiling on her decision, because she had walked only a mile towards Carybridge when she heard a horse behind her and the thrumming sound of cart-wheels coming from Tamerton. She put down her heavy bag and waited at the side of the road and the carrier's cart appeared around the bend on its way to Carybridge, Stowey and a dozen other villages before arriving at Taunton for the night mail. Lydia put up a tentative hand and it drew up with much 'Who-ther! Steady boy!' although the sedate horse was obviously never going to manage more than a gentle canter. The driver was the father of the Tongie girls and took her up gladly. Lydia remembered how welcome Bessie's familiar face had been when she arrived at the Place. Now Will Tongie's face was even more so.

He was ripe for gossip. 'Bessie did tell me about last summer an' 'ow you got the better o' them little ladies! And our Sibbie is expecting again, begging your pardon, Miss Lydie, but I know you will want to 'ear our news. And what about yourn? Oh, we was that sorry we was, to hear you had lost your dear ma . . .'

Lydia felt the familiar tightness in her chest. So many people had known Lucy and been grateful to her for all kinds of things.

She swallowed. 'I want to get to Taunton, Mr Tongie. And then catch a train to Bristol.'

'You just stay along with me, missie! We'll get to Taunton some time. And right to the railway platform!' He smiled reassuringly at her and added, 'You off visitin' then?'

'Yes. A friend in Bristol.'

They trotted on, picking up the afternoon's post at each village until it was quite dark and then went through Bishops Lydeard without pause. At Taunton station, which was run by the Great Western Railway, Lydia bought a ticket for Bristol for four shillings and twopence and the use of a foot-warmer for a penny. She had never travelled on a train before and had only watched its smoke in the distance from Dunkery Beacon. It was like a wild animal hissing along by the platform, but once inside there was a cosiness she had not imagined. Each little compartment was lit by its gas mantel, something Lydia had only seen at the Place. She watched it nervously when it popped, wondering whether she might be poisoned by its fumes then realizing how little that would matter.

It was quite impossible to see anything through the dark windows, so, after some investigation, she pulled the blinds, put her feet on her metal warmer and composed herself comfortably for the next two hours. She marvelled that she could. She still had formed no real plans and she would arrive in Bristol much too late to go to Miss Parmenter's house, yet there was a curious satisfaction in at last going forward. Moving towards something. More like the old Lydia Fielding. For too long now, since that terrible night in Granny Peters's cottage, she had buried her head like an ostrich unable to face the future or the past. This afternoon, when she had fought for her life in the sea in spite of such utter self-disgust, she had been forced to lift her head at last.

In spite of this small cache of courage so hard won, Bristol Joint Station was a frightening experience. Before they entered it, Lydia had pulled up the blinds and gazed in awe at the city lights. By their blaze she could make out the frail-looking iron drawbridge that must be Mister Brunel's last work; the battlements of Clifton Village rose to meet it and at its feet lay the Docks. Then they entered the huge glass arch of the Joint Station in a cloud of demonic steam and Lydia saw that even at this hour the heavy wooden platform was jostling with people. Beneath the staging a hundred shadowy forms darted and squeaked; Lydia was well used to rats but not in so many numbers and she shuddered.

A porter yanked open her door, practically snatched her bag and ran off towards the arched entrance. She thought, in terror, that she would never see him again, but when she reached the ticket collector, there he was waiting for her by a hansom, his hand held out for a penny. There were a great many hands held out: the driver of the hansom, the porter at the tiny boarding house by the river, the sleepy chambermaid who showed her a room and brought her tepid tea the next morning. The people on the Moor had wanted to help her because they knew her: here in Bristol, no-one knew her.

The bed was damp; she guessed it by the smell and went to the trouble of slipping in the heavy mirror from the washstand. She removed it five minutes later, ominously cloudy. The chambermaid, summoned by the bell-rope, was uncaring. No-one had complained before, in fact the gentleman who had slept in it last night had said how comfortable the bed was. She did not wait to hear more but trailed out, yawning blearily. Lydia lay down in her clothes but the chill from this afternoon's immersion seemed to return as the slow hours of the night crept by. When daylight came, she got up and sat by the window, rubbing her arms and shivering as if with the ague.

After breakfast at eight o'clock – lumpy porridge and three gritty sausages – she set out to find Miss Parmenter, leaving her bag in her room. She had no wish to arrive on Miss Parmenter's doorstep with bag and baggage; the boarding house was unwelcoming but it was temporary independence. Besides, she had a vague notion that she should get to know something of the city itself and she did not have the strength to carry her bag around the streets.

The river was as unlike the Stowe as fresh pump water to a midden. As the May sunshine rose above the squat Cathedral, the turgid water gave up its pungent odours insidiously. Lydia knew it was a tidal river but she had never imagined the stinking squalor of the enormous mud banks at low tide. Stuck with every kind of rubbish they seemed to have a life of their own, apparently breathing and gently pulsating in the heat. She left the water and turned up a tree-lined street and into a square. Elegant seats were arranged around a monument in its centre. She sat on one hurriedly, recognizing belatedly her old nausea and accompanying faintness.

She sat very still on the seat, making a conscious effort to fight off her malaise. Traffic circled the square constantly and in an effort not to let her eyes follow it she peered through at some children playing stool-ball on the green. Nurses pushed high baby carriages around them and dogs snuffled excitedly and went from tree to tree . . . and there was a fountain. From being cold, Lydia was now burningly hot and the fountain offered coolness of a sort. She stood up and walked shakily along to the crossing sweeper. He rushed to clear a way for her, then shook his hard hat at her until she dropped a penny into it. Somehow she was over on the strange, hard grass, and there was a seat by the edge of the clean, sparkling water. Not Avon water. Much more like the Stowe. She leaned towards it and she must have leaned too far because the stone parapet was rising to meet her and if she didn't put up her hands quickly it would hit her head.

It was one of the strollers out with her own baby who went to Lydia's aid. The last thing Lydia heard before unconsciousness was the anxious voice above her. 'My dear, are you all right? Let me . . . why, surely it's Miss Lydia Fielding?'

Alice Harper had had her baby in the Hotwells sanctuary early in January and had been a long time recovering; but when she had, Miss Parmenter had taken her into her small house in Clifton Village as a companion, secretary and general factotum. Miss Harper, well used to keeping house at her father's vicarage, had filled all these positions and still managed to care excellently for her baby. It proved a very good arangement, leaving Miss Parmenter free to run the school and still carry out her social duties when Sir Anthony Warren was in the city. Fortunately for Lydia, Miss Harper had received a message that morning from Fanny's father and she had put her son into the baby carriage and walked down to the school with it immediately, crossing Queen's Square on her way back at midday. With the help of some of the children, she got Lydia onto a seat and revived her with her own smelling salts; but it was obvious that Lydia was unwell; she could barely speak and she seemed in some pain.

Alice Harper remembered that her employer

had been with Lydia Fielding that dreadful evening at the Stapleford Assembly Rooms. She hesitated only a moment before calling a hansom and directing the driver to drive slowly to Sion Hill in Clifton and wait for her outside Avon View. She helped Lydia to stumble into the seat and then set out briskly herself.

Lydia lapsed in and out of consciousness during the drive up to Clifton and though she tried hard to remonstrate when Alice ushered her into a bedroom and helped her to lie on a bed, she was incapable of real protest. When she eventually came to, it was to find Fanny herself leaning over her, bathing her forehead.

'Alice fetched me, my dear.' The voice was low and very soothing. 'She's downstairs now making beef tea. You are faint from lack of food. Lie still.'

But Lydia was already struggling up. 'Miss Parmenter—'

'Fanny. We are friends – do you not recall that, Lydia?'

'Fanny, then. I must get up immediately. I have a room at a boarding house in Baldwin Street and I did not plan to call on you until this afternoon.'

'My dear, I beg you. Lie down. It is afternoon. Late afternoon now. And I am afraid you are not well. Alice tells me she discovered you on the green in Queen's Square. She got you here somehow. You seem to be in a lot of pain.'

'Yes. I am in great pain.' Lydia turned her head on the pillow, her mouth suddenly parched. Fanny held a glass to her lips and spoke quietly again. 'We have a little maid. It is her day off today but she will be home in the next hour. I will send her for my physician, Lydia.'

Lydia grasped the thin wrist with a hot, dry hand. 'Fanny, Fanny, please do no such thing. I know what is wrong with me. I cannot tell you now but later . . .'

'Lydia.' Fanny's tone deepened. 'I know what is wrong with you also. You are having a miscarriage, my dear. If you will tell me how far advanced your pregnancy is, then I will know whether a physician is necessary or not.'

Lydia's face flamed scarlet with shame. She turned her head again as if she could hide it entirely.

Fanny said gently, 'I thought you knew me better than this, Lydia. You were coming to see me, after all.'

Lydia looked up, her features twisted miserably. 'I'm not sure now whether I really intended to come to see you. Or whether I simply had to leave home. Fanny, I think I must be mad – I cannot see my way any more!'

'Just tell me how many months . . . how many months, Lydie?'

'Four.' The voice was a resigned whisper.

'Then we will delay the physician. And we will say nothing to Alice. Nor to little Tweenie when she brings your supper.'

Fanny got up briskly and went to the linen chest beneath the window. She opened it and lifted out a sheet. The next moment, to Lydia's horror, she was tearing it massively; then again. She came back to the bed.

'If it is as I think, Lydia, this will be no tragedy for you. I am certain you are losing the child. We must be practical, my dear, especially if this is to be our secret. I have seen a loss at four months before and I think it is no more than a heavy flux. But if it proves otherwise, I shall insist on sending Tweenie for the doctor. Do you understand?'

Lydia remembered Marella and nodded. Fanny looked at her and smiled fleetingly and then turned back the bed covers to slide in the draw-sheets. Lydia did as she was bid, numb with shame, seeing only too well that Fanny's diagnosis was correct. Tears of weakness coursed down her face.

'If only I hadn't come . . . if only . . .'

'Ridiculous child. Everyone on Exmoor would know about it by now if you had not!' Fanny turned back the covers expertly. 'Whereas now . . . ' she held out the water glass again. 'Listen, my dear, I would tend you anyway if I did not know you. How much more eagerly I do so because you are my friend and because I have such need of you.'

'Need of me?'

'You are losing a child, Lydia. But I have thirty children who need you.'

'How can you trust me with them now?'

'Because there will be extra understanding and sympathy from you, Lydie.' There came a

303

tap at the door and she added quickly, 'If you have not been beaten low by life, my dear, how can you understand these little creatures, who no sooner lift their heads out of the gutter than someone kicks them back.' She raised her voice to bid the person enter, and Alice came in with a steaming, spouted cup. 'Ah, your beef tea. Thank you so much, Alice. We have decided that a good night's rest is what Miss Fielding needs, Alice, so do not bother Tweenie when she comes in.'

She stood up, still talking calmly and naturally to cover Lydia's distress. Lydia accepted a napkin and the cup and even managed to drink a little of the brew. Fanny and Alice left her, to eat their own meal, and she lay back and tried to feel some sort of relief that she really was losing the burden of Gus's child.

After a little while, she slept. She had no emotions left.

Eleven

The schoolhouse was a one-storeyed dwelling, huddling behind the gaunt school as if for shelter against the mild rain that seemed to fall so often in Bristol. When Lydia saw it first, it merely added to the sense of complete unreality which had taken her after the sordid reality of her miscarriage. The schoolhouse consisted of a wash-house, kitchen and two other rooms and she cleaned them thoroughly, pausing occasionally to look through the tiny windows across the river to Leigh Woods and wonder where she was and what she was doing. With the same sense of unreality she accompanied Fanny each morning into the school; she wrote hymn words on the blackboard, she tied shoelaces, she even emptied the privy bucket into the river and hardly noticed it. Sometimes she would form conscious thoughts: this time last month I was breathing the high Exmoor air . . . milking the Fielding cows . . . I was unhappy, I do remember that I was unhappy . . . but I was living.

Her present thoughts consisted entirely of what

to do next. There were names to learn: Alice Watts, Jimmy Slater, Maggie Turnbull, Alfred Tassell who was lazy; Lizzie Turnbull, Maggie's sister who was industrious. Ned Parkin who scratched. There was the coal to order and lists to be made out for slates and battledores and bibles.

Teaching school in Bristol was nothing like teaching the Garrett girls at the Place; it was three-quarters organization and only a quarter of actual tuition. Fanny promised that in future there would be some help so that Lydia could use her 'Exmoor methods' and take the children outside. For the present, Fanny herself had her political fish to fry and Lydia was on her own. There was too much to do and the only way to do it was by devising a humdrum routine. It suited the new Lydia.

Now, on a Sunday afternoon in October, she and Fanny sat on either side of a bright fire in one of the small rooms, which was now Lydia's parlour. It was Fanny's habit to call regularly on Sundays; Lydia had not been to Avon View since Alice Harper had taken her there in May. Fanny had tried hard to draw her into some kind of social life, but so far had had no success. Now she was once again trying to awaken an interest in her first love: politics.

'All my activities at the moment are thanks to you, Lydia. If you had not taken up the teaching post I simply would have had no time to give. My dear, the fluff from that skirt is going every-where! What on earth are you going to do with it?'

Lydia was tearing up an ancient serge skirt which had been on the top of a box arrived from Milton Mains that morning. She did not look up: Fanny never lost an opportunity to tell her how fortuitous her arrival in Bristol had been. It seemed to underline their new relationship. Lydia was another Alice Harper; one of Fanny Parmenter's 'cases'.

She said flatly, 'The boys complain that when the girls sit comfortably sewing, they have to finish their slate work.' She smiled slightly as she did sometimes when discussing the children. 'They have to admit that it is because they did not work hard enough at it during the morning! They are very honest boys. But I thought if I found some hand work for them it would encourage them to work on their spellings. Making rag rugs is a fairly manly task, wouldn't you agree?' She ripped again and sneezed and set the skirt aside apologetically. 'Some of the more active ones might try to make a wattle hurdle later on. My father used to spend wet days making hurdles and fencing.'

Fanny applauded both ideas heartily and Lydia flushed and turned the subject back to politics. Her old shining confidence in her teaching methods had gone, long lost in the shocks and humiliations of last winter. She could not believe Fanny's praise to be anything but charity.

Fanny spoke persuasively. 'I know you won't consider attending my tea parties, Lydia dear. How galling it is to realize that nearly all political life consists of tea parties! But this is something different. Charles Bennington is an influential Methodist who has tried to get into the Council Chamber for years. Now he is standing down so that we may nominate a younger man. This will be his farewell speech and he has promised that I may say a few words. I would appreciate your support, Lydia.'

Lydia felt trapped. 'You know I can never refuse you, Fanny. Of course, if you wish it . . .'

'I do! It is settled. The meeting is at the Victoria Rooms next week. I will call for you in a cab.'

Lydia said slowly, 'I did not realize your supporters were of the Methodist persuasion.'

'My dear, we have an uneasy alliance. But minority groups must band together for their own survival. My eventual aim is to see women in the Council Chamber who can divert more of the local taxes into education – besides making their own lot easier. The Radicals, who consist of two camps – the respectable artisans who are mostly Methodists, and the unrespectable working class who are mostly heathen – support me because when the Council eventually agree to female house-owners having a vote, I can bring with me all my lady tea-drinkers! Do you begin to see the method in my tea parties, Lydia?' Fanny was laughing gently now but her mild eyes watched Lydia's face hopefully.

Lydia shook her head ruefully, laughing at last. 'I will come with you to your meeting, Fanny. Do not ask more. I do not understand politics and never will!'

Just then there was a knock at the door and one of the more disreputable of the schoolboys stood there, panting and eager.

'Jest out o' Sunday School, miss, and thought I could fill the hods for the morning!' he said hopefully.

Lydia handed him the key to the school and instructed him not to tread dust from the coal pile. Fanny listened behind her and watched the boy scuttle off importantly.

'He's come before on a Sunday,' she said quietly. 'They love you, Lydia.'

Lydia walked with her to the carriage waiting on the Hotwells road above the school. 'Alfred Tassell fills the coal hods in order to eat some of my Sunday fruit cake,' she said prosaically.

Fanny said, 'Which you make for him.' She climbed into the carriage, ignoring Lydia's denial. 'You certainly would not make it for yourself and you did not offer any to me!' she laughed. 'You are coming to life again, Lydia! Don't forget next Wednesday. Seven o'clock.'

Lydia watched the feather in Fanny's bonnet as it receded down the road then turned up Jacob's Hill and was lost to sight. Fanny Parmenter was like Lucy Fielding in many ways. Lydia turned and walked carefully down the muddy path to the schoolhouse. She could not afford such thoughts. She would make tea for Alfred Tassell and ask him if he remembered his Sunday School text.

But she noticed the next day that she did in fact have a band of helpers who could be relied upon to take over the more menial school tasks.

Alfred saw himself as keeper of the stove and Lydia, noticing from the first day his thin shivering frame, permitted him to sit next to it feeding it coal so long as he kept a reckoning on his slate of how many lumps it took. The first time this had happened he had said with sly triumph, 'I en't 'ad time to do me sums, miss.' Lydia had raised her brows. 'How many coals have you put on the stove, Alfred – twenty-eight? That was a long sum, was it not? And tomorrow, if you put on more or less, I shall need to know the difference between the totals.' Alfred had looked from his slate to her face, then suddenly laughed. 'You're a fly one, miss,' he had congratulated her.

That Monday afternoon Lizzie Turnbull cornered her in the tiny cloakroom-cum-porch. 'Alice bin and wet 'er drawers agin, Miss Fielding,' she said with a sigh. 'If I got to sit with me sewing all afternoon I can't keep me eye on 'er.'

Lydia considered. 'Alice might take the trouble to look after herself if she has some pretty drawers, Lizzie,' she said thoughtfully. 'Would you be able to sew her a pair with frills? I have some lace at the schoolhouse that might do.'

'Cor, miss. Me? Sew proper drawers?'

'They're more useful than samplers. Especially for little Alice.'

'Ah. You're right there.'

So Lizzie came to the schoolhouse and went through the box from Milton Mains and found a petticoat which Lydia pronounced redundant. Together they cut out two pairs of long-legged drawers and salvaged the lace. The box, which had brought with it unwelcome memories yet no letter from her father, suddenly became precious. She took out her silk foulard and hung it in the tiny clothes closet; thumbed through the books.

'What's this 'un, miss?' Lizzie asked, picking up *David Copperfield*.

Lydia told her, smiling as she recalled the poignancy of the story.

'Could you read it to us, miss? While we be doin' hand work?'

So Lydia began readings from Dickens. The boys hooked rugs, the girls sewed, the old stove hummed and creaked and the bare old room was filled with the winter dusk. When David's mother died, Lydia was not surprised to see some of the girls in tears and the boys silent and tight-lipped.

Alfred said sturdily, 'Well . . . I ain't got no ma so that can't 'appen to me.'

Lizzie Turnbull stroked a gather with great concentration. 'I 'an't got one neither, Alf Tassell. But I pretends I 'ave.'

Lydia felt her own tears rise. She was far luckier than these children. She had never had to pretend she had a mother. There had always been Lucy.

The meeting at the Victoria Rooms did nothing to persuade her into politics. Charles Bennington proved to be a wily-looking man

311

who talked of future tactics as if he were planning a chess game.

'We shall be making our nominations for your future representative very shortly,' he told the packed hall. 'He will need to be astute . . . young and vigorous, which I no longer am – ' he waited for the laughter to die down. 'Above all, a man who can fight with whatever weapons we can put into his hands!' Vociferous applause greeted this battle-cry. It died when he bowed towards Fanny. 'And Miss Parmenter who will speak now, ladies and gentlemen . . . Miss Parmenter *is* one of those weapons!'

Fanny stood up. Some of the ladies smiled and clapped. Mostly she was greeted with suspicious looks.

She spoke of collaboration between future women voters and the Radical party, but briefly. Fanny's politics were concerned with people and she was soon talking of children and their education.

Someone shouted from the back, 'You mean girls – not just children, missis! An' what do girls want with book learning?' Raucous laughter followed and several suggestions were put forward for girls.

Fanny replied quietly that most girls grew up to be wives, and as wives needed to be book-keepers, readers of recipes and writers of letters they required book learning as much as, if not more than, boys.

This was not a popular viewpoint even with the more respectable of the audience. When she left the platform she was followed by a cat-call.

Later, Lydia said nervously, 'I had no idea your meetings were such ordeals, Fanny. How do you bear it?'

'When you believe in something, Lydia, it becomes easy to fight for it. Many people would ask you how you bear to teach children who smell – and swear!'

'That is true,' Lydia said thoughtfully, recognizing her commitment to the school for the first time. Then she sighed. 'But you believe in so many things, Fanny. Your public work – and your private life too which is – must be – at such variance sometimes.'

Fanny said gently, 'You mean my engagement to Anthony? That surprised you, Lydia? It surprises many people. Anthony and I hold different opinions about many things. But – ' her smile became diffident – 'we are in love. Besides, there will be no long-term difficulties.'

'You mean once you are married, you will support him completely?'

'Yes – yes, that is what I mean!' Fanny's smile broke into a laugh. 'That is why I must put off the wedding date until after I can have my vote! I must be a house-owner at the next election, Lydia!' They were in a cab and it now halted opposite the schoolhouse. 'I will wait until I see your lamp lit, my dear. Thank you for coming with me. I admit I was nervous. But next week you shall meet the man who will get my vote at the next election. Our new nominee. Then I think I shall recruit a new Radical! Someone who can take my place when I marry and leave Bristol!'

Lydia glanced back into the darkness of the cab almost nervously.

Fanny said, softly, 'Put it from your mind, Lydia. Your work is with these children, they are what matters. And speaking of them, who is this?'

A shadow detached itself from the riverbank and moved forward. Lydia, used to the vast darkness of the Moor, went to meet it without fear.

'Alfred! Alfred Tassell – and covered in mud! Have you been in the river?'

'Nah, miss! I come through the drains. Got nowhere to go, see, so I were waiting for you.'

He made his statements as if they were obvious and put out a hand. Lydia took it; it was slimy.

Fanny leaned forward. 'Alfred, I have told you before, you cannot sleep in the schoolroom and there is certainly not room in the house.'

Lydia smiled into the darkness, this time with confidence. 'It's all right, Fanny, I will see to Alfred. He might agree to stay to supper with me. After he has washed of course. And so long as he promises not to swear.'

Fanny, remembering her earlier remark, laughed softly through Alfred's protestations and told the driver to go on. Lydia unlocked the schoolhouse, lit a candle from the banked fire and surveyed her visitor. His eyes peered out from a complete coating of mud.

'You can explain later,' she forestalled him.

'First, into the wash-house with you, take off your clothes and do the best you can under the pump. I'll pass you a sheet. You can wrap yourself in that for supper. Perhaps I can wash and dry your clothes for the morning.'

'I can stay 'ere then, miss?' Alfred asked hopefully.

Lydia herded him into the wash-house without a reply – which was quite good enough for Alfred. She could hear him whistling and gasping happily for the next half an hour while she boiled up the mutton stew over the open fire and laid an extra plate on her small round table. She caught sight of her face in the mantel mirror and was surprised by her wide smile. She thought, surprised: I'm lonely . . . I've got more people around me than I've had in the whole of my life, yet right inside I am lonely and it's a pleasure to have Alfred's company.

He sat opposite her, swathed in his sheet like an ancient Roman, his hair standing up in wet spikes, his face and hands cleaner than she had seen them before.

'There's meat in this, miss – cripes, it's good! Sorry miss, I din't mean to swear, it slipped out like. 'En't you 'avin' none, miss?'

'I had it for supper last night too, Alfred. I'm glad you're helping me out with it. Now you'd better tell me why you've got nowhere to go and why you've been in the drains.'

Alfred looked at her through damp eyelashes. 'I washed me clo'es and 'ung 'em on the side o' the copper.'

'Good. They can come in here by the fire soon.' Lydia ladled more stew onto his plate. 'Well?'

'Ta, miss. Well, Pa's got this lady, see. A new one. 'E din't want me there. An' it were cold and I went back an' . . .'e walloped me a bit. An' I went back again an' 'e said e'd 'ave me, like. 'E chased me and I went down the drain cover at Christmas Steps 'cos I knows the way from there down to the river, see. An' then I waited for you.'

Lydia was a long time digesting this. She imagined Alfred's father, who worked when he could on the docks: a big man who wore a leather belt, brass-buckled and heavy.

She said as calmly as she could, 'I'm glad you waited for me. But I cannot see why you could not use the road and not the drains.'

'Pa runs faster 'n me,' Alfred said simply, chewing blissfully on a bone. 'But 'e wouldn't come down a drain.'

'I should think not.' Lydia reached for a bowl of russet apples and put them in the middle of the table. 'And neither must you again, Alfred. You could be drowned – '

'Or lost,' Alfred nodded with relish. 'There's miles o' drains, miss. But one o' the mudlarks showed me a way through 'em. Safe as 'ouses when you knows 'ow.'

'No more drains, Alfred,' Lydia repeated sternly. 'Promise.'

Alfred crossed his fingers, then uncrossed them to take an apple. 'Promise,' he grinned.

*   *   *

Lydia had written home at some length back in August. Now she received a reply from Rupert; hurt and offended but also obviously relieved.

'. . . it was necessary for us to marry before Michaelmas,' he printed carefully.

. . . Betty has been persuading me ever since to write to you and offer you forgiveness. Which I do, daughter, though you treated all of us here very badly and deserted us when we might have needed you. I will say nothing of my feelings and I know Betty might have been pleased to have your help, but the way you treated Gus Pascoe was nothing short of disgraceful. You led him on, daughter. I know that for a fact. Everyone knew it. And then you made him look a prize fool. It is for him, not myself, that I grieve. Though as he has now bought the freehold of the farm from Sir Henry Garrett he is my landlord and it would have been easier for me had he also been my son-in-law. However, I will say no more of that as I think it likely Gus will try to pay a visit to Julius once he has finished his summer's work here and will wish to see you. I hope you will be pleased to hear that you have a half-brother. Betty was delivered of an eight-pound boy on September the sixteenth and they are both well. She asks me to tell you that Jinny Johnson had a son at the end of June . . .

Lydia read on through an account of the difficulties of making a profit from sheep these days, then folded the letter carefully and put it on her overmantel. She wondered how long she could keep Alfred with her as protection against a call from Gus, then told herself not to be ridiculous. There were constables walking the streets of Bristol.

As October drew on, the social life in the city accelerated. Sir Anthony Warren came down from Stapleford and stayed with Fanny's parents in Kingsweston Manor and Fanny was a great deal with him. She found time to call on Ned Tassell and have a word about Alfred, with the result that the enormous man came shamefaced to Lydia to thank her for her hospitality to his son and to assure her that it 'was the drink done it'. Lydia, sniffing her small parlour afterwards, could well believe it. She opened a window onto the river and sniffed the dark dank air instead. But Bristol air never had the purity of Exmoor's. She sighed and sat down to write to Jinny. She would miss Alfred, but she had plenty to do.

One of the boys, Jimmy Slater, had an uncle who lived in Shirehampton and had promised a load of withy sticks. They arrived while the children were eating their beavers at midday and with much shouting and laughter were stacked against the muddy bank just above the tide line where they would not dry out. That afternoon Lydia left the girls to their sewing and started the boys on a simple hurdle. They worked out of the weather inside the porch where the children hung their coats and caps, but even so it was a messy, strenuous job calling for an expertise which no-one had. When, through the open door, Lydia saw a carriage stop up on the Hotwells road her heart sank. Fanny and Sir Anthony Warren stepped down, both as smart as paint. She tried to get her small team properly organized.

Fanny's voice, gentle and slightly apologetic, spoke behind her.

'I am afraid we have not come at a convenient time, Miss Fielding. But I wished you to meet our third school manager the moment he arrived back in Bristol. Which he did this morning.'

Horrified, Lydia put her hands to her cap. It was bad enough Sir Anthony seeing her dishevelled, but he knew of her hard work from Fanny; it was just too bad of them to bring a stranger unannounced. She took a breath, dabbed at her fiery cheeks without realizing her hands were muddy, and turned. Facing her, dressed in respectable snuff-coloured breeches and dark coat, was Wesley Peters.

She was conscious of one enormous heartbeat against her ribs and then she was fighting the weakness of a near-faint again. She could not speak. She stared at him with her eyes huge and tragic. He was so familiar; the last time she had seen him he had been roughly dressed in smock and old trousers tied at the knee, but whatever he wore he had that same quiet assurance.

Fanny's voice reached her from some way off.

'This is Mr Peters, my dear. We know you are old acquaintances but thought it best to say nothing until perhaps hateful memories might have faded. Lydia? Are you all right?'

Wesley's hand shot out and took hers. It was strong; dry and warm and persuasive.

'We have interrupted something interestingly familiar here, have we not, Miss Fielding?' He turned to Alfred and Jimmy. 'I think we should tie a frame first, lads. It's not usual but it will do for a beginning.' He drew a knife from his pocket and stripped some bark, and in an instant the boys were around him, watching and helping. Lydia took Fanny's arm and went into the schoolroom.

She had no idea how she got through the rest of the afternoon. Fanny sat her down and opened *David Copperfield* at her bookmark. She began to read and time passed. At one stage she was conscious that Wesley was sitting with the boys at the back listening to her. Certainly when they sang their hymn, she could pick out his voice just above Sir Anthony's, with its broad vowels still distinctively there.

Then at last the children had all gone and Sir Anthony was going through the slates and complimenting her on the standard of work.

Wesley said, 'Lydia, I am sorry. I did not realize my arrival would be such a shock.'

'It is my fault, Mr Peters. Lydia, forgive me. I should have mentioned it the other evening. But Alfred was here and it slipped my mind. You see, Mr Peters told me that if you knew he was a school manager, you would not take the post. So I had to keep it from you at first.'

'I don't understand.' Lydia felt tricked and cheated on all sides.

'I told Miss Parmenter that we were connected by marriage.' Wesley spoke without expression. 'And that after . . . what had happened, there was some bitterness. That is all.'

'Not quite.' Fanny smiled warmly at Lydia. 'He also told me that you were made for the position of teacher here, Lydia. What with Anthony's recommendations also, there was never a more unanimous appointment!'

Lydia knew some acknowledgement was due from her, but could not make it. She closed the stove door and picked up her cloak.

'Perhaps . . . would you care to come to the schoolhouse? I usually make tea at this time.'

Immediately, she wished the words back; it was bad enough to see Wesley here in the bareness of the schoolroom, but among her own things it might well prove unbearable. However, they all agreed to come with her. Wesley did hang back to explain to Sir Anthony the intricacies of weaving a hurdle, leaving Fanny and Lydia to lead the way.

'My dear, I feel I have let you down,' Fanny said unhappily as she waited for Lydia to unlock the door. 'But he is a good man and I feel sure was as distressed as you were at the turn of events between your families.'

'Oh, more so, I imagine,' Lydia said, going straight to the parlour fire and mending it briskly. 'He was devoted to his sister. And I believe was instrumental in saving his father from the gibbet.'

'Oh Lydia.' Fanny took the kettle from her and put it on the trivet. 'And though he is a just man – yes, just – he is also merciful. He told me there had been enough death in both families and that he had to do his utmost to stop it.'

Lydia said nothing to this and went to fetch the teacups. By the time she returned, Wesley and Sir Anthony were sitting at the two places by the table squashed against the wall. Fanny was making the tea.

Sir Anthony said heartily, 'Well, you've made yourself a tight little ship here, Miss Fielding. And the school work seems excellent . . . excellent. You have accomplished a great deal in a short time.'

'Lydia gives the school *all* her time, Anthony dear. Every minute of it. She is completely dedicated.' Fanny took the tea cosy from its hook by the hearth and put it on the pot.

Sir Anthony nodded. 'How well I remember your enthusiasm at Garrett Place.'

Lydia, sickened by what she thought was empty praise, cut across this last compliment with – 'Anyone could do what I do, sir. When Fanny had the school she made far-reaching plans. That was impressive. I simply do what comes to hand each day.'

Wesley said quietly, 'Be proud of what you do, Lydia. You are close to these children and work by instinct. Miss Parmenter worked by design. Both methods are invaluable.'

Lydia let herself glance at him. In the lamplight his hair shone almost silver and his eyes were startlingly blue. She was visited by the same despair she had felt during her long illness a year ago: she loved him and he was completely inaccessible. More than ever now.

She said, 'Shall I make toast – can you stay?' She started to pour the tea; her hand was steady.

Fanny shook her head. 'No dear, not today. We came to tell you some wonderful news.' She accepted her cup and the steam rose about her face, flushing it prettily. It occurred to Lydia that she looked more ethereal than she had when they first met at Stapleford. 'We have a vote, Lydie! At least, the female house-owners have a vote! It is the thin end of the wedge, my dear! There will be women Members in the House during our lifetime!' She laughed at Lydia's expression. 'Oh Lydia, what an uninterested face! But if I tell you that with women able to vote – and eventually sit in the Council Chamber – we shall have more money for those children out there – ' she gestured towards the door. 'Perhaps then the news might waken a spark in those golden eyes of yours!'

Sir Anthony chuckled quietly and put his hand over Fanny's. 'Steady on, my darling. Not too much excitement.'

Fanny said, 'How can I help it? It's what I've worked for ever since I moved into my own home.' She smiled more calmly. 'However, Lydia, we learned of this decision at midday today and Miss Harper has already taken notes to all the dear ladies I have courted so assiduously this past year. We are to have a gathering at Avon View this evening to celebrate – '

'And to welcome Mr Peters back to Bristol as our new Radical nominee for Clifton Ward!' Sir Anthony added bluffly.

Lydia glanced at Wesley again, this time with incredulity at his overriding ambition. He said gently, 'It was put to me, when I began my venture here, that I must arm myself to fight the opposition, Lydie. But I found – as you have done – that when Miss Parmenter showed me the enormous amount of work that needed to be done I could not use my energy simply for my own ends. Clifton Village is a Tory stronghold – a solicitor called Charles Bennington has contested it for years without success and has now retired. Miss Parmenter suggested that with the help of her new voters, there might be a chance—'

'Mr Peters has given work and hope to a lot of people here, Lydia,' Fanny interrupted eagerly. But Wesley would have none of it.

'This is no political address.' He laughed up at Lydia, obviously expecting her to respond. She felt only shock; how could he – how could he behave as if everything were perfectly normal? She did not think she had seen him laugh before: his whole face was transformed. 'Lydia will have to listen to such false eulogies this evening – '

'False? Certainly not!' said Sir Anthony.

Lydia said faintly, 'I am afraid I cannot come.

Forgive me, Fanny. I am very happy for you, but . . .'

Fanny bit her lip. 'Never mind, dear. You were thoroughly put off by the meeting at the Victoria Rooms, I know that. There will be no such catcalls tonight but you have a great deal to do.'

'Thank you, Fanny.'

She could not wait for them to leave; she was completely out of tune with Fanny over political matters and had to admit it to herself now that it transpired Fanny had drawn Wesley Peters into her circle. She watched him cross the muddy bank to the carriage and help Fanny inside. Was she jealous? Was it as basic and simple as that? She went back into her warm parlour which seemed so empty now. There was his teacup. She picked it up and touched the rim with tentative fingers. Then she took the tea things outside, forcing herself to remember how he had used his own sister to beget an idiot child, causing her death and Alan's murder. She held onto the pump handle, cowering over it with a groan as she recalled Wesley's parting words just now – 'Lydia, I am very sorry about your mother. She was good and true.' How could he say such things after what he had done?

She was forcing herself to set work for tomorrow when there came a light tap at the door. Instantly she was alert and trembling, convinced it was Wesley. When she opened the door a crack and saw a female figure huddled there in the darkness, she felt a pang of what might have been disappointment.

'Who is it? Miss Harper?' She held the lantern up high and the light glinted on pale, anonymous eyes.

'It is I, Lydia. Anne Pascoe. Julius's wife, you know.'

The fussy, self-important voice was instantly recognizable. Lydia was surprised and very uneasy. She searched the darkness behind Anne and saw the outline of a trap on the road with someone at the horse's head.

'It's my driver. No-one else. Won't you ask me in?'

She sounded petulant. Lydia stood to one side and lighted her through to the parlour.

'Oh, you're busy. My dear, I've heard about you taking over this school from Miss Parmenter – we might have guessed at Stapleford that you were up to something. How you curried favour with Miss Parmenter!'

'Nothing was further from my thoughts then, Anne.' Lydia took Lizzie Turnbull's sewing from a chair and motioned her visitor into it. 'Miss Parmenter offered me the position after Mamma's death. Even then, my first duty was to my father. But when he announced his marriage plans, I felt free to take up a life of my own.'

'No need to be offended, Lydia!' A small tinkling laugh came from inside the bonnet. 'I was intending to compliment you. Miss Parmenter is odd in many ways, but as far as society goes—'

'Are you staying, Anne? May I take your bonnet?' Lydia said pointedly, standing over the chair.

Anne looked up and flushed. 'No, I am not staying where I am so obviously unwelcome. But I have come to do you a great favour, Lydia Fielding, and I think you had better sit down and listen to me. Then you will change your tune!'

Lydia sat down slowly with a sense of doom. She knew that Anne would not want her in the precious 'family' now that the infamy of Alan's murder hung around her name; so her favour must be something to do with Gus.

Anne folded her hands on her lap righteously. 'This visit is in no way disloyal, Lydia, though you may at first think so. I have the best interests of my husband at heart, I think I am more far-sighted than he is and though his present plans – no, they have not reached plans yet, more like thoughts – might seem to be advantageous to our position—'

Lydia interrupted impatiently. 'Anne, please. Say what you have to say, straight out. I shall not be offended.'

'I should hope not, indeed! There is certainly nothing for you to be offended over, Lydia. Certainly not!' Anne jerked her head like a ruffled hen and settled again. 'It is about this Captain Peters.'

'Captain Peters?' Lydia wondered if she had heard correctly.

'That is what they call him at the Docks.

Wesley Peters, my dear. Your poor brother's . . .
er . . .'

'Yes. Very well. Wesley Peters.' Lydia's hands
tightened together.

'You must realize he is using Miss Parmenter's
kindness to rise above his station.'

'Just as you say I am.'

'Not at all, Lydia. We all know you have no
social ambitions. Why, you have never been out
since you arrived in Bristol and it cannot be
from lack of invitation.' Anne smiled forgivingly.
'No. Captain Peters is very ambitious. Very
ambitious indeed. You know he is a manager of
this school – all legally drawn up, of course.
What you probably do not know is that he is to
be nominated as a candidate for the Council
Chamber itself! Of course, he does not stand a
chance. Not a chance, my dear. I have pointed
this out to Julius, but it seems there is some
spleen between the Peters man and Gus. And
Gus is with us at the moment.' Her eyes avoided
Lydia's. 'He would have called on you, Lydia, but
he is unwell.'

Lydia knew a momentary sense of relief, then
her feeling of danger increased. 'What of the –
the plans – for Wesley Peters?'

'Yes. Well . . .' Anne looked at her twined
fingers and flushed again. 'There will be considerable excitement at the announcement of
his adoption. Excitement. And near-riots.' She
glanced up. 'There are always riots when anything unusual happens in the city, Lydia. The
constables disappear and there are a few sore

heads the next morning.' She looked down again. 'Occasionally, when there is ill-feeling, someone goes into the river.'

'That cools them off, I dare say,' Lydia remarked, frowning.

'They are doubtless dead when they go in. They certainly are when they are fished out.' Anne stood up abruptly. 'Well, I had best be off. I am on my way home from visiting an aunt of mine and I do not wish Julius to know I called on you. Naturally.' She smiled brightly and went quickly into the hall. 'Gus is suffering from toothache and his face is swollen out of all recognition. How vain men are!' She paused and leaned confidentially towards Lydia. 'If they had to put up with swollen stomachs like we do year after year, they could not afford such niceties!' She gave her tinkling laugh and Lydia wondered whether she meant something particular by that last remark. But Anne was not so subtle. 'You have guessed, my dear. Next May.' She took three steps outside and paused again. Her voice rose a tone until it was a whine. 'Probably Gus's face-ache is causing him to be more than usually vengeful. I hope you understand, Lydia, that he means it . . . he means it most seriously. Well. Don't say that I have not tried. I have done my best. No-one can do more.' She went on into the darkness and Lydia watched the trap dip as she clambered into it. Then it rolled jerkily away and Lydia, still frowning, went back to the fire.

Had Anne really been trying to warn her that

Gus and Julius intended to take Wesley's life? It certainly sounded like it. Yet here in Bristol, where since that first awful day Lydia had met with nothing but kindness, such melodrama seemed impossible. According to Fanny, Wesley was a popular figure . . . with the Methodists.

Lydia's frown deepened and she bent down to sweep the hearth. Wesley would not be popular with any of the merchants whose trade he threatened. And though any 'riots' would have to be made by the working class, she had seen just how easily they could be swayed when they had rounded on Fanny at the Victoria Rooms.

Lydia stood up impatiently and began to tidy away her work, determined to give Wesley Peters not one more thought that night. For a whole year now she had banished him from her mind and now it seemed she had to learn the trick anew.

She was lighting her bedroom candle when a tap came on the window. It was the gentle touch of small fingers which Alfred had developed as a special signal and Lydia flew to the door expecting to see him covered in slime once more and perhaps pursued by his awful father. But Alfred stood there, alone and fairly clean, if completely out of breath. He darted beneath her arm and closed the door quickly on the lamplight, then moved to the parlour curtains. He peered out and groaned anxiously.

'What on earth has happened, Alfred? Is it your father?' Lydia set the lamp on the table and blew out her candle. It was proving an eventful evening.

'Nah, miss.' Alfred turned and held his side, painfully. ''Tis Cap'n Peters. 'Im what was 'ere this afternoon – *you* know.'

'I know, Alfred. And he wouldn't hurt you, so compose yourself.'

'But there's them what 'ud 'urt *'im*, miss!' Alfred took a last gasping breath and spoke more clearly. 'I keeps an eye on 'im, see, when 'e's at 'ome. 'E bin good to me, miss. Almost as good as you bin. So I were waitin' outside Miss Parm'ter's place up Sion to get 'im a cab, see. Out 'e comes and asts what I'm a-doin, an' I tells 'im. 'E ses 'e wun't need no cab, cos 'e's gonna walk down any minute now and 'ave a few words wiv you afore you goes to bed! So I thinks I'll come and tell you and 'ave a drink o' tea with you both. An' 'alfway down Jacob's Wells, there's these blokes. One big 'un is the boss like. Shoulders like a bull 'e got and a 'normous face. I 'eard 'im tellin' the others to fan out and ketch Mr Peters when 'e d'come along in 'is cab. Only 'e en't coming in no cab. So I runs on lookin' for a constable 'an' there en't onc. So 'ere I am.'

Lydia felt her own face stretch as wide as his. She swallowed. 'This big man. Did you hear a name?'

'Ah. Can't remember though, miss.'

'Would it be Pascoe? Mr Pascoe? Did the others call him that?'

'That's it, miss. D'you know 'im?'

'Yes. And so does Mr Peters. We must find a

constable, Alfred.' Lydia reached behind the door for her cloak and picked up the lantern. 'Come on. You've done very well. Thank you, Alfred.'

No longer did she question her motives. Once outside, with the tiny schoolhouse locked and in darkness, she took Alfred's hand and held the lantern high and they picked their way carefully over the muddy grass to the road. The winter so far had been mild and wet and the road was almost as bad as the riverbank; Lydia guessed with a sinking heart that even if the Pascoe men had not bribed the constable to avoid this road, it was unlikely it would be patrolled. She and Alfred half ran, half walked almost to the Cathedral without seeing anyone save a solitary drunkard stumbling from the densely packed hostelries of King Street. It was too early for many of those, too late for more respectable folk to be going to the theatre or to dinner.

Lydia turned and pulled Alfred back the way they had come. 'We must go up Jacob's Hill,' she whispered, breathing quickly. 'Perhaps we can slip past—'

'They be all across the road, miss!' Alfred panted back.

'Then I will talk to Mr Pascoe. There is no other way. He will listen to me.'

She got no further. From the steep road leading up to Clifton Village and the broad expanses of the Downs there came a sudden roar of triumph, then a cacophony of laughter, then an all-too-familiar voice yelling, 'Into the river with him, lads! Best medicine for a swelled head!' She heard a rush of feet – steel-capped boots on the cobbles, the clatter of pattens. A gaggle of dark forms burst forth from the mouth of the narrow road and spread across the breadth of the riverbank. It was impossible to distinguish one from another, but above them all, tossed like a boat on a steep sea, was a separate silhouette. As the strange mass approached Lydia and Alfred – now transfixed in the middle of the road – Lydia caught an occasional glimpse of lightness from that helpless puppet. It was Wesley Peters. He was so limp and boneless he could already be dead. Her heart contracted as she lifted the lantern high and let out a cry that topped the roar of the rabble.

'Stop!' The single word pierced the blackness almost physically and the other noise died; the impetus of the men was checked. Wesley came to rest on three pairs of hands. Lydia approached them. 'How dare you behave like this? We have called the constables and they are on their way. Now put that man down and go home! Do you hear me? Go *home*!'

The six hands obeyed her and Wesley's inert form disappeared into the midst of the crowd. Lydia could see now that there were about a dozen men; she could deal with them as she dealt with the children in school. There was one . . . somewhere . . . with whom she could not deal.

He did not detach himself from the others, but his hateful laugh told her where he was.

'Lydia? By God. Two birds with one stone. What luck. It's all right, lads. She is one of mine.'

A few doubtful laughs echoed his. Lydia was beginning to be known in Hotwells as Fanny Parmenter's successor and was treated with respect.

She said coldly, for their benefit and to cover her own creeping fear: 'You choose to joke, Gus. There has been enough joking. Send these men away before they get into trouble.'

His voice was still amused, but deliberately so; the anger showed beneath. 'So . . . we are back to that, Lydia. The game ended . . . and ended well, did it not? Now the joke is to end. You know what that means, Lydie.'

She felt sick. Alfred's hand was pulling at hers; pulling her towards the river. She resisted it because she had to.

She said, 'Send them away, Gus.'

He detached himself from the others at last. He was in his caped greatcoat. Above the high collar she could see his swollen jaw.

'Very well, Lydie. If that is what you want.' He looked deeply at her, his black eyes hating her yet wanting her. Then he turned to the shifting, muttering group and spread his arms.

'All right, men. You can drop our precious would-be councillor in the mud where he came from.' The muttering rose to a crescendo and almost drowned his voice. He was going to have difficulty in persuading them to give up their night's sport. The smell of cheap whisky hovered over them like a cloud.

'Now listen, men!' Gus's spread arms herded them back on themselves and made a space between Lydia and himself. She straightened and breathed deeply. At her side Alfred tugged again and they retreated three paces more.

'Just drop him where he is!' Gus shouted impatiently. 'He won't forget tonight, don't worry, and there's more whisky where that came from—'

'We en't got 'im, guv!'

The single cry came, just as a lithe form snaked at an angle from across the road, snatched Lydia's lantern and hurled it with force at Gus's turning, questing face. Then Lydia, pulled by both hands, was sliding and slipping down the riverbank and uproar had broken loose again behind her. Flames from the smashed lamp leapt crazily for a few seconds before being stamped into a darkness inkier than before.

Lydia gasped, 'Wesley! Are you all right? The schoolhouse – back to the schoolhouse!'

Wesley slithered to a halt, holding Alfred and Lydia back. 'We're almost in the river – can't go to the schoolhouse, Lydie, it will be the first place they look! Can you swim, Alfred?'

'No, I can't, Cap'n. An' them as can 'as drowned in there!'

'Come on then. Keep to the water's edge. There might be a boat—'

Gus's voice shouted behind them. 'Spread out, lads! They can't get away! Get the girl and you've got the man! Down to the river both ends – cut them off!'

Wesley swore quietly into the darkness. His arm around Lydia was like iron; he had not been hurt. He whispered, 'Listen, both of you. It's Pascoe. I've got to tackle Pascoe. The others will melt away then. Will you stay here while I go after him?'

Lydia grabbed at his shirt. 'No, Wesley! Please! You don't understand – his anger is like a madness – '

''E 'ad a crowbar, Cap'n,' Alfred whispered. 'An' anyway, 'e en't goin' to be far away from 'is men in case they scarpers.' The voice became smaller still. 'If it don't matter too much about that promise, miss, I could take you through the sewers. 'Tis quite safe – I knows the way all right. An' even if they tries to follow they'll only get lost.'

A surge of hope made Lydia gasp. 'But it's dark, Alfred. You'll never do it in the darkness.'

She felt him shrug. 'It's never light down there, miss. But you'll get your cloes muddied.'

Wesley whispered, 'Is it safe, Lydie? Could you bear it?'

Far to their left came the sound of splintering glass.

'The schoolhouse.' Lydia felt deep anger as she thought of her small home being despoiled. 'Of course I can bear it. We must get away somehow and bring these men to justice!'

Alfred needed no more encouragement. He took the lead, drawing his two companions along the waterline and then leaving them, to quest up the bank on all fours sniffing like a small animal. Shouts ahead of them were drawing closer all the time and Lydia held fiercely to Wesley's shirt while he kept his arm around her waist. Both of them knew that as a last resort they would take to the water, holding Alfred between them.

Then he was with them again.

'I got one,' he breathed triumphantly. 'There's a grid thing over it but it's only held by wire.' He scrabbled back up the bank again. This time they followed him closely and came to the grating framed in lead and set into the muddy grass itself. Wesley released Lydia and let Alfred guide his hands between the bars of the grating to a twist of wire behind. He bent low and began to work. Shouts and cries were all around them now and it was obvious their pursuers were closing the net. Alfred fidgeted on his haunches and Lydia stood up and put her arms protectively and hopelessly over the two down-turned heads.

Then there was a faint squeak. Wesley stood up, pulled at the grating and it came away with a hideous grinding sound. He pushed it away from them and it fell into the mud with a squelch that was loud in the sudden silence. The next instant Alfred had slipped into the opening like a fish. Wesley followed him and reached back to help Lydia inside. If she had had last-minute doubts, they were scattered by the renewed yells around them and Gus's voice from the road shouting, 'They've gone into a drain! We've got 'em, lads! Rats in a trap!'

As she crawled after Wesley, her hand, already

slimy, clutching his desperately, she wondered whether Gus was right. The air around them was fetid and heavy, the curved walls constantly pressing, first on a shoulder then a hip, and beneath their knees a turgid sludge made progress difficult. Almost immediately, a voice boomed in their ears: ''Ere it is, boys! They can't get fur . . . anyone got a light?' It sounded so near that Lydia expected a hand to grasp her ankle and indeed she did begin to slide back towards the drain opening until she was suspended from Wesley's hand as if they were on a cliff face. The voices were incomprehensible now, shouting and echoing everywhere. She could even hear the rattle of a tinderbox and waited with closed eyes for light to reveal her.

Then there was a jerk on her hand and she was conscious that Wesley had climbed onto something solid; his grip was strong and steady. Then another hand clamped her wrist and she too was being drawn upward and away from the voices. Wesley's face, white and ghost-like, came towards her in the darkness and his voice whispered, 'Give Alfred your other hand, my love.' She reached up and Alfred was there and Wesley's arm was on her waist again and she was drawn free of the mud and was on a ledge with the other two. Alfred's mouth found her ear. 'We're in the main sewer now, miss, and there's like a cat-walk for the blokes to do repairs. We'll be all right now. Keep a 'old o' me collar. Take no account of any scurryings, 'tis only the rats. Walk nice and slow.'

She obeyed him implicitly and behind her Wesley walked just as circumspectly. The darkness was absolute unless they were directly beneath a storm drain when a paler patch would appear above them and they could breathe the fresher air. A strong brown river materialized below them at these moments, frothy-topped, bearing flotsam of every description. Squeaks could be heard too once the sounds of pursuit had died down. After the first ten minutes of careful pacing, one foot directly in front of the other, Wesley said calmly, 'Alfred, what is to stop them following us?'

Alfred said simply, 'They don't know the way, sir. Every second right and third left. You got to know it, else you could wander around 'ere for the rest of y'r natural.' There was a conviction in his voice and Lydia shuddered. The pressure on her waist increased reassuringly.

It took them half an hour; a gruesome, nightmarish experience, but uneventful. Alfred halted suddenly and led Lydia to an iron ladder in the wall. Then he went up and obviously struggled for some time with a heavy cover. She heard a metallic scrape and the next instant a circle of night sky appeared above them.

'Come on, miss! All clear!' Alfred whispered down.

Lydia put one foot on a rung and prepared to ascend. Wesley lifted her clear and turned her to face him.

'Lydie . . . thank you,' he said quietly. 'I wanted to talk to you this evening. My coming

339

this afternoon was too sudden and I could see woke unhappy memories for you. I wanted to know how you felt, whether you had changed. Now I know. There is no need for talk.'

She could just see his face glimmering in the grey light from above. He was safe. It was all that mattered, after all; he was still unattainable. But he was safe. She began to shake and a small sob came with her next breath.

He said, 'Ah, Lydie . . . Lydie . . . Don't cry. So much has happened and our love is the same. We knew it . . . did we not? At your birthday party, we knew it. Nothing shall separate us now, dearest.' He bent his head and kissed her. The tenderness of that kiss was like nothing she had imagined. She had wanted him to kiss her before now, had imagined it often: it had been a demanding kiss asking the same things Gus asked; above all, wanting her. She had imagined her surrender. A surrender without humiliation, but a surrender.

Perhaps there was a faint promise of desire in Wesley's kiss. But far stronger was the tenderness. It asked for no surrender, it stated no supremacy. To turn away from it entailed an act of will as hard as turning away from home on a freezing night.

But there was nothing else for it. She put her muddy hand to his chin, holding his face steady while she looked into it with grief. Then she whispered, 'Oh Wesley. My dear. Everything separates us. You must know that.' He stared down at her as if he would argue, but finally

340

shook his head. 'You are wrong, Lydie. But we will talk later. Can you climb up, my dearest?'

In reply she turned and went up the ladder.

Nothing else that night seemed important. They walked together in their filthy clothes to Avon View, Miss Parmenter's house on Sion Hill. There, Sir Anthony's footman went immediately for the constables and Tweenie prepared baths while Miss Harper laid out food in the dining room. The bustle was reassuring but bewildering. When Fanny led Lydia into the guest room and turned down the familiar bed, she was as confused as she had been the first time she lay there.

'Everything is being taken care of,' murmured Fanny. 'Anthony will see to all the unpleasantness, you can be sure of that.'

Lydia managed to smile her thanks. She wanted to sleep. She wanted – oh, how she wanted – to dream.

Twelve

Lydia woke the next morning to a shaft of watery sunshine across her face. She knew it must be late but she did not move. The children would be arriving at school, finding the broken glass. Still she did not move. The sunshine, its colour, quality, coldness, made her feel very nostalgic and she lay and savoured it, letting it carry her back to particular moods if not definite memories.

There was a tap at the door and Alice Harper crept in. She smiled when she saw Lydia's open eyes.

'Miss Parmenter and Sir Anthony have gone down to school, Miss Fielding. I wasn't supposed to disturb you but a gentleman has called and I thought . . .' She held the brass bed knob, pressing her lips together. 'It's *his* brother, Miss Fielding. Mr Julius Pascoe. His wife calls occasionally and leaves cards but he's never been since I came here. Shall I tell him to go?'

For a moment Lydia had thought it might be

Wesley and in spite of everything, her heart had leapt. Now it steadied.

'Is he asking for Miss Parmenter? Or me?'

'You. I think he must have known there was no-one else here. Perhaps he went to the school-house first. He seemed quite certain you would see him.'

'Yes, I'd better. I'll be fifteen minutes, Alice.'

She dressed slowly, still conscious of the sun-shine, though she was rehearsing phrases for Julius in case he had come to beg for Gus. She drew the curtains and stood looking out at Mr Brunel's bridge hung across the gorge almost casually and glistening in the sun. It was November the first. She smiled as she tucked a handkerchief into her waist and turned for the door. November the first and the world was becoming real again.

Julius's hat, cane and gloves lay on a bamboo table before the window and he stood before the fire, his coat tails held up prudently. His smile was not conciliatory and he did not move. Pointedly, Lydia stood by the door.

'I have not breakfasted, Julius. But I do not expect you will detain me long?'

'Far from it, Lydia. This interview is as dis-tasteful to me as it must be to you. I am your first caller?'

'Obviously,' she said coldly.

'Good. I dare say Mr Wesley Peters will be here shortly so that you can both work out a story that will blacken my brother's name.'

Lydia stared at him. 'Do I hear you correctly,

343

Julius? When you were announced I naturally thought you had come to beg for mercy on your brother's behalf. Surely there is no doubt in *your* mind that he is a blackguard?'

Julius went slowly to the small table and picked up his hat and gloves. He flipped his gloves inside the brim. 'Lydia . . . listen very carefully.' He spoke slowly with a deliberation that was near to menace. 'Augustus has been staying with me. Yes. He wished to visit a dentist in Bristol. He went back to Mapperly yesterday afternoon – ' He paused while Lydia made a sound of disgust, then went on smoothly: 'The cab driver who took him to the Joint Railway Station will remember him. He bought a ticket for Taunton.'

Lydia turned from him impatiently. 'Really, Julius, this is absurd! Mr Peters recognized Gus just as I did. The schoolboy with us heard his name spoken by some of his . . . creatures.'

Julius picked up his cane and tapped it consideringly on the table top; a small piece of bamboo cane fell to the carpet.

'I don't think you understand, Lydia. If you persist in this story, Gus will have to use the obvious defence. You will force him to use it.'

Lydia stood very still. After a while Julius hit the table a resounding smack and it leaned gently towards the velvet curtains.

'I can see I must explain,' he said icily. 'He hoped to marry you, Lydia, and then you left home rather suddenly. Everyone knows that, even your own father. He hears you are in

344

Bristol seeing his old rival, Wesley Peters. He plans to teach Peters a lesson, a harmless ducking in the Avon. To cool his ardour.'

Lydia said, 'You are breaking Miss Parmenter's table. And someone is ringing the doorbell.'

'Possibly Mr Peters.' Julius turned and gripped her wrist very hard. 'Gus tells me you will do exactly what he says, Lydia. If so, you will tell Mr Captain Peters that you do not intend to lodge a complaint against Gus and you will make sure that your schoolboy understands he misheard the Pascoe name. If Gus's influence with you is not so strong as he believes, then let me assure you that if you drag us into any magistrate's court, I will personally ruin you and drag Miss Parmenter with you!'

The door opened and Wesley came in, Alice Harper fluttering behind him. Wesley looked none the worse for last night's struggle, but his face was tightly controlled as he stared at Julius.

'Are you all right, Lydia?' He did not look at her but his hand reached for hers. She pretended not to see it and went to the fire.

'Very well, thank you. Mr Pascoe was just leaving.'

Julius said smoothly, 'I came because I thought there must be some misunderstanding between my brother and Miss Fielding. He had to leave Bristol yesterday afternoon without calling to pay his respects and—'

'What is this, Lydia?' Wesley asked sharply.

Lydia stared into the fire. 'It is true. Gus left Bristol yesterday afternoon.'

'Have you been threatening Miss Fielding?' Wesley started towards Julius, who put up his cane and held him back. Alice Harper said in a trembling voice, 'I'll send Tweenie for—'

Julius cut in smoothly, 'I must leave you to your – er – discussion. Goodbye, Lydia.' He tucked his cane into his elbow and passed Wesley without a look. 'Anne will call on you soon. I believe she wishes to make a donation to the school. For any repairs that might be necessary.'

Wesley said, 'We do not take bribes, Pascoe. I do not doubt your loutish brother will be fined appropriately.'

Julius ignored this too. 'Go on, girl,' he said irritably to Alice. 'Open the door for me.'

Alice drew herself up and looked at him with contempt.

'My name is Harper, Mr Pascoe. Alice Harper,' she said.

At last Julius was out of countenance. He paused for a moment longer then strode down the passage to the door and opened it himself.

Alice's voice was shaking again. 'I'll bring coffee, shall I, Miss Fielding? And toast?'

'Just coffee, Alice. That would be most welcome.' Lydia forced herself to turn and show her set face to Wesley. 'And thank you, Alice. I wish . . . thank you very much.' She had been going to say she wished she had Alice's courage before she realized that Wesley knew nothing of Alice's past. Nor hers . . . for the moment.

As soon as the door closed, Wesley came to

her and would have put his arms around her if she had not backed away.

'Lydia, what is it? Let me help you – at least let me help you! You feel powerless against the power of that – that rotten family! I can give you strength.'

She looked at him with a kind of wonder.

'You do not understand, Wesley. I am sorry. So sorry. In spite of Marella we might have been friends. But there are other things that you know nothing of.' She sat down abruptly in a buttoned chair near the fire. The high brass fender supported long fire dogs. She picked up a brush and examined the beautifully wrought handle. 'Gus Pascoe now owns Milton Mains. In effect he owns my father.'

Wesley's boots moved into her line of vision and she thought he might be going to touch her again. He sat down opposite her. Slowly. She could feel him preparing himself to talk to her for a long time.

He said quietly, 'Darling. Darling Lydia. I love you. When will you marry me?'

She almost jumped with the unexpectedness of it. It was like a sly knife slipping between her ribs and into her heart. Her head jerked back and she looked at him with angry eyes.

'How can you ask me that? How *can* you?'

His own intensely blue eyes were still. 'For the reason I gave. Because I love you. And I believe you love me.'

'And if both those statements were true, would not Marella always come between us?'

347

He said, 'Marella and Alan are dead, my love. We must let them go now. They are, after all, together.'

She controlled herself somehow but her knuckles were blue on her lap. She said clearly, 'Memory is one thing, reality another. Is that it? But *you* caused your sister's death, Wesley! *You* gave her that child!'

For a split second he was still, then his hand shot across and picked up both of hers. He came to his knees before her.

'So . . .' The breath came from him on a long note. His mouth was shaking. 'So, Lydie. That is what you have believed of me all this time.' He put her clenched hands to his mouth and stifled a sob. 'I should hate you for it . . . but I could never hate you. You know me, Lydie . . . you must know that I could never lie with my sister! If the whole world told me that you and Alan . . . I would never believe them.'

She said through stiff lips, 'It must be true. It must be.'

'It is not true, Lydia. When I returned from America my father told me I must not let Marella out of my sight. I did my best . . . and you believed—'

'*She* named you! Marella herself said that you were the father of her child! Why do you think Alan left her that night? He loved her! He loved her in spite of that! Oh God – oh God – it *has* to be true!' She was sobbing loudly.

'My darling . . . my Lydie . . .' He tried to enfold her in her arms but her own limbs were still, bracing him away. 'If you cannot believe me even now, I will find out. My mother will know, Lydie. I will see her and—'

'No!' She shoved her chair back with all her strength and struggled past his kneeling figure just as Alice knocked with the coffee. Alice took in the scene, misinterpreted it, and left hastily. Lydia stared at the silver tray. Alice did not know; only Fanny knew. And Prudence. Prudence with her clothes chest and its secret hoard.

She forced herself to sound calm. 'Leave it. Please leave it. It doesn't matter now. They are dead. The child is dead.'

Again Wesley sat slowly on his chair and settled himself.

He said, 'I see Alice has brought in two cups. Will you pour, Lydie?'

She said, 'I must go down to the school. Fanny is there alone.'

'Fanny is quite used to teaching. And she has Anthony Warren with her. She knows that I will call, I told her so last night. Therefore she wishes us to talk together in private. I think perhaps you are under some slight misapprehension about Fanny Parmenter. If you will pour the coffee I will explain how I met her and won her friendship.'

'There is no need.'

'Pour the coffee, Lydie. Then sit down and drink it. You had a time of it last night and need to rest today.' He watched while she did his bidding. Her hand shook so hard that the coffee spilled onto the tray. He averted his gaze and stared into the fire.

'I met Charles Bennington first,' he said in his quiet country voice. 'It seemed important to me that my father should not be publicly hanged for killing your brother. I thought it would be another barrier between our families and there were enough of those already. Bennington told me that a political ambition could be useful to me in business affairs.' He took his coffee and looked up at her suddenly. 'Lydie – we have formed our co-operative – and it is working! All last summer, when you first came to Bristol, I was riding around the small farms on the Moor collecting wool. I could not pay for it – there is no return until the wool masters pay. But last month I had all the money from them – every last penny! I spent all of October back on the Moor giving those good trusting farmers their wool money – five times what they would have got from the Pascoes!' His face was alight with enthusiasm. 'And Lydie, further up the country in Gloucestershire, they have their own mills. Small, of course. Run by water. We could do that – there are enough streams coming off the Moor to run a hundred mills!'

He paused and she said, 'I am glad. Oh, I am glad. It was what you dreamed of when we talked, was it not?'

He nodded, his eyes hopefully on hers. She bit her lip and turned to pick up her coffee and sit down. She stared at the hearth brush.

He sighed and went on in his careful voice,

'Bennington showed me that politics had been good for his business – he is a lawyer. He showed me in concrete ways. The jury at my father's trial were hand-picked, over half of them Methodists.' He waited, perhaps for condemnation, but she said nothing. 'He introduced me to Miss Parmenter and told us both that we could be mutually helpful.' He made a sound like a laugh. 'Fanny has told you of this, naturally. Her political fervour is so different from Bennington's. It burns her up. Literally.' At last Lydia raised her eyes with a question and he said, 'She has not told you? And you had not guessed? I thought as your mother had it you might have known. Fanny has consumptive lungs, Lydie. That is why she is in such a hurry. That is why Sir Anthony pesters her to marry him so that he can take her right away from Bristol and her work and everything. Fanny is torn in half. She loves her Anthony, devotedly. But her precious work . . . she grabbed at me almost physically. My ideas were hers and I was not so self-centred as Bennington – or so she tells me.' He mistook her appalled gaze. 'She was impressed by the co-operative, Lydie. That is all.'

She breathed, 'Fanny . . . I had no idea. Oh, my poor Fanny! That is why—'

'That is why she wanted you for her school. Yes. That is why she hopes we will marry and take on everything else.'

She gazed at him, stricken.

He leaned forward urgently. 'If it will persuade

you, Lydie, then let it! I would leave Bristol and never consider a political future again if you made it a condition of our marriage. But if you still hesitate because of Marella and Alan, then marry me for Fanny's sake!'

She groaned aloud. 'I cannot! Oh Fanny . . . I cannot!'

He was silent, elbows on knees, face close to hers. Then he said slowly, 'Then the other way. If we go far from here – America – anywhere – will you marry me then?'

She held his searching stare for a moment longer, then dropped her head into her hands. 'Why did you leave me there, Wesley? Afterwards, when I was ill, why did you never come to see me?'

'You had a fever, my love. I would have come the moment it worsened – I asked my mother to let me know. Luke would have come after me.'

'When my mother died and I was alone—'

'My own mother came to you. She told me she stayed with you and watched over you.'

'She prayed by the coffin for a long time. Then she spoke to me in the kitchen. She said I looked older. She told me she was waiting for her husband . . . I thought her mad.' She looked up and met his frowning face for a brief instant, then gestured wearily, 'It does not matter. None of it matters, Wesley. You must have known . . . you saw me that day at Michaelmas. I belong to Gus Pascoe. Like his horses and sheep, I am his property.'

His exclamation was angrily dismissive. 'He

tried to rape you! Face up to it, Lydia. Have you
been cowering and whimpering all this time
because of that? We should have had it out in
the open—'

'I enjoyed it, Wesley!'

The silence was shocking. Lydia felt as if
she had ripped something from her own inside,
physically. She stood up and, still bent with the
pain of it, went to the window.

'I thought you had seen that too.' She watched
some children bowling a hoop down the slope of
Sion Hill. 'Oh, I fought at first. But then . . .
then, I stopped fighting.'

His voice said behind her, 'You were ex-
hausted, my darling. Stop torturing yourself.'

She said coldly, 'You do not understand still,
do you?' The children disappeared around the
bend and she turned and faced him. 'When I
came here – to Fanny's house – I was carrying
Gus's child. Alice Harper found me in Queen's
Square. She was another of Gus's . . . objects
also. You did not know that either? No, I
thought not. I lost the baby and took the job.
But if Gus should ever want me again, he knows
what to do.'

Her brutal words acted like whiplashes on
Wesley and red weals appeared on his pale face.
He put out his hands as if to ward off blows, and
stammered, 'I do not believe . . . it was not like
that.'

She looked at him. Could he not imagine the
terrible loneliness, the sensation of an inevitable
fate? She certainly could not explain them.

He said, 'Lydie . . . Lydie, I love you. And I know that you love me. Does not that mean a thing?'

She felt a faint surprise at his obtuseness. 'What has that to do with it? Alan loved Marella and she loved him, but they were destroyed by something . . . other. Fanny and her Sir Anthony are in love, but the lung death will destroy that. I always thought my parents . . . but my father took Betty Sperring before my mother was dead.'

He looked at her and she saw that his blue eyes were full of tears. She turned away at that and stared again through the window. After a while she heard the door close behind him.

She whispered to the leafless trees still bathed in sunshine, 'If this is being alive again, then let me die, please let me die.'

She did not die. At four o'clock that afternoon Fanny returned in Sir Anthony's coach with messages for Lydia from the children and a humorous account of their clearing-up operations in the schoolhouse.

'The eldest Turnbull girl was the superintendent and I assure you, my dear Lydia, that every solitary piece of furniture has been beeswaxed, every ornament and glass polished, each cup and saucer lovingly washed and dried!' She collapsed in a chair by the fire as Alice brought in tea and crumpets. 'Alice, my dear, how delightful! How is little Edward?'

Alice talked about her baby while she poured

tea but she did not mention Julius Pascoe's visit.

Fanny took up her tale again. 'You will never guess who re-glazed your broken window! None other than Bully Tassell himself! Yes, Alfred fetched him at midday and he had finished by two. I think he is trying to get into your favour, Lydia!' She became serious. 'I am trying to reassure you that your little home is snug and safe again, my dear, and Anthony has been talking to the Chief Constable, who will arrange a special patrol of the Hotwells road. You need not be frightened. But if you are, then you must stay here and go down by cab each morning.'

'Fanny, I am not a bit frightened. Those ruffians were not interested in me. They would not have been interested in Mr Peters if he was not a candidate for the Council! It is as I have felt for a long time – politics are dangerous!' She looked to Sir Anthony for support but he laughed.

'When Fanny marries me she will be trying to convert all my Tory friends to social reform, Miss Fielding! She will have more people after her blood than ever before.' He too became serious. 'Yet I want her to marry me more than anything in the world.'

Fanny waved a teasing hand at him and said something about the election. Lydia watched their fond banter with new eyes. She was glad to be able to help Alice with the tea things. As they went downstairs to the basement kitchen, Alice said, 'No need to mention about the visit from Mr Pascoe, is there, Miss Fielding? Miss

355

Parmenter might become over-anxious about me and I would not want that.'

Lydia said, 'That is thoughtful of you.'

Alice took the tray from her and put it on a scrubbed wooden table. 'Miss Parmenter has been an angel to me. Ever since that time in Stapleford. There is nothing I would not do for her. Nothing at all.'

Lydia looked around the neat kitchen and wished with all her heart she could echo those sentiments.

She said instead, 'May I see Edward? I never have.'

Alice Harper smiled and held open a door. Lydia went through into a small warm sitting room lit by a single candle on the mantel. Alice tiptoed to a crib in the corner and leaned over it to pull down a coverlet. Lydia peered through the twilight and saw a chubby round face, black lashes on rosy cheeks, black curls.

She hardly knew what to say. The baby was so like Gus.

Alice whispered, 'He's beautiful, is he not? Just like my father when he was younger.'

Lydia looked sideways. Alice's nice, ordinary face was flushed to prettiness as she gazed down at her son and Lydia suddenly saw her as Gus must have done. Lydia said in a low voice, 'Yes. Yes, he is a beautiful baby.'

Alice covered him again and straightened.

'And he is mine.' She turned and went back to the kitchen, closing the door quietly. 'He is nothing to do with the Pascoes. But when he grows up I shall tell him. And he will hate them.'

Lydia said, 'As you do.'

Alice shivered. 'Yes. Yes, as I do.'

Slowly Lydia went back upstairs. It was how she hated Gus: obsessively, almost possessively. She knew it was wrong, yet could do nothing about it.

As she went into the parlour Sir Anthony turned to her bluffly and said, 'I expect you heard some names, did you not, Miss Fielding? There must have been a ringleader last night. And the Chief Constable will be only too pleased to bring him to justice.'

She said carefully, 'No, there was no one in charge of the rabble, Sir Anthony. They were drunken louts on the lookout for a scapegoat.'

Fanny looked at her searchingly. 'Are you sure, Lydia? You were so determined last night that someone should be brought to justice.'

Lydia smiled. 'I am sure, Fanny dear.' She remained standing by the door. 'I think I will collect my things now and return to the school-house.'

Fanny was up in arms. 'You will do no such thing! My goodness, there is no fire lit – nothing!'

'Then I shall light it.' Lydia was adamant. She felt her only hope of survival was to return to the life she was building at the school where there had been no thought of the past and no time to consider the future.

Sir Anthony supported her decision. 'Back on the horse after a fall. Is that it, Miss Fielding?

Perhaps you could spare Tweenie to look after Miss Fielding for a day or two, Fanny my dear?'

Fanny smiled thankfully. 'That is a splendid idea.' She got up and left the room to 'arrange things'. Sir Anthony held up a hand to the departing Lydia.

'Miss Fielding – just a word in private before you leave.' He stood up and went to the mantel-shelf. 'I was at Garrett Place last week taking my leave of Sir Henry. Lady Maud was enquiring after your work and your position here and you may be sure I gave a good report.' He picked up a small enamelled box and turned to Lydia, smiling. 'She informed me casually that the cameo given to you by Miss Caroline and Miss Judith was one of a pair and she would like you to have its partner.'

Lydia took the box and opened it. She said huskily, 'Lady Maud is too kind.'

Sir Anthony nodded. 'It is her way of main-taining the connection between you.'

'Yes. I understand.' Lydia felt long-delayed tears rise in her throat. Lady Maud could not possibly write to someone who had been little more than a temporary nursemaid in her house-hold, but with Sir Anthony Warren as a highly respectable messenger, she could send a valuable and significant gift. 'I am so grateful to know I still have . . . good . . . connections . . . with the Moor. Thank you.'

'You have many others, Miss Fielding. Your father—'

She closed the box with a snap. 'Yes, I have

358

many others. But they are all tarnished, Sir Anthony.' She looked up at him. 'I . . . I know about Fanny's illness. Mr Peters told me this morning. I am deeply sorry.'

'Ah.' He retreated to the fire and stared into it. 'Yes. Quite.' He glanced sideways quickly. 'I wonder . . . wonder whether you also know of Fanny's hopes. For you.'

Lydia gripped the small box in her hand. 'I intend . . . I will do my best to run the school as she wishes, Sir Anthony. As for politics . . .'

'I understand.' Sir Anthony was obviously embarrassed. He cleared his throat. 'She – we – will be grateful if you can keep the school going. As for politics, I think we can all rest from those for a while once this wretched election is over.' His smile was suddenly turned on her. 'Let this be a secret between us for the moment, Miss Fielding, but I saw Sir Henry Garrett last week in order to resign my seat in the House. As you know, he is my patron.'

'You have resigned?' Lydia was apprehensive. 'But Fanny – she had hopes of converting your friends. You said so yourself.'

'I hope she will still do so. But outside the rough and tumble of the party.' He spread his hands to the fire, still smiling. 'You see, Miss Fielding, I intend to nurse Fanny back to health. It can be done, you know. There are places on the Continent. But it means no outside commitments, no anxieties of any kind. She has arranged things here so that she can leave it all – after the election, of course – and I have arranged things so that we can leave England for two or three years.' He saw Lydia's expression and said reassuringly, 'Miss Fielding, Fanny could not have countenanced my kind of politics. Did you not see from the first time we met that I was completely bound by Sir Henry's wishes? Exmoor belongs to the Garretts. Whatever change is effected there, must be done by someone from within. Your Mr Peters, perhaps. I could do nothing. I was the Garretts' Toryman, just as my father was before me. Fanny would have been deeply unhappy.'

Lydia bit her lip but nodded slowly. She had imagined Sir Anthony to be entirely ineffectual but the plans he had made for Fanny proved otherwise.

'If – when – Fanny is cured, what then?'

'Sufficient unto the day. We will see. Perhaps Bristol again and local politics? Once Fanny is cured, the world will know her.' He spoke with quiet confidence.

Lydia said, 'This makes me very happy, sir. Fanny, dear Fanny, is in good hands. Thank you.' She turned and left quickly. She too could have had a love like this. If she had waited. If she had been stronger.

School was not the same. In many ways it was better: she was conscious now of her love for the children and theirs for her; she could see how her instincts had proved true and that even when she worked blindly in a vacuum she had still forged amazingly strong bonds of trust and respect between them. She saw the ugliness of the schoolroom and strove to improve it; the children's drawings covered the walls and as Christmas approached she encouraged them to decorate the bare corners with berried holly and garlands of ivy.

But in other ways it was almost unbearable. Daily she waited for a word from Wesley and it did not come. She wanted to hear of his plans for the small farmers of the Moor, she wanted to ask him so much. How easily they had talked on the few occasions they had been together! The naturalness between them; the awareness too. Sometimes in the night she would wake and think of him and her face would be hot with shame. The sheer weight of shame she carried made her feel branded. She cut short Fanny's visits in case she should notice it. Fanny, persevering with her tea parties, thought Lydia was being considerate and made no effort to break through the barrier which surrounded her.

At the end of November, a sergeant from the City police station waited for her outside the school gate. It seemed that a body had been pulled from a storm drain in the city; it was bloated and barely recognizable as human, but it was just possible that it had been one of the miscreants who had hounded Captain Peters and Miss Fielding.

Lydia said faintly, 'Alfred did say that people had died in the sewers.'

'Serve 'em right too, miss. Especially in this

instance, if I may say so.' The sergeant cleared his throat. 'We did wonder if it would be too much to ask you to cast an eye on 'im. In case there was something you could recognize.'

'I saw nothing of individual faces or forms, sergeant.' Lydia walked down her garden path and fitted her key in the lock. 'Perhaps Captain Peters could help you? They had manhandled him before I arrived on the scene.'

'So I understand, miss. But Captain Peters is at Taunton following the death of his father, as I dare say you know—'

'I did not.' Lydia looked round. 'When did that happen?'

'Two days since, miss. Prison fever, so I understand. There will be arrangements. Things for 'im to see to. We can't 'old on to this cadaver, miss. Not after today.'

Lydia stared past his head. So Nathan was dead at last.

She said, 'I am sorry, sergeant. I cannot help you. Good night.'

He stared helplessly at the door as it shut quickly after her. 'Good night miss,' he said ruefully.

Fanny said, 'You will like Stapleford Court, Lydia. It's small – nothing like Garrett Place, fairly near the town so that we can go to Christmas service at the Harbour church which I understand is most heartwarming. And it has no bitter memories for you, my dear, yet you will be near enough to visit your father and friends if you so wish. Perhaps on St Stephen's Day we could all ride over?'

Lydia said, 'Fanny. Dear Fanny. I would so much prefer to stay at home for Christmas. This is my own little house now and I planned to ask Alfred and the Turnbull girls to dinner.'

Wisely Fanny did not press the matter then. 'Think it over, Lydia. I do not like to think of you here alone. Even Mr Peters is planning to spend a few days with his family.'

Lydia looked at her sharply and when she avoided the glance it was obvious that Wesley had spoken to her on the subject of Gus Pascoe. Lydia's heart sank; she had no way of knowing what had been said, but the piece of information about Wesley's whereabouts at Christmas told her plainly that however strongly Fanny had put Lydia's case, Wesley had discounted it. Lydia had little doubt that he would have received an invitation to Stapleford Court and that he had declined it when he knew Lydia might be there.

The small shops that trailed from Christmas Steps to Bristol Bridge were bright with Christmas goodies. Along with the dripping bread and beavers at midday, appeared oranges and apples; Lydia knew the fruit was filched from the applewomen who came in daily from Gloucestershire and Somerset but she said nothing. Instinctively she knew that morals could not be taught to these children by word of mouth. She bought a crate of rotting fruit in the market and spent an evening cutting it up and spicing it with sugar, cinnamon and sultanas. The next day at dinner time, she placed the bowl of prepared fruit on a stool by the stove and, while the children helped themselves ecstatically, she read the first part of *A Christmas Carol*.

'We gonna do this every day, miss?' asked Alfred. 'It's better than running around the freezing yard.'

'We need exercise too, Alfred. We will "follow my leader" for ten minutes after this.'

The latter proved so successful that at the end of the afternoon she repeated it before the children had time to begin their shivering journey home. They were in the middle of high stepping and arm swinging over the grass to the road when a carriage drew up and Anne Pascoe climbed down. Next May's baby was already evident in the backward tilt of her body. She watched in amazement as Lydia began to whirl her arms like windmills, closely followed by twenty-eight imitations.

'My dear, what on earth—' she began. Lydia refused to be side-tracked. She whirled on for another three seconds before halting smartly, turning and dismissing the children. They ran up the road laughing and rosy-cheeked, Alfred bringing up a reluctant rear.

'You drill them like soldiers, Lydia!' Anne lifted her skirts fastidiously as she crossed the grass.

'Hardly.' Lydia watched her own breath steaming briskly before her with some satisfaction. She really must get the children outside more often, it was good for all of them. She felt ready to cope with Anne.

'I have been promising myself a visit with you ever since . . . ever since . . .'

'Ever since you warned me of Gus's intentions against Wesley Peters,' Lydia said straightly. 'For which I thank you, Anne. I might not have taken later information very seriously had you not come that night. I take it Julius knew nothing – knows nothing – of your visit?'

'Of course not!' Anne glanced up in alarm. 'But this time, yes. In fact he suggested it.' She followed Lydia into the parlour. 'Ah, my dear, you have made this tiny place charming. Quite charming. Of course our literary gentlemen started a vogue for tiny cottages and I believe Mr Coleridge himself stayed in this one when he came to Bristol, is that so?'

'I have no idea.' Lydia removed her cloak and bent to lift the banked fire wondering whether she was to be declared respectable again by the Pascoes. Anne's attitude was certainly as condescending as it had been at Stapleford.

Anne watched her as she moved about putting things to rights. She smiled approvingly. 'I am thankful nothing came of the unfortunate attack on the Peters man. Of course I realized afterwards that Gus could have had nothing to do with it, but if there had been any mud-slinging – well, mud sticks, my dear. Most unpleasantly, and, as I pointed out to Julius, education is all the vogue now and you are fast becoming a

well-known educator! Did you know that, Lydia?'
She trilled her meaningless laugh.

Lydia said, 'Miss Parmenter's school is becoming well known, Anne. I run it for her. That is all.'

'Even so, my dear. Even so. You could easily become a vogue yourself. I remember the assembly at Stapleford where you were quite a success.'

Lydia shook her head definitely. 'I do not wish for anything like that, Anne. If you have any plans for making me a – a – vogue, as you put it, dismiss them utterly. I wish to live a quiet, secluded life.'

'My dear, that is to your credit. And safer too. I was merely congratulating myself on having averted a possible disaster for our family last month.' She smiled, at once arch and smug. Lydia sat down and tightened her lips, glancing meaningfully at the pile of slates on the table.

'Quite. Quite, my dear. You are busy. My errand is very brief. We want you to spend Christmas with all of us. At Mapperly. There is to be a Christmas Eve dance – that foulard you wore for the assembly will do very well. And we shall have carols. It will be quite delightful and you will be such a help to me with the babies.'

Lydia could only gape at her. Anne filled the gap with another laugh.

'Do not stare so, Lydia! Surely the breach is healed by now? Certainly it is, on Gus's side. You hurt – injured – him deeply, Lydia, you must have known that, yet now he wishes you to be his guest at Mapperly and . . . well, who knows? Can we not turn the clock back, Lydia?'

Lydia shuddered. 'I hope not. Anne, forgive me, you have never done me harm, but surely you can see that I cannot possibly come to Mapperly? Gus is vengeful and wants only one thing of me—'

'Lydia! Really, my dear!' Anne pretended to be shocked, then leaned forward and covered Lydia's hand with her gloved one. 'My dear, all men are like that. They cannot help it. And it is our duty to—'

Lydia stood up abruptly. 'What happens in your marriage is your affair of course—'

'Oh, I naturally referred to marriage! Did you imagine for one instant that I would countenance – or that Joanna would countenance – anything other than an honourable union for you?' Anne spoke to Lydia's back as she trimmed the lamp angrily. 'Lydia, Gus intends you to spend Christmas with him. If you refuse, you know he will come and fetch you. Why do you not accept gracefully and be done with it?'

'Because . . .' Lydia finished with the lamp and went to the window to close the curtains with a swish. 'Because, Anne, I am already promised for Christmas. I am to spend three days at Stapleford Court.' She turned and looked at Anne directly. 'I assume that even Gus will accept that excuse?'

Anne fidgeted. 'Well, if it's true. Is it true, Lydia? Have the Warrens really invited you there? I had no idea you were on those terms.'

Lydia flushed. 'I am to be Miss Parmenter's

guest, naturally. That is perfectly true, I assure you. I would not stoop to lie about such a matter.'

'No. Naturally not,' Anne murmured. 'Well, in that case, I very much regret that you cannot . . . but I do see.' She stood up and smoothed her cape over her abdomen. 'I only hope that Gus will also understand.'

Furiously, Lydia watched her walk back to the carriage. Now she would have to go to Stapleford. Not that it mattered. Wesley would be elsewhere; she might as well go to Stapleford as stay here.

Thirteen

It was to be a quiet Christmas. Fanny assured Lydia of that. The Dowager Lady Warren would be there with her cousin who had been a lifelong companion. Two daughters with their husbands and small children would take up all the nursery floor. 'Edward and Sibyl Lambourne will be with us for Christmas dinner as their parents are engaged with the Garretts. And . . .' Fanny looked closely out of the train window as they passed the hump of Brean Down. 'I have prevailed upon Mr Peters to stay at the Court and visit his family the day after Christmas.'

Lydia followed her eyes. The sea was flat and grey and strangely unfamiliar. She could pretend no longer. 'Oh Fanny,' she said in a distressed voice.

Fanny turned to her instantly. They were alone in the carriage as Sir Anthony had gone ahead by road, taking the luggage with him. 'Lydia, my dear. Why did you tell him?'

Lydia did not answer until they pulled up at Bridgwater platform. A porter ran along the length of the train plying for hire and a hand-cart followed him, piled with hot pies. She stared at it unseeingly. 'I had to show him it was hopeless.'

Fanny said impatiently, 'It is not hopeless, Lydia! I will not have you give up so easily. Do you imagine Wesley Peters is innocent? After four years in America? And why should it be worse for you than for him?'

Lydia, who had heard Fanny on this tack before, might have smiled at her fiery reply had it been about anyone else. She said, 'My dear, I can forgive him very easily. But he—'

'He forgives you, Lydia! I promise you! Forgive *me*, Lydia for pleading your cause unasked. But I knew you would have put the blackest picture you could before him! I told him nothing but the truth, believe me. But I tried to explain how it was for you in the midst of so many catastrophes.'

'Fanny – he knew what had happened.'

'But he went away from it. He could not imagine how it must have been to be trapped more and more by each and everything that happened!' She spoke in a gentler tone, 'Lydia, had you come to me for advice I would have urged you to say nothing at all of your experience with Gus Pascoe. On the other hand, as the Pascoes are so thoroughly wicked, it might have been that they would have informed Mr Peters themselves. I do not know. In any case, you are much too straightforward to try to deceive anyone. Except perhaps yourself.' She sighed at Lydia's expression. 'Listen, my dear. Will you simply let events take care of the situation over Christmas? Mr Peters wants very much to be with you . . . to talk to you. I have not engineered this, Lydia. When he heard that you were coming to the Court after all, he asked me whether he might change his mind too. It is not so dreadful after all, is it my dear? To see him?'

Lydia looked down. 'No.'

'Then you will . . . do your best?'

'Whatever that means . . . yes. I will do my best.'

She told herself she was glad to be warned. She knew, as the train sighted the high range of the Quantock Hills, that she was simply glad.

The Court was indeed different from the Place. Only half a mile from the small wool town of Stapleford, it had long since given up pretensions to being a mansion and was on the way to being a town house. There was stabling and a paddock for the horses and an orchard at the bottom of the garden, but the home farm dealt with all the livestock, and the portraits in the hall were of statesmen and civil servants and minor diplomats.

The accommodation was more comfortable than that of the Place. The rooms were small and warm, each with its own roaring fire in a modern cast-iron grate, its own gas lamp on a swinging adjustable arm and its own comfortable night commode and washstand. The beds were all full-feather, the carpets very thick. It was impossible not to feel relaxed in such comfort.

Lydia put on her foulard and went down to dinner that Christmas Eve quite unable to quench a small flicker of anticipation; an echo of how she might have felt two years ago had she been invited to such an important house.

Her eyes found Wesley immediately. Everyone had forgathered in the hall and all were sampling the local ginger wine. Wesley was bending over Sibyl Lambourne, filling her glass while she stared at him, openly curious about this unknown guest.

Fanny drew Lydia forward so that Sir Anthony could make introductions; she smiled and inclined her head as she had done often in the last six months. Usually Fanny's friends and political acquaintances made no impression on her; her polite remarks were automatic and made for Fanny's sake. This time the Warren family registered properly. They all had Sir Anthony's slow benign manner, his readiness to praise rather than criticize. Selina Markham, his sister, said warmly, 'We've heard so much about your intellect, Miss Fielding! Anthony quite forgot to mention that you are beautiful!' His other sister, Sarah, said, 'After dinner you must come upstairs and look at the children, my dear. They are perfectly lovely when they are asleep.' They both told their mother that the decorated fir tree was 'completely beautiful' and that her new Persian kitten was 'exquisite'. More than that, they obviously adored Fanny, which was sufficient recommendation for Lydia even if they had disapproved strongly of herself.

Sibyl and Edward Lambourne knew of her as a country hoyden but remembered her with more approbation from the Stapleford assembly. They surveyed her coolly now, not certain whether her survival after the collapse of her family was exemplary or not. Her quiet, almost staid manner reassured them that she was no social climber, but when Wesley Peters was introduced they exchanged glances, scenting intrigue.

Wesley handed her a glass of wine. 'Lydia. Thank you for coming. I must talk to you.'

Sibyl Lambourne arrived at his elbow. 'You are to take me in to dinner, Mr Peters, and the doors are open. Shall we? Edward is your partner, Miss Fielding.' She glanced over at her brother, obviously signalling him to find out all he could during dinner while she did the same. Lydia almost smiled. If Fanny hoped for a quiet holiday with no raking over of memories, she would have to remove the Lambournes.

However, it was simple to foil Edward's clumsy attempts to turn the conversation to gossip. With the arrival of the game soup he probed fairly gently into the true ownership of Milton Mains.

'I dare say the Garretts were furious with you over the whole business. They loathe to see any of their farms run down. They were doubtless thankful to let it go to Pascoe.'

Lydia watched a globule of soup trickle down his chin and said thoughtfully, 'I don't *think* there can be much ill-feeling. Did you see the gift Lady Maud sent for Christmas?' She displayed the cameo and went on to tell him of the first one which had been given to her by the grandchildren. 'I have no knowledge of any business transactions, of course, but we are still friends, which is what matters, do you not agree?' She permitted herself a smile as the globule ran into Edward's collar. During the fish and the beef, he was beguiled into talking of the season's hunting. When Lydia chose the fruit trifle in preference to plum pudding, he said in a low voice, 'I hear old Nathan Peters, the lay preacher, died in Taunton Gaol last month. What a relief for you and your father!'

Lydia said steadily, 'Prison life must be a living death, I agree with you.'

'I understand he put a curse on all your family.'

'I hardly think so. As you see, Captain Peters and I are still good acquaintances. He is a manager of the school in Bristol where I—'

'*Captain* Peters?'

'A courtesy title. Well deserved.'

'Er . . . probably. What is this I hear about a wool co-operative? What does that mean exactly? The Pascoes are absolutely furious and talk of starving out any farmer who joins.'

She looked across the table to where Wesley was replying to a remark from Sybil Lambourne. His face had a closed, withdrawn look and if he wanted friends on the Moor he should be making the most of her ardent young interest. For the first time Lydia hoped he would win a seat on the City Council. She turned back to Edward. 'A co-operative would take some of the power away from the Pascoes when it comes to

374

wool prices. I would say that was a good thing. Competition usually is, surely?'

He grinned. 'The Pascoes have been at the game for a long time, Miss Fielding.'

'Yes and they have always underpaid. My father has spent his life grumbling at their prices.' She tried for a roguish smile. 'Where would your sympathies lie in this, sir?'

He stared into her liquid amber eyes, perhaps remembering how casually he had treated her at Garrett Place fifteen months before.

'I would follow your lead, Miss Fielding,' he said gallantly.

She held his gaze deliberately, then lifted her glass and drank as if making a pledge. She said, 'I hope you will remember that.'

After dinner they went again into the hall and listened to the wassailers from the town. Then presents were piled beneath the tree for the morning and Lydia was conducted to the nurseries to look at the four sleeping children. She went to bed herself, not having spoken a word to Wesley. But he wanted to talk to her. He would talk to her. Perhaps tomorrow.

If she had expected his talk to be about forgiveness she was disappointed. Breakfast, church and midday dinner took up all the time until mid-afternoon when they split into small groups, most of the ladies retiring to their rooms to rest, the Lambournes going out with Sir Anthony on horseback. Wesley declined all suggestions and when Lydia looked likely to be inveigled into a ride, he said, 'I had hopes you would show me the town, Miss Fielding. This is my first visit to Stapleford.' She glanced at him, intending to back out of everything and go to the comfort of her room, then found herself saying, 'By all means, Captain Peters. I will fetch my cloak and bonnet.'

They walked sedately down the drive of horse chestnuts and the steep road into Fore Street. Wesley took her arm when she crossed the gushing gutters and lifted her onto a mounting block when a wagon splashed by and would have muddied her skirt. His touch was such a mixture of the familiar and friendly with the sensual that she was breathless; apparently so was he. They barely exchanged a word.

They came to the harbour, a massive wall of stone blocks very different from the shelving shingle of Listowel beach contained within the arm of its jetty. Far below, the sea lapped, green and glassy. They watched the many swaying masts at anchor for Christmas Day.

Wesley said abruptly, 'Lydia, tomorrow I am going to visit my mother. I want you to come with me.'

Once again he had surprised her. She looked round at him.

'Visit Prudence? I could not, Wesley.'

'Surely you will wish to see your father before you go back to Bristol?'

'Yes. Sir Anthony has offered me the wagonette or a horse.'

'Take the horse. We will go together. But first we will visit my mother.'

'Is this what you wished to talk about? I cannot see your mother, Wesley. I cannot!'

'It is what I wished to say for now, yes. After we have seen Prudence there will be other things.'

She turned to face him. 'Fanny said . . .' Her voice died and suddenly her eyes filled with weak tears. She wanted him to hold her, to kiss her as he had done beneath the stones of Christmas Steps, with deep love and the promise of passion. And with the urgency of desire came the usual shame.

He saw the tears but did not touch her. 'Fanny said?' he prompted.

'She said . . .' Her voice was a whisper. 'She said that you had forgiven me.'

Still he did not move towards her and his voice was hard when he replied. 'I have nothing to forgive, Lydie. You behaved as anyone would have behaved in the same circumstances. Do you not understand that?'

'I – I hardly know what I understand any more.'

'I want you to believe two things, Lydie. Please. One is that there is nothing for me to forgive. And the other is that there is nothing for you to forgive. Until you accept that, we cannot begin to talk.'

She moistened her lips, hating herself. 'I – I accept that.'

He took her hands and pressed his thumbs into her knuckles.

'Lip service. In order to believe you must be with me tomorrow.' He shook her hand as if they were sealing a bargain. 'Now. That is settled. I want you to show me the Staple Hall, Lydie. And the warehouses where Tavvie Pascoe stores the raw wool. And I want to take a good look at this harbour. We might use it ourselves later on.'

She could not adjust herself so quickly to the change of subject and atmosphere. 'I – I'm not certain about the warehouses. The house – Tavvie's house – is up a little, with a view of the harbour. But why do you want to know?'

'We need somewhere to do business if we make this a really local industry. How many wool-packs will the hall take, I wonder? And could we import Irish flax for wool-linsey? And could we start everything off from the cottages themselves? What do you think, Lydie? Would the women spin wool at home for the co-operative?'

She felt again the terrific drive of his enthusiasm. They began to walk the length of the harbour to where the tide levels were marked and the harbour dues printed. She said hesitantly, 'Jinny would. Jinny Roscoe that was – Jinny Johnson now. There must be others like her. She could make enquiries . . . ask people.'

He took her from the harbour up through the town to the Staple Hall, pacing out its exterior measurements and leading her into a discussion on dyeing. When they reached the Court again, it was assumed she would go with him to Listowel on St Stephen's Day. They had a noisy

378

nursery tea with the children. They wore paper crowns and played Ring-a-Roses and Turn the Trencher. Edward and Sybil Lambourne left them to return home. Christmas was over.

St Stephen brought a frost the next day. It encapsulated each twig and leaf and bracken frond, turning the bare uplands into a fairy-tale etching and crisping the air until it tingled as it touched human skin. Lydia, in Fanny's tricorn hat and Selina's riding habit, rode side saddle on a docile mare from the Court stables. Wesley was on a similar hack. They walked the horses up the long pull to the Heights and let them make their own pace on the undulating Moor. Almost against her will, Lydia found herself returning Wesley's smiles as the panorama before them revealed new vistas at every turn.

'Nowhere like it in the world!' he called, reining in by her side. 'We'll build a house up here one day – right on the top!' She held bridle and pommel in one hand as she turned to stare at him. In spite of everything, her heart lifted hopefully. Was there really some simple answer to her humiliation after all? Did Wesley know it? Was that why he was taking her to see Prudence? They were riding high above the great headland of Tamerton and just for a moment she let her gaze slide past him to the tumble of rocks and streams where she had fought Gus over a year ago and then succumbed to him. Wesley urged his horse's head forward so that her view was obstructed. 'You look beautiful in that

379

highwayman's hat!' he said. 'You are the most beautiful woman in the world, did you know that?'

She focused on him, surprised because she had not heard such a gallant compliment from him before. Then she understood.

'I am no great beauty, Wesley. Do not try to divert my thoughts to trivialities, please!'

Unexpectedly he flushed. 'Certainly I wish to divert any unhappy thoughts you may have, Lydie. But not with trivialities. It is important that you know yourself. You are beautiful and in my opinion you are the most beautiful woman in the world.'

Tears threatened her again; how easily he could transport her from one emotion to another. And how well he knew her. Almost immediately he said in a matter-of-fact voice, 'Is that the hunt? They were meeting at Tamerton, I think Sir Anthony said.'

She accepted this gambit, swallowed the tears and looked towards the long, mournful cry of the horn. 'Yes. Sir Henry and Lady Maud will be there.' She pushed her horse on. 'I hope we can strike off the road before the beaters put up anything around here.'

'I should think so. You do not like the hunt, Lydie?'

'When it is in full swing there is a kind of madness about it. Besides, I feel a foolish affection for deer.' She wondered whether one day she might be able to tell him about the stag who had become so confused with Wesley himself.

They took the long slope to the gates of Garrett Place at an easy canter; conversation was impossible and though Wesley smiled brightly at her again she did not respond. Occasionally they heard the call of the horn but it did not come near enough to make them turn off at the Milton Mains sheep track. Doggedly they went past it without a glance and trotted the extra mile to the Listowel lane, past the familiar gate and down the combe. Wesley had stipulated that they should see Prudence before Rupert, and Lydia agreed to this on the grounds that it would be the least pleasant of her day's calls and she wanted it over.

They came to the lane leading to the two Peters cottages. Wesley lifted her down and tethered the horses to an alder. They had encountered no-one on their ride and beyond the muddy track the beach spread itself as emptily as it had the last time Lydia had seen it. She felt the familiar queasiness in her stomach and leaned for a moment on Wesley's arm, head down. He seemed not to notice.

'She is with Granny Peters now, Lydia. In any case we shall not see the others. They planned to visit my father's grave and will have left.'

She straightened with difficulty. 'Granny too?'

'Aye, so I believe.'

Her hope had been that Luke and Benjie's sombre presence and Mercy's garrulous one would have been some kind of protection from Prudence and the awful knowledge which lay between them. But it seemed she was to be spared nothing. She recalled her foolish bargain with God made in this same lane. Well, she had one kind of freedom.

The midden was covered with a network of frost, its obscenities veiled for the moment. When Wesley knocked and pushed at the door, no stench emerged. Perhaps Prudence and Granny Peters no longer had reputations as witches. But the shutters at the window made the tiny room very dark; only when she had followed Wesley inside did Lydia realize there was no fire.

Prudence's voice came harshly from Granny's old chair. 'You agin, Wesley? What is it you want now, boy? 'Aven't you plagued your old mother enough this past week without beginnin' again? What be ee a'-*doin*'?'

'Lighting up, Mother.' Two rush lights dipped and flickered on the table as Wesley leaned over them. The interior of the cottage wavered and settled into place just as Lydia remembered it. Wesley went to the grate and riddled the ash expertly. 'It is bitterly cold in here. Why have you not lit the fire?'

''Tis warm enough with the shutters closed. Only me 'ere today, not worth a fire.'

He rummaged in the corner for bracken kindling. Lydia pressed back against the wall out of the wavering lights, knowing Prudence had not seen her. She was afraid now: Prudence was mad. And she had never liked Lydia.

Wesley reached for a rush light and held it to the ashy mass. There was a crackling and a dozen small flames licked up the fire bars.

Wesley said easily, 'It is a month since I was here, Mother, you have forgotten. We talked. All through the night we talked. Do you remember that?'

She replied sullenly, 'Aye. I remember. You're hard, Wesley. Hard and cruel. We did not have to speak of Nathan like that.'

'It was necessary.' He put some small logs across the fiery bracken and stood up, tall and thin, his crown of hair giving him the look of an angel; an avenging angel. 'Now I have brought someone with me, Mother. And I want you to tell her what we said that night. It is necessary also. Necessary that she hears it from your lips. Do you understand?'

Prudence turned inquisitively and peered past her son. Her nutcracker face lengthened in shock.

'You! What you doin' 'ere agin? Thought you was out the way for good an' all! Good an' all! I paid my debt to you, girl, you know that – ' She clutched her skirt to her face and her voice descended to a mutter. 'Nuthin' but trouble – when 'e first clapped eyes on 'ee – nuthin' but trouble between our two fam'lies – '

Wesley said sharply, 'That's enough of that, Mother! Lydia has a right to know the truth. Perhaps it is best that it stays with her, but she will decide. Now speak!'

Prudence glanced at him, dropped her skirt and spat venom.

'She 'asn't spoke the truth to you, 'as she, my son? Do you know she is a whore? She's a Pascoe woman! She's laid with the Pascoe man and she will lay with 'im agin—'

Wesley leaned down and took the bird-like shoulders and shook them and Prudence's voice rattled in her throat. Lydia gasped a scream.

Wesley spoke grimly. 'I know about Lydia. Now, I want her to know about me. About the taint that is in me. Yes, taint, Mother! Tell her! Tell her now!' He held her up and her shadow jumped on the fireplace wall where Mercy had made nettle tea. 'I have come here to find forgiveness for all of us.'

'Forgiveness?' Prudence hissed. 'What you ask is betrayal – can you not see that? Betrayal of the dead!'

'Mother . . .' He put her back in her chair gently. 'Mother, the dead cannot confess. Speak for them. You kept their counsel before when it mattered, perhaps. Shrive their souls now and speak for them.'

She stared up at him, her chin jutting forward as it had always done, indefatigably, with a kind of hope.

'Shrive them?' she murmured. 'Aye, p'raps . . . p'raps. He were buried in unhallowed ground. Unhallowed.' Shockingly, she cackled suddenly. 'Unhallowed . . . aye, it were always unhallowed. Always. You guarded 'er Wesley, din't you? You guarded 'er well. For someone else. An' you din't even know it. Seen some sights over in the Americies, but you was still so believin' . . . so believin'.' Her voice rose to a wail and died and a sob shook her. 'My poor 'Ella. My baby. My

384

only girl. She were too pretty by 'alf. Just fifteen when I found them first. An' 'e tole me it was the will of the Lord. 'E tole me—'

Wesley said quietly, 'Just say it, Mother. Just say it.'

She opened her eyes widely at him as if surprised. Then she said clearly, 'Nathan. Nathan Peters fathered that idiot child and so killed his own daughter. And went mad 'imself. Nathan Peters.'

Lydia could hear someone weeping. It was herself.

Prudence looked at her and cackled again. 'It was me told her to make up to young Alan Fielding. Me took 'er along to that big party to 'elp out with the serving!' She cringed as Wesley's shadow leapt. 'I din't know they'd love each other so dear! I din't know, son. All I knowed was that she couldn't marry 'er own pa! An' 'e . . .'e'd be disgraced for all time if it came out that he'd laid with 'er! 'Is preachin' were all that mattered to 'im, Wesley. 'Is preaching and 'is little Marella.'

Lydia groaned, remembering Prudence in Carybridge Chapel looking at her husband so anxiously . . . Prudence unregretful at her daughter's death. And Marella calling for her father at the end. 'Nathan!' the single cry.

She might have whispered it herself because Prudence's head came round and her sunken eyes looked across the table.

'Nathan. Yes, 'tis Nathan you must forgive, my girl. Nathan Peters who loved 'is wife and lusted

385

for 'is daughter. An' 'ad to see that daughter with another man. 'Tis Nathan Peters who needs—'

Wesley said, 'Very well, Mother. Enough now.' He looked at Lydia. 'Do you feel faint, my love? You could wait outside while I straighten things here.'

Prudence said shrilly, 'She felt faint before. Din't you, my beauty? Faint with child that was – just like my 'Ella! Only she found your brother to cuckold! An' you'll not 'ave my son! No, not while I've breath in my body! You'll not cuckold Wesley Peters just to 'venge your brother!' Wesley was holding his mother, hushing her. Lydia put her hands to her throat and backed towards the door. Prudence still ranted, twisting her agile scrawny body away from Wesley's soothing sounds.

'Came 'ere for a potion – did you know that, son? Nan Nancombe died in the snow and your gran and me were the on'y ones making remedies. So she came 'ere! Told me she would live wi'out men, then soon as the baby be gone, up she goes off to Bristol to get you!' She turned and held his face in her stick-like hands. 'Wesley – can't you see that there can be no more truck between them and us?'

Lydia backed through the door and let it swing shut behind her. She stood for a moment breathing deeply of the frosty air and letting the sounds of Wesley's quiet voice steady her pounding heart. Then she turned, gathered up the riding habit and ran back down the lane to the horses. The tears were cold on her face and her throat was sore with her laboured sobs. Everything seemed to be spoiled. The careful companionship with Wesley; the unexpected joy of Christmas – the first Christmas without her mother; the luxury of Stapleford Court, even her friendship with Fanny . . . all seemed tarnished. One of the most terrifying revelations of this morning was Prudence's continuing protective love of her incestuous, hypocritical husband, which made her hate Lydia. But the worst, by far the worst, was her own likeness to Marella and Nathan. She was deeply and wonderfully in love with Wesley Peters; she accepted that fully now. But Gus Pascoe was her master. He could wake in her base and animal desires.

She untied the mare and looped the reins over the pommel while she struggled to mount without assistance. The mare was frightened by her panic and circled anxiously. She mounted at last and the horse took to the path alongside the Stowe in an uncoordinated trot much too fast for the icy ground. Lydia lay low to avoid the whipping branches of alder, but even so her borrowed tricorn was whisked from her head before they were halfway up the combe. She sobbed and tried to pull in the mare; it was Fanny's hat, she must not lose it. But the horse had the bit between its teeth and Lydia was not used to riding side-saddle. There was no stopping at the gate of Milton Mains either; they charged past and out on to the Heights road, straight across that and into the bracken and wilderness of the tops.

Lydia held on somehow, praying that the horse would tire before she put a foot down a rabbit hole and broke a leg. To the right and not far away, the hunting horn brayed peremptorily and her horse veered away from it, stumbled and just recovered, changing pace.

'There's a girl,' Lydia forced herself to speak gently, but the words were jerked out of her throat. 'There, that's enough, my lovely. Steady now. Whoa there . . .' She hung on with one hand and tried to rub at the sweating neck with the other. The mare slowed its hectic canter to a trot. The glistening chestnut body began to tremble, then the trot faltered and the mare halted and hung its head, blowing and fidgeting.

Lydia slid down and held the head to her. She wept again and it was as if the mare wept with her. They stood like that for what seemed a long time before Lydia looked around her.

They were on the undulating heath of the top moor, waist high in dead fern and gorse. A few trees grew in the direction of the prevailing wind, gnarled and without branches. To her right two or three acres had been cleared and a few sheep nibbled the winter-short grass, probably her father's. A dry-stone wall girdled a copse of rattling beeches. As she stared and stroked the mare and wondered bleakly what to do, a horse cleared the wall and landed badly in the field. The rider pitched forward but was in no danger of falling. Irritably he drove his mount towards the sheep and seemed to gain some slight satisfaction from watching them scatter. He leaned back in the saddle, easing his muscles and watching them idly. Then he saw Lydia.

As he had cleared the wall she had realized it was Gus. The way he sat and went with the stumbling horse, the expertise of his recovery – it was all typical of him. She wanted to run and could not.

He walked his horse slowly to the edge of the pasture and looked across the barrier of bracken.

'Well. The lovely Lydia Fielding. How do you do, Lydia?'

'I am . . . well.' She forced herself to speak because silence was unbearable, but her voice was hoarse.

'I heard you were at Stapleford and wondered whether you might ride to Milton one day, but this is better still. Were you looking for me?'

'No. My horse bolted.'

He laughed. 'It is fate, is it not, Lydia? You try to get away from me and I try to forget you. It is not to be.'

She could not deny it. She felt the soft nose of the mare in her neck and realized she was leaning heavily on its withers. Her legs were shaking.

Gus called, 'I'll come to you. Wait.' He wheeled his horse and galloped across the field and into the bracken. She thought: I must run, I must get up again and run. But it was useless, the mare was blown and so was she.

Gus dismounted, took her reins and his and

led both horses to a rock. Unsupported, Lydia stumbled and would have fallen but for his arm. He held her casually, familiarly, with none of the tenderness which was in Wesley's touch; there was still a smile on his face but no laughter in his black eyes.

'Hello, Lydie.'

She remembered Prudence's words back in that hovel and thought she should have drowned in Listowel Cove last May.

'Have you nothing to say to me, Lydia? Aren't you sorry for the way you have treated me?'

She whispered, 'Leave me alone, Gus. That is what I would say. If we meet like this by accident, pass me by. You have no more love for me than I have for you.'

'Quite so. What we feel is stronger than love.'

'I resisted you once, Gus. Since then you have been determined to have me one way or another.' She stood very still within his arm. Below them on the Heights road, a horse could be heard. 'Well, you did that, Gus. You won. There is no need for anything further between us.'

He laughed; his hunter's laugh. 'We know that, Lydie. I told others, of course, but though they loved hearing it, the mud did not stick because you went to Bristol and polished up your reputation. So I want you with me. Married or not. I don't really mind. But I want everyone to know you came to me. You left Bristol and the Parmenters and Peters . . . and you came to me.'

The horses had taken to the bracken. Lydia pressed back. 'Please, Gus. Get on your horse and go now.'

He said, 'It's him, isn't it? The Peters whelp.' His arm tightened brutally. 'We'll start with him, please, Lydie. If you don't mind.' His sneer was horrible. 'You will tell him to go away.' He lowered his head and fastened his mouth on hers as Wesley's horse breasted the fern.

She heard his voice like a whip crack as Gus took her hair in his other hand to hold her head still.

'Pascoe! Let her go – let her go, d'you hear me?'

Gus lifted his head but still held her hair; she felt her scalp lifting painfully.

Gus said, 'Are you still here, whelp? Leave us.' He took a twist more hair and Lydia let her head fall back but restrained a whimper. She heard Wesley dismount in a flurry and launch himself at the two of them. It was a desperate attack and though Gus released her at last, he parried it easily and pushed Wesley off and into the bracken with a contemptuous snort of laughter. Lydia too fell but immediately started up, her hand held out pleadingly.

'No! Wesley – no – please! It is no use!'

Wesley was already crouching, ready to spring. Gus was ready for him, thick legs bent and arms arched as if for an embrace. He let the hatred show in his face as he hissed, 'You won't take me by surprise again, Peters! No, not again – never again. You won't get me, Peters, and you won't

391

get the girl either. She's chosen me – she was always mine and she knows it!'

Wesley took two careful steps towards his tormentor and Lydia cried out, 'Please do not be hurt for me, Wesley – I am not worth it! Please!'

But it was too late. Wesley sprang and was clasped by the arms that had wrestled with sheep. He was hugged to the barrel chest like a lover. He was a fitter man than Gus with a sinewy strength that might outlast him too, but Gus was the heavier by far and this was to be no endurance test. Gus dug his thumbs into Wesley's spine and bent the supple body backwards, bracing his own body back at the same time so that there was no chance of Wesley throwing him.

Lydia screamed, 'You will break his back, Gus! Let him go, for God's sake!' She scrabbled up and threw herself on Gus, ripping his sleeve from its shoulder and falling again in time to see him lift Wesley's feet from the ground. As she gathered herself to pull at him again, he swung Wesley's limp body around and hurled him into the bracken. He lay very still.

Lydia said, 'You've killed him!' She ran frantically through the broken fern and leaned over him. He was crumpled, his arm at an odd angle, his coat off his shoulders and blood showing on his shirt. She slid a hand beneath his head; a pulse beat in his neck. She looked up, 'Quickly – go for Tarling – he's still alive! Hurry!'

Gus, bent double, panting, looked up from hunched shoulders. 'Are you mad? I have just rescued you from that sneaking bastard and if he isn't dead then I will finish him off now!' He took a lumbering step forward and Lydia arched herself protectively over Wesley. Gus halted. 'Get up, Lydia. Stop grovelling over that peasant and get up. I should have finished him off two years ago when he first set eyes on you. He's nothing to you, and you know it.'

Quite suddenly the hysteria which had been below the surface of her consciousness for so long now seemed to rise physically through Lydia's body and evaporate in the still, freezing air.

She said in a voice so calm it was utterly convincing, 'Wesley Peters is everything to me.' She spread her arms over him. 'If you kill him you kill me also.'

'Balderdash! Come away, girl! Come on. The whelp will recover soon enough. I will take you back to Stapleford and we can announce our betrothal.'

'Gus. Listen to me. Listen carefully. I fell in love with Wesley Peters on my twenty-first birthday. I cannot explain what happened between you and me. It has cast an evil shadow over my life. I thought I was ruined because of it. But the shadow has gone. I cannot explain that either. Perhaps it is because of Wesley's constant love for me – it does not matter. All that matters now is that Wesley lives. Go for Dr Tarling.'

Gus leaned forward as if he would grab at one

of her outspread arms, then turned it into a gesture of contempt and repudiation.

'If you go from me now, Lydie, you will go once too often. I warn you—'

'And I warn you, Gus! If you do not fetch Dr Tarling very quickly, everything that has happened – *everything* – will come out. I shall not care about my own reputation any more. I shall make sure that your name is blackened throughout the district.'

He stared at her incredulously. 'You really choose this – this *oaf* – above me, Lydia?'

Her voice rose at last. 'I wish I had chosen him a year and a half ago!'

He said, 'You fool . . . you little fool. I will fetch the doctor. But you realize that your father and your home – they are in my hands.'

'Go!' she said contemptuously.

She watched him shamble to his horse, shrugging on his tattered coat as he mounted. The animal pushed through the bracken to the pasture again; she heard the thud of hooves and then nothing.

Wesley stirred and groaned.

'It is all right.' Lydia knelt and tried to hold his head still. 'Stay quiet, my love. I think you have broken your arm in the fall. Dr Tarling is on his way.'

Wesley's upflung arm worked its way slowly over the bracken roots and his hand took hers.

'I am still whole, my Lydie.' He held her astonished, hopeful gaze. 'Are you?'

She said, 'I do not understand, Wesley. He hurt you – you were unconscious.'

'I was winded. No more. Lydia, don't you see? I had to show you where your heart lay. If I had murdered Pascoe, his ghost would have claimed part of you always. You would never have had a chance to forgive yourself.'

'Forgive *myself*?'

'Hasn't that always been the trouble, Lydia?' He sat up and put his arms around her and she knew he had not been really hurt. 'Listen, beloved. We – we *knew* each other, did we not, right from the beginning? But you could never trust me. For one reason or another you felt I was not for you. Am I right?'

She nodded. His eyes were as blue as the Listowel sky when she had thought she was seeing it for the last time.

'But I had awakened a need in you, nonetheless. And when it seemed I could not fulfil that need . . . there was Pascoe.'

'Oh God. Dear God. I am sorry, Wesley, so sorry.'

'No. Not any more, Lydie. You sent Pascoe away many times and then you ran from him. You could have taken the easy way out. Married him. Been the lady at Mapperly. But you did not. You told my mother you would live without men—'

'I almost went with him just now. Until you came . . .'

'And then you chose.'

He stared at her for a second more and then he

kissed her. He was gentle at first and then less gentle. She clung to him, willing to give herself to him there in the bracken. But he held her close and stroked her hair as if she were a child.

'Dearest, when we come together, there will be no fear, no shame. We will never take from each other. Only give. Do you know that?'

'Yes.' She knew that he could feel her tears on his neck.

He put his hands to her head and held her so that he could see her face. 'Ah, Lydie, be happy again,' he said.

She stared at him. His blue eyes seemed to be calling her back to life. They were as steady as the stag's had been, offering her protection and a share in all the delights of his Moor. She too put her hands to his face. They knelt, facing each other in this curious pose that was a true marrying. And Lydia said, 'I am certain of just one thing. I love you, Wesley Peters.'

And he replied as if it were an ancient ritual, 'And I love you, Lydia Fielding.'

After a while he stood up and pulled her up to him. They walked and stumbled through the bracken to where the horses were nibbling the sparse, frosty grass. He reached under his saddle and produced Fanny's tricorn hat. Then he began to tidy her hair, straighten her habit, brush away the bracken bits.

'I had a fall – there will be no disguising my torn clothes. I have recovered – as Dr Tarling will bear out. Apart from that we have had a good day.'

She kept still while he tidied her. Suddenly she smiled. 'We have had a wonderful day, Wesley. We've found each other. We are happy.'

He too smiled and kissed her again and she responded instantly.

'Have I been hard with you, Lydie? I wanted so much to kiss you yesterday down by the harbour. And at Fanny's house when you told me about Gus, I wanted to hold you and comfort you. But I knew you had to see clearly for yourself.' He studied her face carefully. 'You do see, don't you?'

'I see that Gus could not command me – because of you. And now . . . I can think of him without feeling at all, Wesley.' Her eyes widened as she deliberately recalled the bull-like figure and the confident, brutal way he had treated her. 'I am not frightened . . . not disgusted . . . not ashamed!' The smile died. 'Perhaps I should be disgusted, my love?'

Wesley laughed. 'You *should* feel? Oh my dear Lydie. Do not try to command your feelings any more, sweetheart. Feel nothing for Gus. But feel something for me!'

She too laughed and pulled his head to hers then said in her practical way, 'We must go, dearest. We shall get the ague and that would be unbearable just now.'

He laughed at that. They were still laughing as they breasted the rise onto the Heights road. Laughter had probably never come easily to Wesley in the repressed atmosphere of his Methodist upbringing; it had not come to Lydia for a long time now; so it was with delight that they laughed together that winter afternoon.

There was no sign of Dr Tarling.

'Let us ride this way in any case,' Wesley suggested. 'We can cut behind the tops and call on Jinny at Lambourne if you like. Unless you particularly wish to go now to Milton?'

Lydia thought about it, then shook her head. 'Mamma knows.' She touched her heart. 'She told me to choose happiness, Wesley. Almost as if she knew. My father . . . let us wait until tomorrow to tell him. Let us be selfish with each other today, dearest. It is our precious secret. Jinny might guess but she need not be told.'

'Very well.' He caught at her hand. 'Fanny will guess too, Lydie. It is her dearest wish. You know that?' Lydia nodded and he went on, 'She will say nothing, but she will hope that we will go on working together for her causes. Tell me honestly, my love, would you prefer to leave Bristol for good? Begin afresh somewhere else?'

'No.' Lydia spoke without hesitation. 'Our destiny is in this corner of England. I want to help you with your co-operative, Wesley. I want you to help me with the school. There is so much we can do. Together.'

They rode on quietly, talking easily, re-discovering the unique naturalness of their relationship. Far below them, the sea heaved restlessly and the gulls gathered on the rocks overlooking the combes and kept watch on the hapless humans tethered to the ground.

Wesley said, 'Yes. We will build a house up here, Lydie. One day. This is our land.'

She smiled, looking around her. 'It made us, did it not? I would like it to make our children also.'

'There is no bitterness, Lydie?'

'Not any more You and I . . . we – we vindicate what has gone before. Nathan, Marella, Alan, Gus.' She reached across and touched his muddied coat. 'I hope your mother will see that one day, Wesley.'

He nodded. 'She will. If not before, then when she sees our children.' He steadied her horse. 'Oh, Lydia.' He leaned across to kiss her. She felt her body leap at his touch. And was proud.

THE END

A SELECTED LIST OF FINE NOVELS
AVAILABLE FROM CORGI BOOKS

14058 9	MIST OVER THE MERSEY	*Lyn Andrews*	£5.99
14060 0	MERSEY BLUES	*Lyn Andrews*	£5.99
14974 8	COOKLEY GREEN	*Margaret Chappell*	£6.99
14450 9	DAUGHTERS OF REBECCA	*Iris Gower*	£5.99
14451 7	KINGDOM'S DREAM	*Iris Gower*	£5.99
14538 6	A TIME TO DANCE	*Kathryn Haig*	£5.99
14771 0	SATURDAY'S CHILD	*Ruth Hamilton*	£5.99
14906 3	MATTHEW AND SON	*Ruth Hamilton*	£5.99
14753 2	A PLACE IN THE HILLS	*Michelle Paver*	£5.99
14872 5	THE SHADOW CATCHER	*Michelle Paver*	£5.99
14792 3	THE BIRTHDAY PARTY	*Elvi Rhodes*	£5.99
14905 5	MULBERRY LANE	*Elvi Rhodes*	£5.99
12375 7	A SCATTERING OF DAISIES	*Susan Sallis*	£5.99
12579 2	THE DAFFODILS OF NEWENT	*Susan Sallis*	£5.99
12880 5	BLUEBELL WINDOWS	*Susan Sallis*	£5.99
13136 9	ROSEMARY FOR REMEMBRANCE	*Susan Sallis*	£5.99
13756 1	AN ORDINARY WOMAN	*Susan Sallis*	£5.99
13934 3	DAUGHTERS OF THE MOON	*Susan Sallis*	£5.99
13346 9	SUMMER VISITORS	*Susan Sallis*	£5.99
13545 3	BY SUN AND CANDLELIGHT	*Susan Sallis*	£5.99
14162 3	SWEETER THAN WINE	*Susan Sallis*	£4.99
14318 9	WATER UNDER THE BRIDGE	*Susan Sallis*	£5.99
14466 5	TOUCHED BY ANGELS	*Susan Sallis*	£5.99
14549 1	CHOICES	*Susan Sallis*	£5.99
14636 6	COME RAIN OR SHINE	*Susan Sallis*	£5.99
14671 4	THE KEYS TO THE GARDEN	*Susan Sallis*	£5.99
14747 8	THE APPLE BARREL	*Susan Sallis*	£5.99
14867 9	SEA OF DREAMS	*Susan Sallis*	£5.99
14903 9	TIME OF ARRIVAL	*Susan Sallis*	£5.99
15031 2	THE DOORSTEP GIRLS	*Valerie Wood*	£5.99